Praise for the *Brown Sugar* series

A *Los Angeles Times* Bestseller
Winner of the 2001 Gold Pen Award
for Best Short Story Collection

"Audaciously refreshing. . . . From Taylor's insightful and provocative introduction to *Sugar*'s last sentence, each story not only pushes the envelope but also shatters taboos of African-American love and sexuality."
Essence

Brown Sugar is "as smart as it is sexy. . . ."
Honey

"Particularly intelligent, varied and sexy. . . . A stylish anthology. Many pieces weave serious questions of racial and sexual identity into their racy scenarios."
Publishers Weekly

"*Brown Sugar* portrays sex as it is rather than how others envision it to be."
The Boston Globe

"A sleekly-edited collection . . . it sets a noble standard for collections that follow."
Black Issues Book Review (starred review)

"This provocative anthology is as entertaining and original as it is seductive."
Heart and Soul

"Whether subtle, romantic, or graphic . . . *Brown Sugar* represents some of contemporary African American literature's best voices."
Library Journal

". . . *Brown Sugar* is a celebration of sex and sensuality. These 18 stories demonstrate an incredible diversity of settings, characters, and sensibilities. . . . [*Brown Sugar*] liberates black sensuality from typical American standards of love and beauty."
Booklist

Brown Sugar 3

When Opposites Attract

A Collection of Erotic Black Fiction

Edited by Carol Taylor

WASHINGTON SQUARE PRESS
New York   London   Toronto   Sydney

WSP

Washington Square Press
1230 Avenue of the Americas
New York, NY 10020

ISBN: 0-7434-6686-1

First Washington Square Press trade paperback edition January 2004

10 9 8 7 6 5 4 3 2 1

WASHINGTON SQUARE PRESS and colophon are
registered trademarks of Simon & Schuster, Inc.

Manufactured in the United States of America

For information regarding special discounts for bulk purchases,
please contact Simon & Schuster Special Sales at 1-800-456-6798
or business@simonandschuster.com

Brown Sugar 3 is dedicated to
lovers and lovers of fiction everywhere.

CONTENTS

ACKNOWLEDGMENTS

As always, many thanks to my agent, Tanya McKinnon, for her smarts, savvy, and good-humored guidance, and a warm welcome to my new editor, Malaika Adero, who has proven to me that good things come to those who wait. Thanks to my family for making me who I am; without you I am nothing. Thanks again, Ellis, for the martini-and-gimlet-fueled inspiration. My deepest thanks to all the writers who have so diligently and fearlessly created the original stories in *Brown Sugar 3*; you are on the cutting edge.

"Different strokes, for different folks."
—Sly and the Family Stone

INTRODUCTION

Scratch the Surface

You never thought it would happen. You knew he wasn't the one. You were complete opposites. He wasn't your type and you weren't his. But it's the next morning and you're watching dawn break across the bed, fingers of light sliding slowly across the rumpled sheets. As you break through the surface of sleep, you become aware of the arm snaked around your waist, the chest pressed against your back, his breath rising and falling rhythmically in your ear. Your hips are nestled into his, your legs parted by his thighs. You feel his lips nuzzling your neck even in sleep. Then a rush of heat infuses you as you remember everything that led up to last night.

You weren't interested in him when you'd been introduced. It was even easier to talk to him because of it. You didn't feel those pinpricks of attraction when you'd met him and felt free to be yourself, unguarded, open, unself-conscious. Derrick was friendly, unassuming, easy to talk to and easy to walk away from, and you'd done it all evening. He was so different from you, his background, education, his ideals, and goals. He was even bittersweet dark to your milk chocolate. Personally, you'd always preferred brothers with a little more cream in their coffee. That *café con leche* complexion had always been your thing and some light eyes and curly hair would seal the deal. The truth was you preferred men who looked like you, acted like you, did the things you liked to do, and had the same type of background you had.

Derrick was a coal black, bald brother who still lived in the Bronx neighborhood he was born and grew up in. "Not far from my moms in case she needs anything," he'd said with a smile and a shrug. But not only that, as you'd walked around the gallery looking at the sculptures from all over the world he mentioned that he'd never been out of the country. "Why get in a plane for eight hours when I can jump in a car and drive all over America in the same time." He'd shook his head in amazement at the very thought. You'd laughed to yourself. You were already thousands of miles from the island of your birthplace and so was a wanderer by nature. You couldn't comprehend still living in the neighborhood you grew up in and couldn't fathom not ever traveling outside the country, exploring other continents, cultures, and peoples. You couldn't imagine not having met other French, Italian, German, Dutch, and British blacks, seeing how they lived and referencing yourself against them. When he'd said something about driving a bus for the MTA for the last ten years you tuned him out completely and let your eyes crawl over the crowd, already walking away from him in your mind. But he excused himself first, saying you looked preoccupied. Relieved, you watched him walk away, liking the easy strut in his glide, the way his hips and ass moved under his jeans. When he turned and smiled, his teeth white against his deep black skin, you smiled back before you could stop yourself.

Derrick was easygoing, casual. You usually went for intense, have-to-change-the-status-quo radicals, somehow juggling a corporate career and a side gig as a writer, playwright, or producer. You liked brothers who were on the go, who questioned everything, who had too much drive and determination to sit and drive a bus for ten years. You liked brothers who were going places—and *not* as a bus driver—who were gonna change the world, light it up like a rocket blazing into the sky. You liked brothers more like you. An overachiever since kindergarten, you rocketed through school so fast you were in college at 15. In your first corporate job at 19, executive assistant to the V.P. at 22, head of the department at 25, and president of your own division at 30. Now at 35 you had everything you'd worked so hard for: a nice brownstone in Harlem's Sugar Hill, a closetful of designer clothes, six weeks' paid vacation to visit your friends in Europe or to chill in the West Indies, piles of invitations every week, and a fat IRA and enough stocks and bonds to feel secure in an insecure market. You had everything you could ever want, but somehow you weren't happy. Before you can wonder why, Derrick is back at your elbow with a big smile and a glass of red wine. Taking it, you wonder what he's doing here. Couldn't possibly be his scene, could it? Shouldn't he be watching a fight at his mom's house with his other bus-driving buddies drinking beers and eating KFC?

You're a snob, so you surprise yourself when you accept his offer for a lift home. The opening was over, all the hors d'oeuvres gone and the crowd thinning in search of other pursuits that might involve free wine. Most guys you dated didn't own cars.

They lived centrally or were away on business trips too often to deal with one. *I guess driving a bus has its perks,* you think bitchily. When you say yes, Derrick takes your glass and puts it on a table, then he settles you into your coat. Picking up your briefcase, he takes your arm and leads you through the crowd and out the door.

You talk all the way to Harlem as he expertly maneuvers the SUV through Friday night traffic. His patience as other drivers cut him off amazes you. You also couldn't believe he knew who Machiavelli was, but when you'd been talking about corporate politics you quoted him and he'd nodded and smiled.

"So you read *The Prince*. It's my favorite book, next to *The Art of War*. I don't know which I like more. That's what kept me out of corporate America. If the business world was anything like the court Machiavelli described with all its backstabbing and machinations—"

Did he just say machinations? you wonder.

"—then I was gonna stay out of it," he finished. "So I drive a bus. I'm good at it. I'm a simple man with simple needs. I make good money. I have job security. I own my own car and my own place. I work a shift and I'm done. It doesn't stress me and I don't take my work home with me. I've got plenty of time to do what I like, seeing my moms, and taking road trips with my buddies. I'm happy."

He was full of surprises, you thought, but at the end of the day he was still a bus driver and not really interested in being anything else. Meanwhile, for you, the sky was always the limit.

After he watched you let yourself in he drove off honking once in good-bye. He hadn't asked to come in or tried to kiss you, hadn't even asked for your number. You watched him smile one last time before driving away. When he was gone you stood there strangely missing him, amazed at what you could find when you scratched the surface.

* * *

You're not sure why but two weeks later you get Derrick's number out of the phone book. When he chuckles his pleasure down the phone line at hearing your voice, you like that you can hear a growl underneath it. When you invite him to dinner he accepts but only if he can pick the place. Then you end up gabbing with him for hours. You were surprised how well you got along. It didn't matter that you were so different; you had many things in common. You both shared a penchant for junk food, bad sci-fi, and Marvel comics. He was the youngest of four children and so were you. When you hung up the phone you had a smile on your face. It was still there when you woke the next morning.

When he picked you up two days later you still had no idea where you were going, but you were glad to see him. He belted you in and headed for the West Side Highway, heading down-town. He slipped in a CD and slid down the window as you leaned back in your seat breathing in the salty, early spring air. As D'Angelo crooned softly, *Lemme tell you bought the girl, maybe I shouldn't, met her in Philly and her name was Brown Sugar* . . . you realized you'd missed him: his steadfastness, forthrightness, and his easygoing attitude. You liked his calm way of taking control of situations. How he'd patiently let you talk that first night you'd met, how attentively he listened, not trying to rush in to finish your sentences for you, or discreetly checking out the crowd for someone to network with.

Respecting the music, neither of you speak a word the entire drive, sinking instead into a comfortable silence. Thirty minutes later when he pulls into the South Street Seaport, you look over at the inky water twinkling under the city lights and this time it's your turn to smile. You think back to the first night in the gallery you'd told him how much you liked eating on the balcony of the ship permanently docked there. How you used to love walking around the seaport in the summertime with your friends, shopping and eating seafood, killing time watching the sunset. How you hadn't been there in years as busy as you were and how hard it was to get there without a car.

Two weeks after that, when Derrick drops you home, this time from dancing all night at Sticky Mike's in Chelsea, you ask him to park and come up. It's early enough for a faint rosy light to start to brighten the eastern sky. You'd both danced till you were drenched in sweat and funky. The packed first floor of the club had pressed you up tight against each other until you'd thought the deep red of your shirt would bleed onto his white one. The sweat and humidity had frizzed your hair into a halo of kinky curls and you hadn't cared. You both danced like there was no tomorrow, like it was the end of the world. When you stumbled out the door at 4 A.M. Sunday morning drenched in sweat, the cold air making you shiver as you walk to his car, he wrapped his big dark arms around you and matched his stride to yours.

"Not bad for a bus driver," you cracked. "All that sitting must build up your energy for dancing."

He shot back, "And you sure can get down for an uptight corporate sister. I'd never have guessed it, getting all hot and funky. You surprise me, girl. I like it."

And he'd surprised you, too, being more than what you'd thought but always just what you needed.

As you stand in your living room drying off with a towel, the shower steaming up the bathroom, you watch Derrick slowly stripping off his rugby jersey to his wifebeater undershirt. He has nice shoulders and a great back and his oversized shirt had been hiding big strong arms and a really nice ass in jeans barely held up by a thick leather belt. He was honey-dipped, his skin a smooth dark chocolate. His nicely shaped bald head perfectly suits his strong nose, round dark eyes, and full lips. He's good-looking, if you look hard enough. Normally you go for drop-dead gorgeous, but the more clothes Derrick took off, the more he became your type.

Naked, his legs are thick and strong; he has big feet and slightly splayed toes. His legs are sweetly bowed. His chest is wide and curly dark hairs barely discernible against his skin taper down to his stomach and then disappear into his groin. He takes your towel and drops it to the floor, then he pulls you toward him and slips his fingers under your shirt, pulling it slowly over your head. Beads of sweat still glisten on your skin. He licks a trail moist and hot down from your neck to your navel, stopping at the waistband of your skirt. He hooks his fingers into the elastic and slips it down and eases you out of the drenched jersey fabric. Your panties are next and you step out of them. He then stands and looks at you, his hands shaping your shoulders, then your arms and your hips. His skin blue-black in the candlelight appears like velvet. He turns you around, then fits himself against you. Snuggled in tightly he wraps his arms around you and licks another salty trail from the tip of your shoulder up across your neck. He breathes his moist breath against your ear, his teeth nibble chocolate kisses on your lobe. When he hears you moan he picks you up and takes you into the bathroom, shutting the door behind you.

More Courageous Contrasts

Forget everything you think you know about attraction. Forget about your type, about what you are looking for, or what you think you want or don't want. The rules are changing. These days the definition of a "type" are expanding and growing as our world becomes smaller and more global. It's time to forget what you think you know about types of people and character based on looks, status, socioeconomics, religion, color, class, education, and background. These days that's all changed. We no longer wear ourselves on our sleeves. Character is as deeply imbedded in our psyche as our culture, our origins, and our backgrounds. There are as many different types of black people as there are shades among us. It's taken White America decades to figure this out, and many are still unconvinced. Now blacks are coming to the same realization about each other.

Our clothes don't make us who we are; neither do our jobs, our family history, our friends, our salary, our neighborhood, our color, or our class. The only thing that makes us who we are is who we are. And you'll never get that from someone in an instant or even a day. It takes a while to get to know the person behind the facade, the man behind the image, or the woman behind the trappings. There really is no such thing as a type. We are as complex as the world we are raised in among the many different types of people who made us who we are. So to think you have a type and are attracted only to that type is not only shortsighted, it's also self-defeating.

Every day there is a new type of black man or woman maturing and coming into their own, who is completely different from what you think you know and like. And although this new guy looks just like the old guy, get ready, he is absolutely nothing like him and you should be glad. Our world is bigger than where we live, the town, city, country, or the part of the world we live in. If we learn to be accepting and to not discriminate, to choose rather than to merely accept what we are used to, then all the different types of black people around us can be remarkable and fascinating. At best eye-opening, astounding, life changing, at least simply extraordinary. We will then no longer be bound by old rules that don't work, but we will not have lost the flavor of our taste. It's time to move forward, away from the tried and not always true, from childhood familiarities toward more courageous contrasts.

Different Strokes for Different Folks

Brown Sugar 3 explores what happens when opposites attract, because being involved with our opposite allows us to see ourselves more clearly than when we are with someone with whom we share many similarities. It also allows us to see different aspects of ourselves and our world through their eyes.

The relationships I've found alternately most satisfying and most frustrating are the ones where we've been complete opposites: socioeconomically, philosophically, physically, mentally, in our background or our families. That's when I really had to make the effort to understand that person, and for them to understand me. Subsequently I was able to experience things I might not have: other types of music, literature, cultures, backgrounds, points of view.

As I become more involved with men who are very different from me, I find that it is our differences that make our interactions stimulating and interesting. That variety is truly the spice of life. To a southerner, my northern sensibilities were as fascinating to them as their southern traits were to me. How an American finds my West Indian characteristics alternately intriguing and confounding. Or how an African's mannerisms illuminate parts of my own African background though we come from completely different cultures. Who we are goes farther back than our color, shade, nationality, background, beliefs, income, friends, or our circumstances. Just because someone is different from you or from anyone else you know doesn't mean that you don't have many things in common.

The stories in *Brown Sugar 3* celebrate many different strokes, for many different folks. Here you'll find stories of opposites attracting with passionate results. Black, white, Asian, Latin American, African, and African American. The lawyer is drawn to the gangster, the old to the young, the mother to the convict, the rich to the poor, the ethereal to the corporeal, the gay to the straight, the professor to the student, the saint to the sinner, and the intellectual to the street smart. These stories are told by best-selling authors and award-winning literary writers and performance poets whom you already know and love, writing outside of their genre but in their own particular style about characters you'll recognize in places you'll know: Patricia Elam, Denene Millner and Nick Chiles, Trisha R. Thomas, Michael Datcher, Lolita Files, Karen E. Quinones Miller, Lori Bryant-Woolridge, Wanda Coleman, E. Ethelbert Miller, Leone Ross, Tracy Price-Thompson, Michael A. Gonzales, Lisa Teasley, Preston L. Allen, Sharrif Simmons, John Keene, Raquel Cepeda, and Miles Marshall Lewis. What their stories give you are different glimpses into the many different worlds that make up Black America, and each truly represents what makes us tick sexually and emotionally.

The Choices Are Endless

These days I know there's no one type of person who is right for me. I may have preferences, likes and dislikes, that certain something that just drops my drawers. For me it was arty intellectuals; we all have our cross to bear. But I now embrace the many different types of men out there, the gorgeous go-getters, the bookish academics, the B-Boys, the sporty guys, the shy introverts, and the outspoken activists. The movers and the shakers and the solitary writers, changing the world one page at a time.

I'm finding that these men can teach me about their world and show me different parts of my world through their eyes. They allow me to appreciate how different we all are from each other and help me to learn about myself through those differences. The choices are endless for exploration of yourself and your world and the people in it. In *Brown Sugar 3* you will find characters pulled in many different directions toward people they never dreamt they'd be attracted to, with passionate and surprising results. Their stories celebrate brothers and sisters in every size, color, shade, tone, and hue, and they take place all over America and the world. In the gritty city streets and the rural towns of Middle America; in the academic enclaves of the Midwest and the L.A. party scene; in the hip New York spots and the downtown Brooklyn hangouts; on the East Coast and the West, the North to the dirty South, uptown and downtown.

It's Time to Come Correct

Writing about sex has always been an honorable tradition. Many of our best authors have explored the depths of passion and pathos in their writing: James Baldwin, Toni Morrison, Langston Hughes, Ntozake Shange, John A. Williams, Audre Lord, Chester Himes, Alice Walker, Gloria Naylor, Frank Lamont Phillips, Barbara Chase-Riboud, Opal Palmer Adisa, E. Ethelbert Miller, among them.

The stories you are about to read set the stage for seduction with a distinctly new flavor and they are as insightful as they are sexy. Let Wanda Coleman's poetic prose transport you behind prison walls into a strange and tender relationship in "Harold and

Popcorn." Preston L. Allen is back with his gritty and sexy "Who I Choose to Love." If you liked his stories in *Brown Sugar* and *Brown Sugar 2*, then you're going to love Nadine and Johnny's continuing drama. This time, though, you'll start at the very beginning. Then let husband-and-wife writing team Denene Millner and Nick Chiles take you underground in "Play It Again." Their story of seduction is played out in alternating male and female perspectives when an upwardly mobile sister finds herself under the spell of a subway musician whose musical prowess transports her to a place outside of social class. Then follow performance poet Sharrif Simmons's sexy urban romance as his characters, one a lawyer the other lawless, get caught up in "Love and the Game." If you're looking for a Hollywood ending, you won't find it there. In Lori Bryant-Woolridge's otherworldly "Close Encounters," a single mom takes a break from her day-to-day and winds up in a place where nothing is what it seems. In Leone Ross's ethereal "The Contract," we feel the pull between a young man yearning to lose his "virginity" and the "older" woman who grants him his wish; but get ready, this story has a twist. In Trisha R. Thomas's sad and deeply affecting "So Much to Learn," a woman reflects back to her first love, her college professor twenty years her senior, and how it changed her life. Michael Datcher's "Happiest Butterfly in the World" will surprise you. It is a wild ride that ends with a bang as a petite and outwardly proper librarian is drawn to a huge, streetwise young buck barely out of high school. In Lisa Teasley's sexy and sorrowful "Center for Affections," her heroine, a former model du jour put out to pasture once her "African" look passes out of favor, must reassess herself and her sexuality, slowly finding the lost pieces of herself along the way. Miles Marshall Lewis's "Diva Moves" is a quietly sexy morality tale that cautions us to be ourselves, because there is someone out there who will love us exactly the way we are if we'd let them. Raquel Cepeda's spiritual fairy tale "God Bodies and Nag Champa" teaches us that we *can* have a second chance at first love. Patricia Elam's unflinching "Scenes from a Marriage" will make you think twice about the bonds of marriage, sacrifice, and fidelity when a new husband, who's given up his bisexual life to start a family, starts to regret his decision. You're gonna laugh when you read Karen E. Quinones Miller's funny and insightful "Auld Lang Syne," which perfectly illustrates how karma is a boomerang. If you like to watch, then go straight to John Keene's hot and surprising story "Sums," as two wildly different men find themselves pulled into the same fantasy. Then make sure you're sitting when you read Lolita Files's shockingly raunchy "Standing Room Only," where an ordinary night in L.A. takes on a whole new meaning when a sister gets more than she bargained for but exactly what she needed. All you big, bold, and beautiful honeys are finally gonna exhale after reading Michael A. Gonzales's "Crazy Love," wherein a rail-thin brother "finds solace in the exhilarating arms of full-figured strangers." "The African in the American" is Tracy Price-Thompson's perceptive and illuminating story about a young warrior fresh from the shores of Africa who almost gives up trying to find the African in the Americans he comes across, until he finds a woman who embodies the finest qualities of both. Last but certainly not least, journey with poet and writer E. Ethelbert Miller in his introspective and deeply affecting story "Korea," where a man is pulled to a Korean woman and back to a place he though he'd left forever.

You won't close this book unaffected. These stories go beyond erotica, beyond sex, to a place you will find more familiar than not, no matter how far from your own experiences they may be. These are the things that make us who we are in Black America. These are the real souls of black folks and they will take you there in many more ways than one.

So come with me now, 'cause it's time again to come correct.

Brown Sugar 3

WANDA COLEMAN

Harold and Popcorn

*O*n *The Yard the muted pops come in clusters, the smell of hot butter fills the hillside air. We cling-and-clutch beneath the heavy yellow
tarp, a block's length from the gun tower. Against that true-blue heaven
above us, armed guards in olive drab uniforms leisurely pace the deck.
Outside the tarp, other lovers are lined up, eavesdrop on our pleasure,
await their chance to lock lips and legs. . . .*

* * *

Open my eyes and his wavy bushy head is roiling 'tween my
thighs. Raise my head a bit, and I can see the heavily muscled arc
of his deeply dark shoulders and back cutting a dark horizon
against the unfamiliar white bedroom walls. We rock together,
cradled in our need. We are in somebody else's house, the huge
coils of their box-spring mattresses squeaking counterpoint to the
gyrations of my hips.

I had stood before him, bold as lust. "You wanna fuck?"

I said it straight out, like I was askin' if he wanted a smoke.

His head snapped back ever so slightly, but his eyes glinted
and those thick-thick kissables parted, and those perfect white
ivories expanded in amusement.

1

"You don't play, do you?"

"Who has time for play?" I made my voice throaty.

His right hand troubled his lips, in pleasantly shocked consideration, while his other hand teased his waist girlishly, as if to ask, "Who's got the cock?"

But he said, "You're bodacious," eyes traveling my face to my breasts and back.

The word was just coming into vogue out here, but I had heard it recently and therefore understood. "Does that unnerve you?"

"Like—not quite. It might, under other circumstances."

Meaning that he was the prisoner and I was at liberty. Meaning, under the terms of his incarceration, I had the advantage. Meaning that since he had not had a woman in yea months, he was sick to his socks of blue balls and masturbation. Meaning he was about to take this opportunity afforded by state-issued furlough.

"What do I call you?" His eyes danced mine. Somebody in the neighborhood was cooking "Oh Mary Don't You Weep" on the stereo and it was heating up the living room. The other inmates were pairing off, making their selection from those women who were available members of the Criminal Justice Arts & Culture League, as the remaining members, male and female, crept around back to the kitchen table, to chat over dominoes and bid whisk, to smoke and drink.

This was not about whoring; it was about otherness. It was about entrapment at birth. It was about understanding that our society isolates and perverts what it does not understand. It was about salvage if not saving. It was about him and me—my knowing who he is without illusions, and his delight in discovering me.

Without looking, we could sense the tension between bodies drawn together in the rhythm as if magnetized by loneliness. The room vibrated with the soft undertone of voices drunk on anticipation.

I held up the joint of Panama Red. He looked at it.

"Sweet Meat, I don't think I'm going to require any outside stimulation."

Magically, it floated from my fingertips, clasped with a smile and a stranger's hoarsely whispered "Thank you." Harold's eyes never released mine. Shyly, his right hand stroked my forehead, lightly, skipping back to primp my 'fro.

"Feels soft. Like cotton candy."

I will come to know the cool touch of those umber hands against my flesh as well as the cool voids of his black eyes and ripples of hair.

"It's the Injun in me," he explains. "On my father's side. You look a little tribal yourself."

It's my skin, he means, and he runs his hands along my thighs, which will soon become part of our ritual, noting the Sioux redness beneath my Ashanti brown, as if I'd been spanked all over. He licks his tongue out, leaving a wet trail in the swath of his eyes.

"Sweet Meat, you taste like my mama's pecan pie."

"And you . . . you taste like my daddy's blues."

When our lips meet, tributaries merge into a great nameless

river, flooding through us and washing away all distance and difference. We reach into and through one another in that familiar
yet alien space of ultimate knowing. There is a rush from my ears
to my groin, followed by an indescribable series of jolts, and
exquisite sweetness. Upon parting, we share glazed stares, awash
in mutual dizziness as our hearts throb as one.

Radar tells me what my eyes will eventually confirm. Harold is
hugely hung, circumcised, as thick around as my wrist, soft on
the outside, granite at the core, with a swing to the right when
erect, from years of too-tight jockeys made to constrain something smaller.

"Uh-huh," he says; a forefinger rims the black bra peeking
from under my puff-sleeve sweater. "B-cup. Just enough to fill a
hungry man's mouth. Nuthin' hangin'." His other hand hugs me
from below, pushes me close. "Loose booty! Ohmymy!"

He's taller and buffer than what I'm used to, and it feels so
good to be lost in his arms. We're joined at the crotch, swaying.
Someone has hit the lights as afternoon segues into evening.
Someone's located the nearest radio and the room is bathed in the
soul sounds of our teens. We bump and grind in that perfect,
unstudied choreography of an untrammeled Africa working its
way through the American.

As we take a swift turn, we notice a couple tripping over one
another, as they make for a doorway against the western corner of
the room. She giggles, his arms clamped around her waist. I look
up and see his eyes are on them. He looks down and into me.

"We're next."

"Groovy."

"Do they still say that?"

"No. But it fits."

"Yeah. Cuz you sure fit my groove, Sweet Meat."

And we're off whirling somewhere Up There, spinners against the chaos. He is every dreamlover I've ever swooned for in the still of my empty nights. I imagine myself, sitting alone, savoring these very moments, squeezing the emotion from them and into love letters. Listening to The Delphonics sweetly croon as I scrawl his name in my journal over and over again preceded by a Mrs. For this, I am courting a felony.

The particulars go something like this: I'm a volunteer worker in the prison movement. I am divorced, have two children, a car, a full-time secretarial job, no men friends, and am a wanna-be singer. That last item brings me here—presenting my repertoire on program at penal institutions up and down the state. Keeping the spirit of our brothers alive, they call it. Those big beautiful brothers, many of whom are unjustly criminalized for surviving by those any-means-necessary. Harold's an armed robber, doing indeterminate time because of catching several "beefs" while serving his sentence, a beef being a crime or violation committed during incarceration. One of those beefs concerns the murder of the woman who testified against him on the robbery charge. He is suspected, but there is no evidence to connect him with her death. He has less than eighteen months left. His mother and sister cover him as much as they are able without complications involving the law. His father went out for beer and cigarettes when he was nine months old and never returned. Trouble began in high school, with poor grades, bad boys, and nothing to do on weekends. He has children that he claims, and likewise, the ambition to become a singer on the outside, having the looks if unable to carry a note.

Sometimes I give him voice lessons.

We play games of chess and checkers on The Yard. I buy him cherry snow-cone drinks from the visitor's canteen, chewing gum, and packs of Kool filter longs to take inside later. He'll use them for trade. We talk about music, entertainment, politics, and what's going on in the community. We talk about the length of his sentence and the eventuality of parole. Otherwise, we never discuss the future.

One day he will knock on my front door. I will open it and invite him in. It will be curious but not awkward. We will eye one another coolly. We will mutually agree to part as friends. He will go his way; I will go mine.

These are the facts of our lives, but they have nothing to do with our moment.

Kissing is what we do. I am hooked on his thick shapely lips. Take their texture and flavor with me after each visit. Live from one visit to the next by carefully unrolling the details from my mind: his hands—huge and spatulate with nails three times mine. His waist is thick yet narrow in proportion to his tight, full hips. His broad chest sprouts hairs "like a white man," a characteristic he doesn't like but lives with, preferring the smooth hairlessness of most bruthas. His pharaoh's nose—identical to King Tut's—his thick sideburns betraying a touch of the Irish for all the charcoal of his skin's tone. Like me, he is soft-bodied but strong.

*   *   *

There's a magic in his mouth and he moves his tongue in a studied dart and flicker before scorching mine, overwhelms me in his embrace as I willingly drown. We spend a few minutes talking, eating the lunch I've prepared, the rest of our hour or two kissing until my lips blister. Then, alone, I drive the hundreds of miles home to live for that next visit—as if my life is otherwise suspended.

* * *

We spend hours talking person-to-person, three to four times a week. We talk like teenagers in the throes of first love. I don't know how he manages to call me so often. I don't understand the workings of the scam, even after he carefully explains during one visit. I content myself with curling up on the couch, ear pressed to the receiver, listening as he woos me over the wires. I don't dare daydream about this when going about my daily doings, shopping, having the car serviced, going to and from work. I try to block out all thoughts of Harold lest my love come down on me. I do not know that what we are having is called phone sex; I simply enjoy having it. But that doesn't stop our longing for physical contact.

We look enough alike to be sister and brother, and so he arranges for me to obtain the fake identification I will need for our conjugal visit. We will arrive in separate cars. His mother will come with me, part of that first day spent staring out the window on the opposite side of the quarters divided into a bathroom, faux kitchenette, living room, and a bedroom. Mom will sleep sitting up in the chair, he and I in that strange twin bed that strains under our weight.

"What's the matter?"

"I don't know. It's funny, I guess. Just the thought of you being my sister. Even though it's pretend, it turns me off."

I laugh. "Maybe. Plus your mother's in the next room."

"I guess that's it, too."

I follow his eyes as they trace the patterns on the dark beige wallpaper—Spanish stripes and curls.

"Here we are, playing this kind of game. It's so weird. Like I've gotten used to being caged like an animal—in a cell. Like I belong there 'steada here. It's scary."

"Maybe you should go along with it instead of fighting it."

"What do you mean?"

"Remember the first time we were together?"

"Yeah." He smiles, closes his eyes.

"Go back there. We're in that house there—that room."

"On those monster coils. I can still feel them diggin' in my back."

"That's it . . ."

The earth feels like it did when I was a child, the room reminiscent of my great-aunt's. It smells much-lived-in, of old radiator steam and chamomile tea. There's the dresser, the chest of drawers, the night tables. It's rose-colored in the early evening light, deepened by the rose-patterned paper on the wall. We pull back the quilt and laugh at the leavings of the previous couple—two saucer-sized splotches.

"Seems they did themselves proper." He laughs.

I snatch a case from one of the downy pillows and cover their tracks. As I start to turn he pushes me forward, throws up my skirt, looks.

"God—there's enough here for two women!"

My bikini skivvies conceal nothing. He pulls them away, stands to doff his shirt, unfasten his belt, as I scramble out of my dress and bra.

"Emmm, ummm."

Talk about God? There's that instant in which all men seem either demonic or godlike, that stance taken just before penetration—in which he looms and in which a woman resists in pain or surrenders in pleasure.

*   *   *

I can hear the poppoppop of it bursting. There's always music. This time someone's snappin' their fingers to James Brown. I can hear the distant mutter of fifty conversations—men visiting with wives and girlfriends, a few with other relatives. Beneath the yellow tarp the slag gray of the wall nearby can be seen, and two dozen pairs of sneakers, workshoes, sandals, and pumps. I can feel each thrust and turn, up inside me, my nipples against his chest, and he begins to rock steady, moaning softly with the sway, moaning as that surge shoots from the base of his spine . . . as I feel my uncontrollable muscular clasp and release . . . as we vibrate through one another. . . .

*   *   *

The ritual starts the night before. I put on potatoes and eggs to boil for the salad. I cut and fry a chicken until it's crisp. Or I make thick-layered roast beef sandwiches. Or I smother a ham in pineapple. I bake a pie, cookies, or cake—depending on what I brought last time. If it's a cake, I cut out a section of the lower level, and conceal a lid of marijuana inside before applying the icing and the second layer. If it's a pie, I seal the lid in tinfoil and bake it in under the top crust. I know I will be punished if I'm caught. But he has asked this of me, and I am willing. The ritual ends with a bath. I know he's going to shower and shave. So that morning, before seeing the kids off to the sitter's, I take a long luxurious soak in the tub, lots of lilac bubble bath. Then I lotion down and select my outfit for the day.

Snapshot: Harold posing for me, hands to hips, teeth blazing, huge wavy Afro crown. Snapshot: Me and Harold cheek-to-cheek at the picnic table with his inmate-partners Lonnie and Ray-Ray, and their ladies. Snapshot: Me posing in Harold's embrace. I'm wearing a red minidress that reveals my long, thick thighs. He's bulging out of his royal blue tank top and deep-cuffed denims.

When they move Harold upstate, the ritual becomes more adventuresome. It means paying more in sitter and motel fees for the privilege of seeing him. It means timing my travel so that I drive all night. It means sleeping in the car on the prison parking lot until they open the gate. It means turning around and heading back home after the visit, driving hours without sleep, so I can get home in time to go to work on Monday morning. It means sacrificing food and phone money. It's the price I pay to be near him, to prove my devotion.

If there is a theme to this, it is kiss and tongue or tongue and kiss.

Often, when they have simultaneous visits, the inmates and their ladies gather around the same table, flirting outrageously with one another. The men will ask their women to stick out their tongues—to see who has the best, and laughter ensues. Well—her tongue may come to a point, all the better to flick with, or her tongue may have greater texture, all the better to lick with, or her tongue may have a slight tip that makes it advantageous for certain operations.

All I need to come is Harold's tongue scorching my mouth. The way he touches my chin and commands me . . . the way his eyes roll away when enthralled . . . the way he moans from his groin before the thunder. And sometimes, when it's too intensely good, he trembles all over. The way he trembles now, against me, in this eternity.

"Shit, Sweet Meat—Godammm! That was good!"

"Harold, you're trembling."

"I can't help it. That happens to me sometimes. I feel it that deep, I guess."

"Hmmm."

"Like that?"

"Like that."

The prison sprawls eastward, across the valley like an animal of stone. I almost expect it to rise, and rear like a stallion, the men and women inside it thrown helter-skelter. It is a maximum security facility, and unlike the one down south, we meet inside a visitors' room, with redwood walls, windows, and huge picnic tables. There is a courtyard for those who want to enjoy the sun and fresh air, and a popcorn booth set up to provide punch and free, fresh, hot, buttered popcorn to the inmates and their families. Children are allowed, and many recently jailed fathers see newborns for the first time.

"Gosh, I wish I didn't do this. I'm glad the guys can't see me."

"They'd think . . . ?"

"I was a sissy."

Dear Sweet Meat,

I think of us together all the time—just you and me. I imagine all the good things we will make life be. There will be no stopping us. We were meant to be together, without a doubt. The delicious smell of you stays with me hours and hours. I can't get enough of you. The stars in the sky, the birds in the trees, they all spell you. My self-esteem was pretty low until you came along. Now it soars. And with you at my side, I know there is nothing that I can't accomplish. Make a special place for my letters. Keep them near you always. We're one now, after that special day. There's no lookin' back. Other lovers are out of luck. We're more married than married. You know what I mean.

Forever,

Harold

One day, I'm coming through the gate all done up in pink. They check my identification as usual, followed by a light frisk, a check of shoes, purse, and hat. All the while the sergeant is smiling. He knows me well by now. He knows who I am going to see. They carefully and deliberately unpack my picnic basket, make note of the potato salad rimmed with deviled eggs and tomato slices, the ham, reeking of cloves, honey, and mustard, and the peach cobbler, in disposable tin pan, still retaining its ovenly warmth. The sergeant catches my eye as he produces a fresh pencil from his spin together, both of us now imprisoned in the passion that has become bond, in this finite universe, this borrowed room, this borrowed bed.

In his love's waning, Harold trembles beside me, here, which is our forever. My head rests above his armpit, against his right biceps, one arm across his chest, and I feel each tremor ride through him. We are silent. Beyond the door we hear the undertones of rhythm and blues shot through with laughter. His fingers tap out the bass guitar line against my upper arm. No one can touch us in this afterward. This is our now. We are immortals. We are free.

pocket. And I watch as he leans over and pokes it through the center of the cobbler.

I do not blink.

He smiles at me. I smile back.

*   *   *

Huge kernels float past us in the air like Goodyear blimps, crusted with salt and butter, flashing hot like moons orbiting suns. I am in a delirium of pleasure, hold him tightly to me as his erection subsides, as the tremors take hold.

"Hey, Blood—hurry up. Before they get wise to the hookup."

Gradually, normal perspective takes hold, and we turn around to see we've knocked over one of the baskets and our clothes are covered with hot buttered popcorn, a few kernels sticking to our hair. We knock them free, and at the "all's clear," leap from under the tarp and another couple leaps under it. I hear her giggle as the tarp is dropped.

*   *   *

"We have no future, Sweet Meat. You know that, don't you?"

"Yes, Harold."

"But you're willing to do this anyway?"

"Yes."

"You're something else . . . something else . . ."

I quiet him with my tongue. It is coral and shaped like an elongated *u*. I press him back against the sheets and pillowcase, knead his chest. He moans at the promise. I fulfill it, as I glide my groin against his. He springs erect, and I rise up to lower myself, gyrating slightly with the move. He bucks to meet me,

PRESTON L. ALLEN

Who I Choose to Love

*H*e was the handsomest man I had ever seen, like he could be on TV or something. Brother had skin the color of bread just out the oven, and sparkling eyes something lighter than brown, kinda like brown with gray in it. And them long lashes. Them heart-shaped lips. That smile that dimpled on one side. And so old to be a virgin.

I was sixteen and had lost my cherry like three, four years ago already, and he was about twenty when he knocked on my door. I open up without asking who it is, because I'm skipping school and expecting company. But it's not who I'm expecting. It's this pretty boy in a white shirt and tie, with one of them old school high-top fades, a Bible, and a lawnmower.

He says all proper, "I see that your grass is overgrown. I shall gladly cut it for you, free of charge, if you will allow us to come back tonight and have Bible study with you."

I'm checking out the body on this movie star standing in front of me. Tall, like six-one. Wide shoulders. Big chest. Narrow waist, narrow like on football players, who got big thighs but lean waists, so their pants got to be big enough to fit their thighs, but always end up bagging out around the waist. His pants fit like that. Bagged out. Loose. But there's still the outline of a large package swinging between them thighs. I'm like touching my lip with a finger and thinking, *little Miss Nadine don't do church boys*, but this one's got my attention for real. So I'm like, "Sorry, Jethro, but my daddy dog cuts our grass."

He looks kinda familiar, but nobody I know looks that good. He twinkles all cute, then gets serious. "Well, this way your father can rest from his labors after a long day at work. May I speak with him, ma'am? Or your mother?"

I say, "Daddy Dog and the moms ain't home. Plus, they got their own religion, Jethro. They don't have time to be talking to no Jehovah's Witness."

Pretty boy takes offense. "First of all, my name ain't Jethro. It's Johnny. You can call me Brother Johnny. Second, we're not Jehovah's Witnesses. We're from the Church of the Rushing Mighty Wind. And third, ain't you supposed to be in school?"

"I'm home sick."

"You don't look sick."

Jethro's right, I'm wearing a tube top, hoochie shorts, and leopard skin go-go boots. "All right, Jethro. You caught me. I'm skipping."

I catch him checking out my body, but he turns it into a lecture. "You should never skip school. Truancy leads to idleness. Idle hands are the devil's workshop."

"You right about that, Brother Jethro. I sure am idle."

"Brother Johnny," he corrects, pressing that Bible to his chest, looking at me like he wants to help, but I haven't needed help since I was born. He says, "I could pray with you right now if you'd like."

I don't like.

And I don't like the way he's looking at me now. Shifting from lust to high horse like that. I know he's diggin' what he sees. My body is tight. My tiddies look good in this tube and no bra. But naw, he gotta go and ruin it. This is how the righteous get the upper hand on you. He's judging me and he don't even know me.

I peep my gold bangles like I'm in a hurry and they're a wristwatch. I get all sassy with him. "Man, I ain't got time for no praying. My boyfriend's gonna be here in a few minutes to fuck me."

I say it to shock him. It shocks him. Grown man like him, turning away, shame-faced. Haven't seen that one in a while. A man with shame. Man or boy. Most of them I know, look you straight in the eye and tell you what they like for you to do to them and how they like for you to do it.

This big Christian boy from that Church of the Rushing Whatevers, he stumbles backward off our landing, grabs on to his lawnmower, looking at me, blinking like the sunlight is too strong. Behind him, I see other men with white shirts, ties, lawnmowers, knocking on doors. Big Christian boy is leaning heavy on his John Deere with its Jesus Loves You stickers and looking at me with a face that has no tattoos, no piercings, no scars. His eyes are talking to me now. His eyes are preaching to me.

For a quick minute, I'm ashamed. I haven't felt shame in so long. Brother Johnny's trembling beside his lawnmower, looking like he wants to fall on his knees and pray for all of my sins, and all I feel for him is anger for making me feel shame.

He don't even know me. He don't know what I had to do to find love. He just comes here and looks at this house and thinks, middle-class neighborhood. She gots no business acting all wild. Her poor parents must try so hard, and a daughter like this is the thanks they get. Her poor parents must cry for her. Yeah, they cry, and I'm sorry about that. But I cry, too.

He's looking at me and making me feel ashamed that J.H. is pulling up in his ride real slow, because he sees this big fool standing here. He's not sure if it's the cops or somebody Daddy Dog sent to spy on us again, so he's cruising slow until I give him the signal. Then he pulls into the drive and jumps out the car.

The radio in the Eldorado is still jammin' "She's Built, She's Stacked, All the Curves a Man Likes," as J.H. pimp-rolls toward Johnny in a magenta and gold sweatsuit, with his platinum medallions swinging outside the zipper and his lean, mean, clean-shaved head bopping. He's got a joint glowing between his lips, and he's all five foot five of muscular chest, and arms pumped up bigger than his head, and them skinny chicken legs he's too lazy to work out. I can see he's ready to jack-slap the fool with the lawnmower talking to his girl. J.H. is a quick one to jack-slap, no matter how big you think you are. He musta spotted the Bible in Johnny's hand because when he gets to him, all he says is, "Whuzzup witchu?" and throws his arms open in challenge. "Whuzzup witchu, nigga?"

J.H. is scary, but Johnny stands his ground. Maybe because he's got a little size on him. Maybe because he thinks Jesus is on his side. "I was just asking her if she wanted me to cut her grass."

Smoking that weed, J.H.'s too buzzed to notice Church Boy's not scared of him. If he was a little less buzzed, there'd be serious trouble. J.H. looks down at the lawnmower, and then spits on the ground next to Johnny's polished church shoes. He squeezes the joint back between his lips and says, "Cut grass? For real?"

"Then we'll come back later and have Bible study with the family."

J.H.'s eyes are half-closed, sleepy-looking cool. Don't let it fool you. He's jealous as hell. Trying to figure out if I'm doing the preacher boy on the side. "We? A whole group a ya'll? Her daddy's a preacher." He nods at me. "Ain't your daddy a preacher, Nadine?"

"Used to be."

"Well, whuzzup wit this?"

"I don't know. He just knocked and said he wanted to cut our grass. See." I point across the street. J.H. looks to where I'm pointing. My neighborhood of boring-assed pastel houses and two-car garages has been invaded by these gray-headed men looking like lawnmower salesmen with their ties and dress shirts. "Damn," he says, a smile breaking across his face.

J.H. don't smile much, especially not in front of other men. Smiling is a sign of weakness. Smiling is for fools. You smile when you trying to get some pussy, maybe. Or when you finish stealing something. You don't just be going up to other brothers smiling at them. But J.H. is smiling now at Johnny with all his gold teeth showing, top and bottom, because this whole necktie and lawnmower situation is just so whack.

When J.H. signals for me to get on with it, I lock the door, walk past them, and slide into the Eldorado. J.H. is really cracking up now with his chest shoved out and his hands on his hips as Johnny pushes the lawnmower out the yard. Then Johnny stops and turns real slow like he's thought about it hard, and he says, "You know she's too young for this."

J.H. stops laughing. Johnny's made him mad now. Daddy Dog has told him the same thing. Warned him he's gonna sic the cops on him if he don't leave me alone. As though he's making me do what I do. I do it because I want to do it. J.H. don't make me do nothing I don't want to do. Johnny's pushing his lawnmower again, and he don't see J.H. reaching into his waistband where he keeps his gun. He shouts at Johnny, "Preacher Boy!"

When Johnny turns, J.H.'s hand is on the gun butt curving out his waistband. Johnny shoves his hands up in the air like a stickup in the movies and J.H. hasn't even taken the gun out. All J.H. does is yell at him, "Suck my dick, Preacher Boy!"

Now we're both laughing at Johnny with his hands in the air. Brother Johnny ain't so brave now.

J.H. is still laughing hard when he gets back in the Eldorado, because the joke is on all of them, Johnny and Daddy Dog, too. What they don't know is that J.H. is young, too. He just looks old because life's been hard, and he's had to drop out of school, and toughen up like a man to make money and survive. He ain't but sixteen. My sweet baby. And I'm sixteen, and two months older than him, and the day is ours, and we ride, and soon I'm not even thinking about Johnny-preacher-at-my-door no more and the shame he made me feel for being who I am and loving who I choose to love.

At J.H.'s crib, we make love, make love, make glorious love, in the sauna, then on his heart-shaped waterbed wrapped up in silk sheets. I am filled and happy when it's over and he is, too. But some of his boys are out there with them other girls, and as we lay on the bed we hear them giggling and squealing and soon his hand is pinching my tiddies again.

I'm like, "Baby, why you trying to frustrate yourself like that?"

" 'Cause I love you, and I wanna rock your world. If we ain't have to sneak around like this, I could spend all day with you and fuck you like fo' or five times. I'm good for fo' or five."

"You already rock my world, baby. I love how we make love. There's nobody make love like you. Three with you is a lot."

He groans. "Mmm."

I hug his beautiful bald head to my chest to get his mind off these dangerous numbers. Three, to him, *used to be* a lot. Now he has to go for four. He's quiet as I massage him. I pray he's about to nod off to sleep. My prayers are not answered.

"But that other nigga used to hit it like five times."

"I wasn't with him like I am with you."

"Five times."

"It ain't mean shit to me, baby."

"I shoulda smoked his ass."

"What you did was enough."

But it ain't enough. I should never have told J.H. the part about how many times. Onion Man wasn't shit compared to J.H. How can I get him to understand that the past is the past? What we are now is all we need to be. What I did back then was just a thing that happened. What me and J.H. have is quality. All he got to do is smile at me to make me drip. "You're who I love, baby. I choose to be with you."

His movements are angry against my chest. Pushing away. I

should have seen this coming. He rolls over and grabs his gun. Checks to see it's loaded. Clicks off the safety. I sink into the mattress. Look at the clock. It's after two. His scary old grandmother, who almost never comes out, is in the room next to ours. I hear the soap opera turned up loud coming through the walls. I hear her coughing. From out in the living room, where his boys and them other girls are at, I hear squeals of pleasure. Now he's aiming the gun at me. Sighting down the barrel. He loves me. I know he won't shoot. He loves me. I go to the bedroom door. Don't even waste time throwing on clothes. Click the door shut behind me. Exhale.

Everybody looks up at me. The lanky, high-yellow boy is on the leather couch eating out some dancer I don't know while another one is riding his dick. The squeals are coming from the one on his dick. The white girl they call Zilla, because she has Godzilla tiddies. Bouncing up and down on that big dick, moaning and screaming. Them other two of J.H.'s boys are watching the action with forties in one hand and their dicks in the other. They pretend not to notice me all naked because they know how crazy jealous J.H. is, but the action slows down as I grab a seat on a low footstool near the big-screen TV and put my head in my hands.

Then I remember where I know Church Boy from.

The Church of the Rushing Mighty Wind was where Onion Man took us about two years ago for the choir showdown.

Of all the girls in junior high choir, I got to sit up front, not because I was lead alto, but because Onion Man wanted to do something with his right hand while his left hand was driving.

Whispering shit again about why didn't I start bringing my little sister Pam with me to his house. The three of us could have so much fun. Pam would like it, she really would, he said, and my tears fell down my cheeks in the darkness of the van because I couldn't see how it was not gonna happen to Pam like it happened to me. It was OK for me because I was bad and I deserved it, but Pam was just a child.

I sang real good that night. We all did. Our school got some kind of award for it, or something. Brother Johnny was there that night. We had rented out their church because it had television cameras set up. Him and a few other church folk had stuck around to make sure we didn't mess up their equipment and stuff. Brother Johnny had looked at me funny that night from the back of the church when we were singing, and he had looked at Onion Man banging away on the piano keys, too. He kept looking at me, then at Onion Man, like he knew what was up, which he couldn't have because I hadn't told nobody about it yet, not even J.H. And Lord, why did I tell J.H.?

J.H. is hard because life is hard. My sweet baby. His mama died the day he was born. When he was 'bout ten, he watched as the Left Street Boys smoked his old man. When he tried to stop them, they gave him the scar that runs from his ear to his collarbone. J.H.'s hard because life is hard. Because men like Onion Man exist. Someone has to be hard enough to stand up to them. Someone has to say, this is where it ends. You can't do this to her no more. Next time I'll smoke your ass, they'll find you dead where I done buried other motherfuckers like you, you punk ass, call yourself a teacher onion-headed sonofabitch. Someone has to say she's my bitch now, someone has to say, I'll stab you again, leave her alone. After that, Onion Man left the school and never came back. Didn't even take his briefcase or pick up his last check, I heard. Didn't leave no forwarding address. Nothing. That was 'bout two years ago. Just after we had sung at Johnny's church.

J.H. comes out the room so quiet I don't even hear the door open. "Come back in the room," he says.

I don't look up.

He reaches down and pulls me up by the arm, but gentle-like. It's his way of apologizing. I accept it. Again.

Then I'm on the bed with him, massaging his big arms and barrel chest, his tattoos of a fist with a gun in it. We are going for four in our pleasure palace, with its mirrors on the walls and polished brass furniture and gold. I am massaging his nipples and he is sucking mine. J.H. pushes my hand down and we're both surprised his dick is up again. We will go for four. If I get home late, I can deal with Daddy D. I'ma let J.H. go for four because he's the only one in the world who loves me.

I get on top. I suck his bottom lip, I kiss him little kisses on his lips. He reaches under me, I feel him struggling to find the opening, he is not fully hard anymore. I kiss him again to warm him up, but J.H. ain't nobody's fool. I can't even pretend. Nothing pisses him off more than pretending.

"Shit. I need some mo' stimulation." He puts his hand on my booty. "Zilla still out there?"

"Yeah."

"You think she cute?"

"She all right." Not. She's got lips like Mick Jagger. A face like Mick Jagger. I hate red hair. "There's that other girl out there. The dancer. She's cute."

He laughs and slaps my butt. "Naw, I wanna see you with Zilla. I wanna see you sucking them monster tiddies. Go get her."

If there's anything that pisses J.H. off more than someone who pretends, it's someone who disagrees with him. I call Zilla, and she comes in with her thin red hair plastered to her head with sweat, her big tiddies hanging down to her navel like balloons. Except for her tiddies, she's real skinny. You can see her ribs. Her pussy looks all right, though. Nice little shave job, like a heart.

She gets on the bed with us, puts her arms around me from behind, and fondles my tiddies. Zilla kisses the back of my neck. She starts getting into it, moaning against my skin, trying to make the hairs stand up. She wants more. I stretch my neck so we can kiss. She kisses all right. But she smells like cologne. I'm not into Zilla at all.

J.H. gets off the bed and sits on the chair, watching us. He is naked except for his magenta socks. He has his dick in his hand, and it is hard enough that the head is peeking through the fore-skin. Zilla lays me on my back and props my head up on a pillow. She whispers: "It'll be all right. I know what's up."

She does know what's up. She's good at loving tiddies, even small ones like mine. I kiss her, and she kisses me. Her arms go round me, tenderly. Time becomes timeless. A warm feeling comes over me. I think about love and kindness and happy things. Then she goes back and sucks them tiddies hard, bites on them till it hurts just right, and I get all horny skanky and think about the good stuff like sucking dick and thrusting my hips and fucking my lover so hard my pussy hurts and he can't catch his breath and sucking his tongue and opening my legs for a bigger dick, or two dicks, or clever fingers, a woman's lips, ass fuck, and my hand goes down to my clit, but her hand is already there, and her fingers are clever and tender.

Then my man says, "Come over here, Zilla." I feel her go away from me. I'm not ready for her to go. I open my eyes. He is kissing her, she is kissing him. He says, "Suck this dick for me, Zilla." She says, "I gotta go, man. I gotta take that math test sixth period or they gonna flunk me this time for sure." "Come on, Zilla." "Naw, not with that crazy bitch here," she says, looking at me. "I heard about her." I'm crying and crying and the girl is saying, "What's wrong with her now?" And my man is saying, "She gets like that sometime. Suck this dick for me, Zilla. Forget about her. Why everybody getting all crazy over a little dick suck?"

She's sucking his dick now with her back to me, I watch her pussy lips from behind, I close my eyes, I curl up in a ball. I'm crying, and nobody cares.

J.H. gets me back home before my folks get there. He's apologizing about what he did. This kinda shit just keeps happening. But he's my man, and I love him, and he says it was the reefer made him do it, and he promises, promises, promises he'll make it up to me tomorrow, which is not true because tomorrow is the day they will pick him up for what they say he did to Onion Man.

But as I'm getting out of his car, neither of us knows that. Onion Man's body hasn't been found yet, and J.H. and me are still boyfriend and girlfriend not separated by prison bars, and he's sorry about what he did, and I've got this feeling in my heart like emptiness, which he ain't filling like he used to. We kiss, and he dips so my old man won't catch him at the house again. I go inside and strip out of my hoochie clothes and go-go boots and hide them under my bed for tomorrow, which is never coming again, and put on the blue dress I wore the last time I went to church. I sit on my bed. I listen to the sound of mowing.

I'm empty. Empty.

I hear someone knocking at my door. I step in my slippers and go downstairs. It's Church Boy Johnny in his polished church shoes and tie. He is beautiful. Beautiful. But life is not beautiful. I am not beautiful. Jesus does not love me. He gave His life for me, but for Onion Man too, and I think Johnny knows this. I brush back tears as he says: "I couldn't stop thinking about you all day after you left with that guy. You lay heavy on my heart. The Lord put you on my heart, and I should've done something. I want you to tell me the truth. Are you all right? Did he hurt you?"

The sun is high in the sky behind him. His shadow stretches inside the door. The church boy who couldn't get me off his mind all day. I smile.

"He's my boyfriend," I say.

He shakes his head. "He looks like bad news to me. You shouldn't be with somebody like that. He has a gun."

"True dat."

"People could get hurt."

"True dat. Who should I be with, then?"

"At your age? You shouldn't be with anybody."

I'm looking at him hard now. He looks good with the sun over his head, like a big, fine angel. "You trippin'," I say.

"But it's true. You're so young."

It comes out kinda sad when I say, "Everybody's got to be with somebody. Even you."

"Not if you got the Lord."

"You ain't got nobody?" I say. "One of them church girls ain't scoop you up already? Fine as you are?"

He kinda blushes, and I notice his hands. He's got big hands, long, slender fingers. His hands seem nervous now. He keeps rubbing them together or shoving them in his pockets. He says, "What we are on the outside is not as important as what we are on the inside."

"But you're so young," I throw back at him.

"I'm older than you."

"I know. Duh."

"You know? Then why'd you say it?"

I shake my head. It's trippin' me out that he doesn't get it. He ain't as smart as J.H. I like the way his brows knit up when he gets confused. "I'm just saying, is all."

"Just saying what?" he asks, his brows all knitted up.

"Never mind, Jethro. You were worried about me? That's nice. But why? You don't know me."

"I just wanted to make sure you were OK. There are people in the world who care."

"That's sweet, but I already got parents."

"You seemed upset when he brought you back, is all."

"You saw that?"

"I was across the street."

"You were spying on me." I push right up to him. He's beautiful, with that dimple. Smelling all like musk, cut grass, and righteousness. "You don't know nothing 'bout me."

"I'm not trying to make trouble. I'd better leave."

"Yeah. Get your ass off my property."

"I'm sorry." He lowers his eyes, backs away. I watch him for a while, see if he's really gonna leave. He's at the edge of our walk now. He's leaving. He looks good leaving, he looks good coming, but that's only the outside. I'm wondering about his inside. Wondering about him.

I holler after him, "Jethro."

He turns, hands stuffed in his pockets. "My name is Johnny."

"You can cut my grass for me."

He looks surprised. "For real?"

"Yeah, and do Bible study with the old folks and all that."

He takes his hands out of his pockets. "OK, let me go get my lawnmower."

I lean out the door. "You're sweating. Come inside, let me get you something to drink. What you want, Coke, apple juice? Plain old water?"

He's looking at me with his head kinda tilted to one side, suspicious, then he straightens up. "Apple juice," he says.

I go in the kitchen, and I listen to him walk inside the house. I'm thinking J.H. would fucking kill me and Johnny if he saw this shit. My hand is kinda shaking as I open the fridge. The apple juice bottle is empty. Thank you, Pam, drink all the damned juice and leave the empty bottle in the fridge. My voice is trembling. I don't know why. "How 'bout some Coke? The apple juice is finished."

He doesn't answer. The house is quiet. I begin to think that I only imagined him. I turn. He's standing in the living room looking at the family portraits on the walls, me in pigtails, Pam in Afro-puffs, Daddy Dog and the moms in suit and church dress. His hands are stuffed in his pockets. "Coke is fine," he says.

I pour him the Coke and hand it to him. "You can sit down. Damn, brother. Have a seat. You're making me nervous." I knock the stupid vinyl-wrapped cushions off the couch to make room for him. He sits. I stand in front of the door, slyly pushing it closed with my booty. He's holding the Coke in his hand, just looking at it, but at least he's sitting. There's room enough right next to him for me, but I don't know how to play this. I don't know how to do a church boy. I'm standing there with my hands behind my back. "Drink," I tell him. "It ain't poison."

He drinks in big gulps, emptying the glass, and I'm still just standing there.

"So," I say.

"So," he says.

I smile down at him.

"I'd better go get my lawnmower."

"So, you really ain't never had a girlfriend?"

"I never said that."

"You have a girlfriend?"

"No."

He starts to get up. I sit down next to him and put my hand on his shoulder. "Let me show you something," I say.

He turns to me on the couch. "What?"

I reach for the album on the coffee table. I put it on my lap and open it so we have to sit close to look. This is the boring album from when I was young. I'm looking down at family pictures and explaining who everybody is. Here we are at church. Here we are at the zoo. Jesus, it's boring, not like the album under my bed with the pictures J.H. took of me naked. He's nodding like he's interested. I'm trying to figure out what church boys like. I know what I like. I like the way his chest swells so big. I like his pretty-boy face, his innocent eyes. When we come to the last page, I close the book. "So," I say.

"So," he says.

Then I kiss him.

"Shit."

"Jethro, you cursed!"

"I'm sorry. Lord forgive me, I didn't mean to say that."

I'm holding his hand so he can't get up. "You kiss nice."

"It was you kissed me."

"Your tongue tastes good. You got sweet lips."

"I have to go."

But it was too late. "It's all right. It's all right," I soothe. My arms encircle his chest. He resists, and I put my lips against his neck. He likes that. He groans. "You like that."

"No," he lies, shaking is head. "I have to go."

"Please don't go. I'm so happy you're here with me. Don't you see how happy you're making me?" I take his hand and place it on my heart so he can feel how fast it's beating. We do that for a while, and he's OK with that, and because I'm angry and I'm starting to hate him for judging me, I stop pretending that his hand over my heart isn't touching my tiddies through my thin church dress. I make him rub it real good, make him feel the hardness of the nipple, teach him that he's a man and not a faggot talking about he ain't got no girlfriend. He's pulling away, but not hard enough. I see tears, and I know that he is struggling with something, too.

"Why you crying?"

"Why are you doing this to me?"

"I need help. I need you to help me. Ain't that what church boys are supposed to do?"

"Not like this."

I close his mouth with a kiss. His hands move on my chest. I like his slender fingers on my nipples. He's a quick learner. He says, "This is wrong." But he keeps playing with my nipples. He's not so different from me.

I shift on the couch, slide my collar down and put a nipple in his mouth. "Yeah," I whisper to him, "that's good, baby," when he starts to suck. Church Boy's got natural skills. Pretty soon he's got my ass twitching all over the couch real nice. Then I'm kissing his mouth all hungry.

He's whispering back, "This is so, so—"

"Good."

"Mmmmm."

"You think we should go in the bedroom?"

"For what?" With them knitted-up brows.

"You know. Duh."

"But what if—?"

I rip open his shirt. One of the buttons pops off. I kiss him again. "Don't worry. We still got about forty minutes before the moms and the daddy dog get home. Thirty minutes before the bus drags my little sister home."

"We're gonna get caught."

"We ain't gonna get caught." I reach down and feel his excitement. "Come on. Let's go."

I lead the way upstairs and into my bedroom. When I look back it's kinda funny, him standing there with his clothes all pulled out of place and the crotch of his pants inflated like a circus tent. I pull my dress over my head. Step out of my panties. He's watching it all and breathing all shallow. When I lay down on the bed, he comes over to me. "Take off your clothes," I tell him.

"But—"

"Oh damn." I reach up and rip the rest of his shirt off his chest. Unbuckle his pants. He got a big dick. Real big. Curved to the right. Uncircumcised, too. I know how it's gonna be. This little Bible study won't take too long. It's his first time. I figure, a minute. Sixty seconds of bliss. The second time, I will begin to teach him how to be a man. How to last longer. How to use his mouth. I'm gonna make him suck my pussy till his mouth fills with my juices. And what my mouth will do to him—! The third time, I may even enjoy it, but the third time—that will have to come tomorrow.

Yes, he will be here with me tomorrow and tomorrow and tomorrow after that. I'm not gonna let this one go. He won't wanna ever leave me. I hate him so much.

I take his big hands and teach him how to work me right. Soon, my ass is winding slow circles on the sheets. I'm sucking his tongue and gushing on the fingers he got pushed up in me. I'm coming real nice. I want those heart-shaped lips on my pussy so bad, but he's not ready for that today.

I pull him down on the bed. I kiss him. He kisses me. I put my finger in my pussy, and scoot back so he can see it good while I play with it. I'm all gushy. Juice dripping down my thigh. "Look what you done, Johnny. You gonna have to fuck me now. You gonna have to make me come."

I lay back, and he gets on top and shoves it in with one hard push.

"Jesus!"

"You OK?"

"Yeah, nigga. *You* OK?"

"Yes, I'm fine."

"Then do it."

"Oh my God."

"Just do it. Push your dick in. It ain't gonna hurt me. Don't worry about me. I like it."

I am filled with him. He begins to thrust. Lotta chest and face movement, not enough hip. "Like that?"

"But harder."

More hip movement now. He's so big, he slips out. He hurts me a little bit trying to put it back in. I hold him, guide him in, kiss him on the mouth. Then he does it right. He fucks me, and fucks me, my bangles jangling, my head pressed into the pillow, I'm screaming, it is glorious, and sixty seconds later, he comes, still thrusting like crazy. Then he flops on the bed, kinda smiling, nervous, thinking about what he did, but there's no time to think. I'm jacking him, and *boing!* He's ready again. He fucks me and fucks me, and I'm kissing his chest. Then I push him off, roll over, and teach him doggy-style. He rides it hard. He's making sounds like he's praying or something back there, but I don't care because it's so good with his big hands on my ass, his sweet breath on my neck. I twist my neck around and take his tongue in my mouth. He is so good, he does not know how good he is. I'm coming hard for the first time today for real. I think I could love him if I didn't hate him so much.

Then he can't find his clothes, and when he finds them, he puts them on funny. He holds his Bible like it's burning his fingers. Then he cries, the big stud cries. I drag his horse dick out of his incorrectly belted pants and suck him till his hips begin to push. He fucks my mouth like a pussy. I stick a finger in his ass. He moans, his hands press down on my head. His dick spits come all over my face, my bed, and his pants. He's come all over himself. Oh, he's crying now, and scrambling through the house looking for water. When I show him the bathroom, he ducks in there with his dick sticking straight out, and I'm laughing, laughing. It's so funny.

"And you better hurry," I tell him, "because I hear a key in the door."

It's only my little sister, Pam, but he freaks, and goes running out the back door, and I'm laughing because he left his drawers behind. And I'm shouting after him, "Don't forget to come back tonight for Bible study." I'm laughing. Laughing. Because he had no right to make me feel shame. He didn't know shit about me. What gave him the right to look down on me? I'm laughing.

I'm laughing at Brother Johnny, the Christian I de-Christianized.

Laughing because I don't know that J.H. went back and killed Onion Man. Laughing because I don't know that J.H. will go to prison for life. Don't know that I'm pregnant with his child. Don't know that in less than nine months Johnny will be my husband and firmly believe that he is the father of my baby.

I hated him that day I took his virginity. Hated him for most of our courtship. Hated him when I gave birth to "our" child. Hated him when I got tired of being married to him after two years and told him the baby wasn't his. Hated him when he said it didn't matter who the baby's father was because he loved me and the baby. Hated him when I broke down and started crying, crying, crying, and he was there for me, still teaching me how to love, and all I could teach him was how to fuck and get fucked over. Hated him because he was always there whenever I needed him. Hated him because I had never experienced that kind of love, not even from the moms and Daddy Dog, though Lord knows they tried.

I hated him because I hated myself and he was the only one who could get me to see that, and still love me. Oh, how he loved me. I made sure of that. I hated him because he made me love him. I hated him because he made me love myself.

DENENE MILLNER AND NICK CHILES

Play It Again

She

My mother had told me from the day I first learned the power of words that my mouth would write a check my ass couldn't cash. That was true when I was little, and Mom would give my little behind a working out for things like calling a classmate a scumbag. Never mind I hadn't a clue what a scumbag was. And it was true this afternoon, when I told my boss that she wouldn't know shoes even if I put my size $7\frac{1}{2}$ in her ass. Well, I didn't exactly say that word for word, but the sentiment was apparent. It's just that on this particular day, I needed her patronizing, self-aggrandizing attitude to take a backseat. But no, she had to insist that the four-page special on designer shoes that I'd planned for the fashion section of our newspaper wasn't "realistic." "The women who buy this newspaper," she'd said matter-of-factly, "are mostly people of color, and people of color do not buy Jimmy Choo shoes because a lot of them can't afford them. They buy Nine West."

Well, am I not a person of color? And do I not have a closet full of designer shoes that would shame Imelda Marcos? Okay, they're shoes that I probably could ill afford, what with the cost of living in New York City. But I'm young. I'm single. I don't have kids. Why not indulge myself with a sexy, strappy pair of depth-defying Chanel sandals, or knee-high, military-style Cole Haan boots, or a sensuous pair of Salvatore Ferragamo mules? That's what young women with a little disposable income do in New York City—they spend their cash on clothes and shoes, so that they can look good while they're partying. But my boss wouldn't know that, seeing as the only black people she's ever around are me—yes, I would be the lone African American in the entire features section of the newspaper—and the people who clean the toilets in her Upper East Side manse. She's yet to recognize that the black folks she reads about in the crime section of this shitty newspaper aren't the only black folks in town. No, the other black folks in town actually appreciate some of the finer things in life, just like white people do. Now that's what I told her.

And that wasn't smart. Because no matter how foolish she is, my boss is one of those white ladies who doesn't like getting told off—particularly by me. First of all, against her bitter objections, her boss—the guardian angel who hired me and told me he was going to make me a star—promoted me to run the women's section of the newspaper. She had been planning on putting a white girl in the slot. Since then, we've butted heads so much that I'm sure she's going to find a way to fire my behind. She'd tried it before. Surely, she would try again after today's blowup. And that's one check my ass definitely can't cash right now. I can't afford not to draw a salary.

I figured I'd better get out of her face and cool myself off, too, before we came to blows. But I didn't want to go home—nothing there for me. No boyfriend to rush to—unlike stilettos, single, straight, worth-something black men are rare. No friends to talk to—all my girls live in my hometown, P.G. County, and my roommate is a lunatic whose boyfriend has her going suicidal damn near every other day. She's not worth unburdening my troubles to. And both her stupid cats—Flick and Switch—got diarrhea. In fact, one of them shit on my brand-new Air Force Ones. No, home wasn't the place to be. The bar around the corner from the office, that was.

* * *

I was inebriated and feeling really sorry for myself when I finally decided to make my way into the subway. Normally, I would have simply hopped into a cab—I didn't like traveling in nobody's funky, nasty subway—but I'd spent the last of my cash on an apple martini and I didn't want to walk to the ATM because my feet were killing me and I was a little wobbly. So the subway it was. I was part running, part stumbling down the stairs, jostling with other commuters getting a head start on their way home, when I heard the most beautiful, melodic sound—like an angel drawing me to heaven. It was Stravinsky's Violin Concerto—the lively classical piece my father played for me almost every night after he read me my bedtime story. Daddy had made a point of exposing his only daughter to the classics early—Bach, Mozart, Chopin, Stevie. Well, Stevie wasn't a classical musician in the tra-ditional sense, but he's as brilliant as any of the dead white musicians my father had played for me. Instinctively, I stumbled toward it, the sound of the violin ringing in my head, passionate, inviting.

I rounded the corner and struggled to look through the crowd that had gathered around the violinist. Just then, the train came, and the platform cleared. Like the drawing of a curtain, before me stood a wondrous sight—a large, dreadlocked black man, his eyes closed, swaying gently as he tenderly cradled the violin. He was wearing several layers of rumpled clothes and his face was covered by a dark, heavy beard. In other words, he didn't look at all like the smooth pretty boys I usually found myself sitting across from over watered-down drinks at the club. But something about his movements, the soft and sensuous way he held his instrument, the obvious joy on his large kind face, snaked down and touched me in surprising places. I felt a familiar tingling below my belly that startled me back to my senses. I quickly glanced around to see if anybody was witnessing this embarrassing scene—a grown woman in a business suit getting juiced by a grimy subway musician. What the fuck was wrong with me?

He

I saw her watching me. She was new—definitely not one of my regular ladies. The light *tap-tap-tap* of her footfalls had caught my curiosity as I paused for the second movement of the Stravinsky concerto. From experience I could identify her footwear as expensive and exquisitely constructed, and surely so lovely as not to disappoint. I had a carefully planned playlist worked out for the day—I was saving the Prokofiev for after five—but I decided that this lady, this caramel vision in beige, should inspire a change. I paused and looked down, catching another glimpse of that sensuous heel. Never had I seen one so well-shaped and perfectly groomed. Oh, she was wearing light-brown Ferragamo mules, with a textured look that almost gave them the veneer of antiques. I had not yet dared to take in the face, but already I knew she was special.

Usually by 3:30 I was trying to fight off the boredom. Sometimes boredom was my greatest enemy underground, the hornet that constantly buzzed around my head. If it stung me too strongly, I'd just put Sarah—the name I'd used for my instrument since the original Sarah walked out on me—in the case and move on, back to the dreary little room. There was no use plying her until my neck could barely move if the whole thing was going to bore. I had already tried that one—ignoring my instincts and stomping on my personal happiness. That's how I got into this predicament in the first place.

Three things kept me going: the music, the money, and the mules. Roughly in that order. Let me take the last first. The name isn't meant to be offensive, just a little shorthand I came up with to describe a particular interest of mine. Shoes. More specifically, the footwear favored by the ladies of the evening—business-women. Those sensually designed shrines to the female foot. Among the elite—pumps, stilettos, mules—mules were the lingerie of the group, the sexy nightwear that set my heart racing.

I'm not afraid to admit my preoccupation—by confronting it, perhaps I can tame it. Or at least keep it from getting me into too much trouble. I'd had a few close calls already. If there had been a police officer nearby when I followed the brown-eyed darling in the black suit and the red-and-black Manolo Blahniks, I probably would have gotten hauled away. I didn't mean her any harm—she was so perfect, with the most fetchingly wonderful ankle and sensually rounded heel, that I felt I had lost control. I was drawn to her like the tide to shore—or a crackhead to the pipe.

The ladies who flooded the subways and platforms after 5 P.M., gliding along in their short-skirted suits and perfectly sculpted calves, regularly grabbed a sizable proportion of my nonmusic consciousness. (I had long ago divided up my brain into the music sphere, which sometimes threatened to crowd out even the instinct to eat, and the nonmusic everything else.) Maybe I have some kind of masochistic impulse to yearn for the unattainable. I don't pretend to understand it. But I knew if I could last until five, a certain energy seemed to infuse my playing. Because after five, my senses were overwhelmed by the sea of intoxicating feet, heels, ankles, and toes, all dancing before me like stars twinkling on a clear night. It was enough to take my breath away. And to send me into paroxysms of the most passionate, beautiful violin playing that my fingers and hands could muster. Sarah would lift up arias that filled the stuffy, florid subway air with notes and tones so moving that I'd stop to see more than a few tears on the faces to go with the inspiring feet.

Mine was an instrument that could draw women in like a snake charmer, could send them off into exquisite fantasy. I saw it every day, the vacant look that stole their eyes, the sensuous droop of their lower lip as they watched me and Sarah, transfixed, listening to her desperate, soaring cry. A violin, played right, was as affecting as a lobster dinner and a $400 Bordeaux. Believe me, I speak from experience.

But that was before the breakdown, before the hallucinatory spells, before I lost everything. My days at second chair for the New York City Opera were now a distant memory—a decade of scraping together coins and single dollar bills on the New York City Transit–owned platforms had kicked away every ounce of my once-considerable dignity. All I had now was the lovely jolt of surprise I got to witness almost hourly when I played. New Yorkers thought they knew everything, had seen it all. But their narrow little worlds hadn't prepared them for a master violinist who happened to be a tall, hulking, dreadlocked black man who just might need a shower. In my big hands, on my hamlike arms, Sarah looked like a vulnerable little nymph. I loved the surprise, but I also knew it partly came from a reaction to my unsavory looks. It hurt, but I chose not to dwell on it. The women used to call me *fine*—now they tried to avoid looking at my face. Before, I had to ignore their stares—sometimes with an expensively suited suitor at their arm—for fear that their obvious hunger would distract me. Now, while they listened, their eyes would wander everywhere but to mine—almost like they were embarrassed to have such feelings inspired by the playing of a common subway bum.

Of me, they knew nothing. Did they disturb me with their pretensions, their need to not see me? Well, I had worked hard over the years to escape that truth. The most I was willing to say was that I was now used to it. I had no choice but to be. A brother had to play; a brother had to eat.

The money was sometimes very good. I'm not going to lie about that. Of course it couldn't compare to the six figures I pulled in at the Opera and the various smaller ensembles and chamber groups I played with in my heyday. I was striding on top of the world then, romancing a different woman every weekend, buying threads that fell loosely from my muscular frame, keeping my locks silky and sweet-smelling with an array of expensive oils and creams. Could any woman—black, white, Latin, Asian—resist a strapping, dreadlocked violinist who dared to play outside of her apartment window at midnight? I smile at the memories.

In the corner of my eye, I saw Miss Ferragamo inch closer, sliding those lovely feet nearer to my money-laden instrument case, almost like she wanted me to see her. This was unusual— they usually stayed at more than an eyeball's length, sometimes even preferring to lurk behind a column. Especially the white and Asian women. As I prepared to launch into vintage Prokofiev, Violin Concerto No. 1, I dared to take a better look. I repositioned the instrument on my shoulder and took her in fully. What I saw almost brought tears to my eyes.

My God, she was the most incredible creature I had ever encountered, underground or above. Her skin was a burnished, glowing walnut, as if a carpenter had buffed her with his rag when he completed the job. Big ovals dominated her perfect face, sitting atop her high cheekbones like windows to her haunting soul. Her shining dark hair was coifed to within an inch of its life, no curl out of place, not a strand misbehaving. And then she did something so rare that it almost scared me—she smiled. A broad, welcoming smile that shook me down to my raggedy boots. Her teeth gleamed and deep, twinkling dimples beckoned. Against my better instincts, betraying my well-nurtured fear of rejection, I smiled back at her. So afraid was I of how thoroughly I might have screwed up, I didn't even bother to wait around for her response. I closed my eyes, took a long deep breath, and launched into the most inspired, most yearning version of Prokofiev's first concerto I've ever played.

As if they had their own brains, their own free will, my fingers flew over the strings, my hand stroking the bow as tenderly as a mother's touch. The mood of the first concerto is wistful yet mysterious, hushed yet energetic. I touched them all, zipping over the strings with a manic drive, wringing every ounce of charm out of Sarah's phrasing. I wanted desperately to know if I was reaching my walnut fantasy, but I dared not open my eyes; I couldn't risk the distraction of those brown ovals boring into me. I played on.

She

It was one of the most incredible sounds I had ever heard, a heartrending wail that simultaneously made me want to cry and do a slow grind between the sheets. I felt like a queen, standing atop my throne as this magician with a violin for a wand poured out his heart for an audience of one. I watched his fingers and hands tense and relax, sliding over the strings and deftly maneuvering the bow. I had never seen such a gifted violin player this close—it was much more athletic and rigorous than I ever imagined. There was something almost primal about the vigor and speed required. Before I even knew where my mind was headed, I was overcome by a vision of this man hovering over me as I lay prone beneath him, trembling with the anticipation of those firm yet gentle fingers hitting the right notes on my eager flesh.

As he moved his torso up and down to press his whole being into a particularly forceful sequence of notes, his dreads flew away from his body and framed his face like a lion's mane. He was one of the sexiest men I had ever seen, and yet I knew he might as well have been standing on the other side of the world. What was I gonna do with a subway performer, even if he could make his instrument produce noises as beautiful as any Aretha ever unleashed? I was looking for a longtime man—one who could keep my heart singing and my closets laced at the same time. I looked down at the crumpled dollar bills and glistening coins in his instrument case. Not many pumps or mules in there. Not even a new pair of stockings. I almost convinced myself that it was time to move on, to stagger my way back to my apartment, pull off these clothes and collapse on the couch with a bowl of ice cream in my lap.

But then he dipped down and did some kind of undulating motion with his back as he raised the instrument up to his shoulders. It was the shoulders that did it for me—as wide as a doorway, but lithe and spry enough to undulate. I could think of dozens of strong backs that I had clutched in abandon as their owners made me scream at the ceiling. Well, maybe not dozens. A big, strapping, muscled shoulder moved me like the waves of a pounding tide—the feel of them, the look of them, the handle they provided a woman who needed to hold on. I could see Mr. Violin was well endowed, shoulder-wise. The upward slope of his jacket on both sides of his head told me that he could make me happy.

With a theatrical flourish, he brought the song to a mournful close, the last note lingering in the air for what seemed like minutes. His eyes opened again and took me in, this time more fully than before. I stared back, noting the angular contours of his face under the beard—if I didn't know better, I might have guessed that a pretty boy was hiding underneath the hairy jungle. I don't know where I got the inspiration for my next move—maybe it was the accusation of my last boyfriend ringing in my ear that I overplanned my life down to the second, leaving no room for spontaneity, for unexpected joy. Or it could have been the memorable description that my wild friend Carmen laid out for me one night over a bottle of tequila in her apartment: a blow-by-blow accounting of the most fantastic sexual encounter of her young life—getting her pussy eaten by a handsome thug one night in the corner of a deserted subway car. I stared at the violin player, then I turned and, just before he left my line of sight, I gestured with my head for him to follow me.

As I walked toward the end of the platform, my mind was so overcharged that I couldn't even try to fathom what I was about to do. I heard his footsteps behind me and I smiled. I looked up and saw a big wide pillar at the end of the platform, almost like it had been rushed onto the set by stagehands for my bold one-act play.

He

The gesture seemed unmistakable, but still terror loped through my veins, slightly buckling my knees. She had moved her lovely head in a beckoning lure, commanding me to follow. And to make sure the message had been received, she sent me a lingering gaze just before she turned and walked away. I watched the slow departure of the Ferragamos, feeling my heart thrum as I saw the subtle tensing of her sculpted calves while she glided away. I had no choice but to follow—I sensed that the ragged remains of my life might never again meet a moment brimming with such delicious promise.

I glanced around quickly, noting that we were alone, save for a few teenagers toward the other end of the platform. I gave a second's thought to the fate of my money, which might surely disappear if left unattended. But there was no time to kneel and collect the coins and bills, and such a grubby move would taint the salacious perfection of the moment. I placed Sarah on the cold platform, not even gentle with her placement. She was my rainmaker, but her assemblage of wood, glue, and wire—albeit a finely crafted assemblage—was no match for those faultless calves and heels.

As my footfalls echoed hers, my chest pounded with the tense thrill of sensual possibility and a palpable fear of impending doom. For Miss Red-and-Black Manolo had also seemingly gestured to me, and then glided away, and when she turned to see me leering at her back, her scream had sliced through the air like a machete, battering my well-constructed defenses and sending me tumbling to the ground in defeat and terror.

Miss Ferragamo was about to run out of platform, but she kept going. A large faded-gray concrete pillar stood about three feet from the wall announcing the platform's end—beyond loomed the dark menace of the tunnel. Miss Ferragamo slipped behind the pillar and disappeared from my view. But I knew she waited. I inhaled deeply and stepped around the pillar to confront her. Her eyes were tightly closed but her face offered a gentle smile. I looked down to see that her white blouse had been unbuttoned past her lacy cream bra. The lighting was dull but her neck and upper chest glistened, the globes of her sizable breasts straining against the confining cups. It looked like an image from one of those soft-core porn movies on cable—the swooning woman opening herself to the handsome stranger, head held back, neck and chest waiting to be consumed. Slowly I moved my mouth toward a small, pert mole that sat above her right breast. As my lips touched her skin, I heard a soft gasp, a gently feminine intake of breath. She then sucked in a mouthful of air when I let my lips caress a trail from her breast all the way up her neck to the sensitive spot just below her right ear. I moved my lips down again to her breasts. I glanced up at her face—and saw her light brown eyes staring intensely. She grinned bashfully, apparently embarrassed that she had been caught watching. Then she shut them tight again.

I breathed deeply, savoring the subtle fruity flavor of a fragrance I could tell probably cost more than all the shabby clothes I now wished I could strip off my body. The scent brought me back to tantalizing late-night trysts in the midst of the opera season, when I'd be flying so high from three hours of dancing with Puccini or Verdi that I would dive into the many willing female partners with the delight of a wine connoisseur traipsing through a French vineyard. I hadn't been so close to such a beautiful and exquisitely scented neck in a long time. I felt a familiar rush in my loins and had to take a momentary pause to stop myself from emptying a month's supply of ejaculate into my drawers. (Frustrated and embarrassed by a growing addiction to masturbation, I had pledged that the next time I emptied my loins it would be inside of a woman—or at least a condom that was inside of a woman.) I was tempted to reach up and release her breasts from their confinement, but I didn't want to risk such presumption. I would take what she offered and enjoy the hell out of it.

She

As I felt the tickling of his lips and breath blazing a trail across my chest and neck, I got a whiff of his musky scent. I was more than a little surprised that he didn't stink. The look of him, the clothes, the fact of what he did for a "living"—I wasn't even sure if it could be described as his "living"—all led me to expect stink. But what I got was a manly musk; deodorant mixed with the sweaty bouquet of a workingman. It brought me back to a scandalous summer a few years back, when I was fucking a construction worker who used to visit me during his lunch breaks. We'd go to the park, to a spot we'd carefully scouted—a small gazebo near the zoo that was surrounded by a thicket of bushes and trees. I would pull up my skirt and sit astride my man as he gripped my ample butt cheeks with his strong, coarse hands. The calluses on his fingers would chafe my skin, making my booty feel like it had been assaulted by a sheet of sandpaper, but it was a sensation that I grew to crave. And the smell of a workingman stayed in my nostrils even after I had to kick homeboy forcefully to the curb when he started getting increasingly possessive and belligerent. He had messed around and caught real feelings. In my mind, from the beginning he was just a fuck buddy. A reason to carry condoms in my bag.

I thought about ripping off Mr. Violin Man's shirt and caressing his broad chest and shoulders. In fact, I yearned to do exactly that. I hadn't yet reached out and touched him, even as his mouth became familiar with every inch of my upper body. I was enjoying the attention immensely, but there was a line I was still hesitant to cross. I didn't even understand why.

Slowly, he moved up and softly nuzzled a tender spot right below my left ear. It was a spot that had caused me trouble from the very beginning, since the afternoon fifteen-year-old Raymond Stamps stumbled across it down in his basement and my panties ended up bunched in the corner. I usually blocked access to it— most men didn't deserve it. When Mr. Violin Man hit it like a homing pigeon, I almost peed myself. Without thinking, I reached out my hand and yanked at his shirt. I opened my eyes long enough to catch a glimpse of his chest, brown and bulging, as I expected. With a violence that surprised me, I grabbed at his chest and raked my fingers across it, almost as if I were trying to take a piece of him with me. I wanted to bite him, to take a big hunk of him between my teeth. I felt a rumble in my throat, almost like a growl, and a wave of passion surged down and through me. I wanted him to do something to me, to make me feel something.

He

As the delicious pain coursed up from my chest, I was surprised to look down and see that she had drawn blood. Several parallel red marks were forming across my chest and stomach. Instead of anger or concern, I felt a strange sense of pride and glee. The stranger had left her mark on me, more permanent and indelible than any lipstick kiss or mere hickey. My excitement jumped to another level, one I didn't even remember having anymore. I was overcome by a rush of that all-consuming need to ingest her, to swallow this woman whole so that she could never leave me. I imagined pulling up her skirt, tugging her panties to the side and plunging my tongue between the juicy folds of her middle, not stopping until she yelled her submission. I dreamed of standing up, grabbing her fleshy ass with my hands and roughly pulling her to me as I stabbed her with an erection that couldn't possibly get any prouder. I did none of that; what I did was slide my attentions southward, down past the hemline of the skirt, past the delicate knee. I stared at the Ferragamos, savoring their sculpted perfection. I lifted a hand and slowly ran it over the textured surface of the shoe, then I moved the hand to the heel and softly pulled it from her foot. I repeated the gesture with the other shoe, hearing what I plainly detected as a quickening of her breath.

There had been a funky little flutist, a short curvaceous lady from northern California who was a combustible mix of Italy and Egypt, and during a memorable night in my East Village loft she had slid her left foot into my mouth while she was putting in work on other parts of me. I had always appreciated a well-shaped foot in a sexy shoe, but my flutist turned me out, kicked me hard into a new obsession, like the dealer giving the church girl her first hit of the crack pipe. When I looked up and saw her leg extending from my mouth, when I tasted the smooth salty toes and felt them wiggle sensuously on my tongue, I gave my heart over to the feet. One might assume that a foot fetishist might ply his addiction with ease, given the omnipresent nature of feet, but such an assumption would be wrong. Yes, I saw tantalizing feet most everywhere I turned, particularly in the warmer months when the boots were stashed in the closet to make way for the mules and flip-flops (oh, the naked ecstasy of the barely there flip-flop), but they were not exactly accessible. The combination of visible yet inaccessible spelled terrific sensory frustration. I was like a drunk staring through the closed liquor store window.

I lifted the brown foot, noting the doll-like taper of the ankle and the elegant protrusion of the big toe, and slowly drew it toward my lips. I ran my closed mouth gently across the side and the heel, feeling a warm flush spread down from my face. The foot was softer than I could have imagined; obviously its owner took regular care to soak and stroke and pamper it with an array of delicious creams and lotions. It was almost too fantastical to imagine, hidden in a corner of my domain, the city subway platform, with unfettered access to the feet of a beauty queen; the passion throbbed so forcefully between us that I lost all fear of rejection.

I opened my mouth and slowly slipped her foot inside, making sure she could feel the ministrations of my tongue and the soft sucking of my cheeks. At the contact, her moan rumbled through me, leading to a moan of my own. I heard a faint rustle and dared to open my eyes. At the sight before me, the blood rushed from my head and a faintness overcame me. My lady's skirt was pulled up and her fingers probed underneath the black silk of her panties. A heart weaker than mine might have stopped from sheer ecstasy.

She

I had never considered having my foot eaten. You walked on your feet, you slid them into shoes, you rubbed them every night to ease the pain from the shoes, but to plunge them into a man's mouth? To have the toes sucked and instep licked? I had no idea. I opened my eyes and saw half of my foot in his mouth. Powerful sensations raced up my legs. I became aware of a stirring dampness between my thighs, so moist it almost felt like I was dripping.

My right hand moved on its own, sliding downward as if I were lying alone in my bed. I saw his dreaded head bob back and forth as my foot went in and out; the sight produced a deep moan that I couldn't stop. My fingers slipped inside my panties and quickly separated the folds of my pussy, moving over familiar terrain in a hurry. I stroked and touched, grabbed and tickled. He moved to the right foot, repeating the sucking and licking. This one was even more sensitive, the connection to my vagina even more direct and intense.

I felt the familiar rumblings deep in my gut that told me something powerful was coming. I looked down and saw piercing light brown eyes staring at me in wonderment. He looked down and watched my fingers moving inside my panties. I didn't know I liked being watched, but I did. The hunger in his eyes was so open and honest, I was almost tempted to pull him to his feet and wrap my legs around his waist, letting him plunge inside me for real. But that was a line I couldn't cross.

The wave slammed into me at once, starting at my submerged toes and rushing up my legs in a torrent. I heard the loud roar of an oncoming train hurtling through the dark tunnel, the warning din ratcheting up the sexual tension, pushing me over the edge. I dropped my head back against the pillar and unleashed a deep-throated scream. The orgasm and the train hit at once, the roar of the train hiding the piercing scream of my orgasm. It was so overwhelming, I had to reach back to the pillar to keep from falling to my knees. When I glanced down again at his dreaded head, which was turned away, I got an idea and I acted on it. I slipped my hand into a breast pocket on my jacket. It was an act of whimsy that I hoped I wouldn't regret.

He

As I walked away from our hidden corner of the platform, my nerves tingling, my legs weak, I looked down and saw something white sticking from my breast pocket. It was a business card. I plucked it out quickly, squinting down as I stepped into a swarm of departing passengers. When I saw the name, I staggered and almost fell. With no regard for the people around me, I let out a loud, guttural roar—part laughter, part scream. I felt my body shake and I shook my head wildly, in wonder and delight. I barely saw all the worried looks. The clenched hand of fate had finally found me. Who was my subway lover, this delectable vision, this ghost lady of my daytime dreams? Her name was Sarah.

SHARRIF SIMMONS

Love and the Game

I've watched love turn
oceans into puddles
turn daylight into dark caves
his hand shook
as she opened the door
her anger was all he had left of her beauty
so he fell

Nothing worth while comes easy, Eric, nothing." Slapping her hand on his broad chest, she jumps out of bed and storms into the bathroom, slamming the door behind her.

"C'mon Maxine." He jumps up to follow her, his muscular build tightening with each motion. His manhood, awake with the morning, points like a compass to the bathroom door. He's determined not to let it go to waste. Not this morning. Not for the same old argument. He finds the door unlocked. Slowly turning the knob, he whispers playfully through the slight opening. "Maaaxiiiiiine . . . are you in there? What's wrong with my booboo?"

"Kiss my ass, Eric," she yells out, trying her best to sound serious. "Just leave me alone." He walks in. She rolls her eyes at him and turns to look into the mirror. Maxine is beautiful. Her hazel eyes sparkle like diamonds. Her dark hair, pulled into a tight bun, shows subtle streaks of red highlights. Eric appears behind her. His penis pushes up against her back. He gently touches her neck with one hand, caressing her naked thigh with the other.

"No Eric . . . I gotta get ready for . . ." He greets her resistance with a soft kiss on her shoulder blade.

"Relax, baby, we got time."

Her attempt at anger vanishes, replaced by the thought of what was about to happen. His strong arm slowly snakes around her waist, like an anaconda preparing its prey to be consumed. She closes her eyes and leans her head into his chest, surrendering to him. He lifts her left leg up onto the sink, rubbing his hand across her round ass, inching his way toward her vagina. She can feel him growing, his breath caressing her spine. His fingers find her walls. When he feels her wetness, he leans forward, rubbing his rock-hard dick across her pussy, teasing her clit with its head.

She slides her hand across her breast and squeezes a nipple, sending a wave of pleasure through her body and moisture between her legs. "Fuck me, Eric," she whispers through clenched teeth. She grabs the back of his cornrowed head and raises her leg higher so she can take him all in. He moves rhythmically in and out of her, his legs, like two stone pillars, anchor him firmly in place as he pulls her waist back and forth, her pussy dripping over his throbbing erection.

"I love you baby . . . you feel so good. . . ." His voice is thick and sincere. Their bodies bang together, their fleshy sounds echoing off the bathroom walls. Maxine feels her body trembling with her coming orgasm. She rubs her clit, holding herself steady with one hand braced on the mirror. When she comes it lasts for what seems like a whole day, her mouth open, her hips quivering. When he feels her coming, Eric presses himself deep inside her. When he feels his own orgasm he turns her around and Maxine kneels in front of him. Taking him in her mouth, she sucks until his warm cum hits the back of her throat. He moans in ecstasy, his every muscle shaking with satisfaction. They fall to the cold bathroom floor, holding each other tightly, laughing at the depth of their passion.

* * *

Nothing worthwhile comes easy. He's been hearing that most of his life, mainly from people who've always had it easy. The love of his life was no exception. Her daddy, Mr. Real Estate, her mommy, Mrs. Psychologist, gave her anything she wanted. No matter how far she fell, they were always there to catch her. Like the year she dropped out of law school to sing backup with the funk band Blue Dragon. The band eventually left her ass stranded in Thailand in the middle of their tour, broke and alone. But all she had to do was call her parents.

Eric didn't come from that. His father disappeared when he was eight, leaving him and his sister with a mother who saw kids as burdens rather than gifts. His childhood had been anything but easy. He learned the value of hard work from the lessons of a hard life and resented anyone who thought differently. Maxine meant well, though. She didn't always understand where he was coming from, or why he was the way he was, but she loved him, despite their differences.

"Don't forget your briefcase, baby." Eric stands at the door in his bathrobe, holding her black leather case. He watches her in awe as she walks toward him with the grace of a supermodel, her black skirt accentuating her voluptuous curves.

"Thank you, sweetie," she answers, grabbing a fistful of penis before walking out. "Keep yourself ready for later." She slides her tongue across his lips, then jets toward the elevator.

The subway is crowded as usual. Maxine is grateful for her seat, her legs still weak from the morning workout. She crosses them, closes her eyes and leans her head against the car window. She's in the bathroom again. A warm feeling moves through her as she thinks about Eric filling her up. She sees his beautiful body in her mind. She smiles, appreciating his way of avoiding conflicts with humor, lovemaking, and tenderness. He's perfect, she thinks, fighting off the rush of denial that seems intent on destroying her fantasy. But it's too late. She's back in the real world. A world where she is a prosecuting attorney and the love of her life, the man of her dreams, is a dope dealer, a hustler, a straight-up thug.

*   *   *

"Yo, fuck that B, you tell that muthafucka I said I'm gonna see him fa sho, this is the second time he's pulling this bullshit." Eric screams into his cell phone as he walks across 125th and Lenox. "I'm tellin' you, Rick, talk to your boy . . . talk to him!" He slams his phone shut, eyebrows mashed together like crumpled paper, anger seething through his veins. He inherited more from his father than good looks and street smarts; an explosive temper also came with the package. For now, he needs to calm down, put his mind on something pleasant.

* * *

"Maxine . . . would you pass me that file, please." Mark Pearl is the new assistant district attorney. "This case is gonna be big . . . I'm talking interstate trafficking, extortion, kidnapping, and the big one . . . murder, all of it coming out of Harlem, U.S.A." His face is glowing like a child's at Christmas. Maxine swallows hard. Her stomach always tightens when drug cases come through the office.

"Hey, Mark . . . you mind if I look at the case file when you're done?"

"No prob . . . just put it on my desk when you're finished."

"You got it."

* * *

She chooses to face her fear head-on. As she reads through the file, her mouth dries out, her breathing increases. Had she really thought it all through? What would she do if her nightmare came to life? Break the law, warn her man, quit her job? She's never felt this way about anyone. She knew the risks when she met him, that fateful day in court. His brown eyes had devoured her from the defense table, his confidence supported by his impressive build. She decided then and there that she had to have him. He looked beautifully dangerous, like everything her parents had ever warned her about.

Thinking of him sends a chill down her slender arms; warmth gathers between her thighs. She finishes the file. There is nothing this time. No name in the file, no open investigation. She sighs and returns the folder to Mark's desk. She then goes to her office, closes the door and calls her man.

"Leave your message at the beep . . . peace."

"Hey, baby." Her voice is seductive and sweet. "Just checkin' in on you, hope you're being good . . . call me."

Her phone rings seconds after she hangs up.

"This is Maxine," she answers excitedly.

"This is Eric." He mocks her excitement.

"Where are you . . . when are you comin' to get me?"

"Let me know when I can . . . you know I want to get you, baby . . ."

"Well, I get off at five, but I can make other plans if—wait . . . hold on a second."

Her office door is slowly opening. Maxine covers her cell phone, annoyed that someone would walk in without knocking.

"Hello . . . I'm on the phone in here—"

"Not anymore."

Eric walks in and smiles, showing off a set of straight white teeth. He decided to surprise her for lunch, needing to see her. No matter what was going on or how bad he was feeling, Maxine always made him feel better.

"Oh, you're good . . . you are real good."

Maxine can barely contain her excitement. She jumps into his arms, kissing him like she hadn't seen him just four hours earlier. "Let's get out of here," she whispers into his ear. She grabs her purse from behind the door and heads toward the elevator as she yells out, "I'm going to lunch."

* * *

The cab ride is more of the same: their mouths, pressed together like Chinese kissing fish, arms intertwined like vines. Eric runs his hand underneath Maxine's blouse, pinching her nipple as she fondles his erection through his jeans. He moans with excitement, slowly raising his hips up and down, following the motion of her hand against his penis.

The cab driver has seen enough. "Excuse me . . . ma'am . . . which side of the street is good for you?" The two of them come up for air.

"Right here will be fine." Maxine removes a twenty from her purse. "And here . . . keep the change."

They step out of the cab and head into the brownstone. Eric follows Maxine up the stairs. Inside, she teases him, walking backward as she slowly unbuttons her blouse. He grabs her arm and pulls her into him. His large frame absorbs her body like a pillow. She jumps up and wraps her legs around his waist, working her tongue inside his mouth. He carries her over to the bed, gently laying her down, pressing himself on top of her.

"Now where were we this morning?" He rises to his knees and unbuttons his shirt. She helps him pull it off and throws it to the floor. She thrashes her tongue around his left nipple, biting and pulling on it with her teeth. Their passion takes over. Making love to him has become Maxine's obsession. He makes her feel so alive, like she's always on an adventure.

"Get that fuckin' skirt off."

"Yes, baby."

"Now open your legs and let me see it . . ."

"Here it is."

"Rub it for me, baby . . . let me see you rub it."

Maxine slides her fingers across her wet vagina. She rubs it slowly, her back arching. Eric runs his tongue around her ankle and up her thigh. He kisses her hand as she masturbates for him, then places the finger in his mouth. He sucks it hungrily, tasting her juices. His tongue replaces her hand. Finding her clit, he licks it purposefully. Knowing what she likes, he is sending waves of pleasure up her spine. Her moans excite him. His tongue presses into her like a worm burrowing into a hole, moving in and out, driving her crazy.

"Give me your dick, baby . . . please . . . give it to me."

Eric takes off his boxers, his dick is as hard as marble, its veins bulging with blood and excitement.

Maxine spreads her legs wide, inviting him inside her. She wraps her legs around his waist as he pushes into her opening. It feels so perfect. They fit together like they were made for each other, like a mold of themselves had been separated at birth. He rolls her over, still deep inside her. She's on top of him now, grinding her hips back and forth.

"I love you, Maxine, I really do."

He's never felt like this before. Trust, loyalty, love, they all betrayed him early in life. Not feeling for anyone was easy. It kept him sharp, clear, let him do what he wanted, when he wanted. But Maxine mattered. She made him feel like being a better man; he needed her comfort in his loveless world.

"I . . . I'm coming, baby . . . I'm . . ."

"Yes, fill me up, Eric . . . fill me up."

He bursts inside her, pressing his penis deep into her body, lifting her in the air with his powerful legs, his back arched like a bridge. She comes right after him, collapsing on his chest, their juices running down her thighs.

"I love you E . . . I really do."

"I love you, too, Maxine . . . I love you, too . . ."

I've watched love turn angels into demons
turn rhythm into straight lines
I'm going out of my mind
he repeated as she hung up the phone
another sad dial tone
another long walk home

Maxine sits on the side of her bed, staring pensively at nothing. Eric can feel her heaviness and reaches for her shoulder. "What's on your mind?" he asks, but doesn't really want to know.

"What would you do, Eric?"

"Do about what?"

"C'mon, baby . . . you know what I'm talking about."

Eric changes his tone. He knows where she's going and he isn't in the mood for it. "I mean, what's up with you, Maxine? I'm not going to tell you again; don't go there with me . . . aiight?"

* * *

He doesn't want to get upset. He already feels like the world is against him and doesn't want to add her to the list.

"Don't be like that, Eric. I just worry about you. It's hard. I don't want to lose you over—" He cuts her off.

"Yo, I told you, don't talk about shit you don't understand." He stands up, stepping into his boxers. "How many times I gotta tell you that? . . . Damn."

"Don't be like that, Eric. I know what I'm talking about." She's trying not to get upset, not to push him away, but her emotions betray her. "Where are you going? Why do you run away when you don't like what you hear? You're not a kid anymore, Eric, talk to me."

"Talk to you about what . . . what! What do you want to hear?" He's yelling now. "You want me to buy a suit and work for some muthafuckas downtown? You forgettin' where we met . . . c'mon, don't start trippin' on me."

"I'm not tripping, Eric, I love you, and I know you love me. You're acting like that doesn't matter." Tears well up in her eyes. "How long do you think you can last out there?"

"Why don't you ask yourself how long you can put up with me? That's where this is going . . . right? You know what the fuck I do, shit, I've never lied about that, so what's this all about?" Eric is fully dressed and heading to the door. He's heard enough. Time to get back to work. "I'll call you later." He speaks without even looking at her, then walks out, slamming the door behind him. Maxine wipes her eyes and falls back on the bed. She pulls her long legs into her chest, curls up and cries herself to sleep.

*   *   *

It's been raining all afternoon. Eric is looking out of his apartment window, thinking about Maxine, his feelings, and where he should go from here. Love. How could this have happened? The pretty-boy thug, caught up in emotions. *Please,* he'd been with more women last year than he could count. They'd all been the same, easy screws looking for a payday. Maxine was different. The last eight months have been brand new to him. He's attracted to her like steel to a magnet. She was like gravity, pulling him uncontrollably to her. It had never been like this. He'd never let it get this far.

*   *   *

"All rise for presiding judge Earl Dresman." The bailiff's voice boomed through the courtroom, grabbing everyone's attention but Maxine's. Her thoughts are not with her. Mark, the assistant D.A. on the case, has to nudge her to stand up. "Hey, you all right?" he asks, concerned.

"I'm fine," she lies, trying to clear her head.

Maxine hasn't heard from Eric in three days. Did he know how much he was hurting her? She wasn't eating and could barely do her job. How could he be so selfish? She doesn't want to think the worst, but anything is possible.

"You may be seated." The bailiff approaches the bench and places a case file before the judge.

"Will the defendant please rise." Judge Dresman removes a pair of reading glasses from his robe and places them on his liver-spotted nose. "Mr. Rick Tubin, you are charged with . . ." Maxine's heart skips a beat. She's heard this name before, from Eric. What the hell was he doing here? Her imagination begins to run wild, her palms and armpits moisten. She leans over and whispers in Mark's ear.

"I've got to make a call."

"Right now?"

"It's an emergency."

"All right, I'll cover you, but make it quick."

Maxine grabs her purse and rushes out of the courtroom. She speed dials Eric on her cell phone. "Eric . . . I know you're mad at me but I thought you might want to know that your friend Rick is in my courtroom right now. I'm sorry about what I said. Can you please just call me back, I'm so worried . . . just call me . . . please." She hangs up and walks back into the courtroom.

*   *   *

Eric is walking down a long hallway. His cell phone sits in his jacket pocket; it's turned off. His 9mm pistol is fully loaded and tucked discreetly in his waistband. He knocks at room 467.

"Who is it?" a heavy voice yells from behind the door.

"It's E. Open up."

Eric puts his hand on his pistol and braces himself in front of the door. Several locks are undone and the door opens a crack, the chain lock still in place. Eric steps back and kicks the door open. He pulls his gun from his waist and bursts into the apartment.

"Don't move, muthafucka!" he yells. The man on the floor throws his hands in the air. Eric points his pistol at his face.

"Don't shoot me man . . . don't shoot."

"Where the fuck is Tony?"

"Tony who?"

"Oh . . . you wanna fuck wit me . . . that's what's up . . . Stand up . . . get up!"

Eric pulls the terrified man to his feet and places the barrel of the gun to his temple. He cocks the hammer.

"What's it gonna be, homes? I'm asking one more time . . . where is he?"

"He went to re-up in Queens. . . . H-h-he said he'll be back at midnight . . . th-th-that's all I know man . . . that's it . . ."

Eric slowly releases the hammer.

"All right . . . calm down . . . you did good . . . now pack up all this shit and give me every penny in here," he says, motioning with his gun around the room.

Eric leaves the apartment with a duffel bag full of drugs and money. He's willing to shoot whoever stands in the way of what is owed him. That's how the game is played. You play with fire; you get burned. Tony was lucky he wasn't there. He still had an ass whippin' coming though. Today just wasn't the day for it.

*   *   *

Back in his apartment, Eric listens to Maxine's message. How did she know who Rick was? Must've heard him on the phone. More importantly, if it is Rick, what the hell was he doing in court? Things were getting thick. He thinks about Maxine, how much he misses her. He doesn't feel it can work. Their lives are already on a collision course. She works for the law, and he works outside of it. That simple.

There is a knock at the door. Eric grabs his gun from the table and stands with his back against the wall next to the door. "Who is it?" His voice is calm. He pulls the hammer back and waits for an answer. "It's Maxine." Her voice surprises him. He tucks his gun into his waist and lets her in.

"What you doin' here?" His tone is dry, indifferent.

"Why haven't you called me, Eric? I know you got my messages."

"Why you doin' this . . . you're the one with all the questions . . . what you expect? I don't need nobody tellin' me what to do . . . you know what I mean?"

She takes off her jacket and throws it on the chair. She walks over to him and reaches for his face. He pulls away, avoiding her touch. She reaches for him again. This time he doesn't move as her hand caresses his cheek. "Don't fight us, Eric . . . I love you . . ." They stare into each other's eyes. Eric steps back abruptly, as if snapping out of a trance.

"What's this shit with Rick? How do you know who he is?"

"I've heard you talk about him."

"What does he look like?"

"Is he about your height, with dreadlocks and a goatee?"

"Sounds like him. Damn, what was he there for?"

"He skipped six meetings with his probation officer . . . nothing major . . . but it made me worry about you, since you hadn't called."

Eric's shoulders loosen up. He takes a deep breath and relaxes. Maxine moves in closer, kissing him softly on the cheek. "I'm not your enemy, baby. I care about you. You can do what you want,

Eric . . . let's just be there for each other, OK?" He looks away from her. His thoughts swim around in his head. She means a lot to him, more than he realized. He kisses her back. "I'm with you, Max . . . I'm with you."

Eric pulls her into him. They sink into each other's kisses like birds returning to the nest. He kisses her neck and starts down her body, slipping off her blouse in the process. His tongue explores her belly button as he reaches under her skirt and removes her panties. She unbuttons her skirt. It falls around her ankles and she kicks it aside. She stands before him like a statue, her body aching for his touch.

He lifts her leg onto the kitchen counter. He runs his tongue up her thigh, his middle finger caressing her clit. She grabs the back of his head with both hands, as he plunges his tongue into her vulva, licking her roughly. She moves with him, fucking his face as he fingers her ass, her juices splashing across his lips. She turns around and props her ass up for him, leaning her long caramel body across the kitchen table. He enters her from behind, her moans arousing him. He fucks her ferociously, holding her thin waist still as he thrusts in and out of her. It feels so good he has to stop himself.

He pulls out and sits on a kitchen chair. She turns to straddle him, slipping his dick back inside her. He stares into her eyes like a sinner seeking salvation, surrendering to the weight of his love for her. She feels him in her stomach. He raises her up and down his shaft, licking her nipples as her breasts bounce in front of him.

"You're in so deep, baby . . . it feels good . . ." She moans. Her voice pushes him over the edge. His muscles tighten; his back arches off the chair. He comes like a natural spring releasing years of pressure. His liquid fills her cavity with warmth, causing her to climax uncontrollably. Her legs stiffen as she comes over and over. "Don't move . . . please, don't move," she begs.

They sit still on the kitchen chair, their sweat fusing them together.

Eric smiles. "I guess we've made up."

They laugh so hard they almost fall off the chair.

* * *

It's raining again. Eric puts on his coat and heads to the store. It's time to get back to the grind. He's got to move the product from his apartment as soon as possible. His partner Rick is out of the picture for a minute; that means he's got to pack it all up and take it to the Bronx himself. The bodega is crowded. He grabs a paper and tosses fifty cents on the counter.

Eric is waiting to cross the street when his cell phone rings.

"Yeah."

"Hey, baby."

"What's going on?"

"You . . . What are you doing? I miss you already."

"Getting a paper . . . getting ready to head back to the crib."

A blue Caprice pulls up to the curb and stops in front of Eric. The limousine tint on the windows makes it impossible to see who is inside. Eric is speaking on the phone, oblivious. The back window slowly rolls down and a familiar voice calls to him. "Yo, E . . . Check this out."

He looks up. Three gunshots ring out. Eric has no time to react. The impact lifts him off his feet and throws him against the side of the bodega wall. His cell phone crashes to the curb. The blue Caprice pulls out in a cloud of burning rubber.

"Eric . . . Eric . . . Noooo!" Maxine is screaming on the phone.

A crowd surrounds him. Someone yells, "Call 911!" He feels like his chest is on fire; it's getting harder to breathe. "Maxine," he whispers.

"Don't try to speak, bro," a stranger insists; the man then folds his jacket and places it under his head. Eric's thoughts are calm. The game has caught up to him. He knows who shot him; it was Tony. A surge of anger runs through him, and then, he passes out.

Rainbows have it easy
They appear after the storm
And smile over the city
At the end is a shining pot of gold

Maxine holds a bouquet of roses. Her eyes, wet with tears, are bright red. She walks into the elevator and presses five. Her phone call to Eric runs like a tape endlessly looping in her mind. What could she have done differently? Why didn't she stay with him? She leaves the elevator and approaches the nurse's station.

"How do I get to room 514?" Maxine can barely speak; her voice cracks with every word. The nurse points down the hallway to the left. "Thank you."

She reaches the room and pushes open the door. The sight of him almost stops her from entering. The tubes protruding from his nose and mouth are connected to the machines that are keeping him alive. His once-strong body now lies fragile in his hospital bed, his broad chest wrapped in blood-soaked bandages. If she ever denied the reality of his world, she could do so no longer. But she loves him, and everything that comes with it. She knows that now. Maxine places the flowers on his bed, sits at his bedside and waits for him to wake. She plans on being there when he does.

LORI BRYANT-WOOLRIDGE

Close Encounters

I'm not sure if I'm losing my mind, because let's face it, it's entirely possible. I'm a forty-four-year-old single mother and a card-carrying member of W.O.W. (Worn out Women). I won't say my life is bad, just busy as hell and boring to boot. I've had two failed marriages (and have absolutely no interest in a third); a boss who *thinks* I'm his damn wife (and we're definitely not talking the trophy edition); two teenage sons who assume my only reason for existing is to cater to their every whim (a trait honestly inherited from their father); a Mastercard bill that's fast approaching "priceless"; and breasts and a butt that are beginning to droop like snapdragons in the Sahara.

So when this . . . this freaky encounter happened, it was too out there for me to decide if it was real or some twisted fantasy from my overwhelmed, starved-for-excitement mind. It was so bizarre and yet so incredibly fantastic that I don't know if I should call the loony bin to commit myself or contact *Ripley's Believe It or Not*.

It all began when I decided to run away from home for a couple of days. My boys were visiting their father for the weekend, my house looked like the aftermath of hurricane Floyd and I didn't feel like cleaning or looking at all that mess for the next two days. So I decided to book a room at the downtown Le Meridien Hotel for some much-needed "me" time. I figured I'd do a little window-shopping along Chicago's famous Magnificent Mile, stroll along Lake Michigan, and enjoy the pleasant fall weather while doing some serious thinking about how to restructure my life.

I checked in around noon on Saturday, hit Marshall Fields and the beach, and then returned to take a long, hot bubble bath. I have to tell you, there is nothing I enjoy better than a serious soak in a tub I don't have to clean. Relaxed and refreshed, I putzed around the room for a couple of hours—watching television, reading Eric Jerome Dickey's newest novel, but mainly doing not a damn thing. And you know what? It felt great. The only thing that would have felt better was some mind-blowing, knee-buckling, too-decadent-to-tell-your-best-girlfriend sex.

It's been a while since I've done the do, and the longer I sat around thinking about fucking, the more depressed I became. With divorce number two in the can, it was clear that I had no success when it came to men and was woefully unlucky in love. It was also becoming increasingly more difficult to hide the fact that I was lonely and desperately afraid of being an even lonelier (and hornier) old woman.

Suddenly the hotel room felt entirely too claustrophobic, so around six-thirty I decided to get dressed, go downstairs, meet some new people, and pick up my spirits with a cocktail or three.

Forcing myself out of this self-actuating funk, I slipped into my favorite charcoal-colored dress—a fine silk knit with a flattering ballerina neckline. I loved it because it graced my voluptuous curves, hid my numerous flaws, and matched the gray in my short crop of salt-and-pepper twists in a fashion that made me look hip and funky, not old. I dabbed on a coat of rambling rose lip gloss, added a generous spritz of White Linen cologne, grabbed my silk shawl and purse, and hit the hallway knowing that I may be unlovable, but I was still plenty damn cute.

My ride down to the lobby was uneventful as was my foray into the hotel bar. Despite my raging hormones, I wasn't looking for action, just to get my flirt on, so entering a nearly empty room was disappointing. Besides the bartender and pianist filling the room with his rendition of Stevie Wonder's, "A Ribbon in the Sky," there were only seven other people in the bar: a group of four guys who looked like used-car salesmen, each hoisting a bottle of Budweiser to his lips; an older gentleman sitting solo drinking whiskey at the bar; and a couple snuggling in the corner and having a hard time keeping their hands off each other.

"What can I get you?" the bartender asked as soon as my behind touched the stool.

"A gin gimlet, please, straight up." I watched as he chilled my glass and began combining the ingredients for my the-hell-with-it-all cocktail. Forget ex's, bosses, bill collectors, and kids. I took a sip of that velvety, cold gin and decided that I was going to get quietly drunk and then take myself upstairs, order room service, and get a good night's sleep in a bed I didn't have to make.

I was about halfway through with my drink when the most incredible-looking woman I'd ever seen walked into the bar. She paused for a moment to survey the place and then sashayed confidently through the room oblivious that all eyes were pointed in her direction. You'd have thought that Dorothy Dandridge had just risen from the dead the way they were gawking, but I couldn't blame them. Even *I* had to sneak a peek.

You couldn't help but notice her—not the way she smoldered. She was wearing the ultimate little black dress (the kind you search for all of your life and always find on someone else's back). The dress was tight enough to accent her even-J.Lo-would-be-jealous figure, but loose enough to leave you wondering what lay beneath. She had the old-fashioned hourglass kind of figure. A real woman's body. Not the wildly popular surgical version of eye-popping, faux breasts planted atop a narrow-hipped twelve-year-old's body.

The woman had a way of walking that made every body part of interest sway with come-hither appeal. It was a walk that brought men to her side and sent women into private places to practice. I felt both jealousy and admiration toward this diva. Talk about paling by comparison. Suddenly I didn't feel so cute.

As she approached the bar, I could see that she was more striking than beautiful. More sensuous than sexy. To my dread and surprise, she sat down next to me. I could feel the heat emanating from her body as she crossed her long legs and issued the bartender a spellbinding smile with her drink order. When her flute of champagne arrived she turned in my direction.

"To love," she said lifting her glass into the air.

"Cheers," I replied, thinking it to be an odd toast between strangers. I raised my drink to hers and stole a good look. Her skin was the shade of peanut butter, her facial features a delightful amalgamation of sharp and round. I guessed her age to be early thirties. She was obviously a woman of color, from where I couldn't tell, but there was definitely a foreign air about her. She had short, glossy black hair with a fringe of bangs cut to frame a pair of sparkling green eyes. They were the hue of the finest Arizona peridot and had the same amazing refractive qualities of diamonds.

Definitely contact lenses, the envious bitch in me decided.

One of the salesmen orphaned his brew and practically came running over to the bar. He stood several seats down from where we were sitting and immediately sent the object of his desire another glass of the bubbly. When it arrived I ordered another drink, all the time wondering why of all the barstools in this town, did this woman have to pick the one next to mine?

I watched her handle her admirer, graciously accepting his drink with you're-so-sweet-but-it's-never-going-to-happen smile, and then gently sending him back to his friends feeling like a winner. I realized then that the key to her irresistible charm was confidence. She was a woman totally at ease with herself. A woman to study and emulate, not envy.

"Men. They are definitely from another planet," she commented simply.

"You got that right," I mumbled into my glass.

"I'm Haley."

"Like the comet."

"Something like that," she said, once again capturing my gaze.

"Thea," I said, forcing my eyes away from hers. Haley's penetrating look was disturbing and the intensity of her stare caused me to pull my scarf protectively around my exposed shoulders.

Then the weirdest thing happened. She smiled at me with a hypnotizing, magnetic grin that was different from any other I'd ever received. It began with an uplifting twitch of her mouth, which parted her full lips before igniting her eyes and sending a flush of electric illumination coursing through her body and pouring out through her skin. The woman was glowing! I mean literally sitting there surrounded by a luminescent force field.

"You are beautiful," Haley commented, her mesmerizing eyes flickering with delicious possibilities.

I nearly fell off of my stool. Was this incredibly seductive woman hitting on *me*—Ms. Conservative, churchgoing, lover of men, divorced mother of two? It sure felt like it, but I wasn't exactly sure. I'd never had a woman outside of my mother, hairdresser, and the bitch who sold me the most hideous evening dress I'd ever owned, tell me that I was beautiful. I know that bisexual and lesbian lifestyles were now all the rage among the Hollywood crowd, but this was new territory for me.

All intelligent replies were jammed in my throat, so I drained the contents of my glass, hoping to wash down the surprise and confusion that were blocking my voice. Glass empty, I motioned to the bartender for a refill, causing my shawl to slip from my shoulders.

In one smooth as Italian gelato move, Haley reached over and repositioned my wrap, managing to brush my breasts and caress my naked shoulder. It happened so quickly and so subtly, I couldn't be sure that her hand had actually come in contact with my body. But if it hadn't, why had my nipples begun to swell and my clitoris been placed on alert?

"It has been a while since you've made love," Haley stated as she parted her lips with her tongue, bringing attention to her delicious mouth. She leaned in close and I swear I could smell roses on her breath. "It's been even longer since you *felt* loved. Truly loved," she whispered in my ear while lightly running her finger across my exposed collarbone for emphasis.

An audible gulp of gin and Rose's lime juice was my only reply. How did this complete stranger know these things about me? And where on my body was the frigging neon light flashing LONELY, HORNY, LESBIAN?

"I can make you feel that way again," she promised. I felt the tip of her hot tongue feather dust each intricate curve of my ear, sending an urgent message to my vagina to cream up and prepare to get busy. Her come-on was seductive and tempting and so damn unnerving.

By this time every head in the place was turned in our direction. Even the couple making out in the corner had stopped to watch. And I can guarantee you that every guy in the place had a hard-on the size of a sequoia, just thinking about the idea of the two of us together. This girl-on-girl fantasy even had me turned on. But I was also embarrassed. I had to stop this runaway train before I got myself derailed.

"Haley, I'm not quite sure what you're thinking. . . . I mean, I'm flattered . . . look at you . . . you're beautiful . . . anyone would be attracted. . . ." I had to pause and douse myself in one final gulp of liquid bravado.

"Thank you, but I'm not that way. I like men. Tall, handsome black *men*. Granted, I have shit for taste when it comes to picking them, but you know, men will be men, and that's what I like. Always have, always will," I said, rambling through my refusal like an idiot.

"But by loving me, you will know the joy of loving yourself. No man can give you this gift," Haley promised with the practiced insistence of a sexual vagabond. Her compelling eyes once again captured my gaze, but there was more to it than just desire. Behind the longing was need . . . almost desperation.

Whoa. Now that sounded pretty deep, even though I really didn't know what the fuck she was talking about. But I needed to depart because I was damn close to tiptoeing over a line that I wasn't prepared to cross.

"It was . . . uh . . . nice to meet you, Haley . . . uh . . . have a . . . good night." I stuttered my good-byes as I gathered my belongings, stepped down off the stool, and made a beeline for the door.

"Thea," she called after me in a silky voice impossible to ignore. "The soul knows. Don't be afraid of the body."

I heard her comment, but again wasn't quite sure what to make of it. All I knew was that for the first time in my life I felt attracted to and desirous of something I'd always considered morally wrong and spiritually corrupt.

I headed straight for the bank of elevators and frantically pushed the call button at least fifty times, all the while praying that she would not follow.

Alone inside the elevator my imagination took on a life of its own. Tantalizing visions of what could have happened with Haley overtook me. I imagined the sleek satin texture of her thighs, the feel of her soft breasts in my hands, her warm tongue in my mouth. My feelings were a study in opposites dueling—the nasty and adventurous, decadent side of me tussling with my heterosexual, ethically upright, good girl.

The Girl Scout won by a hair. When it came to my apparent attraction to another woman, dismay had conquered intrigue.

"Fantasizing does not make me gay. I am not a lesbian. I am *not* a lesbian," I repeated, quoting every magazine psychiatrist I'd ever read.

The elevator ascended for several seconds before stopping to answer a summons on the eleventh floor. As the doors parted, a frosty chill swept through the car, causing me to shudder. I lowered my eyes to the carpet in order to hide my flushed and flustered state. When we were once again on the move, I lifted my gaze again to find a tall brother standing directly in front of me and I must say the rear view was exquisite. He was wearing white linen slacks and a well-fitting crisp white shirt. Biceps were bulging, back muscles were rippling, and his ass was kickin'. One could only hope that with a body that fine, he had the face to match.

Now this is where it starts to get really weird, so stay with me. We continued to ride for another few floors, and the whole time I was checking out this stranger's taut physique. Okay, if you're thinking that I was trying to transfer all the guilty lust I felt for Haley to this much more appropriate target, I'd agree. So I'm busy checking out his derriere when I felt and heard an electric current crackle inside the lift and cause the hair on my arms and neck to stand at attention. Then there was a loud, grinding sound and the elevator car came to a sudden stop. The wild movement threw me forward and into the hard body of my fellow passenger, before tossing us both to the back of the elevator and onto the floor. Then the lights went out.

We huddled together for a moment, until the elevator settled itself. Feeling panicky, I felt around the darkness and located my handbag. I dug in and retrieved my keys, which were attached to a thin, credit-card-sized flashlight. I pressed the corner and the dim light was enough to illuminate the man's attractive face. His nut-brown skin provided a smooth canvas for his broad and masculine features. I was momentarily mesmerized by his plump inviting lips until they parted and just like Haley's had, set fire to his eyes and skin, filling the space with a dreamy, diaphanous light. His eyes, the color of sky-blue topaz, had the same jewel-tone quality and magnetic draw of Haley's, and I found myself unable to pull away.

I still felt sexually overwhelmed by my earlier experience, but was strangely at peace sitting on the floor of this dark box with this nameless man. He had a cool, detached demeanor and an erotic aloofness that I was finding difficult to resist.

I started to introduce myself and then realized, who cared? I was tipsy and horny. I didn't want his name . . . I didn't want conversation . . . I wanted HIM. And his eyes let me know that anything I wanted, he wanted, too. But I was paralyzed by indecision. Just how do you sexually ravish a stranger in the elevator? I mean, the social etiquette of such a situation was beyond my knowledge.

Before I could act, he exhaled an icy breath that chilled my face and caressed my eyes closed. Wafting under my nose was the aphrodisiac blend of spearmint and lemon—a mix I found quietly revitalizing and totally empowering.

I pounced on my manly prey like a lion on the Serengeti. My lips immediately found his disturbingly beautiful eyes, kissing each one shut, before nibbling at his nose and then devouring his mouth like a famished contestant on *Survivor.* His mouth was cool and welcoming and slipping my warm tongue inside was like diving into a glacial pool on a hot, sweaty afternoon. And behind the mint and citrus was the faint aroma of sweet roses— just like Haley's.

Stop fantasizing about that woman, I commanded myself as I quickly unfastened his shirt, damn near ripping away the buttons in my haste. Exposing his skin released his scent. Bracing, herbaceous notes filled the elevator and combined with the gimlets to further intoxicate and embolden me.

With not a single word uttered between us, my hands reached for his shoulders to remove his shirt and upon contact the gauzy light from his body enveloped mine. I traveled south with my mouth, forging a trail of kisses down his chest and stomach. Each kiss left my lips feeling icy hot and deliciously burnt. I ran my hands across his hairless, muscular chest. His skin was soft and smooth and with each touch cooled as mine warmed. It was as if all his body heat was being transferred to me. Perspiration began seeping from my pores and the removal of my clothes was paramount. I stood up and quickly slipped off my dress, leaving me naked but for a pair of black, sheer panties.

"Don't move," I commanded. My ever-active imagination began to spin scenes from HBO's *G-String Divas.* But this time, it was me doing the dirty dancing. "We're going to play a little game. But the rules are no touching and no talking."

Still standing in my heels, I straddled his body, put my hands on the back rail of the elevator and I lowered myself onto his lap. Just like I'd seen on TV, I leaned forward, making sure my breasts hung above his face, my nipples hovering over his mouth in a tempting cocktease.

With my eyes shut tight, and our hot spots separated by the fabric of our lives, I rode his crotch like an erotic dancer in the infamous Champagne Room. I pressed my pussy into his pelvis and began to grind gently, circling twice then rocking back and forth. Pleasure threw my head back and I moaned, feeling his dick get hard beneath his trousers. My nipples now stood defiantly at attention atop two engorged breasts daring him to take a forbidden bite.

I placed my index finger into my mouth and sucked gently. The seductive suggestion of oral sex had just the impact I wanted. He let out a whimper and clenched his ass together. I could see the restraint on his face as he forced himself to keep his hands still and endure the exquisite pain of remaining motionless.

"Ohhh," I sighed as I ran my tongue provocatively across my lips. He moaned in return as his eyes softened and his dick jumped in cruel anticipation of satisfaction denied.

I now understood why so many women loved exotic dancing. It was the pure sense of power knowing that you were in complete control of every man who begged for your attention. It was a high that no drink, no illicit pharmaceutical could ever deliver.

I was really getting into the power trip when he broke the rules and gathered my breasts into his hands. His icy tongue traveled round and round my areolas, soaking them with his sweet saliva before exhaling like the wind on Mount Everest. His glacial breath turned my nipples into icicles and sent a thrilling shock throughout my body. That zinging jolt traveled straight to my clit, kick-starting something deep inside and turning me into a woman possessed.

Nothing mattered more to me at that moment than to feel this man inside me. I disengaged from his lap long enough to pull down his pants and reveal the most fabulous penis I'd seen in a very long time. It was thick, smooth, and shiny. A true Goldilocks dick—not too big, not too small. Just right.

I was out of control as I once again straddled his hips and allowed his hardness to enter me. His penis was stiff and frigid like an erotic ice sculpture, and its frosty delight shocked my vagina into overdrive. With zero inhibition I zealously rode his dick. My pussy was like a furnace and the heat of my hunger engulfed him, causing a steady stream of liquid to flow from my vagina. His silent but exquisite display of facial contortions revealed his readiness to explode. I clenched the muscles of my vagina tight and the flames of my inner muscles licked and tickled his shaft into orgasm. A massive gush of sex juice exited my body as his erection melted away.

My desire for satisfaction consumed me and I continued to grind into his pelvis, but could no longer feel his member within. I prayed like hell that he wasn't the typical shoot-your-wad-and-lose-interest type of brother. I wanted to be sated and needed to arouse him again as soon as humanly possible. Who knew when they'd get this elevator going again? But even if they did pry those doors open to find asses in the air, I was getting mine!

With blind determination my mouth searched out his pecs, captured one nipple and began to suckle while rolling the other between my thumb and index finger. I heard an audible groan, but instead of the growing erection I expected to feel, my mouth and hand became full with the swollen breasts of a woman.

Shock opened my eyes and I looked directly into sparkling peridot and realized that I was fucking Haley.

"Haley? But how? When?" I asked, confusion coloring my face. Once again her eyes detained my questioning gaze.

"The soul knows," she repeated in a whisper.

That was good enough for me. As bizarre as this all looked it *felt* right. No longer hesitant, I gave in to my undeniable craving for this incredible woman who had aroused my desire and captured my imagination.

Our eyes locked as I lifted my face to hers and she gently consumed my lips. Haley's saliva tasted like rosewater and her tongue, intertwined with mine, felt smooth and velvety like a carpet of flower petals. In her arms my body began to lose its feverish impatience and cooled to a simmer.

Haley slowly lowered my back to the floor and covered my breasts with hers. Heart to heart, I felt every bit of the earlier control I'd coveted disappear under the delectable and drugging effect of this woman's soothing touch. I closed my eyes again as she slowly and seductively caressed my body, reintoxicating all of my senses and leaving me feeling deliciously languid.

I was blown away by how different this all felt. With Haley there was no fantasizing necessary to carry me away into sexual bliss. I was lost on another plane . . . momentarily existing in another dimension of myself. Yet, I was completely in the moment. And the power of now was awesome.

After thoroughly exploring my mouth and face with her lips and tongue, Haley began a seductive journey down my neck and across my shoulders until her lips came to rest on my large, chocolate nipples. She nibbled with practiced expertise until I heard a lazy groan escape my lips. Each tug caused a pleasurable nagging sensation in my groin, causing my hips and pelvis to instinctively tilt upward in search of hers.

Slowly, luxuriously, Haley bathed my torso with her tongue as she lightly ran her fingertips down the length of my inner thigh. She slid her hand between my legs, coaxing apart the swollen lips of my dripping pussy. Lubricating her finger with my juices, Haley fondled me in a soft, circular motion, stimulating me to the verge of paradise.

"Open your eyes, Thea."

I obeyed her request and with wide-eyed wonder was immediately transported into another world. Haley, emulating her male form, exhaled and the sweet scent of roses gently assaulted my face, stripping it and the rest of my body of all skin, bones, and muscle. I became a hologram of energy, my form supported by the love and light within. Stripped down to my spiritual essence, I felt ecstatic and vibrant.

Our ocular intercourse was more sexually intense than any physical coupling I'd ever experienced. I was filled with the sensuality of the universe and as the intensity of my feelings began to overwhelm me a blinding white light filled the elevator.

Wave after wave of beautiful, limitless energy flowed through my body. The shake and tremor that consumed me sought release in a deep, primal outcry as my entire mind, body, and soul began to climax into the most potent, God-inspiring orgasm I'd ever experienced. Its power dissipated the light and I found myself staring into my own face.

I was beautiful.

My eyelids, heavy with contentment, once again drifted shut. It took several moments for my heartbeat to return to normal and even though I was back in my body, nothing felt the same. I could feel myself smiling and when I looked up again, Haley's eyes were blazing into mine.

"But how? Where is . . . was he *you?*"

She nodded affirmatively.

"But why?"

"Because that's what you needed to feel comfortable."

"Or maybe a woman is what I've needed all of my life. No man has ever satisfied me this way."

"Man. Woman. Penis. Vagina. It doesn't matter. You humans have it all wrong. You get caught up in the costume and then deny yourself or others the truth. The act of love is not about bodies connecting, but rather hearts and souls."

The way she said *humans,* as if excluding herself, should have shocked me, but somehow it didn't. Instinctively I knew that she was otherworldly. Maybe because this sister from another planet had certainly rocked my world.

"Can I tell you something? I mean something crazy?"

Haley smiled as she nodded her consent.

"Right as I peaked, I opened my eyes and I was looking at *me*."

"Because tonight you gave birth to your own spirituality. You experienced your higher self as love's true source."

"I'm confused."

"Thea, making love is witnessing and loving the goddess within. You simply gave yourself permission to love and therefore the greatest of loves was returned."

Haley stood up and reached out to help me up from the floor. My lids dropped and our naked bodies melted against each other as we kissed, long and deep. We stood, arms wrapped around each other for what seemed a lifetime. This experience had been so erotic, sensual, and highly spiritual—a word I'd never once in my life connected to sex. And I wanted more of the same.

* * *

A melodic and celestial chiming roused me from my daydream. The elevator slowed to a stop to deliver the brother with the beautiful body to his destination, which just happened to be on the same floor as mine. I followed, treating myself to the sight of his tight ass moving down the hallway until he stopped at his room. Just as the lock clicked open, he looked up and caught me staring.

He grinned widely, extracting the same in return.

"That smile is full of light. It's stunning," he said with a deep buttery timbre as he tilted his head slightly toward the room. His subtle invitation elicited a flirty giggle full of shyness and satisfaction.

Great teeth and a great ass. Do I dare obey my thirst?

I smiled again and winked in response before stepping past him and continuing to my room. Just knowing he was interested was gratification enough. Despite my earlier craving, I now felt spent, satiated, empowered, beautiful, wise, confidant, and above all, loved.

I continued to grin broadly as I pulled my shawl close and wrapped myself in an affectionate, self-affirming hug. Maybe I was all that and a salad on the side. After all, I'd left a beautiful diva who could have any man and most women this side of the Mississippi downstairs lusting after *me*, as did the superfine brother with major T&A.

Who'd have thought that a lazy weekend in town and a little attention from a couple of strangers could make me feel so damn good? I slipped into my hotel room and immediately kicked off my shoes. Life was all good and so was I.

LEONE ROSS

The Contract

I got into this coma thinking about sex and I guess I'm still thinking about it. Typical guy, huh? My body's lying there on a hospital bed and my mom can't stop crying her eyes out but all I can think is, wake up, wake up, damn it, you gotta get laid, you can't . . . well, you can't *go* without getting some. That's all my body seemed interested in before my brain went crazy and short-circuited on me. My body's been down there in that bed for about a week. I've been up here since then, floating, flying, getting into people's business.

It was the flu, first. I was watching BET over Adrienne's shoulder, one eye on the TV, the other on Adrienne's friend Jennie. Jennie's really hot. She wears short skirts and sometimes I think she's bending over and flashing me a little, but that could be my imagination.

Anyway, I was watching videos and Jennie and thinking I needed an excuse not to do homework yet. Mom was doing her Homework Stroll, what Adrienne calls her Ho Stroll. At around seven she starts walking around dusting and looking at us out of the corner of her eyes. The TV's usually on, or Ade's online, and the more Mom dusts and the more we keep on doing what we're doing, which is *not* homework, the madder she gets. The clock's ticking and homework time is passing, and she's strolling around, cussing under her breath how we don't appreciate a good education, didn't she teach us to do our homework first thing, but no, we just lying up in here watching her cable, and eating all her food. I guess I like it when she fusses like that. It's a pain in the ass, but I like it. Her Jamaican accent comes back and she gets all puffed up.

I did have an excuse. I'd had a headache in one eye all day, and I was starting to feel that wooze you get when flu's coming on. Your fingertips feel like they're getting bigger and your head swims and everything looks weird—very far away or very close up. When you walk it's like gliding on cotton wool. Mom came closer to me, and she was like, well, homework? That's when I said I thought I was sick. At first she just snorted, then she felt my head and admitted I had a bit of a fever. Ade cut her eyes at me; she thought I was faking. Jennie grinned, and her lips were all wet and kinda fat and pretty. I wasn't lying, man. With every step to my room I felt worse.

I was in bed all day sleeping and thinking about sex. Like, how hard it is to be a VIRGIN and how nobody else I know is a VIRGIN, except for Ade, who despite all those boys hanging around and calling her, *better* be one. I'm eighteen, nearly a man. I'm going to Howard when I graduate, we're just waiting for those SAT scores, and I'm going to go to college a VIRGIN? Beau is always up in my face, what, you ain't done it yet, dog? He's a ladies' man. They all like him, with his doo rag and cool strut and all. I can't do that.

Not that I'm not OK, plenty of girls at school make eyes at me. I've had girlfriends, and I've got some. Plenty of action above the waist, sucking nipples and stuff. But I haven't gone any further, even if they insisted. Girls tell me I'm fine and they want me to give them a baby. Don't these girls have any ambition? I've seen what happens to girls who have babies. It's really, really hard to get anywhere in life. I keep telling them that I'm not one of these New York guys. I might have been here for three years, but I'm Jamaican; we have standards. And I'm going to college. Or maybe I'm not going anymore, considering the hospital bed.

This is how it happened: I was in bed, popping aspirin because my head was killing me, trying to get into the porno channels, but Mom had blocked them a year ago after somebody ran up like sixty dollars worth of charges. Actually, I don't think it was me. I watched one with Beau and then a couple by myself, but I bet it was Ade and her friends. I don't even want to think about that.

Mom thought it was me, of course, being a boy, and she cut that shit quick. She was actually pretty cool. She sat me down and said that she understood I was a growing boy, but she couldn't afford my libido. That made me laugh. That's when we made The Contract. She says she's been saving up, and she'll give me ten thousand dollars if I make it to twenty-one without getting anyone pregnant.

That's part of the reason why I haven't done anything yet. Ten grand isn't what 50 Cent and Nas and all those rappers are making, but it could make a real difference in my life. I think it's a good deal, if Mom keeps her word. But it's hard. One girl called

Shania came up to the apartment and took off all her clothes in front of me, rubbing on me, telling me she was ready to give it up. I freaked. Her titties were in my face, all round and brown and the nipples were hard. I was trying to be cool, but the baby stuff was just running around in my head. And Beau wouldn't think this was cool, but I want it to be nice. There are a lot of fools out there who treat girls really bad. I know, because I have quite a few friends who are girls, and they tell me. Furthermore, I've seen Ade crying over her first boyfriend. She kicked the bedroom door shut, and kept yelling at me to leave her alone. I finally got in the room and stood way over the other side while she was crying and hiccuping and telling me how she really, *really* loved him, and he said it back, and now he's taken up with some other girl. At the end, I was like: Sorry, Ade. And she gave me this weak grin. She lost about ten pounds over this fool. So I wasn't about to break anybody's heart, not even Shania's. I packed her up and sent her home and told her that guys were dogs. And so there I was, still a VIRGIN. Sometimes I think I'm an idiot. There's easy pussy out there, and condoms work. But you know.

I jerk off a lot, to make up. I think I'm setting a record. It's weird to do that when you've got flu. Feels like you're in a dream, and when you cum, it's slow motion and soft, almost absent-minded. Then you wonder if you really did it, so you do it again. Mom was at work. She left me with juice and aspirin and said I should read a book, and I was like, yeah, right. She grinned at that. "Well, I always live in hope," she said.

I popped pills and popped myself all day. Mom had asked me

if I wanted to go to the doctor, but I figured I was OK. I seemed to be getting better. Yeah, right.

Then Ade came in, yelling about what, you still in bed, get up you lazy fool, stop faking, and I tried to push her, but I couldn't hold my hand up. She got scared and phoned Mom at work, and while she was phoning, I could feel myself leaving. What I mean is that it felt as if I were splitting—like there was another me inside of me, stretching through my skin, reaching for air. Then I guess I must have passed out, because I don't remember anything until I was looking down at me in a bed, with everybody bawling. Dad's even coming up from Jamaica tomorrow. The doctor says I have something called Reye's syndrome. It's rare, but you can get it if you overdose on aspirin when you have the flu. It fucks up your liver and your brain, and it comes on quick.

I wish my mother wouldn't cry. She worries about her weight, but from up here she looks pretty good to me. And she hasn't been eating. That's the great thing about up here; I seem to be able to go anywhere. I followed her and Ade home and watched Mom cook but nobody ate anything. By then I was getting the hang of this thing, and it's like being in space, you can fly, you can sit down next to people, you can make yourself go through things. I flew through the computer and got this great fizzy feeling, down to my toes. Electricity. There don't seem to be any rules. But thank God, I can still jerk off. Halle Berry came on TV and I sat down on my own bed and knocked one off. Then I felt guilty—I'm still thinking about sex, when everybody's sad? But I can't be sad, because I know I'm coming back. I've got to. It's all very well to fly over Manhattan—I did it three times today, looking at all the girlies—but you know, I've got to come back. This coma is a temporary thing.

Dad says you have to take advantage of your every situation, make the best out of it, which is his asshole excuse for leaving Mom. But he had a point. So I set myself a project. First I promised myself that when I get back, I'm going to get laid, no question. Put seven rubbers on and just do it. It's just that I want to be good. That's the real problem with sex. I'm gonna say it: It makes me scared. You want to be good, you don't want any girl pushing you off and laughing at you, calling you a minute man. I don't want to hurt anybody, either.

My friend Tanya said she once had sex with this guy and it started hurting, and she said stop, and he just kept going, talking about how he was going to spank that ass. I mean, how insensitive can you get? The boy's a fool. What I didn't know was that it could hurt a girl. I thought their pussies were made for that. She wasn't a virgin. And even though he wouldn't stop, she said it wasn't rape, exactly. But it hurt her. She was trying to tell me that pussies get dry sometimes, you run out of juice if the guy doesn't know what he's doing. Tanya got pregnant, too, a year ago. She had an abortion. It was hard to see her afterward, she was so upset. So I don't want to hurt anybody. I want the girl I make love with to get really wet and cum all over the place. That's what'll make me happy. I could really get off on that. I would suck pussy for days if that's what she wanted. She'd just have to show me how. And I'd last and last and try to keep some control so I could see what she wanted, how she was feeling, so I didn't do it too long. And I'd bring her flowers, too.

My project was to find out a little bit more about what girls want. First I went online, but I kept hitting porno sites. Then I stole *Hustler* and *Playboy* off street corners. That was shit. I found a book about girls' fantasies, but it was a lot to read, and it's not like being in a coma gives me magical powers. So then I went everywhere and sat down next to women in parks and restaurants. I even zooted into people's houses, sat down on their sofas and listened to girl talk. But of course no one was giving any classes on how to be good. You know, girls are mad with guys, man. Somebody didn't pay rent, or somebody hit them, or somebody forgot Valentine's Day. But they give us all these things to remember. It can be hard.

I was sitting on top of a gym down the road from our apartment, thinking about all the things I need to remember, when I saw her. Remy. She's very, very pretty. She has curly hair, cut short, a sweet face, and an ass for days. She goes to the gym and pumps iron. She looks like she's about thirty-five.

A woman.

I watched her for an hour, the first day. Just girl-watching, like I've been doing. Watching her lift weights and smile at the guys smiling at her. When she got on the bike I wanted to be closer to her, so I hopped up on the handlebars. That's when it happened. She leaned her body forward, all sweaty and out of breath, and brushed those titties against my chest. Then she fell off the bike.

I was as shocked as she was. I didn't know anyone could feel me. I keep trying to hug Mom, but she walks right through me. I tried to pat Ade, but she kept on staring at the computer screen, reading about comas and the chances of coming out of one. But

Remy, she felt me. She picked herself up and stood there for a couple seconds, and I swear I could almost see a question mark over her pretty head.

"What the hell?" she said.

Then she looked right at me. Right into my eyes. I've never seen a woman look so surprised. "What the hell?" she said again, and then she leaned in closer, and really looked. That was when I lost it. I was shaking. I didn't realize I was so lonely out here. She had fear and disbelief in her face, but then her eyes just kinda melted. They were the kindest eyes I've ever seen.

"Are you all right?" she whispered under her breath. "Are you there?" Then, "Tell me I'm not crazy."

I opened my mouth, but no words came out. I guess that's when I fell in love. She was so fucking sweet. I mean, you see a—what am I, a ghost?—and you ask it if it's all right? Then she reached out and her fingers were against my chest, long, slim nails, touching me. That's when I was up and out of there, fast, climbing above buildings, into that air, filling my lungs. I was trying not to cry.

I try not to think about the body in the bed. It's not me.

*   *   *

I found her next time in the sauna. She was wrapped up in a towel, her legs dark against the white, hundreds of sweat beads on her face, running down her beautiful arms. The towel over her breasts was soaked. She was in there with a girlfriend, and I got there just in time for the good stuff. I made sure I sat myself behind her so she couldn't see me. I wanted to watch her, listen to her voice.

"So I haven't seen you for a while," she was saying. Her friend was a skinny little thing with squinchy eyes and a tough mouth.

Tough Mouth grinned. "Yeah, well."

Remy grinned back. "So what's up? You found a man?"

"You could say that."

Remy rolled her eyes. "OK, you're going to keep it to yourself, that's fine."

"Oh, c'mon. You want to know."

"Then tell me!"

"I met him about a month ago. Girl, he is sooo pretty, I don't even know what to do."

"I bet you do know what to do."

"Yeah, and we been doing it!" Tough Mouth stretched out one leg, then hugged herself. She looked very happy. "That's the thing about these young guys, they know all the kinky stuff."

"Kinky stuff?"

"Yeah, he eat for days, Rem. He loves that shit. Snacking on me like I'm a neck bone."

"That's not kinky, that's good." Remy ran her hand through her hair. I really liked her hair all short and curly. I don't like weaves.

"So what do you mean, young? You going for guys in their twenties now? Given up on the men?"

Tough Mouth leaned forward like she had a secret. "That's the thing. He's not in his twenties."

"What? You're only thirty-four."

"Yeah, and I said he was young, girl. He is all of nineteen."

I started jigging right behind Remy. This was the good stuff. *"Nineteen?"*

"Why not?"

"You could be his momma."

"No I couldn't!"

"Just about."

Tough leaned forward. "I don't believe it. You mean to say that you never looked at a young buck all bright on the street and felt something?"

Remy sat down and shifted in her seat. "We-ell . . ."

"See?" the other girl cackled. "I *knew* it!"

Remy looked a little freaked. "It's not like that. Just that yester-day . . ."

I held my breath.

"Oh I know you be looking at the young brothers and wonder-ing how you can bring them in." Tough Mouth was kind of deter-mined. I decided I didn't like her. *Stop cutting her off*, I thought. *Let her talk.*

"No. Really. Well, only this one time . . . but isn't that weird?" Remy's face got serious. I really liked that she was thinking about it. But she didn't know. Beau once had an older woman for two weeks, and we were all jealous. The guys were like, whoa, Beau be *pimpin'*.

Tough stretched her arms above her head. She did have nice arms. "What was he like, this one-time guy?"

There was a little silence. I spent it admiring the way Remy's thighs dipped in and the way she wiggled her toes. She was going to tell. Tough Mouth wasn't going to let her get away with it.

"The weirdest thing happened to me yesterday," Remy said. She paused. I think my heart nearly popped out of my mouth. "Oh, it's stupid."

"Tell me."

Remy shook her head. "You're going to think I'm crazy." She was rubbing her hand up and down her stomach, but I don't think she knew she was doing it. "I was on the bike in the gym and I got this strange, really strong feeling that someone was watching me."

"Men be watching you all the time."

Remy smiled. "This was different. It was in the air. And then I leaned forward . . . and I . . ."

"What?"

"I . . . bumped . . . into somebody."

"So?"

"No. I mean, there was no one there."

Tough Mouth's eyes were big. Not as big as mine.

Now it all came out in a rush, and I could lean over her shoulder and smell her perfume and something spicy on her breath.

"There wasn't anyone there. Just the bike. But I was next to somebody, I could feel them and then I fell off and looked up and I swear, Katy, I *swear* I was looking at the prettiest boy I have ever seen in my life. He was sitting on the handlebars. And I was looking into his eyes, the saddest, darkest eyes . . ."

"For real?"

I wanted to dance. She thought I was pretty. That was so cool.

"I swear. He couldn't have been more than eighteen, and he had the slimmest waist, these gorgeous shoulders." She grinned. "Skin the color of sandalwood . . ." They shrieked with laughter. "Oh my God, Katy, those pretty *eyes* and he was tall. I just stood there, thinking this is crazy, but the main thing I thought was

God, let him be real so I can touch him . . ." She shook her head again. "I need a man. I am so horny I am seeing things!"

"You got that right," laughed Tough Mouth.

I was so happy I could have high-fived the sun.

Remy stood up. That was when the towel fell off.

*   *   *

I went to the hospital and looked at myself. My head was full of Remy, but I had to look at me, because something was changing. My stomach felt light, and Mom hadn't left that room for days. I forced myself to look, because I'm a man, and men look at things and face them. She was all curled up in the chair next to my bed, curled up in a ball, like she was holding her heart inside, to protect it. Dad was there, too, and I couldn't believe he was crying. That's when I got scared. I never saw my father cry, and it was like he couldn't stop. He was leaking. He kept running his hand over my head, saying wake up, young boy, wake up. You have to. But I couldn't feel his hand, and I wanted to scream. And my mom, she wasn't hissing at him, like she did before he left her, she was just dry, and curled up.

"There's not much time," said the doctor. "He's getting ready."

"No," my mother said. "He's not ready for anything! He's not."

The doctor turned away and I looked at me. I was glad Remy couldn't see me like that.

I stayed all night, and my mother couldn't feel me. Even when I touched her face. Even when I kissed her cheek.

*   *   *

I found Remy at her apartment in Brooklyn. She walked around naked, and I loved her for it. When the towel fell in the sauna, I could have cried, she looked so good, and here she was again. Her breasts were round and they stood up a little and dropped down a little, but they were perfect. She had this stomach, man. The softest-looking thing, like I could fall into it and come out new. Her thighs were long and strong, like dancer's legs. She talks about my skin? This was skin. Light bouncing off it in big waves. Maybe that's 'cause I'm up here. But I'd like to think she would have looked like that anyway.

I watched her drink herb tea, smoke weed, and laugh at a movie. I didn't know how to come to her, but I had to find a way. Sometimes she sat with her legs wide open, and I wanted to look. I never looked at wide-open pussy before, but it was a dance, me always behind her, so she wouldn't see me just yet.

In the end, I just did it. I stepped in front of her, between her and the TV.

"Oh my God," she said. She grabbed a cushion from the couch and held it over her breasts. "Oh shit. Oh my God." Her eyes filled the whole room.

I made myself speak. "Hi," I said. "My name . . ." I had to be strong. I wanted that kind look in her eyes again. "My name's Leo."

I talked to her like I never talked to anybody, not Beau, not Tanya, not Ade. I told her stuff you think is gonna sit in your head alone, forever. That I was scared, and how pretty she was. I told her I wanted to bring her flowers, but my hands didn't seem to work for them, and I tried to get them for like half an hour, my hands going through the roses and the tulips. How I was never going to college, so I wouldn't get a chance to work out what I was going to do. Ade knows she's going to be a pediatrician, but I'm still coasting, thinking actor, lawyer, businessman. I'm never going to have another Christmas. Or bring a special girl home and watch Mom try to be polite if she didn't like her. I'm never going to *go* anywhere. No more eating fish on the beach in Jamaica. I'm never going to look back and see what I learned, or sit down with Beau and laugh like crazy at what we did as kids. There are going to be new movies I won't see, and new friends I'm never going to make. I won't ever pump up a sound system and drive, drive down the road by myself, singing like a crazy fool. I'm never going to know any more stuff. I'm never going to get it right, none of it, none of my life, because there is no more, and I wanted to get it right. It was stupid, but it was fine. And she listened, and I could see the fear running off and away from her, like water. And I wanted to be sure I could still touch her, so I put my finger on her ankle. And it connected. Real, solid. Full of blood and breathing.

* * *

She was smooth and hotter than anything I ever touched. And she was calm. She slowed me down. She whispered to me in her bed, a long whisper that never seemed to stop. She kept telling me it was OK, that I know things, that I know so much already, I know what I need to know. She made me taste everything. Taste the feel of her elbows, even though that sounds funny. She made me suck the dimple in the small of her back, and look into her eyes as I touched her. She kept the lights on so I could see the shadows between her thighs and watch her open up, and it's silly, but I thought this was the most perfect pussy ever, it was like a flower. When I put my fingers there she was wet and getting wetter and I was like OK, oh Jesus. I tried to please her. I did everything she wanted. I kissed her thousands of times, because I wanted every one to take with me wherever I was going. I licked her toes, sucked so hard the polish came off in my mouth, and it didn't matter. Go slow, she said, see everything. So I did. I saw how her nipples got big and puckered up as I slid them into my mouth and when she arched her back and sighed I did it again. I saw how her stomach got all tight when I pushed my thumb inside her, and felt her pussy grab it. She tasted like warm things, and when my neck started aching from the licking and the searching she showed me how to put a pillow under her ass so we could tilt it right and I could get to eating better. I rubbed my face into it and she brought me up and kissed me and I was like, wow, she likes the taste of herself, too.

When she reached down between my legs, I couldn't hold it in. I shot it all over her hand, up her arm, into the air. That's it, baby, you've been holding it in, she said. It was OK; she wasn't mad. She put oil on her fingers and rubbed me, like she loved me, and I was hard again in no time. I was steel. She put me in her mouth and my ribs collided with my heart. She put her tongue in the slit and I could feel sweet rocks in my mouth, fizzing and breaking like the computer when I walked through it.

She sat on top of me and inched me in, and I bucked up, like a crazy fool, and it was all right. She sat there, still, just smiling down at me. The muscles inside her felt like they were showing off, just for me. Grab and pull. Then she let me roll her over, and I was up and above her, all the way inside her, gritting my teeth against her wet cheek, and all the time that whisper: I see you, I feel you, you're fine, honey, oh baby, you feel so gooood, oh God, Leo, Leo, it's so good. She pulled my hand down so I could feel the little bead in between her legs and she showed me how to rub her, and I was holding on, thinking of SAT exams to try and control myself. I imagined her clitty was a ruby-red bead, lined with gold. She was getting all bad and jerking and I was like, wow, this is sex, I'm not a virgin anymore. Then I ran out of words to think; I was just caught up in *knowing*—knowing I was good at this, and that I would have been good at other things, too. There was a bright light in my head, and the smell of sweat and what I think was love. And just as I broke into pieces inside Remy; I think I broke for real, somewhere in a Brooklyn hospital bed.

I hope Mom gave the ten thousand to Ade. Just gave it to her, without any strings. Ade won't do anything stupid.

I didn't.

TRISHA R. THOMAS

So Much to Learn

The first day of school at the university brought an excitement to the air, students rushing, flowing, like a resurgent river. She would get there early, find a seat in the front, she thought, as five or six other students propelled her through the double doors of the classroom. A tall lean man stood with his back to the class printing his name on the chalkboard. He looked over his shoulder, his eyes sweeping the room before resting on her. He turned his attention back to the board. *Professor Gordon Stokes, Equality and Ethics, August 29, 1976.* The bend of his elbow worked up and down as he wrote: Books required. Highly recommended reading. Suggested reading. When he was finished he tossed the worn bit of chalk into the trash can near his feet.

For the next few minutes students filed in taking seats at scattered distances. When choices became limited someone sat next to Victoria. She said hello to be polite but was too busy intently watching the professor to say more. At his desk he organized notes and books, laying out several more pieces of chalk. After a while, she began to worry that she was in the wrong classroom. From his preparation, she feared an advance course instead of the simple intro to ethics class she'd signed up for.

As if he sensed her confusion, he stood up and walked around to the front of his desk. "This is Business Ethics 101 and I am Professor Stokes. Welcome to my class."

He spoke directly to Victoria, "What's your major?" His voice was deep and professional. He was a tall, slender black man with skin the color of shelled pecans. His thick mustache nearly covered his flesh-toned lips. His Afro was neatly shaped, his body slim underneath.

Victoria swallowed nervously before she could answer him, "Fashion Merchandising." The class had quieted.

"What exactly does a fashion merchandiser do?" He folded his arms over his chest, smiling slightly.

She sat there, the blank stare on her face. She had no answer for this man who obviously knew everything, but at this moment pretended to know nothing.

He turned his attention to the rest of the class, "In any case, I'm sure the practice of goodwill will be necessary in the world of fashion as well." He smiled, then squeezed Victoria's slender shoulder as he moved past her.

She was left with a warm tingling around her face and shoulders. Her armpits began to moisten. Embarrassment shrouded her ears, blocking any other sound, although she knew he continued to speak. His opening, she was sure, was neither impromptu nor rehearsed, but simply a ritual for the first day. Her crime was in choosing the wrong seat.

For the next hour, Victoria heard and said nothing. She stared blankly, straight ahead, numb with the fear that he might find her again a fitting example. By the time he returned to the chalkboard, he was announcing the end of class. "Thank you, and see you on Wednesday."

Victoria stood with her purse clutched to her side, gathering her blank notepad when he approached her.

"I'm sorry if I embarrassed you."

"You didn't." She wished she'd taken the time to put on the mascara and lipstick her roommate had offered. Her plain brown skin felt open and exposed. She leaned forward to let her thick hair fall, shielding her eyes. She'd never practiced the art of beauty. There was no need in the secluded suburb on the outskirts of Los Angeles where she'd grown up. Not many black boys to impress. The few she knew only liked white girls.

A knowing half smile appeared on his face. "So, will I see you on Wednesday?" He rolled the chalk between his two palms.

Victoria found the nerve to stand straight, her shoulders back, with one elbow leaning on her narrow hip that carried the weight of two books. She wore a simple red, white, and blue striped top. The body hugging Angel Flights revealed the benefits of youth. Everything would have been perfect if she had just taken the lipstick her roommate had offered. But red? She'd learned her lesson early on about attracting attention. Red attracted bulls.

"I'll be here." She noticed his glance toward her chest. She shifted her books, cradling them in her arms as a shield.

"I'm assuming it won't be here in the front though, right? What a loss for me." His voice grew softer as another student passed between them. "I apologize if I embarrassed you. A proper introduction is required," he held out his chalky hand. "Gordon Stokes."

"Victoria Crane." She took hold of his hand with a firm grip.

"I'd like to talk to you about career choices, if you don't mind staying." His smile tilted on one side, taking the weight of his thick mustache with it. His lids lowered with his voice to let her know he didn't offer his counsel to just anyone.

"What about my career choice?"

"I just think it's a little wide-eyed," he answered. "You know that Virginia Slims' ad, you've come a long way, baby . . . that's only an ad. I wouldn't take it literally. There are many appealing directions a woman can go and become successful, law, medicine, but they require dedication and hard work."

She politely shook her head no. She was tired of people assuming because she was young she didn't know what she wanted out of life. She'd had this conversation already with her father, who worked as an engineer for the city. She needed to major in something realistic, like teaching or nursing. Her plan was to earn a fashion merchandising degree, work for a department store in retail, become a buyer, and to one day have her own high-priced boutique with dresses Alexis Carrington from *Dynasty* would be proud to own.

"I'm not trying to sell you anything. I'm just letting you know." He rocked on his heels. "If you plan to eat regularly and pay rent, a light bill here and there, you might want to investigate other options." He smiled, the creases around his mouth reminding her more of pecans. Her mind drifted, nothing wrong with pecans. Pecan Pie. Sweet Pralines.

She blinked to erase the imagery. "Thanks for the advice." She moved to the door and stopped. "See you on Wednesday."

Relief washed over his face, a smile as well, from what Victoria could see as he turned and went back to his desk. She left quickly before whatever spell she'd cast wore off.

Weeks passed before he talked to her again in the same way, a soft hand on her shoulder, the direct line of his eyes finding hers.

"How about some coffee?" He asked almost apologetically, maybe for ignoring her, maybe for giving her attention in the first place.

She didn't think it was a good idea, not with the dreams she'd been having about him. Whether day or night, she felt his breath in her ear. His slender hands, she imagined, underneath the curve of her breast. She'd fantasized about the words he'd use to seduce her: *I want you, Victoria. I want to come inside you.*

She would have let him if he'd asked. Gordon Stokes was special. He wouldn't treat her as Alex Barry had. He'd only wanted one thing. She'd hated him for tricking her, making her believe she was finally being noticed after she'd talked her mother into buying her new white vinyl boots. She'd already owned the plaid wool skirt and the red turtleneck sweater. But the boots, she thought, were the inspiration for Alex's offer to give her a ride home.

They'd ended up parked near a dry canyon with their tongues down each other's throat. She'd ignored his hard unkempt hands clumsily pushing past her panties, jabbing and prodding. When she refused to finish what she'd started, she found herself fighting him off, his broad athletic shoulders closing out the noonday sun. He'd shoved her skirt up around her waist, pulled her panties down around her ankles, and pried her legs apart. After failed attempts to penetrate her tight flesh, he gave up. She'd cried all the way home, sitting in the back of his car. If only he'd asked, she would have told him, just touch me here, lick me there. There wouldn't have been a fight, no need for struggle. No need to tear her stockings or leave scratches on her thighs.

It always worked fine at home, first one finger and then two, sliding with ease within the well of moistness while the other hand did the slightest dance around her breasts. Her nipples held the power, like queens dictating over the land.

But Gordon Stokes, Professor Stokes, who knew everything, would know where to touch her, and how.

* * *

Over tea in the café across the street from the campus, Gordon Stokes took the time to know a little about her. But in those short two hours, she felt she knew everything about him. She understood his desire to teach, to give, to lead. It came natural to him, unlike Victoria, the youngest of three who thrived on being ignored and relished being invisible. Gordon Stokes was the oldest of eleven children. The man of the house, the man of his classroom. He was used to speaking and being heard. It was a way of life, an expectation. Gordon Stokes needed to be seen, understood, and appreciated. Living and working in the small desert community wasn't his first choice. But here, he could stand out, be valued. A black professor in the late '70s wasn't completely rare, but here, he was the only one, the exception, and that made him special.

As they drank tea he touched her cheek, wiping gently with

his thumb. "The powder from the doughnuts," he explained. They sat on the same side in the cloth-covered booth. She slid in as close to the wall as possible, leaving him plenty of room, but he left no space between them. Small gray hairs were preparing to come through the thick curve of his chin, growing out of place as well on his slender neck. She couldn't believe he was old enough to begin graying, stuck somewhere between the middle and end of his life.

"I'm glad you stayed in my class."

She smiled innocently, as if she hadn't made those words fall from his lips. Wished them to fruition. "Why wouldn't I stay?"

"I thought I might have scared you off."

She had thought about dropping the course after the first day, but admitted to herself there was a pull she couldn't deny. A future already determined. She didn't want to alter that path.

She'd thought of his other possibilities. There was the Asian girl who sat on the right of Victoria, snapping her chewing gum and throwing her dark, straight hair over one shoulder, then to the other, as though set to a timer.

Or Gina, a classic dark-skinned beauty with a square-cut Afro, raising her hand with unnecessary questions, her silver bracelets jangling as they fell against her elbow. "Professor Stokes, so are you saying we have a responsibility to more than just our community?" Each word spoken slowly, dragging into the other. Her Diana Ross eyelashes fanning for attention. Her shiny pink lips always partially open, as if to speak.

No, Victoria wouldn't allow it. She was his first choice. She would remain close. As close as the first night they'd kissed, standing in his classroom after hours. The lights off, only the sound of the clock ticking above their heads. His body, pressed against hers until she had no choice but to lean on the edge of his desk, gripping the sides for support. His full lips swallowed her whole and stole her air. Her head swam.

The weight of his penis grew heavy with the promise that he'd carry out more than a simple kiss. His hands pulled at the tail of her blouse trying to get past the waistband of her pants. The heat of his palm cupping her pubic bone, and sliding between the fold that was hot and slick.

His hand, she thought, what if it still had chalk on it? White chalk made of salt and sand, pushed inside of her, mixing with the clear liquid that saturated her panties.

"Have you thought about me?"

She couldn't answer with his mouth on hers. Yes, she'd thought of him every day, every night, wanting him, and hoping he wanted her as much.

"Touch me," his hand guided hers, still moist and sticky from her juices. He unzipped his pants and covered her hand with his, slowly curling her fingers around the smooth skin of his erection. Full, heavy, the weight in her hand gave her power. The ability to make decisions, cause actions and reactions.

"Squeeze it, just a little," he whispered, breathing into her mouth, taking in her air. She concentrated on getting it right, friction. Heat. Hold it gently but not too loose, grip it firmly, but not too tight. She moved against the length, down, then back up.

"That's right, mmmm, feels good."

She felt the pressure of his hands on her shoulders pushing her down. "Please, kiss it, please," he whispered.

Victoria shook her head. She couldn't do that. For a brief moment she thought of Alex's penis, pushing and bumping against her groin, then Gordon kissed her, deep and open, his tongue swirling around hers, dismissing her fears.

He stopped and looked into her eyes. "Do you want me to be your boyfriend, Tori?"

She nodded. No one had ever called her Tori, only Victoria or Vickie.

"Then you have to do this. Do you want me to be with someone else?"

She shook her head furiously. Not Gina. Not the Asian girl. She shook her head no. She fell on bended knees to the hard acrylic floor, the cold seeping through the thin fabric of her polyester pants. Face-to-face to the wide perfect tip of its head. She leaned in, kissing it slightly, pulling away quickly when she felt a moist drop meet her lips.

"Please," his voice thick from expectation and need.

She opened her mouth, sliding as much as she could hold against her tongue, feeling the immediate urge to cough, to gag. Tears squeezed through her eyelids.

"It's okay. No, don't cry." He pulled her up, holding her against his chest. "You've never done it before?" She shook her head.

"What about sex? Have you ever . . . ?"

She closed her eyes, letting the tear slide down her cheek. He kissed her sweetly, wiping the moistness off her face before helping her adjust her clothing. Without another word, he slipped his shirt back into his pants. The sound of his zipper closing stung her ears. At least he hadn't teased her for being unsophisticated. For that she was grateful.

*   *   *

Two months passed and Gordon had not asked to be alone with Victoria again. He stopped looking in her direction when he spoke, spending the better part of his lecture facing the opposite corner of the room. She didn't bother asking him why. She knew. She hadn't bothered to give dirty looks to his new point of interest. Even when he and Gina lingered near each other as the class ended. Victoria studied her rich voice mingled with the deepness of his, softly laughing, and the chronic sound of her silver jewelry falling into stacks on her wrist. With her eyes she traced the soft neat line of Gina's Afro, wondering if Gordon's lips had pressed against her neck, her shoulder. If she'd kept her jewelry on while he fucked her.

The pain was so strong it left Victoria numb, void of any thought beyond putting one foot before the other. By the end of the semester, she had wiped away any hope of Gordon Stokes. He gave her an A in the class while the rest of her grades reflected the truth. She had been a failure. She'd thought about dropping out, transferring somewhere else at the least, but that would require an explanation to her mother and father. How could she explain without it sounding so small and infantile, a professor. It happens all the time. It was the natural order of things for a student to fall in love with a teacher, the most natural, and yet, most frowned upon, seen as incestuous and manipulative. Her mother would believe it was unrequited love and now jealousy on her part.

It happened all the time, she constantly told herself. *Let it go.*

The dry winter cold overtook the campus, turning everyone into hermits. The bitter chill in the air felt foreign to Victoria, who had a scarf wrapped around her face but flip-flops on her feet. She walked from the cafeteria to her dorm taking in the desert night sky, which seemed clear and endless.

"Victoria, can I speak with you?" Gordon was near the science building, coming toward her with his hands resting in the pockets of his heavy down jacket. He stopped a safe distance away and waited patiently while she gave it a great deal of thought before nodding her head yes. Her thick unkempt braid hung over her shoulder. She toyed with it while she watched Gordon. He stepped in close, then took her face in his hands. "I've missed you," he said huskily, then kissed her forehead.

She wanted to laugh but decided to cry. "What happened? I trusted you." The cold wind made her tears burn as they rolled down her cheek.

"I knew it wasn't appropriate. I knew you couldn't handle it."

"Then why are you here? What now?" She wiped her face with the sleeve of her sweatshirt.

"*Now* I don't care. I'd risk my career for you. I'd quit teaching if I had to choose. I would rather have you." He reached out to pull her into an embrace.

She pushed his hand away and studied his eyes. He didn't blink, as if daring her to doubt the sincerity of his words.

"How many other students have you said that to?" she asked angrily.

"Victoria." He spoke sharply as if to a child. It caused her to step back. He thought twice before his next words, measuring them in tiny pieces. "I'm sorry for hurting your feelings. I'm sorry." He said it again, admitting no guilt. "I'm sorry, I wanted what was best for you."

Now her ears were stinging, the cold, or possibly from the blame in his apology. She understood. She wasn't stupid. He was laying the fault and responsibility on her. If only she'd sucked him and fucked him right then and there, he wouldn't have needed someone else.

No different, she wanted to scream, *you're no different,* but her lips wouldn't part.

He took her by the arm. "It's too cold out here, let's go inside." She felt her feet moving in baby steps, her toes engorged from lack of circulation.

The bright light inside the science building was an assault to her eyes. Gordon walked down the hall checking doorknobs, looking for an unlocked classroom.

"Here." He pulled her inside. He grabbed a chair and sat her down. He kneeled in front of her and pulled off the flip-flops she was wearing. He took her cold feet into his palms and rubbed them for warmth. All the while he muttered about her inability to take care of herself. She needed him after all. Didn't she understand that?

"Please believe me. Everything about you is what I want. Your touch, your love. Tori, please." Gordon's strong stand from moments earlier had been reduced to pleading, begging. "Do you understand—I need you?"

She didn't have to understand. She didn't have to do anything she didn't want to do. For once she held the power and it felt good.

The heat that swelled between her legs came from her want, *her* need. She allowed his hands to move up her sweater, his thumbs tracing the bones of her rib cage. She helped him guide the fabric over her head. She was still so cold. He hurriedly wrapped his arms around her, pressing his face into the smoothness of her stomach. He kept whispering, pleading. His breath against her skin increased the swell of her breast.

"Gordon." Her tone slowed him, but didn't stop his motion. "Gordon. I can't, not here. Somewhere nice." She spoke into the air while his lips finally parted from the wet tip of her nipple.

"Your place, can we go to your house?"

"Somewhere nice would not be my place." He pulled Victoria up to stand with him. His hands trailed over her hips. "I know a place. Just promise me you won't change your mind."

She promised . . . her fate now sealed.

*   *   *

The shiny green Buick pulled up in front of the A Building, idling softly. He squeezed her in a long hug when she got into the car. Their first time would be at a motel on the beach in a room facing the rushing tides.

Victoria stood outside in the blue-black of the night, listening to the constant movement of the ocean and wind. She was determined to take in every sight, sound, and smell. She wanted to remember every detail. The chill against her skin, the way he pressed against her from behind, wrapping his arms around her waist.

"You're going to stay out here all night, freezing?" He took her hand in his, leading her through the thick sand of the Mission Viejo beach. They'd driven over two hours to get there. She hadn't asked why. It seemed appropriate to be a million miles away from the life she'd lived before, the girl who was nothing, believed herself to be invisible. Here she would become a woman with infinite possibilities like the stretch of ocean she watched through her tear-filled eyes.

"I do love you, Gordon."

"Yes. That's why we're here," he whispered in her ear while pulling the sweatshirt over her head. She didn't help him, not with one piece of clothing. He'd patiently stripped her down to her bra and panties, and himself down to his wrinkled cotton boxers. She thought how wrong they were for Gordon. Someone like him should be in silk, perfect silk with three buttons up the front and elastic around his streamlined waist.

But then again, what must he have thought of her simple white bra, the simplest that JCPenney carried in stock. Packaged in a box with no ornate detailing. Her mother had piled six of them on the counter, 34C, in black letters across the top, Comfort Fit. Six pairs of matching panties, one for every day of the week, except washday. Flat, plain, and cotton like the bras. They'd spent the day shopping for her life away from home, she and her mother, as if she'd remain the same person needing the same plain underwear away at college. No. She'd held her breath with each and every day that passed in the summer of 1976, hardly able to stand it. The thought of being free of her mother's constant assessment, identifying every pattern of her behavior, concluding her life before it had even begun. Someone like you is going to end up like that . . . if you continue with this or that or the other.

She bet her mother never guessed someone like her would end up with someone like Gordon, or had she? Had it already been read into her future and she, so adeptly skilled at not listening to her mother's words, completely missed it?

While he stood in front of her, his hands traced the line of her form, appreciating the defining curves that she'd cursed that very morning looking into the full-length mirror behind her dormitory door. She concluded that her mother would have never guessed someone like Gordon would love her, every stretch mark and line of her breasts that had come too early and the slim hips refusing to catch up. Her mother would have never guessed that a man, a professional man of stature and education, would tell her that she was perfect. What he saw with his eyes and hands, what he heard in her voice when she laughed, what he understood in her words when she spoke, flawless.

It struck her only now, so many years later, that he was nervous that first time by the ocean. His heartbeat had danced erratically off rhythm against her chest. His fingers shook before unhooking the double clasp of her bra. He pulled at the straps sliding them over her shoulders, then to the end of her wrists, letting the cotton fall to the floor. He edged his hands to her waist, the beginning of her hipbone, kissing her as he knelt to remove the panties from around her slender ankles.

"Everything about you is beautiful," he'd said, while guiding her backward to the hard square bed in the center of the room.

She remembered being able to hear the rush of the waves outside the motel even with Gordon's breath in her ear. He'd shifted on top of her, positioning himself to meet the tight smoothness of her insides. His elbows shook with his weight. But now, yes, he must have been nervous. She was young, a student; he was an older professor. What if she became confused and claimed to have been coerced, sexually assaulted, or simply announced to the dean she'd slept with Professor Stokes.

He'd kissed her as if sealing a bargain. He guided her to turn over on her stomach, positioning her for penetration. She arched her back, instinctually knowing his intentions. His fingers massaged the folds of her moist skin then stretched along the line between her buttocks, lingering with the natural lubricant. His tongue rode the base of her spine to the pink fold of her skin, glistening. Before long she was scratching at him, moaning for him to be inside of her.

"Please." She murmured quiet whispers of desperation. It was her turn to beg.

He asked her over and over with each thrust to be sure. "Is this what you want?"

Yes, there could be no greater love. Only someone in love could endure this searing pain, a pain that called upon every cell in her body. She screamed in the mouth of the pillow, falling into a darkness where light didn't matter as he gently pushed himself inside her. Every breath she took rewarding her with deeper despair, pulling her down into a vast freedom, spinning out of control.

Is this what she'd asked for? Love. She'd wept as he held

her, ssshing in her ear. Quiet now. It won't hurt as much next time.

But it did. It always hurt.

Especially after she'd found out why they never went to his place. She could never turn him away. So many years later, his children grown, his wife of thirty years still not caring as to where and how he spent his evenings.

Gordon belonged inside of Victoria, burrowed like a tic in her skin. Her blood was his nutrition. His need was her fulfillment. Ten years.

The knock at the door startled her, even though she had been waiting. She said a little prayer of thank you as she did every time he found his way back to her. Back into her arms and her bed.

She opened the door to the tall slim man with the salt-and-pepper hair. The mustache had been shaved completely off when it would only grow white hairs. His eyes creased in deep lines with his smile when he saw her. Ten years. How time flies when life has stopped. For her it had ended on the day he ripped open her soul, filling her with the weight of his flesh, thick and hard.

She had dreamed of a husband and children. A home with cupcakes in the oven and steamy hot cocoa waiting to be poured. Her dreams stolen. No, she had to be honest with herself. She had given them up willingly. Her dreams in exchange for Gordon's visits. She'd finished college and stayed near, where there were no big department stores to manage, no pretty little boutique with her name on the outside sign. She processed student loans at the university. She worked quietly all day with only one thought, one mission, one reward. Ten years.

He held her in his arms as she closed the door behind him.

He the teacher, she the student.

There was still so much to learn.

MICHAEL DATCHER

The Happiest Butterfly
in the World

People-watching is the only benefit of morning freeway traffic. Corsetta has mastered secret staring. Her hazel, crossed-eyes provide the camouflage. With a slight neck twist, her peripheral vision becomes panoramic. A husky, coal-black brother, in a canary Mustang convertible, parked in the adjacent lane. Bald head.

He has a keloid scar running along his forehead hairline. It looks like a long, overweight, earthworm has burrowed beneath his shiny scalp, stretched, and fallen asleep. Corsetta examines the raised tissue, while simultaneously reading "Exposition 1 Mile" on the green freeway sign up ahead.

She imagines the man was kidnapped by CIA scientists and given the cloned, cerebral cortex of e. e. cummings. Her favorite poet with a heavy black penis.

An imperceptible neck shift. His left hand clutching the steering wheel comes into full view. Massive knuckles. *My God*, she thinks. Corsetta visualizes the swart hand with a fist fulla her hair; her jaws stretched wide around his stiff gangsta goblin—as he recites "Somewhere I Have Never Traveled." Abruptly, his Mustang pulls out and merges right. Traffic interruptus.

Corsetta is thankful for the distraction, no matter how fleeting. It helps her tolerate Iago's Silent Treatment. She hates when they argue in the morning cuz he always pulls this junior-high shit. It makes the drive down from Pasadena ridiculous. Iago hasn't said one word through all this traffic. Corsetta knew her husband was gonna go Marcel Marceau when he didn't open the car door for her this morning. She calls it his Asshole Alert. The absence of early morning chivalry means expect no conversation on the ride to work.

Iago won't even make eye contact.

They finally exit on Exposition, make a right onto Figueroa, and enter the campus through Gate 5. The University of Southern California is the only exclusive gated community in South Central. The tall, wrought-iron bars enclosing nearby apartment complexes make those gated communities feel more like caged communities.

Iago parks the car and jumps out. Corsetta knows not to wait for him to walk around to her side. Like his vengeful father, Iago commits to his grudges.

With a metallic pop, she opens the waxed 1988 black Saab Turbo. Corsetta carefully places her legs out the vehicle. Her calves have tightened on the incremental drive down the 110. She pauses to admire them. Her small bones exaggerate the curve of her calves' sinewy tendons. High school track team discipline never left Cross-Eyed Corsetta Carew. These days when her alarm sounds at 5 A.M., she pretends she's still rising for practice.

Years of early morning hills have honed her formerly sticklike figure. The brawn rises through her calves, into her hamstrings and curves up an annular ass.

Corsetta stands, stretching her fingers high above her head. A slight grimace. Her fibrous abdomen will be sore until after lunch. She closes the locked door. Both hands smooth the pleated gray skirt, which is just long enough to show no skin. Corsetta bends her sixty-one inches at the waist. Using the Saab's tinted passenger window as a mirror, she unties and reties the gray ribbon bow that tightly closes her high-neck white blouse. Corsetta's crossed hazel eyes remind her how ugly her attractive brown face is. She jerks erect.

Corsetta turns to find an impatient-looking Iago a few steps from the hatchback trunk. He has retrieved his king-sized, black leather briefcase and Corsetta's lunch-pail-shaped, gray Prada purse is slung over his shoulder. His free hand is on his hip. As she walks around the car, she is tempted to tell her white husband that he gets mad like her grandmother. Instead, she silently reaches up and transfers the purse from his shoulder to hers.

She wonders if he'll hold her hand as they walk toward the library. He doesn't. Corsetta walks alongside Iago as they descend the parking garage stairs and start the ten-minute walk across campus.

After twelve years of repeating this trek, the stares still prick. The odd couple is timeless. Corsetta sneaks a glance at the first man who she really loved—and who really loved her. *We are an odd couple,* she thinks. Iago's skin is as pale as the underbelly of a boa constrictor. Hers as brown as a doe.

She was happy when he cut his hair bald last year. It gave him a more rugged look and gave her more head. His peach fuzz skull, moving in ovals over her clit, probably saved their marriage—or at least her monogamy.

But walking across campus, Iago's multipurpose dome makes him look like a forty-seven-year-old, five foot five neo-Nazi, with a candy-store belly, and a sweet tooth for chocolate.

They reach Iago's office door, mute. She glances at her husband's name above the large block letters: HEAD LIBRARIAN. Corsetta pauses, then continues toward her cubicle.

"Setta."

Corsetta stops and turns.

"I know you can do the job."

Holding his gaze, she hesitates, then walks back over until they are in kissing distance. He gently moves the back of his hand across her cheek. He is unaware of the smile on his face.

"It's not about *doing* the job, I *deserve* this job, Iago—and you know it. There are only so many lateral moves I can make after fifteen years. No one has more institutional knowledge but you—and you've already got your promotion."

Iago's hand leaves her cheek and softly taps her temple with his index finger.

"All your institutional knowledge should include a section on appearances, especially at a private school. People will cry nepotism despite your qualifications."

Corsetta slaps his finger off her temple and takes a step back.

"Why'd you even interview me then?"

"Because you deserved the honor of consideration."

"But not the honor of what's fair and right? We both know I'm not getting a real shot because I suck your dick at night. That's how a lot of people get promoted, Iago."

Corsetta turns and walks briskly to her cubicle. She sits down at her computer and starts a hyperactive foot tap. Many keys jingling. She hears Iago's office door open and lightly close. She wishes she had a door to slam. He's the one who said get a degree. He ain't been the same since.

Corsetta starts up her computer, then impulsively kicks over the wooden wastebasket beneath her orderly workstation. Balled up paper ricochets into her field of view. Corsetta reaches below her desk and raises the gray skirt above her knees. Her toe tap accelerates. With her right hand, she blindly checks the pelvic straps and repositions the Happy Butterfly a little lower, so it hangs over the hood of her clit. She retrieves the spare remote from the back of the bottom desk drawer. The black plastic, candy-bar-sized device has just one button: a red butterfly with a Louis Armstrong grin. Under the cover of her desk, Corsetta cocks her muscular thighs wider. Sets the remote on the mouse pad. Just as she is about to depress the grinning butterfly, she hears two voices down the hall. The library staff is starting to arrive. She hesitates. Corsetta snatches a Kleenex from the box at the upper corner of her desk and lays it atop the remote. Her right hand casually rests on the single Kleenex. Her forefinger finds the happiest butterfly in the world.

The soft, gel-filled, pea-sized "pleasure point" hugging her clitoris begins to vibrate in the pulsing manner that makes the Happy Butterfly a perpetual best-seller. Her foot taps faster. Corsetta becomes conscious of her mouth opening. She doesn't fight it. She feels the pleasure point heating. The crimson gel inside is the same potion that motion lotion is made of. The more it vibrates the warmer it gets. Corsetta's Winnie the Pooh bear sits on the desk, a stuffed voyeur. With her left hand, she squeezes Winnie's head beyond recognition.

The hallway voices are drawing near. A rush of sensation shoots up Corsetta's arching spine. She hopes someone leans over the cubicle and says hello. She imagines talking to a colleague, while butterflying with her dress pulled up over her hidden, wide-open thighs. The image has Corsetta punishing Pooh.

"Hey Corsetta, how was your weekend?"

It's Paul Johnson from payroll, leaning over the front of her cubicle. She's startled because the voices were coming from down the hall. He's looking her dead in the eye, wondering about her arched posture and parted lips. Corsetta's mouth is already open, but she's afraid to speak. She's concerned that the vibrating pleasure point will add a telltale vibrato to her voice. Paul's puffy face hangs in front of her waiting for an answer. She has to say *something*, but not too much. She drops her eyes to her computer monitor.

"Gooood."

"What did you guys do?"

"Mooovies," she lies.

He can't ask me another . . . . ohh noo. Corsetta sees Paul's perplexed eyes shift over at Winnie the Pooh's disfigured face. Distracted, she's forgotten that Pooh's golden head is in the Grip of Death. A common side effect of the Happy Butterfly. Paul's gaze cuts back to Corsetta. She keeps her eyes glued to her monitor. She can't just release Pooh now; it'd be too abrupt and necessitate an explanation. Besides, Corsetta's so aroused that the Grip of Death is what's holding her orgasm at bay. Paul's eyes linger on Winnie under duress. His face grows serious, troubled.

"What film did you see?" he says, still staring at the abused bear.

The vibrating pleasure point continues to warm. Corsetta can't risk an answer. She stares into the monitor like a crossed-eyed Alice into the Looking Glass. Still waiting for an answer, Paul's gaze shifts to Corsetta's face, then to Winnie, back to Corsetta, then Winnie.

Paul straightens and backs away from the cubicle. As soon as he's out of sight, Corsetta simultaneously takes her index finger off the remote and liberates Winnie the Pooh.

"Whhrewwwww," she exhales.

That was so exciting. Involuntary tremor. Corsetta completely wraps the remote in the Kleenex and drops it into her purse. She looks over her shoulder before reaching down and gently repositioning the pleasure point a couple of inches above her swollen butterfly nest.

"May I speak to you in my office, please," Iago cautiously says over the front of the cubicle wall. Another close call. A startled Corsetta snatches her wrists from beneath her workstation, and grabs her lower back with both hands.

"What's the matter?"

"I just felt a sharp pain shoot up my back."

She stretches by making her back concave. Iago starts to walk around to enter the cubicle. She raises a halting hand.

"I'll be okay. What did you wanna talk about?"

He gives her a gimme-a-break look.

Corsetta stands, exits her cubicle and follows her husband down the hall. He opens the door, so she can enter first.

"Have a seat, Setta," he says, extending his outstretched palm to the wooden chair in front of his huge 1940s desk.

Iago pulls the chair out for his wife, then walks around to the leather chair behind his oak workstation. On it rests a framed 8 x 10 picture of Iago and Corsetta kissing just after completing their wedding vows. It's proudly facing out for visitors to see. Neat piles of books line the left and right edge. On the wall, behind Iago, hangs his silver-framed diploma from Arizona State's Ph.D. program in English literature.

"You have to understand the position you're placing me—"

"No, your own hard work has placed you in this position, and this position requires you to fill the assistant librarian vacancy that you created when you got promoted."

"You know what I'm talking—"

"But do you know what I'm talking about? My marital status shouldn't disqualify me from a job that I deserve. You got promoted from assistant to head librarian because your record warranted it. I've never had anything less than an excellent evaluation in fifteen years—and now I have my library science master's. My record warrants your old job—and in some eyes, warranted consideration for your new job."

"Whose eyes are those?" he says, raising a brow. Surprised.

"That's not important. The point is that the new assistant librarian that this library needs is me. No one will do a better job because no one is as prepared, and no one wants the job more."

Iago takes a long look at his wife. He smiles. With his encouragement, she has changed from an insecure twenty-year-old girl who struggled to make eye contact in the initial interview with him, to a grown woman willing to stand up to her mentor—who also now happens to be her husband. Witnessing the hard decisions that led to her gradual transformation has inspired Iago to deal with his own disappointments and move forward. After five years, he has stopped looking for a teaching position. A hard decision that allowed Iago Slovin to focus on being the best assistant librarian in California (and one of the few with a Ph.D. in English literature). A hard decision that now has him focusing on being the best head librarian in the state—with the best staff.

"Setta, let me think about it and—"

"What is there to think about? You've met with all the candidates in the final pool. You know everyone's skills and credentials. You—"

"Setta," Iago barks. "I said I'll think about it. Don't keep trying to push me. Now let me get to work."

Corsetta stands up silent and slow. Her abdomen is still tight from her morning run. She walks toward the door, opens it, then turns back to Iago.

"Since I got my master's, you've been trying to slow my roll. I want you to know—that I know."

Corsetta leaves without closing the door behind her. She grabs her purse from the cubicle, exits out the back, and walks around to the front entrance of the library.

It's Monday, 8:25 A.M., five minutes before the doors open. She wished she smoked. Or drank. Or cheated. Anything to scrape the frustration from the base of her neck.

Corsetta sits down on the third concrete step leading up to the library. Her sore legs are stretched out to the walkway and crossed at the ankles. She looks nonchalantly across the courtyard and back again—trying not to look like she's looking for someone. I hope he comes, she thinks. He didn't show up once all last week.

Corsetta sees a black male student walking from the fountain to her left, toward the library. She casually gathers her knees to her chest, leans left and forward. He's still too far away. She can't quite tell. She reclines again, extending her crossed ankles back onto the walkway. In case it's him, as a ruse, she looks to her right. There she sees Largesse LaSalle exiting the campus coffeehouse seventy-five yards away. At six foot four, two hundred fifty pounds, he's hard to miss. Six foot seven if you count the unruly mass of curly hair, fashionably uncombed. An image quick-flashes in her mind: his big hands snatching her small waist in the air, and slamming her up and down on his forty-five-degree-angled dick—as he strolls across campus with her in his arms. Now that should be a ride at Disneyland, she smiles to herself. The thought causes a slight shudder.

He's strolling straight toward the library steps, chugging on a bottled water. She loves to watch how a man handles his body in motion. Corsetta hears the lock turning on the library door above her. She checks her watch. It's 8:30 A.M. She has to get to the information counter. She turns her head to see the students filing in.

"Shit."

Corsetta reclines again, resting on her elbows. She uncrosses and recrosses her ankles, while squinting her crossed-eyes just off center. Her panoramic peripheral vision allows her to study the rolling dip of Largesse's stride. He's in extra baggy, blue velour sweatpants. An XXL blue Tennessee Titan jersey hangs from his unusually broad shoulders. And from those shoulders, a tan leather backpack. The dimples in his caramel apple face could swallow the tip of a tongue.

Twenty yards from the ornate stone building, Largesse spots the librarian who's always so helpful, sitting on the steps. The other library people treat him like he got a tail. He towers over them, but somehow they do the talking down. They smirk at his nonstudent library card and runaway-slave hair. That's why he only goes to the cross-eyed sister.

Largesse finger rolls his empty Evian bottle into the trash can at the base of the steps, and purposely makes a wide arc so he can walk right past her. He's weirded out by his attraction. *She's probably about Mom's age,* he thinks. *But dammn, those big pouty lips.* He wished her eyes weren't all messed up. Largesse begins to ascend the steps only a foot from a reclining Corsetta, who's looking in the opposite direction. He pauses on the third concrete rectangle. Just before he speaks, Corsetta's nose picks up the subtle sweetness of his Egyptian Musk body oil.

"Getting a little prework sunshine?"

Corsetta turns her head to answer, but she trips on Largesse's eye-level crotch. The velour imprint of his thick, semierect phallus is hanging all the way down past his mid-thigh. If he were naked, and started doing the twist, his wide penis would slap her repeatedly across her face. The thought makes her curl her toes inside her BCBG flats. Her stare makes him glance at his penis. Corsetta breaks free and looks up to make contact with his brown eyes.

"Yes, I'm inside all day so I try to sneak in as much sun as I can get. Everyone complains about the heat, but I can't get enough of this September sunshine."

She was staring at my dick, he thinks. Largesse quickly tries to think of something to keep the conversation going to see if she'll look down again. Before he can get his response out, he catches Corsetta's eyes shifting down to his crotch, then back up to his face. His cock immediately stiffens. He has to move his right leg up to the fourth step, so the penis straining against his blue sweats can run parallel, the length of his thigh. The move brings his dick six inches from Corsetta's lips.

"Yeah, if the sun can make a rose bloom there must be something powerful about it," he says.

Her eyes involuntarily jump from his face to the huge cock inches from her. She feels a rush of wetness beneath her long gray skirt. Largesse keeps talking to see how long she will stare. He leans in slightly.

"That's why during the long Alaskan winters, those people get so depressed," he continues.

"Unnhunh," Corsetta says without being able to tear her eyes away—which arouses Largesse more.

"I'd better be getting in," she says abruptly. Corsetta jumps to her feet and rushes up the steps through the heavy wooden double doors.

Largesse is so turned on, he has to wait for a few moments. He pulls the jersey over his erection, then decides to sit and calm down.

Because he's such a big guy Largessse has always liked petite girls. He finds the joining of extremes exciting. He likes to pick them up and control their tiny bodies as they ride his massive cock. He loves the look on their faces when he first pulls Mr. Hyde out. The intense lust he sees in their eyes. He usually snatches them by the nape of their necks and forces his dick into their mouths. He loves watching the petite girls getting aroused as they witness their jaws working to stretch around Mr. Hyde.

Last year, when little Lashawna gave him head behind the bleachers, he looked down and watched her wide eyes follow Hyde down her throat. She started choking and coming at the same time—which made him come. It's been petite or nothing ever since.

When Corsetta arrives at the information booth, five students are in line looking around impatiently. She hurries through the swinging wooden door and places her purse beneath the counter. Just as she's about to help the first student, Iago walks up.

"We've been paging you. I came down to cover."

"I was out front. I—"

"Corsetta, it's 8:43 A.M."

The students cut their eyes at each other.

Iago storms away toward the administrative offices. While helping the first student, Corsetta simultaneously watches her husband blast through the staff door. He can be a cool boss to work for, but the one thing he will not tolerate is tardiness. He fired Tom Jenkins, the only other black staff person, for his habitual tardiness, which consisted of being late twice.

Iago looked at Corsetta's lateness as a complete betrayal. How could he be hard on other employees and let his wife slide? As it is, she knows everyone is scrutinizing them. Though he can't recall her ever having been late in the fifteen years she has worked at the library (they've arrived early together for twelve of those years), this CP Time madness is unacceptable and will not be tolerated. As the staff door swings back and slams shut, Largesse rolls and dips through the library's main entrance.

Corsetta is still helping the first student. Her line has grown to eight. Largesse dips into the number nine slot. His broad torso towers over the other coeds. Corsetta can feel his stare subtracting the twenty feet of space between them. She wonders if his big dick is still hard. She fakes a sneeze to disguise her body quiver.

"Bless you," the big-breasted, braless blonde says. It's Heather, the sunny volleyball player (with the completely unfair cup size) who works part-time in the library. A straight-A student without an ounce of common sense; Corsetta forgives her because Heather is so nice.

"Thanks," Corsetta replies, sneaking a glance up at Largesse. "You know you don't have to get in line, Heather."

"Well, it just seems like the right thing to do."

Largesse is watching Corsetta with lusty intensity that makes her start to quicken her pace. She wants him closer to her. After years of going the extra mile for students at the information booth, she finds herself running them off the road.

"Try the second floor, next. . . . That's what *Encyclopaedia Britannica* is for, next. . . . I'm sure it's on the shelf, go look again, next."

Corsetta runs through the students, until Largesse is second in line, behind the girl asking if anyone has turned in the library card she lost Friday. Corsetta shoots a quick glance up, and catches his stare on her chest. Even breast men have loved her small breasts, because each fleshy nipple is the size of a bouillon cube.

Corsetta never suffered through a lack of foreplay. Her high school sweetheart, Tee Mack, would get drunk after the football games and religiously sneak through her bedroom window (after dropping Corsetta off to her father at the front door) to suck and nibble. Tee was completely fascinated by how huge and dark the nipples looked on Corsetta's mouthful titties. If she was especially turned on, her bouillon cubes swelled to regulation-sized dice.

When her crossed-eyes made her feel really ugly, she would, like Heather always does, go braless in a tank top and walk around the Fox Hills Mall. During one of her and Tee's week-long breakups, Corsetta let the defensive line coach pull her tank top down and suck her titties right in the weight room—and he came. On many a late night Iago has started snoring with a hard nipple in his mouth.

"The lost and found box is empty," Corsetta tersely says, pulling the bare shoebox from beneath the counter to show the girl. As the student looks into the box, Corsetta glances down at her breasts. A healthy pair of dice are indenting her bra and white blouse as Largesse steps to the counter.

He's tucked his jersey into the blue velour sweatpants. His fully erect cock is angled up so that the fat head has made a tent in the white lining of his right pocket. A wet pre-come spot confirms, for Corsetta, that he's not wearing any underwear. Corsetta's cross-eyed peripheral does a quick check to see if anyone else has noticed. If so, no one's telling.

"I'm looking for a good book on heart disease," Largesse says, staring brazenly at the dice in Corsetta's blouse. He doesn't even make eye contact. Corsetta takes the opportunity to glance at his cock. She inhales the Egyptian Musk.

"Let me show you where the medical books are," she says, trying to get him out of the area before a small viewing party forms.

Largesse's half-lidded brown eyes rise to meet Corsetta's crossed hazel pair.

"Thanks."

Even though Heather will be clocking in at 9 A.M., only a few minutes away, Corsetta doesn't like leaving her purse when she has to leave the information booth. She reaches down and shoulders the Prada lunch pail, then walks through the waist-level swinging door, and around the counter. Largesse takes a step back to allow her to pass in front of him. As she passes, he catches her sneaking a peak at the swollen head saluting from his right pocket.

Corsetta leads them in silence toward the 1920s staircase. The braided ponytail reaching the center of her back has a silver butterfly pendant at the bottom that swings and jumps with each step. She has a yellow No. 2 pencil behind her left ear.

As they ascend the cherry wood stairs, Largesse is captivated by how small her waist is. Both of his football playing hands could completely encircle her, with thumbs meeting at her spine and his big-knuckled fingers interlocking across her abdomen.

"Are you considering majoring in biology?" she says, over her shoulder, even though she knows his green library card means he's not a student at USC. And he knows she knows.

"Actually, I'm still officially in high school."

Corsetta stops climbing the stairs so hastily that Largesse's hard dick comes inches from bumping into her firm buttocks. She turns completely around and studies his face. It's not just his full mustache and goatee, it's his command over his physical being that announces, "Grown Man." He smiles at her reaction.

"Yeah, I know, I look all old to still be in high school. My eighth-grade coach told my mom if she held me back a year, it could help me eventually get a full scholarship and everything. You know, 'cause I'd be bigger than the other kids. It happens a lot. I—"

"How old are you?"

"Nineteen."

Corsetta turns around and continues up the stairs. *He's just a baby,* she thinks. *He hasn't even gone to his senior prom.* A tidal wave of guilt makes her exhale deeply and shake her head from side to side. Largesse follows, watching the sway of her hips.

When they reach the fourth floor, they turn right, down the narrow aisle closest to the wall. The built-in bookshelves, which extend from floor to ceiling, are filled with old, oversized books. Largesse has never been to the fourth floor. He alternates between reading the wide leather-bound spines—*The Human Body, A History of the Brain, Anatomy and the Races*—and examining the sweeping motion of Corsetta's gluteus maximus. The combination of her small-boned, five foot one frame and tiny waist, makes her high-riding bubble ass look like an overinflated basketball beneath her gray skirt. *She must work out,* he thinks.

Every thirty feet, they have to squeeze by the cockpit-like desks often found in school library stacks. Only a few are inhabited. They reach the book-filled back wall, turn right and squeeze by one grad student, then another. Halfway down the aisle, Corsetta turns right again and slows down. She runs her small hands along a series of books.

"These texts, here, deal with the basic structure and functions of the heart," she says, talking to the bookshelf. When she swings to face Largesse, her yellow pencil slides from beneath her ear and falls to the floor between them. She squats to pick it up.

"Are you doing a science project or—"

Pencil in hand, Corsetta finds herself eye-level with the wet lining of his pocket. The pre-come has soaked the white cotton, so that the entire engorged head looks like the unanimous winner of a wet T-shirt contest for cucumbers. She feels Largesse's gaze. Still squatting, her body remembers the last time she sat on a broad black dick like the one in front of her. She bites her bottom lip hard to keep from sticking her tongue out.

Pencil in hand, she rises, science project sentence unfinished. The hooded stare she meets is full of raw lust. God, this young boy wants to fuck me. She looks down at the cucumber again. It twitches. Iago's face flashes in her mind. She takes a giant step back.

"There's also a medical reference section a coupla aisles over," she says, turning to walk away. Largesse starts to follow.

"I'llgetit," she says, her rising palm and pouty lips moving much too fast. "You browse, see what's available here, and I'll bring the books back over."

Corsetta quickly steps down the aisle and turns right at the back wall. Passes two aisles and turns right again, then abruptly stops, leaning her back against the shelves. A fast glance down the aisle. The coast is clear.

Corsetta puts her foot up the third bookshelf in front of her. Slings her purse so it hangs on her side. Another quick glance right. She reaches toward her ankle and pulls the long gray skirt up to her thigh. Reaches underneath and repeatedly runs her middle finger in a tight circle on her clit. The motion forces her mouth to a perfect *O*. Involuntarily, her head jerks back into the books on the fifth shelf.

Corsetta shifts her fingers and brings the Happy Butterfly down so it rests on her swollen clit. She puts her leg down and smoothes out her skirt. Her crossed-eyes scan the shelves. She selects *Diseases, The Body of Man,* and *Cardiology* and holds the heavy leather-bound books to her breast. Corsetta makes two fast lefts and finds Largesse at the end of the long aisle standing profile, completely engrossed in *The Life Muscle*. His dick has softened. His tent has folded.

Corsetta stills her steps and reaches her right hand into her purse. Her forefinger locates the happiest butterfly in the world. As she studies his athletic build, the gel pleasure point gently pulses beneath her skirt. She feels like her whole torso is quivering. Setta monkey-claws her toes, digging into soft leather.

He must be six-seven, she thinks. Corsetta examines his curly uncombed hair, and eyes his thick neck, veins popping with concentration. Her pussy is a desert hot spring. Largesse's shoulder, closest to her, looks like a blue cassava melon beneath his jersey. She finds his biceps grotesque. The muscles lump in various directions at once. They dwarf his thin forearms. His massive thighs fill out the loose-fitting sweats. She wonders what his pubic hair smells like. She bets it's musky.

Corsetta continues walking toward Largesse with her hand in her purse. She's afraid to speak in full sentences.

"Heerre," she vibratos, sliding the books' spines onto the shelf near him.

Largesse looks up from the text.

"Thanks," he replies, and looks down again.

Corsetta leans her back against the bookshelf, out of his peripheral vision. She swivels her head, checking both sides of the aisle. Largesse is oblivious. He studies the diagram's left ventricle. The aorta. The shape of the pulmonary valves. The right ventricle.

He's been obsessed like this since he found out last month. In a weird way, collapsing at practice may have saved his life—or maybe not. Doctor Fargas said you never really know with an enlarged heart. It would take at least six whole months before he knew if the lisinopril and digoxin were working. He certainly couldn't tell now. Some days he would feel so lethargic. A pressure would build in the center of his chest that would make him immediately have to go lie down. On other days, like today, he felt as strong as the all state middle linebacker he was—or used to be.

Mom thought he would trip about having to give up the scholarship. But Largesse was much more concerned about busting the nut that could be the end of him. Death by ejaculation. Dr. Fargas said, "Absolutely no strenuous activities." But shiiit, fucking was one of the few things that made him feel like his old self. Made him feel like the man he was on his way to becoming. He only knew how to have sex one way, and that was like a middle line-backer. That's why the girls liked him so.

Oddly, his sessions had been even more exciting since he found out. Each time he was doggy-style-deep in some tight, wet pussy, he knew it might be the last time—a fear that brought a heightened urgency to the pumping.

Largesse suddenly becomes conscious of Corsetta behind him. He realizes that she has been there ever since she brought the books to him. He gets the feeling that she is staring at him. Checking him out. The thought arouses Largesse. The conserva-tive librarian, with the nice ass, is showing some love.

Largesse keeps his eyes on the page and tries to focus on his reading, but now he's distracted. What if she's a closet freak? He feels his gangsta goblin hardening.

Corsetta is doing a poor job at pretending to read *Principles of Phrenology*. It rests open in her left hand, near her waist. Her right wrist is stuck deep in her purse. Corsetta's wiry back is leaning against the bookshelves, legs positioned wider than her shoul-ders. The crimson motion lotion inside the Happy Butterfly's pleasure point has made the vibrating gel as warm as a well-spanked ass.

Corsetta's completely ignoring the open book. Her crossed-eyes, which had been slowly scanning up and down Largesse's backside, are now fixed on his thick thighs and buttocks. He has the body type of Tee Mack, to this day, *still* the best chicken-wing partner she ever had.

Tee Mack was starving for her in the way post-puberty boys hunger when hormones are raging. An intensity that made Corsetta want to have sex wherever they could find a place. As soon as the final bell would ring, they'd rush from school and go to the house of one of Tee's teammates. Right to the bedroom. Corsetta and Tee would then fuck like teenage gorillas on Ecstasy.

Tee Mack liked to start by grabbing the back of her head and forcing his huge erection down her throat. It drove Corsetta crazy. Sometimes she would come, there on her knees, bobbing up and down on his cock. She had learned to swallow the whole shaft (she practiced on peeled bananas), by relaxing her larynx and breathing deeply through her flaring nostrils.

Tee Mack would stand there, shouting eyeballs looking down, watching his entire dick disappear again and again inside those pregnant lips. He always felt weird about exploding in her mouth. He would try to pull out as he was about to ejaculate. Corsetta would respond by aggressively grabbing his butt cheeks, with both hands, and ramming the engorged head past her tonsils. The stream of come blasting against the back wall of her tickled throat reminded Corsetta of her shower massager. Tee's bass Tarzan howl reminded her of her power.

As image-conscious as Tee Mack was, he didn't seem to care if his friends heard his jungle lovemaking. When they first started dating, Corsetta knew that the other football players sweated Tee for going steady with Cross-Eyed Corsetta Carew. But after hearing enough gorilla shouts, she was sure his teammates stopped teasing. Instead, they all wanted to fuck her doggy-style too—and get their whole shaft swallowed.

Corsetta's proud she never gave in to the players' flirting, because she certainly considered it. Their attention kept her bras in the bottom drawer.

A football player in the next room was a high school aphrodisiac. One moment she's talking with Tee and the guys at lunch; ten minutes later, the same guys are listening to Tee's pelvis slapping against her taut buttocks and ear-hustling the raunchy orgasms that ensued.

She knew the fellas had their ears pressed against the door by how quiet they'd get. Sometimes, at the height of intense sex, Tee would make her give a play-by-play for the fans in the cheap seats. Mid-stroke, he'd snatch Corsetta off the bed, position her on all fours facing the door, and continue pumping hard. A breathless Tee would shout, "Repeat after me: I'm on my hands and knees!" And Corsetta would scream, "I'm on my hands and knees!" Tee would roar again: "Repeat after me: He's fucking me doggy-style!" A hyperaroused Corsetta would yell, "He's fucking me doggy-style!" This continuous call and response would go on for an hour with Corsetta's narration casting sexual positions onto minds attached to ears, hustling for space against a thin bedroom door.

Just as Corsetta was jerking toward her final climax, Tee would bellow: "Repeat after me: I want you to hear how I come!" The truth of that statement (coupled with her favorite position) would rhythmically snap Corsetta's back from concave to convex, from concave to convex as she repeatedly shrieked: "I want you to hear how I come, I want you to hear how I come, I want you to hear how I come . . ."

Largesse's eyes glance off the right of the page, down to the Cucumber Wet T-shirt Winner tenting a full five inches out of his right pocket. He becomes conscious of Corsetta's controlled breathing behind him. Largesse nonchalantly looks over his right shoulder. He finds Corsetta still leaning against the stacks, hand still in purse, exhaling deeply through her open mouth. Her half-lidded, crossed-eyes fixed down on his cock. She doesn't even try to look away. Every few seconds her petite body does a slight shake. Largesse has seen this kind of trance-like lust before. A flash of memories has his forearm hair at attention.

Largesse sticks *The Life Muscle* back in the shelf, takes a quick glance down the narrow aisle, and turns to face Corsetta, who is six inches from him. Her eyes leave his full pocket, scan his abdomen, then chest, and finally lock with his brown eyes. Her shortness of breath forces Corsetta to keep her mouth open.

Still staring, Largesse athletically drops his six-four body into a wide-legged, sumo wrestler squat. Looking up at Corsetta, he reaches under her gray skirt and wraps his big hands around each of her widespread ankles. In one quick motion, he snatches both ankles six inches wider.

"Hhhanh," involuntarily rushes from her mouth.

Largesse's tight fists slowly slide up her leg, incrementally raising Corsetta's skirt in the process. He inched up her runner's calves. Still looking into her eyes, he abruptly squeezes the dense tissue. Corsetta breaks the skin on her lower lip.

His large hands continue deliberately over her knees. A quiver. Looking down, her wide eyes examine him examining her. She's usually in long dresses, long sleeves. Largesse is seeing Corsetta's naked kneecaps for the first time. He feels his swollen penis pulsing.

Corsetta's open thighs are slippery from a mixture of sweat and vaginal secretion. Squeezing hard, Largesse slides northward. Her breath quickens. He becomes conscious of his own heavy breathing, but he's oblivious to Heather Ross's bouncing breasts stopping silently in her tank top at the end of the long aisle. Heather's mouth opens, too.

With Corsetta's gray skirt draped over his forearms, Largesse's damp fingers massage toward her pussy. His eyes leave hers. He sees the black straps circling her innermost thighs. Excited, he aggressively thrusts the dress above her waist.

"Uhhhhh," Corsetta shrieks, her arms shooting wide to brace herself against the bookshelf—her right hand still clutching the remote. Largesse's mouth drops open. The Happy Butterfly is a vibratory blur on Corsetta's bald pelvis. In one motion, Largesse liberates Mr. Hyde, grabs Corsetta's waist with both hands, and springs from his full squat, swiftly raising Corsetta four feet off the ground. Corsetta rushes her left hand over her mouth. On her way down, she watches her stream of come splattering his blue jersey.

"She's a squirter," he meant to say to himself, but the excited words are already out of his gaping mouth. Heather pantomimes "Oh-my-God." She's never seen a cock so thick and long—and she *only* dates black guys. Corsetta's dripping pussy slides down hard on Largesse's stiff ten inches of girth. Heather visualizes her own shaved vagina slamming down on the massive penis. Largesse is in a tantric trance. As if he's squeezing a naughty rag doll by the waist, the middle linebacker jerks Corsetta up and down, up and down on his gangsta goblin. Up and down. Her long ponytail braid is flying around like the end of a bullwhip. Up and down. She screams into one cupped hand as the other cups the remote. The happiest butterfly in the world hangs on for dear life.

"Wow," says the husky grad student, now standing next to Heather. Corsetta's head shoots toward the voice. She involuntarily drops the remote, and with her free hand, starts slapping Largesse about the face, trying to make him stop and put her down. Her blows just arouse him more. He starts slamming her down on his dick harder and faster. Corsetta's white come is speckling all over his blue Tennessee Titan jersey, droplets group on the floor like wet Rorschach dots. She's a rag doll blur, up and down, swinging increasingly inaccurate roundhouses. Another grad student steps up to ringside.

"Damnnn," he says.

Largesse hears nothing. His eyes are glazed over. He's sweating and thrusting, ignoring the slaps that have turned to fists in his face. Corsetta begins to panic. The punching and the open lust from the front row is turning her on more. She feels another wave coming. A look of real terror stretches her eyes wide. At that moment, on the upward stroke, Largesse spins her on his dick so her wide-open thighs are resting on his biceps, and she's facing the bookshelf that her back was previously on. As he fucks her doggy-style-deep, Corsetta is forced to remove her left hand from her mouth to hold on to the wooden shelf, to stop from ramming her face into the stacks. She lets out a guttural roar so primal that Heather unconsciously reaches right down her own miniskirt and starts feverishly rubbing her clit. The husky grad student rests his hand on his cock.

Still pumping like a linebacker, Largesse takes one hand off Corsetta's waist and reaches up for her ponytail braid, snatching her head back. Stimulation overload. Corsetta's crossed-eyes roll back into her head, and she begins to howl toward the ceiling. A steady stream of come arcs and splatters against the old leather books on the shelves and puddles on the floor beneath her.

Just as Heather starts to come, the two other fans' heads jerk toward the stairway. Someone's rushing up from the ground floor. Heather knows it's Iago, because he sent her to look for Corsetta. His clicking footsteps add a hard jolt to Heather's orgasm that makes her grimace and say aloud, "Mother Fucker." The two grad students' heads immediately swivel toward her come-face. Heather momentarily grabs the bookcase to steady herself, then flees the scene down the back aisle as Iago reaches the top floor. Sensing that fleeing the scene may be a good idea, the grad students rush after Heather.

All the activity breaks Largesse out of his trance, but he's about to come. He can't make himself stop pumping. He loves it doggy-style. Largesse lets go of Corsetta's ponytail and puts his hand over her mouth to stop her from screaming. He hears the clicking heels coming in their direction. So does Corsetta. Her head snaps down the aisle. Largesse's eyes shoot to all the medical books in front of him. He's so turned on that he's afraid to come, which turns him on even more. Looking to her left, eyes now wide open, Corsetta starts hitting behind her, trying to writhe and jump off ten inches of black cock that she's been missing for so long. Iago turns the corner and stops in his tracks. He meets Corsetta's wide, crossed eyes and open mouth. The head of Largesse's pumping cock swells up inside the best pussy he has ever had. Iago's mouth drops wide open. Largesse's mouth drops wide open. Tarzan howl. He comes hard, slamming into Corsetta's tight, wet pussy like she's a sweating running back past the line of scrimmage. With her eyes locked on Iago, Corsetta's mouth drops wide open. The scream comes from the very center of her abdomen; the stream of come arcs to the very center of the leather-bound spine announcing, *Structures of the Heart*. The sharp pain starts in the very center of Largesse's left ventricle. He reaches for her ponytail braid just as his smile starts to form.

LISA TEASLEY

Center for Affections

U te Kerina, an only child, arrives in New York from Namibia, Southwest Africa, via Germany when she is sixteen years old. Her father, Helmut, a journalist of the Herero tribe, would consider her occupation as a model scarcely above that of prostitute. Her mother, Seksidia, of the Ovambo tribe, secretly applauds Ute's escape. Although both parents assume she will finish her education in Berlin, this is never Ute's intent. Had her parents the occasion to peruse magazines like *Marie Claire, Elle,* or catalogs such as Hermès, they might be shocked to see her gracing the shiny, slick pages. But Seksidia dies by the time Ute is nineteen, so she misses her strong-willed daughter's professional eclipse.

At age twenty-two (and still no idea she is motherless), Ute is booked less and less frequently to runway, her "elegant savage" look quickly passing out of vogue. Now her eyes are seen as too widely spaced, her bones too sharp, her expression and mulberry skin tone not requisitely blank-canvas. In Paris, where societal tolerance for the African is brittle enough, she finds herself without a single job on the catwalk. One designer actually tells her that the unusual length and thinness of her neck joined to the apple-shaped head, makes her look utterly alien, not unrelated to

ET. Back in New York, feeling like a freakish cow put out to pasture, she senses a chance for reinvention, rejuvenation, re*juicing,* the moment she meets Felicia Brown.

Ute assumes she is slumming at a bar on Ludlow. She sits nursing a beer, listening to the pleasant chatter of one of the more sympathetic assistants from the agency, which will soon be dropping her. In sashays Felicia, barefoot in low-slung jeans. She is clove-brown with wide hips, flip-flops sticking out of her straw Gap bag, two willowy and straggly East Village–studied white boys on either side. While one of the boys—chin in hand—looks rapturously into her round, dewy face, Felicia straddles the chair like a cowgirl. She pulls out a small notepad, begins making lists. Bored, the other boy surveys the room, spots Ute, then seductively smiles. Felicia catches him, swiftly turns around. Blushing as if it might show, Ute grins, her narrow mouth almost too small for her strong, white teeth. Felicia warmly returns the hello, batting her unnaturally long lashes.

Instantly recognizing her from magazines, Felicia moves in for the kill. She goes over and introduces herself as a manager, pointing out the fey boys at the table as one of her bands. Over margaritas on the rocks with no salt, Felicia describes her adventurous girlhood in Dallas, her mother's football clubs, her father's timid, scholarly ways. Ute sits quietly, her lips apart, afraid to speak of her own past for fear she'll get it all wrong. Ute has little memory, but even if she had clear access to her history, she would not willingly divulge.

Playing with the day-old chips, the modeling agency's assistant asks Ute if they should leave. Ute insists on another beer. The assistant glares at the half-full bottle in Ute's hand, shrugs, then tries asserting herself into the conversation. It is no use. Felicia switches sides of the table, so that she can sit nearer to Ute. And although she is used to being stared at, she shrinks her marvelously long body, melting with embarrassment, into the seat.

Felicia asks Ute if she can sing. Ute swallows, shakes her magnificent head. She looks from one of Felicia's eyes to the other, flitting back and forth like a butterfly avoiding the net. Felicia asks her if she's ever tried belting it out in the shower, letting her voice rise full and sensuously with the steam. The cat still holding her tongue, Ute shakes her head, again embarrassed. Felicia says the boys really could use a new lead singer, and that with Ute's looks and presence, and their experience, they couldn't help but get a record deal. Felicia pulls out her pad, this time to sketch a cartoon of Ute. The likeness is striking, capturing the high-browed insouciance of her face. And if Ute could ever really compare to an apple as the designer once suggested, then Felicia conveys on paper the freshly dipped hot chocolate caramel Red Delicious, dripping down the stem, oozing over the hand of the beholder, in ecstasy. Behind Ute, she sketches the boys with barely more detail than figurative sticks. On her way to the bathroom, Felicia slides the cartoon in front of Ute. As she shuts the door behind her, the agency assistant exclaims, "What a pushy bitch!" But Ute's lips are parted in expectant further surprise. She *loves* the sketch, and is sure that this is only the beginning of something sensationally wild.

When Felicia reappears from the bathroom, Ute tells her how much she likes the drawing. Felicia replies, "But I've always adored your face; I probably know it by heart." Abruptly she returns to the two boys who are now thick in conversation. Ute folds the cartoon to put in her purse, and then regrets she doesn't have a book to press it in.

Felicia did not forget to write her number on the back. Ute calls her the requisite, nondesperate two days later. They get together at Felicia's between Avenue C and D walk-up, where the only chair is in front of the computer. Red and orange velvet pillows are scattered all over the floor, a majestically ornate burgundy kilim hangs on the wall. Felicia offers Ute some pumpernickel bread, prosciutto, Gouda cheese, and cheap Pinot Noir. When she's gotten Ute lulled and drunk, she rolls a joint, gives her a mic to sing anything against the boys' tracks.

To impress Felicia, Ute sings unrelated English and German lines of poetry she'd memorized. Surprisingly, the result is an artful cut-up method style. She begins every phrase off-key, then finds her way back to the proper tonality. Side to side, Felicia moves her neck, her head, Southeast Asian style. Ute sways her hands in a confident storytelling mode, her eyelids growing heavier, her smile more tantric.

Felicia grabs her camera, shooting circles around Ute as she sings. As the Polaroids eject, she throws them everywhere about her on the floor. Both women are getting giddy. To steady herself, but more so to touch some of that glistening coconut skin, Ute reaches for Felicia's wrist. She latches on tightly to Ute's hand, laying back her weight, so together they spin. Tiny beads of sweat form like dew around Ute's lips. Her legs quiver. They fall to the pillows, laughing hysterically, Felicia's breath in Ute's face.

Ute's nipples stand at attention; Felicia lovingly brushes the line of Ute's jaw to her neck. She closes her eyes, her mouth in welcome. But rudely and abruptly, Felicia stands up, tells her she is tired.

Felicia continues to tease Ute this way, erotically, down the short, swift road to fronting the band. Felicia keeps her tightly under rein; Ute finds herself playing clubs the likes of which would bring her shame in Okahandja. The strangely sinister chemistry between Ute and the boys initially creates an exuberant interest. Record company A&R execs circle, and close in. The frequent write-ups take notice of Ute "the model," but after some time the press goes against her. The boys blame her for getting all the attention, and finally then for losing it. Before the hot producer can fully rework their under-contract demo, the record company drops them. Ute holds her guard through the nasty, falldown, drag-out breakup. She finds another drummer, guitarist, and bassist, but this quartet never makes it out of rehearsal. At the age of twenty-six, Ute is forgotten by the public, and Felicia is still her most desperate crush, unconsummated.

Seeking the best revenge, Ute licks her wounds and moves to Los Angeles to pursue a career in celebrity. She rents a small Spanish-style home in West Hollywood, buys a convertible BMW, and becomes a lover of sun and plants. Through music and modeling contacts, Ute finds her way to the kind of pretentious clubs where commercial and film agents prey on young, pretty girls. Ute doesn't realize these are also the kind of places where if they knew her age, they would consider her already over the hill. Neither does Ute know that here is where any madam can be the best pimp. So before Ute has the chance to lie about her age to CAA or ICM, M. A. Katz, short for Mildred Aurora, bags her.

M.A.'s girls can make $5,000 to $10,000 a day, since all of them are "model gorgeous." At the very least they are bilingual, can speak intelligently in social settings, and are at their most comfortable with wealthy men. All of them are trained to fuck exquisitely for one to one and a half hour sessions, or the much more costly all-nighters and weekenders. Their well-honed bodies are marathon-ready for the wear; their knowledge of positions and kinks are worthy of a *Kama Sutra* graduate. As many men that want to see two women together, M.A.'s girls—if they didn't start out at least bicurious—become enthusiastically bisexual by only one month's training. Ute does not expect to love her new career, but she is soon amazed to embrace not only the thrill and power of seduction—as Felicia must have always felt—but the infinite pleasures of sex, which Ute suspects Felicia never did.

With still no idea she is motherless, Ute is fucking every client with the kind of guilt-free abandon she never imagined possible. Movie stars, businessmen, diplomats, politicos—some days she has three, four, or five men. Sometimes only one. Once she had a party of seven in one evening, each one coming two or three times, which adds up to quite a bit of squirt. She cannot walk the next day, but this is an exception she does not regret. From time to time, there is also the vice squad cop who doesn't pay M.A., but for whom M.A. pays Ute. This is the only client who wants to tie Ute up; more often than not her bondage clients would rather play slave to her mistress.

She never falls for drugs—coke dries out her membranes; her

tongue becomes too heavy to obey, making her zealous performance less than excellent. Heroin is even worse, robs her of
appetite as well, when eating has always been her most sensual
pleasure. And Ute, never a drinker, can stop at two glasses of
wine. So self-discipline is her only master. And due to extremely
bad memory, self-esteem is not yet an issue. Especially since the
price she commands is paid with the anticipation of carnal bliss.
She is lucky for three consistent years, never to find the john who
pushes her head into a toilet, makes her eat shit, or push any
inanimate object up her pussy that isn't made to stimulate.

In fact, by her thirtieth birthday she thinks of herself as the
Happy African Hooker, and in celebration a client takes her back
to Berlin where she hasn't been since the age of sixteen. This ami-
able, and even quite emotional client—with whom she'd gone to
Paris, Sydney, Geneva, and Majorca—is now proud to treat her
with the chance to speak her second and most-loved of three
tongues.

With his credit card gift of $150,000 max to spend, Ute
walks out into the ritzier streets of Charlottenburg, taking a
cab to Potsdamer Platz for remnants of the Wall, then wander-
ing Kreuzberg for spice, but winding up in Mitte. Not yet has
she spent a dime outside the taxi fare, nor felt the misery of the
cold, gray day of mostly indignant and bitter faces. She would
rather wait to go shopping on her favorite client's well-woolen
arm. She finds a dark wood café with deep night, forest green
walls, and delectable club sandwiches of fluffy white bread,
melodious chicken, and bacon. Ute sits satisfied with a full
belly, warmed with red wine and sweet lips of crumb cheese-

cake. This is when Klaus catches her eye from the lounge bar where he sits.

He asks his waitress to find out what Ute is drinking, and to give her another of whatever she desires. Ute toasts him in the air with it, and he smiles, his mouth like an obscene bruise on his face. When she joins him in the lounge, she finds that Klaus is forty-five, and much paler from a distance. He is rosy-cheeked, strong, well-heeled, and well-schooled on pleasuring a woman. Experienced as she is, the latter she can sense. He is married to an American, and working as an architect in his native Berlin. Ute does all the interviewing, without allowing him his own line of questioning.

Following him to his home on Fuggerstrasse, Ute feels a deep painful guilt in anticipating a delicious fuck with another man while on her favorite client's tab. She is surprised to find so many bicycles at the foot of his apartment stairwell, and walking up the cold stone steps she begins to wonder how much money he really has. It is a false alarm, as he opens his fine, carved door. Everything in this apartment is of the most exquisite taste. He thrusts his palm just beneath her armpit so that his wrist scrapes her breast as he pulls her to him to bite and suck her neck. His cock is already out of his pants, as he pushes her down on the coffee table, tasting her juice with his fingers first, then sucking her off, making a cum mustache. He fucks her slow and hard for three hours before she gives a thought to her favorite client. Exhausted, she dials him from the architect's kitchen. She has to shush Klaus, upon getting her client's voice mail. Klaus continues the history and design report of each room, and the ancient date of the tile. And she realizes it isn't his home at all, but a small fuck palace he's kept for occasions like this.

Same time, next day, she meets Klaus. Five hours later of more in-depth fucking, he takes her out for some air to a gay bar in Schöenberg. Ute is fascinated by a wall-length encased diorama of elephants in a stone cave. Watching two men kiss, as he warms his hand between her thighs, for the first time she allows him some real conversation.

"I come from just above South Africa. A place called Okahandja in Namibia. Most of us are German bastards, really," Ute says, making a circle with her finger around the rim of the wineglass.

"Really? You don't look it. What a perfectly smooth, *dark*, and velvety skin."

"Thank you," Ute says, red and heated inside with the fucking, but a perfectly stoic expression memorializing her face.

"Isn't that the region where the natives still wear German dress? Even nineteenth-century hoop skirts and soldier's uniforms? It's quite tragic, isn't it, the begging for a mere pfennig of German aid, which would end up quite carelessly spent."

"What gives you the right to say *'carelessly spent'*? Germany hasn't even apologized for genocide, much less sexual slavery. My great-grandmother was a comfort woman! And they subjected children to racist genetics studies; they stole millions and *millions* of acres!"

"I can see we would do well not to talk at all." Klaus smiles, holding her palm open in his hand. "It's sad about all of Africa, it truly is, and it is always the same story: poverty, self-destruction, and disease."

"You're right, it's better we don't talk about it," she snaps. "I've been thinking of opening up a center for young immigrant girls trying to find their way in America. A place where they can come for advice on shelter, family planning, food, and career," Ute says, sorely missing her mother.

"Really? A career girl like you?"

"Yes, *fucker,* a career girl like me." Ute stands, throwing to the floor the Paul Smith cashmere scarf he'd lent her from home.

*   *   *

Ute flies back to L.A. with her client, who never finds out about Klaus, nor does he miss any of her attention. She continues to see him, but answers less and less of M.A.'s calls regarding other clients. She does not care how badly she is pissing off her boss, as now she intends to be her own. Ute finally buys a new computer, and gets rid of the ancient Mac her modeling agent had handed down. She researches 501(c) 3 nonprofits, sets up a website; "Center for Affection" is already taken, so Ute becomes www.centerforaffections.org. She leaves her idyllic West Hollywood home, buys a smaller duplex in Echo Park, moves into half of it. Begins learning about new funds for the money she'd long ago invested, then took out of the market for real estate.

Ute leaves flyers in shelters, halfway houses, employment agencies, and AAs. She gets help from a client who has influence over the Department of Immigration. After eleven months of hard work and notice of one grant, Ute now has three girls: one from Guatemala, another from Ecuador, and one from Brazil.

"When I first saw dis name, you know, I t'ought it was for

pros'di'toot," the Brazilian says to her on the third week of group counseling.

"I never saw the word 'affection' as anything sexual whatsoever. I saw it as the action of affecting, of *influencing*. The sound of the word has power to me. And I wanted it to be something that came from me to you, and you to her, and so on and so on and on forever," Ute says, sitting back in her hard desk chair, her arms folded over her champagne cup breasts.

By Ute's thirty-third birthday, seventy girls and five different assistants have come through her doors. She has secured funding to last her the rest of the decade. Ute has also given up all clients, but not the relations. Guilt is the main source of her power— wealthy men thinking back over thousands spent on sex with girls when they could also use their money to make a fresh new crop perhaps go the right way. Ute's influence remains potent to this day. And D.V. becomes one of the more interesting characters she meets through her good work.

He is a film soundman of independent means. He walks through Ute's doors, with the director who is planning a documentary on nongovernmental help centers. He is exactly her height, trim, except for the love handles he cannot work off. He has a pinchable chin, and soft, wavy hair, the color of light brown butcher paper that always looks as if he has just gotten out of bed. He tells Ute people call him either Danko or Vlado, and that she could pick whichever she liked, so she renames him D.V. They go to a nice lunch together, where she learns he was raised mainly in Paris, but his roots are Croatian. He tells her fascinating stories about his New York period—living in a houseboat at the pier in Battery Park, and how he used to do odd jobs around the city just for the grit. Because Ute holds back personal information, they don't find out until the third date that they have German in common, since he lived briefly in Berlin.

D.V.'s house in Silverlake is mostly glass, with a lush, unkempt yard and lumber everywhere. Mint grows up his hillside, which he chews for sweet breath. Ute spends more and more time at his house, mothering his plants, and slowly trusting him with her thoughts. For D.V., like Ute, is originally from a place of regrettable horrors one can never forget. And so not forcefully Eurocentric, D.V. does not offend her even once regarding Africa, women, or race.

He buys Ute a bicycle to match his own, and they go riding through the neighborhood, fighting cars for the right to the bike lane on Sunset Boulevard. D.V. makes her laugh in cafés, at his friends' dinner parties, during the trailers at the movies, and in the grass of her backyard. They go for walks in Elysian Park, goof with salsa dancing at El Floridita, and play basketball at the Y. Without knowing, he teaches Ute how to kiss without precision or sadness.

She finds herself utterly comfortable. Relaxed. And it is around this time when she is thirty-six years old, that she musters enough courage to write her parents. In a month, she receives her father's painful list of each letter that never reached her. The letters are catalogued by headline and theme, and the most devastating, of course, is the news of her mother's death, now seventeen years past.

Though it has been three years, Ute makes a breakthrough in

her lovemaking with D.V. Something tells him to whisper, "stay with me, *stay* with me," just before orgasm. He knows that in her head, while they move together, she travels from state to state, country to country. But this time, she is no one else but herself, and the man inside of her is no one but the one she has chosen.

D.V. accompanies her back to Southwest Africa, and he holds on to her thin, sinewy arm when she breaks down in wracking sobs as they step off the plane. The weight of the air, the colors and smells overwhelm her senses, the connections challenge her brain. The flood of recall is more than she can bear. Her father, standing in front of her, is as delicate as she'd known. His hands vibrate like a hummingbird, his disposition and manner bordering that of a neurasthenic.

At lunch, her father introduces Ute and D.V. to the young journalist he has mentored. He is small with a sculpted body, and a very fine head. His teeth are naturally straight; he speaks with a lisp. He is deferential to her father, and charming with D.V. When Ute looks into his face, she imagines that it is a mirror.

Back in their shack of a room, Ute climbs on D.V. with the frenzy of her first working days, fucking him with vigor as if she were the one with the cock. She is too high to hear him gasp the same words he uses whenever he feels she might get away, for Ute is ecstatic to remember the joy of role play. *How beautiful it would be to have a brother,* she thinks. The image of her father's handsome apprentice in her head, as she is now on all fours on the floor. Why has it never occurred to her to have a baby, she wonders. Why can she not control her mind to embrace the space of peace to excitement?

It is not long before Ute is fucking the mentee, bringing her father to shame. For this abominable act in the eyes of society, her father shows her a frank, intense hatred. His rage goes beyond his ability to lecture, shifting speedily to a desire to disown her. D.V. is torn between his own pain for her betrayal, and hers for the loss of both parents. She does not readily show her vulnerability, and in fact is quite insolent over her mistake. If no one is to blame for her mother's death, and if there is nothing that can bring her back, then why should Ute be taken to account for her every trivial whim? Why should she cry over all the lost years?

She is a stunned and blocked mess. In first class on the plane back to L.A., D.V. sits patiently, silently at the side of the open wound that is Ute. Weeks later she is near lucid again, and realizes the support he shows is beyond loyalty. Beyond even romantic attachment. What D.V. gives her is perfectly unconditional. When Ute goes into therapy over this—her inability to receive all that is pure and good—she hands the Center over to one of her assistants to helm. Her cheating on D.V. not only touches upon her late prostitute years' fears of being a sex addict, but also grips her in the realization of emotional cause and effect. His real love is what she constantly rejects.

They hang on to each other throughout her changes of four different therapists, ignoring the two who advise they should separate. Ute binges on sweets for days, then eats nothing but vegetables and fruit for weeks. She loses fifteen pounds, and D.V. cries. He pulls her back into the garden, the weeds now overgrown, her favorite blooms having died long ago.

No longer taking a salary from the nonprofit, Ute is financially dependent on D.V., and not unaware of that danger. Ute is forty, and completely out of touch with the Center for Affections for a period now just short of a year. This propels her to take another in-depth look into its primary goals and definition. Her assistant wholeheartedly welcomes her back. And since Ute's eating disorders have brought her to the shore of self-loathing, she calls on the strength of her self-will to buoy her through crisis. The Center's girls give her love, and she finally learns how to take it.

Ute remains an expert of sensual pleasure. She is a master at triggering for herself multiple orgasms, and for D.V. an insistent erection. The skin they bake, the scents they make in the luminous heat, glow through their flesh as they mate, as if welded together, and trying to remelt. He does not try anymore to orchestrate whether she is in the act of loving or fucking. He does not monitor the sweep of her emotional recitals. He just loses himself in her landscapes, in her touch, while Ute loses herself in their boundaryless bed, the heart.

MILES MARSHALL LEWIS

Diva Moves

*L*ori asked him to wait for her, as she settled her bill with Dyaspora hair salon. She had already accepted a business card from DJ, a summer associate with the law firm Dewey Ballantine, and hoped to continue their flirtatious banter on their way to the Columbus Circle train station. Ordinarily, she would have hailed a taxi back to her Greenwich Village dorm, but styling her curly brunette tresses left its usual dent in her purse. ("It's naturally curly," she'd told him. *Naturally expensive,* she'd thought.)

An hour earlier, Lori was sitting at a hair dryer, waiting to be moved up front, when she'd first noticed him. DJ sat in a high chair some thirty feet across from her, laughing with a beautician whose fingers fidgeted deep in his thick bundle of shoulder-length locks, twisting new growth at the root. His conspicuous male presence in the beauty parlor was amplified by his good looks. Lori thought he resembled Maxwell, the R&B singer, with his slight frame, almond-colored complexion, angular jaw, and the straight teeth in his bright smile. She'd once read that Maxwell had his hair styled at Dyaspora, and here was his doppelgänger, smiling widely at her.

His fixed gaze drew Lori into the conversation, about some

recent movie or other, and it continued when they were seated next to each other a half hour later. He said his name was Djidaje, DJ for short. He was a native New Yorker, from Park Slope in Brooklyn, and a Hampton graduate. He was about to enter his final year at nearby Fordham Law School in the fall, and had been growing his locks for the last three years.

Lori wondered if DJ was a regular at Dyaspora, and if anyone there knew his real story. His tales of Fourth of July vacations on Martha's Vineyard, time spent studying abroad in Paris, and partying at record industry soirées were almost too good to be true. Her experience with brothers in New York City included its fair share of boasting and wishful thinking, especially when they found out that Lori hailed from Opelika, Alabama. Still, the chemistry was there, DJ was fine, and Lori wanted to ride the wave. *There's nothing wrong with a summer love,* she'd thought, and she definitely wouldn't mind fucking "Maxwell" till fall semester. So Lori Tony reinvented herself.

"I work in the A&R department at Sony Music Entertainment. . . . My uncle is Sidney Poitier and he pulled some strings for me. . . . I went to Hampton for a while, too, but I wasn't really checking for it, so I transferred. . . . Yeah, I pledged Alpha Kappa Alpha. . . . Actually, I'm a singer—like a cross between Sade and Fiona Apple—but I wanna get my sound perfected. . . . Sony keeps trying to offer me a contract. . . . I'll probably change my name from Lori Poitier; I don't really want the industry to know. . . ."

Then she threw in a friendship with Lauryn Hill, for good measure. If DJ could be a globe-trotting, Cosby-bourgeois, talented tenth template, then Lori had the right to redesign her own world as well, she'd felt. In New York City, all things were possible, and all the things Lori said were just as likely to be true as not; who's to say? The city's cosmopolitan population made it easy to accept such bold pronouncements at face value, and DJ seemed accepting and completely unfazed. Plus, she doubted DJ would be interested in her if he knew her real job was a receptionist at Sony Music Studios.

The night before, Lori celebrated the absence of her summer school roommates by blasting Lauryn Hill's *Unplugged* album on her egg-shaped portable stereo while bathing in the tub, soapy water drenching her mocha skin golden under the candlelight. For Lori, Lauryn Hill represented the archetypal strong black woman of the hip-hop generation. (In fact Lauryn used to have her hair styled regularly at Dyaspora, too, Lori had read.) Singing along to Lauryn's songs of heartbreak, redemption, and empowerment, Lori felt a sense of aspiring to something higher. If Lauryn Hill could make miracles happen at twenty-seven, why couldn't Lori Tony, at merely five years younger? Lori did actually sing, despite the embellishments she'd told DJ, but hadn't come close to conquering the industry. That, she knew, would come.

*   *   *

The very next evening, watching Lori across his kitchen banquette, DJ couldn't keep his eyes off her ample bosom. By design, a jade pendant fell strategically between her breasts and she laughed to herself every time he pretended to admire her necklace. Accepting his invitation for a home-cooked meal gave Lori an indication of what the night might entail. *What brother cooks for a woman he's known for less than twenty-four hours?* she thought. She'd come prepared to do the dance, anticipating what might happen later.

"So what are you doing single, Mr. DJ?" She took a forkful of chicken slathered in cream of mushroom and stuffing. The mushrooms set it off; DJ was scoring in every area. It was good to meet a man in the big city who could cook worth a damn.

"You wouldn't believe me if I told you," he said. "Or you would, but it's a little too soon for the battle-of-the-sexes conversation. We just met, after all," he said, winking.

Who winks? DJ was too cute, his long lashes and all. "Uh-oh. This might be headed in the wrong direction," she teased. "You haven't messed up yet. But tread verrry carefully." She swirled her first taste of Merlot around in her mouth, then swallowed slowly and smiled.

"Basically, I don't have the time. The first year of law school is the hardest, but only because it takes a while to adjust. I made that adjustment, but I still have a lot of work to do. So much that I need to wait till graduation before I can even think of being with a woman or in a real relationship."

"I can understand that," Lori said. "But that's not sexist, and not the real deal. What's really on your mind?"

He laughed.

"Okay, for real? After spending four years at school in Virginia, sisters in New York City are stressing me. They're complicated and fickle. Where are you from again?"

Lori almost fabricated someplace, but decided against it. *After all, he's checking for southern girls,* she thought. "Don't laugh: Opelika, Alabama," she answered.

"That's cool. I have a frat brother from Alabama. I didn't know Sidney Poitier had family down in Opelika," DJ said, an eyebrow raised. When Lori didn't respond he continued. "It seems that women at these record industry parties are all about status. They want guys with money, or if they're superfine then they feel they shouldn't settle for anyone less than, I don't know, Damon Dash or Q-Tip or somebody."

"Really," she said, wondering how much this had to do with DJ's own insecurities.

"That's just my experience," he said laughing, raising his wineglass. "I don't have a car, I don't make that entertainment law money yet. And I don't wear enough Prada for a lot of these women in New York."

"Cry me a river, huh?" Lori joked, and they both laughed. "Why are you after women like that anyway, DJ? You seem to have so much going on from what you've told me. I'm surprised a brother like yourself would be attracted to superficial star-fuckers."

Their eyes met on the *fuck* in star*fuck*ers, and Lori felt naughty for bringing sex into the conversation. They each took a sip of wine while the word lingered in the air.

"You have a point," he admitted. "I guess I'm just like the next brother drawn to attractive women, and it seems like most fine city girls up here are into material things. Or their heads are gassed into thinking they shouldn't settle for the average brother because so many stars are walking around that they can get with any one of them. Or they're so caught up in their own fantasies you can't tell what's real from what's not."

"Well, maybe you should broaden your search beyond industry parties, DJ. Or even beyond city girls."

"I thought that's what we were doing," he said, as their eyes met.

Looking across at Lori, DJ took stock of his good fortune in having met her. He loved Lori's strikingly pronounced features: her luminous, Baldwinesque brown eyes; her suckable full lips; the cute smirk that crept across her face when she was amused. Lori's body was nice and compact for her short height, tempting DJ into wondering how far things might go later. He had the feeling she was stretching some truths. But for the time being, he found his curiosity over what lay beneath her sundress and how her rich curves might feel to his touch overwhelming. They finished their dinner in silence, the night's possibilities lingering in the air.

*   *   *

"So you rented us *Before Sunrise*! Excellent choice," Lori said, fingering the DVD case on the coffee table.

"Don't tell me you saw it before. Oh, no!" DJ replied, actually hoping they wouldn't have to watch the movie at all.

Lori spied his Hampton diploma hanging on the living room wall. To the right, she could make out the Eiffel Tower in a framed photo on the decorative fireplace. Next to it dangled over a dozen all-access passes to various movie premieres and record release parties. She recalled their phone conversation the night before, and her attempts to counter DJ's ambitions and accomplishments with her own trumped-up success story. Charmed at first by his good looks and his taste in jazz and cool films, Lori was starting to feel she was digging a hole for herself now that DJ was turning out to be who he said he was. She remembered Chris Rock's old standup line that when you first meet someone, you're not really meeting that person, you're meeting their representative. But in this case DJ truly had it going on, and Lori's attraction to him was deepening.

"I wouldn't mind watching it again," she said. "What I like about that movie was the talk mostly, you know? The whole two hours, walking through Vienna joking around, sharing their dreams, getting to know each other. It's pretty romantic."

"It's totally romantic," DJ agreed. "They had just met on the train with no idea about each other's background, but they were still totally honest and up front about their lives, exploring each other. I've never been to Germany but it reminds me of studying in Europe—"

"DJ," Lori interrupted, feeling uncomfortable with the turn the conversation had taken, "we could watch this together, but today was a long day at work for me. Tommy Mottola quit and things are really bananas in the office. Maybe I should just go," she said, not really wanting to.

"That would be a shame, Lori. Our night's just beginning. Why don't I give you a massage? Work out some of that tension."

Lori agreed, her heart racing. Carrying their wineglasses, DJ soon led her into his bedroom.

Moments later Lori lay on her chest in DJ's queen-sized maple sleigh bed. He sat astride her backside, deftly kneading the muscles of her back beneath her gray chiffon dress. Relaxing in the candlelight and the sensuous sounds of, yes, Maxwell playing softly, Lori thought back to her first taste of New York City three years ago. Her freshman semester at New York University, rolling with newfound girlfriends to spots like Joe's Pub and Lotus; the city had seemed like some foreign country to her. One of the biggest thrills was her new anonymity. No one who knew Lori Tony from Opelika had followed her to NYU. She could be as loud at parties as she dared, as brazen, self-mythologizing, and free as she chose. No one back home would know.

To her, New York was a playground. Lori felt little guilt about her fabrications, even though she now knew DJ was everything he claimed, a cultured, well-traveled entertainment lawyer-to-be. *Guys don't care so much about truth in advertising where females are concerned,* she thought, *as long as they get the product.* Lori slipped the straps of her dress off her shoulders and pulled it off. *He's awfully good with his hands,* she thought, settling back onto the sheets.

DJ got up and put on an Alice Coltrane CD, then slipped off his shirt. He then got a bottle of baby oil from a pot of boiling water on the stove. As he walked back toward the bed, he freed his locks from the band holding them off his face. The spiritual, almost vocal, arpeggios from the tenor saxophone drifted softly through the air. Taking another sip of wine, Lori fantasized about the possibilities of the night, a rare vulnerability softening the lines of her face. DJ was doing everything right. She hoped they connected as well in bed as they had over dinner.

Lori lay on her chest again, as DJ knelt over her, the warm oil poured into his hands seeping through his fingers onto her back. He rubbed his palms together, then laid them on the smooth surface of Lori's skin. She moaned as a harp danced with a sax, a flickering flame danced with the shadows, and they danced with each other.

He kneaded her back, his fingers deftly moving back and forth over her body. Sliding his hands around her sides, he felt the fleshy expanse of her breasts. Lori rose up, and he cupped them in his hands, taking her nipples between his fingers. No words were needed, this was a scene they'd already rehearsed dozens of times since meeting the day before. His hands slid down to the small of her back, and the rise of her voluptuous behind. There was no protest as he slid off her G-string.

Lori turned between DJ's legs, looking up at him. He looked back at her, his fingers tangling in her hair. Then he took a sip of wine and transferred it to her waiting mouth. Lori felt drunk, as much by DJ as by the Merlot. Yet she retained a cool detachment, prolonging each moment, savoring the summit of what she had hoped for while riding the F train on her way to Brooklyn. DJ kissed her breasts softly, inhaling deeply the remnants of her perfume as he circled the raisinlike flesh surrounding her nipples with his tongue. Lori closed her eyes and moaned with more urgency. He quickly slipped out of his slacks and boxers, and slid into bed next to her. As he pulled her to him he licked warm, wet traces over her neck and chest, his oily hands massaging the inside of her thighs. They rubbed and kissed and stroked one another as the scent of sex mingled with the burning incense.

Sitting up now, DJ lifted her onto his lap, and, looking deeply into her eyes, slowly entered her. She began to call out rhythmically at first, while he worked to accommodate himself into her tight space. Her breathing was at first staccato and abbreviated, until her flow increased. Then from a slow and measured pace, their rocking began to shift their foundation.

He entered her more deeply inch by inch, as a child might dig deeper into the sand on a beach, the sand becoming more dark and moist with the depth. They held each other, Lori whimpering softly as he moaned in response. Excited by the sounds of their journey, his rhythm quickened, the moist slapping of their bodies growing louder, the squish of her wetness increasing. Their sounds of love, the hushed sobs and whispered words of pleasure excited them. DJ thrust hard inside Lori, gripping her shoulders, tearing into her as a rush began to overtake him. She cried out, overcome by her own orgasm. When he felt her muscles tighten around him like a fist, he surrendered to his own rush in waves, coming hard inside her with the force of his final thrusts.

Then they lay together in silence, each knowing something incredible had just happened and wondering what it would mean.

* * *

The digital clock radio on DJ's desk read 11:31 A.M. As Lori sat checking her email with DJ's iMac, in one of his colorful Moshood T-shirts, her violet G-string exposed her butt to the cold seat of the black wooden chair. By the time he returned from the bathroom, carrying a burning stick of sandalwood, she was already toward the end of the most recent postings to an unofficial Lauryn Hill fan website.

"This will only take a minute," she said as he stood behind her, massaging her shoulders. "This is part of my job at Sony," she lied, "to check out these websites every once in a while. It's fun to log on anonymously sometimes and set the fans straight. Listen to this girl, for instance, calling herself DivaMoves."

DivaMoves: Hey, y'all! I'm not jealous or anything—LOL— and I don't want Lauryn lovers jumping all down my throat, but it seems to me that Lauryn Hill is guilty of making some major diva moves. The world is making her out to be all that, but she used to be just another girl from New Jersey. It seems like a calculated rise to the top, to me. She's having kids with Bob Marley's son to mix with that royal bloodline, and she's been dissing, I mean distancing (LOL), herself from her roots in the Fugees ever since she blew up. I like her music too, y'all. But I can't get with her changing herself into a cultural icon, trying to be somebody she's not. Be true to yourself, Lauryn!

"That's just her opinion," DJ said. "I don't really mess with web-sites. It seems like chat rooms are constantly full of this kind of gossipy stargazing. It always seemed to me that these people should have something better to do with their time, like live their own lives."

"But people change," said Lori. "Just because you were a cer-tain way once doesn't mean you have to stay that way forever. I know Lauryn, so maybe I'm taking this too personally. But she's the sweetest person. She should be allowed to grow and live her own fantasies just like anybody else. Don't tell me that if you had the chance to be somebody else, you wouldn't go ahead and take it."

DJ was silent, giving Lori a long look. Then he answered slowly. "Lori, I remember a girl in high school asking me, 'Which member of New Edition would you want to be?' My reaction was that I wouldn't want to be any of them, really. I like who I am, I told her. I think it's important to be proud of who you are and where you come from. Maybe I should ask you that question. If you had the chance to be someone else, would you take it?"

Lori just looked at him without answering, her heart in her throat, as the question lingered in the sandalwood-scented air.

*   *   *

DJ picked Lori up from her dormitory near Washington Square Park days later, on a humid, starry Tuesday night. Lori hoped he hadn't noticed the director's chair at the desk in her cluttered room, emblazoned with L. TONY on its canvas back, a parting college gift from her uncle back home.

"I forgot to bring your work number with me to the firm today," DJ said as they walked toward Broadway to catch a cab to Amy Ruth's restaurant.

"Yeah, I was starting to worry when I didn't get a call from you all day," Lori joked. They had spoken daily since meeting at Dyaspora the previous Friday. "I was hoping we were still on for tonight." She stopped at the corner of Waverly Place, noticing the skinny strap of her white Bernardo sandal had come unbuckled. She rested her foot on a streetlight, balancing herself on DJ's shoulder. When he noticed the undone strap and secured the clasp for her, Lori brightened inside.

"Well, I still tried to call," he said. "I dialed information for the number to Sony. They gave me the main number. I asked the Sony receptionist to put me through to Lori Poitier, and she told me they didn't have a Lori Poitier on the roster. In fact, they couldn't find your name anywhere."

"I don't know what's wrong with them," Lori said quickly. "I just started a few weeks ago, so maybe I'm not in the system. You should've just asked for A&R." Despite the sandals and her light floral sundress, Lori suddenly felt warm, her throat dry.

"I asked for A&R," DJ said, looking expectantly at Lori. "They put me through to somebody else who said you didn't work there." When she didn't respond, he turned away and hailed a cab.

Why couldn't DJ have waited until after dinner for this? Lori thought. An uncomfortable moment of silence snailed by while Lori sought to feel DJ out. *It's just a game,* she thought. *Don't new couples do this all the time?* She felt the seconds crawl by while she wondered if she should be honest. After all, she did like DJ and didn't know how long she could keep lying to him. A cab jerked to a halt, and she stepped from the curb as DJ held the door open.

"That must've been an intern," she said, not meeting DJ's eyes. "I swear they can never get anything right."

"One sixteenth, between Fifth and Sixth," DJ said to the

Pakistani driver as he got in next to her. Lori, thinking she heard a trace of annoyance in his voice, changed the conversation to the first thing to come to her mind: the announcement of an upcoming concert performance by Lauryn Hill in Jamaica.

*   *   *

It was Lori's routine to check her email account before crashing for the night. Firing up her weathered Epson, she discovered a solitary email from DJ:

> Lori, you've been dishonest with me, and I've known since the beginning. I have friends who work at Sony, and all their extensions begin with 833—the work number you gave me didn't.
>
> All week I've given you opportunities to tell me the truth. Instead you've lied to me again and again. I would've liked you for you, but you never gave me a chance. The whole Lauryn Hill thing, the job, the Poitier thing—I don't know why you couldn't trust me with the truth. I handle my relationships with more honesty, and maturity, than this.
>
> I didn't do this by phone 'cause I figured we could both walk away easier this way. I can't fall for someone I can't trust.—DJ

Lori felt her face flush. She stared at the screen for a moment, rereading the message, then deleted the email. She wandered around her messy room, busying herself with other thoughts, but her mind kept returning to DJ, his warm smile and sense of humor. She turned off the light and got into bed but couldn't sleep.

A rush of thoughts crowded Lori's mind. He'd known since the beginning, she thought, her face flushing again. She regretted dragging out her little game longer than she should've, but it had quickly taken on a life of its own. She liked thinking of herself as already living where she'd hoped to eventually arrive in life: a singer, a player in the arena that DJ seemed to take for granted. He appeared so confidant and accomplished, Lori rationalized; what was she supposed to say? Lori felt ashamed of herself and her own insecurities and she regretted the end of their brief relationship. She thought to reply to his email, to somehow blame her behavior on self-protection or something, *anything*, but decided "no more lies." Besides, what's a fine, successful brother going to see in a simple girl whose flower hasn't quite blossomed yet? She'd found it difficult to discuss her hopes and dreams with DJ after having pretended that she'd achieved them already. And she'd never thought she'd fall for him, but she had. She rubbed the tears from her eyes, clutched a pillow to her chest, and went to sleep.

* * *

DJ found it impossible to rest with the scent of Lori in his bedsheets. At an all-night laundromat in Brooklyn, he sat tapping his feet absently to the Thelonius Monk music from his headphones, his sheets tossing and tumbling in the wash cycle. The email was hard enough to send, but getting Lori out of his head was even harder. They'd felt so right together. Chemistry like that is hard to come by, and Lori had the package: intelligence, beauty, and wits.

What nonsense, he thought, the statistics that three of every four black men were either addicted to drugs, gay, or in jail. DJ didn't find packs of women falling on his doorstep as a result of these misleading numbers. It made Lori's dishonesty even more painful. He'd spent so much time trying to find the right woman, and when he thought he'd found her, she wasn't at all what she made herself to be. He failed to understand why Lori would claim to be something that she wasn't. Still wondering, he tried to lose himself in the piano riffs and the hypnotic rhythm of the washing machine.

* * *

Window-shopping through SoHo in September, carrying a plastic bag filled with several textbooks for fall semester, Lori froze in front of the Museum for African Art. She'd spotted a young woman admiring a hand-carved, wooden Gye Nyame stool, often the first gift of a husband to his wife among the Akan of West Africa.

The slight-framed woman wore a worn pair of faded blue Levi's with a vintage T-shirt emblazoned with *Sesame Street* characters. Ornately designed gold earrings, bracketing her close-cropped Afro, barely grazed her lithe shoulders. It was Lauryn Hill.

Lori thought about what she considered Lauryn's recent public growth, and her own private evolution. The old Lori Tony might've rushed over asking for her autograph or gushed shamelessly all over her. But the new Lori knew she had a chance to be someone special too, to make her dreams happen in time. Lori thought about this for a minute, then mentally filed the moment away alongside her other New York celebrity sightings, and continued her walk down Broadway.

RAQUEL CEPEDA

God Bodies
and Nag Champa

For Margarita

Anthony threw a pen down in front of me, then his book of rhymes that I hated as much as I loved him. My knees burned from the friction and my back contorted into an awkward arch trying to gauge what he meant by it. We had been tripping for at least the full day, and my eyes were glazed with a film of sweat and ecstatic tears. He moaned, full lips dripping with blood and mucus down his beautiful long brown neck onto my back. A freshly plucked tampon a foot's distance away, by the portrait we bought in Salvador da Bahia that summer. A sweet flushed morsel we'd enjoyed for the first time—and whom I christened Butterscotch because she was so delicious—sat on his bed watching and writing lyrics, strumming her guitar and her clit, bewildered, cumming and singing in falsetto.

*   *   *

I mean, *man,* not only had we all dropped E for the first time together, we had been in the park not even an hour ago talking about Assata's notion of interdependent communities. I actually thought for a minute I'd won him over on the ideal that he was finally claiming responsibility for the thoughts he sampled from other people. We decided to collaborate on a story about Assata's life, with me on script, Anthony on score, and Butterscotch penning the first single. Still tripping, we got this idea to plot a most noble act in honor of the Egyptian spirits entrapped at the Met; we wanted to set the mummies lying all alone behind the glass partitions free because it was the right thing to do. I knew it was the right thing to do because Che Guevara had visited me in a dream. It was the very night I took my five-year-old son (who I named Che because he was charismatic and ironically enough, asthmatic like his namesake), to check out the permanent Egyptian exhibition.

Guevara walked in and sat on the edge of my bed with a copy of Jon Lee Anderson's epic tome *Che Guevara: A Revolutionary Life*. He looked down at the cover of the book and confided not being able to get through it because, *coño*, it was ramblings made possible by an intrusion into his personal diaries and interviews of people who could speak of him, and for him, *only* in his absence. Che said he was still consumed by the misery of the common man, the masses, and couldn't rest in peace until every person on the face of this wretched earth was independent from imperialism. And not until the mummies trapped in purgatory were set free. He then got up and said, "I am one of three guardian angels in your son's lifeline. Be careful that he doesn't inherit my depression. Keep him clean and *siempre pa'lante*." Yes, I agreed, always move forward. Guevara then walked out the door, back to wherever he'd come from.

* * *

"*Mira papito*," I said, "you know that shit ain't right having these dead corpses on display like that." Anthony gave me a piercing look because the only other person who called him *"papito"* besides his *abuelita* Doña Lila, was his late Puerto Rican mother. We used to call her *"La Lupe"* when we were kids growing up in Inwood because she was as tragic as she was bewitching. But unlike the real *La Lupe,* she didn't find Christ before she passed away, rather staying faithful to *Ochún,* the *santo* that crowned her platinum-dyed mane. Lupe was beautiful, tall, with an onion butt and a creamy *café con leche* complexion. Every boy at St. Jude's grammar school on Tenth Avenue had a jones for her and Anthony spent many days in detention for fighting in her honor. Anthony got his looks from his father Moreno, whom I had seen in one faded picture that was laminated underneath his skateboard.

Anthony was dark brown with red undertones like his dad, who was from Samana in the Dominican Republic—a peninsula settled by two shiploads of freed American slaves in the 1820s. Anthony was only up to my shoulders back then, but *damn,* he was always so cute. We met every single day after school, went to Inwood Park and hiked up the Indian trails looking for arrowheads and other signs of life from its original settlers. Then we would go to Mighty Burger and eat on my father's tab. We were best friends until he simply disappeared one summer. After not hearing from him for two weeks, I went to his apartment building on Indian Road and screamed "¡Papito! ¡Papito! ¿Papito?" every day for three straight weeks. No one came to the door until one day this young blond *gringa* opened the window and said she was the new tenant. I was so hurt. I didn't see him again for a decade.

* * *

We were ecstatic, high on this park-bench revolution we were having in some other murky, giddy dimension. So the plan was set. Although Anthony dug it, he maintained that he was an athe-ist, that God left him in the womb. I still wasn't used to having him in front of me though we'd found each other, in the oddest of ways, several years earlier. Butterscotch, who we met at the ASCAP Awards dinner a few months earlier, was cool, too. He, on the other hand, was kismet. "Synchronicity," I'd dubbed it.

* * *

I can't remember how we got to his basement apartment on the corner of Greene and Cambridge Avenues, several blocks from the Sacred Heart cemetery I hated to cross, and a thirty-minute walk from the Fort Greene park benches we had just built on. I always wondered if the bodies buried there had somehow scat-tered throughout the neighborhood—underneath all the beauti-ful brownstones and bodegas—from years of erosion. "Stop talk-ing that shit, girl, you're freakin' me out," Anthony said, whose dark buck-eyes and long eyelashes were pretty enough to dedi-cate several haikus to. Butterscotch shook her head, smiling, and said in that soft southern drawl, "Well, babies, it *ain't* the dead ah *fear.*" In that moment, I kind of thought he might have liked her more since she didn't remind him of his Lupe.

* * *

But here I was, my lips fluttering like a trapped butterfly trying to escape its captor, while he throbbed, thrusted his entire being inside of me from behind screaming, "Please, *mami,* write it down. Just one thought for me."

I wailed in haiku:

God body, please take
that forty ounce out yo' mouth
and fight for freedom

Butterscotch agreed, leaned across the bed and whispered in my ear, "thank you," as she traced over the dream catcher tattoo on my rib with her supple tongue and long, black tresses. Then she licked her way to the Eye of Isis etched on my side, then down my spine, sucking the cocktail of blood and sweat pooling in the small of my back from the clave-like rhythm Anthony and I were conjuring. I was afraid I might die, piss on myself, or at least pull a muscle, if I came one more time. Right there and then, I made a decision to leave my body and regroup, meditating on the sounds of wetness and the pungent odor stifling the room like midday in Santo Suarez, Habana, where there is little shade. My hands, barely able to hold the ballpoint pen he used to scribe his last hit single "The Insurrection," managed to form these words while I stood in front of myself in levity:

My hips divine with the righteous
mathematics of polyrhythmic ecstasy
and still not even I

can get next to me
when these spirits turn the beads of sweat
in my inner thighs into cosmic braille

And when I swirl in honor of Oya
hurricanes start to form off the coast of Africa
and when I swirl in honor of Oya
the dust that was my legacy swirls
to show momentary images of folks
I've been privileged to come forth from
and they say "God bless your soul"
before blowing through my
fingers and on my skin baking like the Sahara

I have a gift of swaying my hips in such a way
that stretch marks turn into khemetic alphabets
that tell tales of the art of telling tales
depending on the gyration
I can go on
I am truly blessed

The pen ran out of ink.

*   *   *

And then as Anthony flipped me over and they both began gnaw-
ing, lapping, and licking me, stopping only to suck each other's
tongue, I remembered. My *madrina* Margarita told me, right
before she died, that her *indio* told her I couldn't sleep with a man

who lived in a basement apartment because I was a daughter of Oya, the goddess of the wind, who kept watch at the gates of the cemetery. Margarita received all kinds of information every morning in her bedroom, as she sat still on the floor in front of that dusty glass she puffed smoke on that laid atop a round table once belonging to her mother. Her *mesita blanca,* or spiritual altar, was covered by a white cloth and had on it a few cheap cigars and a beautiful little gypsy doll wearing an eighteen-karat-gold necklace and cross pendant. Margarita would make me chant these corny prayers I learned at St. Jude's like *Our Father* and shit, then shower me with sweet-smelling *agua de Florida* as I headed out to chill with my girls Lazara and Josie on the corner of Isham and Sherman. Margarita helped many people out in the neighborhood, but her own luck wasn't so good. *Madrina* couldn't, like most *espiritistas,* pick up passages floating in the wind about her own future, and so she died alone in her sleep last summer. Maybe it was for the best, since her man Junior had died on an ironically gorgeous sunny day on September 11.

* * *

While I was confused by the randomness of the spiritual jewels Margarita dropped on me from time to time, I tried to heed *Madrina's* advice, respecting her *aché,* or supernatural gangster, if you will. The good thing about the jewels, though, were that they always came accompanied by a story. *Madrina* said I came from a long line of daughters of Oya, whom I only really knew about from reading this copy of Jorge Amado's *War of the Saints* Junior had lent me. It seems that, on the surface, we were warriors, fierce women who had the ability to make just about anything happen, sprouting like lotus flowers in urban swamplands like Washington Heights. I could dig that. Plus, daughters of Oya had a connection to *los muertos* parallel to none. That's probably why Margarita visited me on her way—I prayed—to a more peaceful universe.

*   *   *

On the night she came and sat on the edge of my bed, Margarita told me I must never sleep with a man who lived below the ground because it would give light to a negative female *egun*, or ancestor, of the man who would retard any other relationship outside that union. The spirits told her that our cousin Prisilla fell in love with such a man and it drove her into a depression that she never crawled out of. She was like Alice in Wonderland falling into a deep bottomless hole of despondency. "*Porque,* you see, while your spirit becomes arrested," *Madrina* said, "his continues on its path, only stronger because his *egun* is being lifted by your presence. So if he's a cheat, a thief, a *cabrón,* you're stuck." Talking about *cabróns* reminded Margarita that she had to leave, to pay a visit to this lady down the block—who shall remain nameless—who had mothered two sons with Junior, to scare the shit out of her. I said, "*Bendición Margie, te voy a dar luz para siempre,*" promising to always honor and give light to *Madrina's* spirit. She blessed me, "*Que Dios te bendiga.*" Then she walked out of my room as I held back the tears swelling my heart numb.

*   *   *

The years went by and I became a senior director of publicity at an independent P.R. firm called Exposure. Actually I was a jaded baby-sitter to a slew of young, ofttimes untalented record company crafted two-hit rappers. So-called socially conscious artists were the worst except for the folks I knew to be on some other plane from jump like Mos and Kwali. We were headlining New York City's freshest hiccup of time where poets like Tony Medina, asha bandele, T'Kalla, muMs the Schemer, and Saul Williams performed on the same bill any given night, at any given venue. But now, too many pseudo-revolutionary-Peter-Pan Africans—to humbly sample Mos—sporting the dippest Donna Karan dashikis and Polo kufis, penned at least one antiestablishment track per album as penance for the cold hard cash capitalism afforded them. I'm not "hating," just simply stating the facts. Our short attention span enabled us to jump on the Mumia Abu-Jamal bandwagon one summer and Amadou Diallo's the next. Not even ensuing terrorist attacks moved the hip-hop community to do anything other than make a lot of ill-informed speeches, even while continuing to support the genocide by and to Africans in their quasi-celebrated Motherland with all things that bling and sparkle. But that's another story.

*   *   *

This rather hypermasculine woman named Angela, who swore up and down she'd fucked every female rapper and R&B singer who lived on Billboard's hip-pop charts, owned Exposure. I knew I should have never taken the gig, but I needed the money and to stay in the loop while I wrote the great Latina flick that would star

Rosario Dawson, John Leguizamo, and Benjamin Bratt, so God/dess help me. Eagle Eye, a Belizian born rapper/producer whom I would eventually befriend, along with his wife and twin toddlers, read two pages of the treatment one day after a strategic planning meet-and-greet luncheon with the dickheads at his label that I had planned to tease the fanzines. Without a word, Eagle gave me back my script and notes as one editor after another came in and headed straight for the buffet. Several weeks later at his Eckō-sponsored record release party, Eagle pulled me aside and told me that he loved the treatment so much that if he were to sell a million albums, he and his wife would serve as my executive producers.

*   *   *

Eighteen months later—in a hip-hop minute—Eagle sold *ten* million albums, became the international ambassador of hip-hop, a fucking hero in his homeland, and wrote me the first of three checks for $250,000. The night after he won a Grammy for Best New Artist of the Year, we dropped Che off with my parents and went to Mr. Chow's to celebrate. We called Angela on the cell to announce, once our contracts were up, we were leaving her firm to form our own production company. Exhaling now.

*   *   *

We barely sat still at our table, waiting for one of Eagle's boys, who he just signed to his new label Nymphflo, and who I would develop in time for his debut at summer's end. Eagle dug into the pocket of his vintage beige sheepskin and pulled out a mini disc player for me to hear some rough cuts of what he promised were going to be musical biscuits. *"Girl, you got me so high like I'm flying in the sky,"* whispers Pharrell Williams in falsetto on chorus. Then this voice chimes in, *"I wanna lie with you / go to war for you / lace you with diamonds and shit / wanna dig your back out / want us to wild the fuck out / 'cause you make me so high / so high, I wanna touch the sky."* I could have written the video treatment right there on my napkin.

* * *

Picture a shirtless homoerotic homeboy by a tropical waterfall, surrounded by his fully clothed posse toasting him with bottles of Courvoisier. In the background, a spring chicken and her horny crew gyrate to the groove, making eye contact only with each other and dry humping the beautiful wet rocks on the river's edge. And then, just when homeboy walks over to her to profess his love, Pharrell slips in to take his girl away from him, 'cause you know, bitches ain't shit. I was not impressed.

Eagle's homeboy finally walks in to the joint and over to our crowded table, gives him a pound and his wife, Joan, a firm hug. We make eye contact.

* * *

Anthony was back in my life just as abruptly as he had gone, his eyes as intense and wide as I remembered, only now he was at least three inches taller than I. The noisy backdrop went mute as I stood up. Eagle Eye and Joan sat dumbfounded, as we stood there in total awe. After the longest two minutes of awkward silence in my life, he spoke:

"*You*

        are

             so

                  beautiful.

You look exactly the same as you did when I last saw you but more like a woman, I don't know. What would happen if I were to tell you I always knew we would be together somehow, someday?"

"Thank you," I said, stunned. "Why did you leave? I have a son. Are you back in my life? Is this for real, *papito?*"

"We found Lupe in the living room next to her altar; she died of a broken heart the last day I left you at the park," he answered. "Are you with your son's father? I went to live with Doña Lila in Corona. I couldn't come back."

"I'm so sorry, so sorry. No. I mean yes, I am, sorry. My son's father and I were never together. Still, Che, our son, is my greatest creation." This couldn't be real. I had to know. "Do you have a girlfriend? Kids? How do you know Eagle? *Papito,* I am supposed to work on developing *you.* I hate the shit I heard so far, it's corny, contrived." Then I whispered in his ear, "Time and space are concentric with the last thirty-six thousand days."

"I have thought about you often over the years. Do you believe me? A crush doesn't last this long. I don't know what I feel. No, I do. I feel sick; you're reminding me of Lupe. I go out with this white girl from Oakland but I want to come back home. Your eyes are sad and pretty. Why don't you like my songs? Eagle and I have known each other since I moved to Corona. I've compared all my women to the person I thought you might have grown into, so nothing ever worked. Can we get out of here?"

* * *

Without even saying good-bye, we bounced to the tiny apartment I was renting back in our old 'hood uptown. It was his first time back. We walked up to the second floor of my small, overpriced apartment and we sat right down on the hardwood floor. There we were, in the dark, by the entrance in front of the statue of Ellegua, the god who lived at every crossroad, who he had not seen since Lupe was alive, and started crying.

* * *

I was torn. All I had as a reference of how Anthony had grown was a sampler of product I could peddle but not accept. How would I reconcile my personal politics with his self-righteous sac-charine bullshit? On the other hand, I've learned from experience that what artists rap, sing, and rapsing about is rarely a reflection of their own truths, but who really wants to deal with a Gemini rising? Adding a white ex-girlfriend into the mix, Anthony's first single, "Brown Girl, Brownstones," and my own red-bone issues, made me disgusted with him. And yet, I felt, right there, right then, that not a day had passed since I had seen my soul mate. None of that shit mattered. *Wait, did I just say* "soul mate," *out loud?* I wondered. Then he turned around and cupped my face in his large callused hands, and said, "soul mate."

*　　*　　*

The phone rang, breaking the comfortable silence we were melting into. It was Joan. "What the fuck? Are you *there*? Pick up the phone if you are [pause]. OK, call me." We smiled. Then he slid his hands down to my shoulder, and leaned over to kiss my chin, my cheek, my collarbones, and my lips. We stood up then, frantically kissing, licking, and biting each other.

*　　*　　*

The slick, asymmetrical purple and green Grammy dress my favorite designer, Mara Hoffman, made for me fell to the cold floor exposing the Taino goddess Atabey tattoo her boyfriend Joshua Lord had etched on my left rib. Anthony knelt down, my fingers wringing his soft, tight curls, my other hand pulling off his red Zoo York sweatshirt. Anthony kneeled and lifted my leg over his shoulder, making it difficult for me to balance on one foot, in the purple Jimmy Choo stilettos he hadn't slipped off my aching feet. His tongue traced my Cesarean scar, down to my swollen clit, then he began to suck and bite, and suck and bite, slipping his index and middle fingers in and out of me. When I came, the tears rolled down my face, and into his beautiful mouth.

*　　*　　*

We spent the next season between my place uptown and his basement duplex in Brooklyn, where he drank way too much.

There was a dark energy in his place, and we never got too much done other than drinking and arguing about why he was drinking so much. "You ain't my mother no matter how much you remind me of her," he yelled once, "so shut the *fuck* up already." I would have walked on out anybody else who spoke to me like that, but something—I don't know—arrested me.

* * *

His home office, where we spent most of our time, was downstairs and fully equipped with a Fender rhodes, drum set, several iMacs, and some studio equipment. A smaller room in the back served as a guest room and den, where we stored several thousand CDs and some art we collected from touring where Anthony opened for Eagle Eye. Oddly enough, he rarely drank on the road, in the studio, or even at the countless open-bar industry parties we frequented. Anthony taught me about working on a strict schedule, how to focus, and introduced me to science fiction and cooking.

* * *

I shared with him books like *Pedagogy of the Oppressed* and *The Autobiography of Assata Shakur,* and world music. We wrote together, and I sat in on many sessions, sometimes with Che, who took an immediate liking to Anthony. Strangely enough, Che physically favored Anthony more than his own dad, Djabril— though little man looked more like my twin than my seed. Luckily for me, Djabril was too preoccupied with his own personal life and quest to beat me to the altar, to give me drama about dating Anthony. He'd recently gotten engaged to a very nice, subservient Italian girl named Drea because he was in love with the idea of being in love.

* * *

Anthony and I, regardless of what was going on in the world, took things very slowly. I mean, I didn't want to change him, I just wanted us to grow together. His upcoming LP, which we dubbed *The Hypnotic* was developing into a mature, lyrically superior introspection track by track. At any given time, Electric Lady Studios swarmed with more hip-hop royalty than all three of Puffy's thirtieth-birthday bashes. And every major magazine and music television station was vying for an exclusive after the buzz on his single "The Insurrection"—off the *Empire* sound-track—propelled it to multiplatinum status.

* * *

The challenge remaining was trying to knowledge Anthony to the world outside of New York, issues like the diamond conflict in Sierra Leone and South Africa, and how the hip-hop community supported the genocide to and by Africans, at least indirectly. Sometimes Anthony, preferring blissful ignorance, couldn't see the rain forest for the trees. Honestly, I couldn't blame him some-times for not believing in a God.

* * *

The door slamming upstairs behind Butterscotch woke me out of delirium. The air was thick with the smell of pheromones, cum, dry blood, and nag champa. Several hours had passed, I think. After I'd come back from wherever I had gone to, I opened my eyes to find Anthony lying naked next to me, twisting strands of my long dark curls, kissing my forehead lightly with his swollen lips. He mounted me, I sucked his tongue as hard and deep as I had his eleven-inch *pinga* earlier. We were down for each, regardless of his shortcomings and my, at times, self-righteous quips.

*   *   *

Madrina warned me not to sleep with a man who lived belowground because I was a daughter of Oya. It was too late, and I never could bring myself to tell him because I was living in the now.

PATRICIA ELAM

Scenes from a Marriage

When Baron told Lily about his plans to spend extra time with their daughter, Poem, she felt slightly jealous. He had never taken a whole week off to be with her. Why, they hadn't even had a real vacation together, just the two of them, since their honeymoon almost five years ago, and what a disaster that had been.

There they were sunning themselves in the beautiful Cayman Islands, yet she spent an inordinate amount of time watching Baron drooling over some guy on the beach. When he turned up later at the nightclub where they were sipping tropical drinks, Baron pushed away from the table, and followed him into the crowd. After more than ten minutes Lily went looking for her husband. She panicked after walking around the entire club and still hadn't found him.

When she decided to go outside, she glimpsed two figures on a gazebo a short distance away. Tears scalded her eyes as she walked resolutely toward them. The night air felt heavy, but it was softened by the tranquil breeze coming off the ocean. The blue moon cast a seraphic haze over the gazebo. It was a perfect night for lovers. Just not the ones she had in mind. If Baron had been any closer to the young man they would have been in an embrace. Lily stopped herself from thinking about what they had just finished or were about to begin. Instead she stood at the bottom of the steps and called out to Baron. The first time she said his name, only a choked sound came, so she repeated it clearer, louder.

Baron had the nerve to be impatient when he came over to her. He said he'd planned to come right back but China Doll asked him to step outside for a minute. (China Doll was the name she'd given the guy because, although his skin was dark brown, his kohl-lined eyes were slanted and narrow and his lips appeared to have been stained by purple Kool-Aid.) His long body was thin and fragile-looking. That Baron could be attracted to him confused her because China Doll didn't appear to be very manly.

She and Baron stood arguing in the middle of the sandy path between the gazebo and the nightclub. "I can't explain the attraction," Baron had said dismissively, until he saw the shimmer of her tears. "It's not going to make sense to you, Lily. You always ask these questions when you don't really want the answer. It will only make you feel worse."

"Try me," she said, disregarding the truth of his words.

He attempted to rest a hand on her shoulder but she brushed it away. "There's not just one type of man I'm attracted to. The fact that this guy looks like a woman but is a man underneath . . . I don't know . . . it does something to me." When she only gave him a blank stare, Baron shrugged. "I told you I couldn't explain it."

"This is our honeymoon, Baron. For God's sake, don't you have any respect for that?"

"Lily, I *know* it's our honeymoon. Why do you think I didn't go any further? I realize you hoped my feelings for men would dry up when I stuck a wedding ring on my finger, but it didn't happen—I just don't act on them. What you don't realize is, in a way he was doing us a favor."

"How?"

"Well, he, you know, made me hot."

"And so?"

"So let's take a blanket and go lay down on the beach. I want to make love to you."

*   *   *.

The thing she couldn't really explain to anyone, not even her best friend, Olive, was that in a way Baron's attraction to men turned her on, too. She didn't want him to actually be with anyone else; she just wanted him to come to her with the desire someone else had ignited in him. But she was always brought back to the same question Olive had asked when Lily first told her Baron was bisexual. Why would she get involved with him? She tried to explain how it felt to have a man in her life who simply wanted to be her friend, without an ulterior sexual motive. Initially, that had meant freedom. Freedom to talk, freedom to listen and share long-buried feelings. When their intense talks turned into make-out sessions, it was like having a boyfriend and girlfriend all rolled into one. Yes, they took AIDS tests, she'd told Olive, so everything was fine. After they married, though, the hunger for what she could not fully have troubled her like a bruise that had become infected.

Baron did find certain things about women attractive: the brave way they could invest their emotions and risk being hurt time and time again; their versatile options with clothes and hair; their bodies when they were slim-hipped and small-breasted like Lily. "I once read that the most perfect breasts are the ones that fit into a champagne glass, and that's what you have," he remembered telling her, holding out a flute to measure with. He liked kissing Lily and pressing their bodies together like palms in prayer. And, best of all, she had a formidable clit, which he often pretended was a small dick, making sucking on it a delight.

More than anything, he had wanted a family. Lily was a great friend who listened intently to him and seemed to care about his many attempts to relegate his gayness to the far corners of his life. He knew she would make a good mother because she had so much energy but was also extremely patient and kind. She was compassionate as well as passionate, laughed a lot and seemed to really feel joy, something he envied. Baron had been with other women before her who eventually grew tired of not being a sexual priority, but Lily seemed untroubled by that, back then. Nowadays, though, she was often irritable and frustrated with him. Had he killed all her joy? Did she sense he was spending more and more time thinking about the beauty of the male body and frequently wishing he was holding on to one?

* * *

It was late Saturday morning and Baron couldn't believe he and Lily were still talking about the week he wanted to spend with Poem. He finished cleaning out the refrigerator, tossing the spoiled food into the trash. He rolled up the newspaper he had padded the floor in front of the refrigerator with and told Lily she should be happy they wouldn't have day care costs for five days.

"Why does life have to be so complex?" she said, opening the dishwasher.

He didn't know what she meant. "Everyone's life is complex," he said, his mind drifting far from the kitchen where they were talking and Poem was sitting at the table in her booster seat, playing in her cereal. He thought about how he'd like to go to a club later in the evening. He hadn't been out alone in almost a month, trying to be the dutiful husband. One night at The Mill in Northeast or Wonderland over in Southwest could last him for another month. He knew he had to approach it strategically though, as if it were a military maneuver.

"Yes, but we *made* our lives complex. We chose to add complexity to the complexity that was already there."

"Sometimes I can't figure you out, Lily. I thought you'd be glad to have a husband who wants to be with his kid. Think about your coworker who always complains that her husband doesn't do his share. You don't have that problem." He didn't say that many times he contemplated what his life would be like with only Poem in it and that the upcoming week would give him an opportunity to experience that. He glanced over at Poem, wondering if it was unwise to have this conversation in her presence.

She looked up at him and said, "I'm eating all my food, Daddy." Her eyes, surrounded by soft, lush lashes, always eased his anxiety or stress.

"Baron, let's do something we haven't in a long time. Please. I want us to talk, really talk. Can we spend part of today just talking?"

He didn't want to think about, never mind talk about, what was on Lily's mind. He knew it already, like a fortune-teller. Baron let out an exaggerated sigh. "We *talk* all the time and we get nowhere. You complain about the same things and get frustrated with my answers."

"I want to go on the swings," Poem said, struggling to climb down from her booster seat. "I want to go outside."

"Get back up and finish your cereal, baby," Baron said, going over to help her. "Daddy will take you on the swings after that."

"Come on, Baron. What were your plans for today?" Lily leaned against the sink, watching him.

He shrugged. He didn't really have any plans. He had thought about jogging because a few pairs of slacks seemed a little tighter in the thighs lately, or maybe washing his car, then buying some yellow paint for Poem's room. But mainly, he thought again about calling his friends who hit the gay clubs most Saturday nights. They were from his pre-marriage days and teased him sometimes about getting a "weekend pass." He'd laughed it off but he was definitely overdue. So he decided to grant Lily's wish and talk through her concerns. It seemed like he had to do this more and more often. Lily's problem was she spent so much time thinking about the future instead of taking one day at a time.

Indian summer, he thought, wondering why it was called that. It should be called lazy summer. The heat wasn't the ferocious kind they'd had in August. Instead it was as if summer had decided to just take it easy for a while. He and Lily each held one of Poem's hands as they walked outside, even though she hadn't finished her cereal. "Spoiled girl," Lily chided, smiling. They then took turns pushing her in the swing and helping her dump her crate of toys into the sandbox. From all appearances, they looked like a normal family, Lily thought, and drew temporary comfort from it.

She left them and began to pull weeds from the garden in the rear of the house a few yards from the sandbox. Baron went back inside to make iced tea. Then he brought out the pitcher of tea and glasses and set them on the wrought-iron table next to the steps. "All right, Lily, now what do you want us to talk about?" He filled the glasses, leaned against the back stairs, and looked down at Lily getting her hands all dirty with the weeds.

"I just want to know if what we're doing makes any sense. I want to know if you want to get old and gray with me. I want to know that I'm not a fool." She was on her knees, staring up at him.

"And you think I can answer those questions?" He turned around to check on Poem, who was singing to herself.

"All right." Lily held up her hands, then continued. "One question at a time then: Do you love me? I know you love Poem, but do you love me?"

"You always ask me this. I wouldn't have married you if I didn't love you." He stared at the top of her head, not doing a good job of hiding his irritation. Lily's hair was pulled haphazardly back into a short ponytail. He liked when she wore her hair this way; it made her forehead prominent, her wide eyes seem smaller, and gave her a less delicate look. Baron poured himself more tea although his glass wasn't empty. Lily hadn't even tasted hers.

"Okay. But are you *in* love with me?" She moved around on her knees, yanking at the weeds trying to strangle her petunias.

"What does 'in love' mean, anyway? Why is it different from just plain 'love'?"

"Oh, who are you now—Bill Clinton?" She looked up at him to see if he was kidding.

He laughed. "See? I *love* your sense of humor, Lily. You can make me laugh even when I don't want to."

"I'm serious," Lily sighed. "I want to know if you're in love with me."

"I don't know how to answer because I'm not sure what you mean." Baron hiked up his shorts and got on his knees in the dirt with Lily.

"Daddy, Mommy, come play with me," Poem called out to them. She had a pail of sand raised high and ready to pour onto her doll.

"Hold on, baby," Baron said. "I'll come in a few minutes."

"Think back to someone you might have been in love with. Like that guy in high school you told me about," Lily said, turning to face him.

"But that's the point—I was in *high* school. What did I know?"

"So what. What was it you said? You craved him 'every waking moment.' " Some of the weeds were so entrenched in the soil, Lily needed two hands to pull them. Tired, she stood up to shake out her cramping legs.

"You don't forget anything, do you?" Baron shook his head. "I haven't felt like that about anyone since. Thank God. It wasn't healthy."

"I want you to want me but I can't be a man." Lily glanced over at Poem, who was covered with sand but happy. She squatted back down, resting her hands on her knees.

Baron brushed off his hands and stood up. He didn't really like the feel of the dirt and his knees weren't in the best shape. Plus the conversation was not new. He needed to reassure her without compromising himself. "I married you because you're the perfect woman for me. And you were willing. I don't want to hurt you, believe me. We have a unique situation here, Lily, one that most people think won't work. It's like we're persevering against all the odds, going where few have gone . . ." He reached out a tentative hand and smoothed her hair.

"So we're pioneers?" She smiled hesitantly, glancing up.

"Kind of. I mean, obviously you're not a man. If you were you couldn't have given birth to Poem and she's . . . everything." He watched his daughter dump some sand outside the box. "Don't do that, baby. Keep it inside, okay? But, Lily, to be honest, lots of women couldn't be as courageous as you." They looked into each other's eyes. "And I love you for that."

"I know," she said, feeling better.

"Maybe I don't say that enough to you. I love you. I appreciate you."

He drew her up off the ground, into his chest. She clung to him in the hope that it was one of those times when the forces converged to make him actually desire her (or seem like he did). She knew by heart the three times it had happened in the five years they'd been married: on the beach after the China Doll incident, the night he cleaned out his closet and found a joint in a coat pocket that they smoked for old times' sake, and the time they stayed up well into the next morning confessing unrevealed details of their previous relationships. "You'd hold on forever, wouldn't you?" he said.

As usual, he let go of her first, just as Poem yelled, "Help, Daddy! There's a bug in my sandbox."

*   *   *

When Poem was tucked into her bed for the night, Baron went to his study and made some phone calls to see where his friends would be hanging out. He didn't reach anyone directly but left several messages. Maybe it was better that he couldn't get in touch with any of them. He'd have a couple of drinks at a bar alone and would get back home earlier than if he hung out with his buddies. He showered without mentioning his plans to Lily, but when he came out of the steamy bathroom, she was perched on the edge of their bed wearing every sadness she owned on her face. Was he not supposed to do anything without her, or was it because she didn't trust him? He didn't consider himself having been physically unfaithful to her. Now, mentally, that was another story.

"Going out?" she asked, even though the answer was obvious. She loosened the scrunchie that held her ponytail in place and ran her fingers through her hair, letting it fall like a curtain across her face. She wasn't sure how to act but was glad that she felt somewhat in control. If she responded the way she felt she would yell at him about staying home with his family or ask why they couldn't get a baby-sitter for Poem so she could go along with him. She didn't want to start crying because lately it had no effect. He used to hold her and try to soothe her. Now he'd sigh and stay away from her until she finished. Once Baron made up his mind to do something, Lily knew she couldn't stop him. He'd ask why she gave him such a hard time when she could go out anytime she wanted with her girlfriends. And sometimes she did but she usually didn't want to. Her girlfriends had their own families who they did things with, she'd say.

She decided to remain calm, not expend the energy it would take to fall apart, and act aloof instead. He would know, probably, that it was an act. "All I wanted was to be a family with you," she said, instead of everything else she was thinking.

She surprised him. He had expected a storm. Even though there was an edge to her words, he could handle it. He sat beside her, feeling his own weight as the mattress yielded. "We *are* a family," he said. "I won't be out late, I promise." Then he kissed her cheek, which she did not turn to him.

"Who's going with you?" she asked, trying to sound nonchalant.

"I don't know yet," he answered, knowing he'd better make his exit hasty before she broke into a thousand pieces. He rose, grabbed his pile of underwear, slacks, and a lightweight sweater and dressed in his walk-in closet, watching himself in the mirror. *I'm still attractive,* he thought. *Someone at least should want to talk to me, buy me a drink, give me a phone number, something.* Mentally listing his possibilities made him hard. He wouldn't do anything to screw up his family, though, he reminded himself before he rushed from the house.

* * *

Lily was proud that she hadn't broken down in front of him. She was hurt that he'd dressed up, primped himself for a club full of men. She hated to admit that he looked good. His sweater hid the slight paunch he had developed, so he appeared more toned than he was. The gray hair creeping into his locks and beard seemed to glisten when he had sat down to kiss her. She didn't want to think he'd actually have an affair. But there was something he obviously needed at the clubs. To flirt, to pretend he was free, she didn't know exactly what. Baron seemed to sparkle when he was in there, so carefree and happy. She had gone with him once in the early days but watching the men grinding and sucking each other's tongues was more than her heart could take. Was that really what her husband wanted to do? She just wanted to be with him. Why did she have to love someone so unattainable?

She fixed herself a bath, then turned on the Jacuzzi. She had read somewhere that you could achieve orgasm by positioning yourself just so, beneath the jets. She knelt and moved near the forceful stream of warm water and closed her eyes, gripping the side of the tub. Images of Baron masterfully eating her pussy enabled her to climb to ecstasy amid the porcelain and the water. When he was in the mood, he lapped and sucked her so well, she didn't even mind that he couldn't fuck her as hard as she liked. Despite everything else, he loved her pussy. Long after most straight men would have called it a day, Baron would keep on licking, making her come again and again.

Before she turned down her bedcovers she checked on Poem, asleep under her Winnie the Pooh comforter with her mouth open. Lily kissed her softly on the forehead. This was the reality of what she had of substance with Baron: Poem, and that was it. She didn't know how to make it be enough.

*   *   *

Baron drove to the Wonderland club with his car stereo blasting Jill Scott; he sang along at the top of his voice: "You can't get in the way of what I'm feeling . . ." His cell phone rang. Probably Lily, ready to let him have it. He glanced down at the digital display and saw it was his friend, Carter. He hooked his hands-free into his ear quickly, "Hey, man, been trying to reach you. I'm on my way over to Wonderland. Can you meet me?" Carter couldn't. He was at the airport about to fly to New Orleans for a twenty-fifth college reunion.

"Damn, any other time," he said. "This is a rare occasion I would have made sure not to miss." Baron didn't say anything in return, just took the tease.

"How are your girls?" Carter asked.

"They're fine."

"Okay, well, I hope you find whatever you're looking for tonight."

"I'm not looking for anything."

"Yeah, okay. I'll call you when I get back in town, see what you caught without looking."

The club was darker inside and louder than he remembered. Nelly's "Hot in Herre" was blaring through huge speakers. Baron started sweating immediately so he pushed up the sleeves of his sweater. He was feeling slightly awkward, alone in the cavernous club. Wonderland was, without accoutrements, basically one large warehouse room with a wooden dance area. Every inch of the place was packed tight with male bodies. The crowd was mixed tonight, though there were more black men than white. People were feverishly dancing in every available space. He got bumped more than a few times as he headed toward the bar. Along the way, a particularly agile young man was expertly doing the "Harlem Shake" as other admiring men gathered around, egging him on. Baron made his way through the gyrating bodies for a closer look.

The man at the center of it all was beautiful and quite young. He was bald with smooth, glistening light brown skin. Baron thought about what it would feel like to rub up against his bald head. Perspiring profusely, the man, still in constant motion, stripped off his shirt and tied it around his waist, revealing a perfectly chiseled chest. Baron was captivated.

The circle of onlookers began closing in around the dancing machine. Baron was forced to the front by the crowd. The young man began pulling people toward him, trying to get them to dance with him. Most turned him down, afraid to challenge him. Baron just wanted to look at him. Surprisingly, he felt his body moving in rhythm with the young man's. Ordinarily, Baron couldn't do the "Harlem Shake" worth a damn (his nephew had tried to teach him to no avail). Somehow with the combination of Nelly's beat and such visual inspiration, Baron became aware that he was doing it. He smiled and let his body do its thing. Baron closed his eyes, allowing the music to engulf him, then he felt a touch. The man was reaching out to him, grabbing at his sweater, tugging on his elbow. He grasped Baron's hands and drew him closer. The crowd parted around them. Baron focused only on the young man, letting his body drift toward him. The man yelled something to Baron. "What?" Baron cupped his hand to his ear.

The man moved in close and grabbed Baron by his shoulders. Baron could smell alcohol on his breath. "You're drenched. Why don't you take that hot sweater off?" he said. Although Baron loved looking at the young man's six-pack chest, he certainly didn't want to strip himself. Not here, anyway. But he was flattered that this beautiful young man was coming on to him. After all, from what he could see, this boy was the hottest thing in the club! Baron had barely gotten his foot in the door and someone wanted him. He could almost leave now; he had gotten what he needed. Somehow living with Lily, pretending that he could live without a man's touch, felt like he had given up part of himself. Or more accurately, ripped out the very core of his being. This guy's interest in him filled that empty place.

The young man put one hand on Baron's waist and began dancing against his leg, writhing around him like a snake on crack. He took one of Baron's hands and put it on his sweaty bare chest. Baron could feel how fast his heart was beating. This experience alone was worth what he'd have to go through with Lily in the morning. The DJ played another song, something he didn't recognize and couldn't dance to as well. He contemplated leaving again.

As if reading Baron's mind, the young man took his arm and led him off the dance floor. "Don't get lost," he said as they made their way through the crowd. Baron tried desperately to keep up as they stepped through the maze of lively, uninhibited men.

They walked into a smaller room in the rear of the club with red leather chairs and couches and another bar. Barry White was playing back there, rather than the house music up in the dance area. Couples were scattered about the room in a myriad of positions. Some were locked together in heated embraces on the couches. Others were deep in conversation at tables along the walls. There were no empty seats so Baron and his new friend leaned against a wooden pillar covered with painted renditions of Cupid. His name was JQ and he was a professional dancer who had even been in a Kelly Price video. "You were looking so serious on the dance floor," JQ said. "I wanted to bring you out of your funk. You out of it yet?"

Baron laughed. "Is that how I looked?"

JQ nodded, looking past Baron. "Hey, there's a booth," he said, pointing across the room. Baron followed his finger to two men who were leaving a tip on a table close to the bar. Baron sat down first, expecting JQ to sit across from him; instead he scooted in next to Baron, their thighs touching briefly under the table. Baron leaned his elbows on the table, pretending to study the plastic art deco frame listing the mixed drink prices.

"Want a drink?" JQ asked.

"I think so," Baron answered. "I got all worked up out there. I guess I was looking serious because I was concentrating so hard."

"I saw. You were definitely saying a little somethin'-somethin'." They both laughed, easing the tension Baron had felt leaving the dance floor. He now took in all JQ's fine points. His smoky eyes with eyelids at half-mast as if he were high or very sleepy and his swollen lips beneath a curly mustache that made Baron wonder what his pubic hair looked like. Could this fantasy dream lover really want him? He needed a drink to calm himself.

JQ caught the waiter's attention without even raising a hand but then he could catch anyone's attention. By the time the waiter returned with their drinks, JQ had asked about Baron's wedding ring and Baron had told him the truth, that he'd been married five years.

"So I'm curious—what happens when you get that insatiable craving for a man's lips, shoulders, thighs, and beyond . . . ?" JQ whispered, leaning in close to Baron.

"I take matters into my own hands," Baron said chuckling.

JQ wasn't chuckling with him. He looked at Baron intently. "You're fooling yourself, man. Do you mean to tell me you haven't touched another man for five damn years?"

Baron felt a little uncomfortable. He hadn't told anyone what he was about to tell JQ. It was a relief though, he realized, as he spoke. "Nothing heavy. I've gone to a couple of clubs and done some rubbing and grinding and hugging up in the dark. I've had my shit sucked a couple of times, jerked off in the same room with somebody. But no, I haven't gotten that ass in a very long time, if that's what you're asking. This is actually my first night out in a while. I feel like I should be satisfied with my family and my work. Think about it—there's nothing out here, really, except a bunch of horny men. Society at large treats you like crap, so why bother? I'm not telling you anything you don't know. I took my time, got it all out of my system, screwed my brains out. Thank God I didn't get AIDS . . ."

JQ turned toward Baron and studied him. "You sound bitter, man. And you obviously *didn't* get it out of your system."

"I guess not," Baron agreed, somewhat reluctantly. "I just always wanted a family. And in terms of what I was seeking to accomplish with my life, I thought a wife and kids would make things easier. They're like the currency you need in this world."

"Okay, so now that you've got your currency, it's all right to go prowling around in gay bars?"

Baron just shook his head. It didn't matter whether he was telling his story to someone gay or straight. No one ever understood except for the time he had gone to a meeting of gay married men, but they were all white. Their wives, for the most part, acknowledged their lovers and in a couple of cases the lover even lived with them part-time. Baron didn't want something that extreme. But he did want the occasional freedom to step out and mingle for a few hours without feeling guilty. And he sure wished he could do something about the raging heat he felt from JQ's thigh being wedged up against his. He knew the best thing for him to do was to go on home. He glanced at his watch. "I gotta go."

"Now?"

"Yeah."

"Before you get into trouble?"

"No, just before it gets too late." He reached into his pants pocket for his wallet and placed a twenty-dollar bill on the table. When JQ covered Baron's hand with his, Baron found himself unable to move. Something inside him that had been tucked away, banished, and nearly forgotten, seemed to break loose as JQ's long fingers wound themselves around his. Luther Vandross was crooning, "It's so amazing to be loved. I'd follow you to the moon and the sky above."

"Can I give you my card before you go? I dance at private parties." JQ's eyes sparkled mischievously. The waiter returned to see if they wanted refills. JQ did, Baron didn't. Someone was laughing outrageously in the booth behind them and it annoyed Baron. He turned around but it was too dark to make eye contact. A couple in leather vests, who had been humping against the wall since Baron and JQ sat down, moved away from their post, apparently in need of a more private spot for their transactions. Baron tried not to think about it but he wondered briefly what it would feel like to not be undercover, to walk out into the night with JQ and allow the feelings to ebb and flow naturally. He took the card JQ handed him. JQ Rawlins/Entertainment Services, it read. He stuck it inside his wallet.

"You want the truth?" he said without thinking. "Sometimes I hold my wife and I wish I was holding a man. I touch her and wish she had a dick. If it's dark enough I can pretend. It's fucked up, I know. What the fuck am I doing to her and to me?"

JQ didn't answer, just continued caressing Baron's fingers,

hand, and on up his arm. Baron was sure his goose bumps could be felt through his sweater. "Well, you obviously care about her," JQ finally said.

"I mean, don't get me wrong. I guess I'm still somewhat bisexual because she can get me hard and everything but not as hard as when I'm with a man. I can come but I don't explode, if you know what I mean."

"I know exactly what you mean," JQ whispered, his hand slipping down near Baron's crotch.

Baron gently pushed it away. "It was great meeting you, bro," he said, feigning nonchalance. "I gotta go."

"Give me a kiss first." JQ turned toward Baron, blocking his exit.

Baron cautiously pecked at JQ's cheek. "Okay, now let me out."

"I know you can do better than that. Give me a real kiss, then I'll let you out."

Baron stared at the smoothness of JQ's skin, the thickness of his lips, the way they were slightly parted, waiting. He looked around, his heart pummeling his chest. No one was paying them any attention. Baron moved in closer and bent his head to meet JQ's. He sighed when their lips touched, at how soft they were, at how perfect the kiss felt. JQ leaned forward and slipped his tongue inside Baron's mouth and Baron sucked on it until he couldn't stand it anymore.

"All right. That's all you get," Baron said, abruptly ending the kiss.

"That's all I wanted, motherfucker," JQ laughed.

*   *   *

Lily had called Olive but reached her voice mail and left a message. It didn't really matter. How could she expect people who weren't in their situation to understand it? There had to be some way to make it work; she just hadn't figured it out yet. Meanwhile she hadn't been able to sleep. Lily glanced at the clock. Two-thirty A.M.. He had left a little before midnight. She switched on the television and finally drifted off watching an old Alfred Hitchcock movie on the A&E channel. Then the phone rang, cruelly waking her from what felt like the briefest nap.

"I'm sorry, Lily. I must have been sleeping when you called. You said you needed to talk?"

It made her feel a little better to know that Olive cared. But she didn't want to talk now, she wanted to sleep. So she said good night, promising to call in the morning.

He should be home soon, she thought as she hung up the phone. She hoped he'd want her when he came in. If he came to her tonight, she promised herself she wouldn't ask him anything about what he'd done, where he'd been. She slipped out of bed and went into the bathroom. She stood in front of the mirror and traced the areas she wanted him to touch—her ears and neck, around her breasts, her belly and between her legs—and then she perfumed them with scented oils. She loved her husband a great deal and wondered, as she slipped into a nightgown, why sometimes that seemed like a crime. When she heard his key turning in the lock she switched off the beside lamp.

Baron entered the bedroom and lit a candle. Its flame seemed to beckon to her from the dresser. He undressed silently and then slipped into bed beside her, propping himself up with a pillow.

"You sleep?" he asked softly. She slid close to him and clung to his waist. "Take your nightgown off," he commanded in a whisper. When she raised it above her head, he began slowly kissing her neck, sending waves of sparks down to her inner thighs. She wrapped her leg around one of his and began pushing her pelvis against him, moving until she located his hardness.

"Yes," she sighed, closing her eyes, opening herself all the way, so that he could take her at anytime, all of her, more than her, whatever he wanted or needed. He held her tightly, kneading her shoulders with his hands and bruising her lips with his, ramming his tongue between them. One hand left her shoulder and found its way down to her clit, rubbing until it throbbed and swelled in his grasp. Then he turned her over and mounted her from behind.

"Is this ass mine?" he breathed into her ear, sucking at the lobe.

"God, yes."

"Is all of it mine?"

"Yes, Baron."

"Does it feel good?" he asked

"Yes, Baron, it's good. Oh, it's so good. . . ."

"Baby?" His breath was coming in quick snatches then.

"Yes. Yes . . ."

"Can I . . . ?"

"Yes, whatever you want."

"Can I call you JQ, baby?"

With his eyes closed, Baron could almost believe he was holding JQ until he felt Lily's tears. This time he cried with her.

Standing Room Only

Rena took a long hit of weed. She sucked in deep, allowing the skunky mist to filter down into her lungs, back up her trachea, and take a final dance through her nasal passages. She let it linger there, savoring the aroma, holding her breath as she studied the joint in her elegant, French-manicured fingertips. She watched the fiery red ash crackle and spark as it released its pungent funk into the air.

"Puffpuffpass, bitch, puffpuffpass. Damn." Anisette plucked the joint from Rena's hand and took an impossible drag that revealed far too much about her favorite habit. She talked without losing an iota of smoke. "This is my shit, you know. You're hitting it like you know I got some more."

Rena ignored her and exhaled. Of course there was more. Anisette was never caught without her lah. Even her stashes had stashes.

Rena sipped her Cadillac margarita, the fifth one in less than an hour. The room was spinning, but she could still make everything out. She was broke off, but functional.

"Whose party is this?" she yelled.

"For the last time, fuck if I know," Anisette said. "And I wish your drunk ass would stop screaming at me. I'm two inches away from you. Fuck."

She walked off, taking the wonderweed with her. Rena almost cried, just watching it go. She didn't care about Anisette leaving. Even though she was Rena's best friend, when Anisette got blazed she became bitchy and short-tempered, which wasn't much of an improvement from her natural state.

For Rena, the result was the opposite. She didn't smoke much, but when she did, weed worked just the way it was supposed to, with the requisite *h*'s in full effect: happy, high, horny, and hungry. She was always all four. More horny than anything. Mad horny.

Like now. She was hornier than ever these days. But she didn't have a boyfriend, and sex with anyone outside the convention of a real relationship just wasn't her thing. It had been a minute since she'd had that kind of intimate interaction. More than a minute. Dog minutes. It felt like years.

Her senses tonight, compliments of the weed/margarita combo, were operating on red alert. She was aware of everything. Negligible shifts in temperature translated into alternate moments of her skin breaking into a minor sweat, then catching a chill and her nipples bricking up beneath her thin silk top. Eau de toilettes collided with eau de stank, overwhelming her ability to breathe.

The room was the typical, dim-lit L.A. club scenario, stuffed to the gills with The Beautiful Ones. This was an S.I. party: Somebody Important. Some comedian/athlete/singer/designer/celebrity. All the you-knows-in-the-who-knows were there. Cristal was poppin' and Belvedere was flowing free, along with Courvoisier, Grey Goose, or whatever the liquor of the moment was. Rena was glad that weed never changed. It wasn't trendy. It was what it was and that was that. If anything, a better, stronger version emerged. No brand names necessary.

Everything tonight was a blur of color. Overstuffed couches in private rooms, too much titty, too much thigh, a whole lot of makeup, real hair, real weaves, bulging pecs, the outlines of six-packs and biceps rippling beneath formfitting shirts. Sparkling cocktails with glow-in-the-dark ice cubes, the glint of gold and bling-bling, platinum chains, platinum teeth, things that had no business with precious metal wrapped around them. And black, everywhere black. Black tables, black chairs, black sunglasses, black hair, black eyes, the crack of a black ass in a black dress that plunged way too low in the back.

The noise was what affected her most. The music was sheer cacophony, a series of unbearable beats that no longer differentiated one song from the next. Everything was loud. The whole room was a din. With her senses this heightened, it was as if she could hear hearts beating, toilets flushing, gossip flying, lips smacking, nuts being scratched. Every speck of sound seemed enhanced, magnified for her listening torment. She needed a diversion, something to shift her focus from the mayhem. Perhaps, she figured, she'd order another drink.

Rena wobbled, apropos of nothing. She recovered quick and looked around to see who noticed. A gaggle of near-naked super-hoes next to her smirked and looked off. Rena giggled. Yup, this was it. This was the elusive one. The nirvana she'd been searching for. Anisette wasn't joking when she said she had some bomb chronic. Rena was zooted. She was high, high, high, high, hiiiiiiiiiiiiiiiiiiiiiiiiiiiiiiiiiiiiiggggh, like the song playing at that very moment declared.

She scratched a phantom itch at the back of her neck.

"Dick nails," said a husky voice close to her ear. It was a whisper, but in her current state, the pitch of everything was at peak volume.

Rena jumped, sloshing some of her leftover drink on a woman next to her. "Sorry," she stammered, as the leggy chick stormed off. Rena licked the juice from her fingers and turned around. She found herself staring into a pair of hazel eyes hovering above an incredible sexy grin.

"Wha . . . ?" she muttered.

"Dick nails," the sexy grin repeated. He was stroking her left hand now, turning her palm around. "You've got dick nails."

She was too stunned to react with logic. Any other time, she would rebuff an uncouth statement like this and the guy who made it, but something about him gave her pause. His tone was quite pleasant and matter-of-fact, like he was commenting on the cut of her hair or the turn of her heel. She didn't get the usual creep vibe that signaled the need to exit, stage left. She gave him the once-over, the twice over, the thrice.

He was eye level, her height, just the right size. His hair was a shock of curls, begging for fingers to get tangled in it. He was beautiful, the color of deep honey, a golden god who seemed to materialize from nowhere, dressed in black from crown to heel like a fucking super-ninja. Black turtleneck. Black slacks. Black shoes of the most exquisite leather. Thick black lashes framing luminous eyes. His build was perfect, a balance of solid and slight. Not one of those towering hulks of overexercised meat working the room, but choice USDA. One hundred percent lean beef.

A sudden image flashed in her head. It was a scene from one of her favorite movies, *Pulp Fiction*, a close-up of the words written on Samuel L. Jackson's character's wallet: bad motherfucker. Yeah. This cat in front of her right now? He was a bad mother-fucker.

In the midst of her high, Rena had great clarity. She willed herself not to reach out and touch his hair. Instead, she cleared her throat and took another sip of her drink.

He smiled again, bringing her hand to his lips, pressing them with light pressure against her skin.

"What are dick nails?" she asked.

He held up her fingers as if on display.

"These," he stated with authority, "are dick nails. Look at them." He moved her hand to and fro as if it belonged to him. She watched him maneuver it, an entity outside herself, almost like it wasn't a part of her body.

"Your fingers," he said, "are nice and slender, very ladylike, and the nails are well-manicured. Long, but not vulgar or ghetto." He looked her in the eye, his voice calibrated with undisguised suggestion. "You just know that a hand like this knows how to hold a dick. Knows how to treasure it." He turned it around and kissed it again. "This? This hand right here? This is man's natural cradle. Dick nails and all."

Rena threw her head back in laughter. What he'd said was absurd, but it was smooth. The smoothest, boldest thing she'd heard in a while.

"That's interesting," she said. "In the eighties it was my eyes. 'You've got bedroom eyes,' was all I heard. I didn't know what those were, either."

"You do," he said, peering into her face, tilting his head a little. "They're nice. Very suggestive."

"Whatever. Then, in the nineties, it was dick lips. 'You look like you can suck a mean dick,' was the line. The fact that I like mine glossy didn't help the situation."

Rena noticed him studying her mouth.

"But this is some new shit," she said. "This is definitely extra. I guess dick nails are what's happening in the new millennium, huh?"

She drained the last of what was left of her sloshed drink and laughed again. As the happy gurgles worked their way up her throat, she felt her left hand being pressed against a bulge.

No, he does not have my hand on his dick, she thought. *OhmiGod. He has my hand on his dick.*

She didn't move, and neither did he. Instead, he pressed her deeper into the folds of his slacks, and her hand, no longer needing any guidance, conformed itself to the shape of him, the thick, long curve of his shaft. She followed the bronze dick road. It veered a little to the left.

They stared into each other's eyes. He was smiling. So was she.

"You want another drink?" he asked.

There was something different for certain about him. A lilt in his voice, a kind of musical quality that came at her from an angle she hadn't noticed at first.

"Where are you from?"

"Would you like another drink?" he asked again.

Rena ran her nails along the tip of his dick, right at the head, toying with the slit in the surface she could feel beneath the fabric. She squeezed. He gasped, his eyes closing with instinctive pleasure.

"Shiiiiiiiiiiiiiitt."

"You're from Shiiiiiiiiiiiiiit?" she whispered. "And where would that be?"

He opened his eyes. The dark lashes framing them created a spellbinding effect. His pupils danced with a wicked gleam as he pressed her backward into the bar counter behind them. Her hand was still on his dick. His hot breath was on her neck, just below her ear. She couldn't tell if the sensation of his tongue against her skin was real or wishful.

"What are you drinking?" he persisted.

"Cadillac margaritas. Where are you from?"

He gestured to the bartender for a repeat order. His face was still pressed into her neck as his tongue, with delicate flicks, made its way up her chin, around the perimeter of her mouth. Rena couldn't believe they were even doing this. It was like she was outside of her body watching herself. This was the kind of stuff white people did in the club, that public making-out shit. Black folk didn't do this, did they? At least, she didn't think so. But times had changed, and she was kind of out of the loop.

Something about this man was unleashing her inner freak.

Yeah, she was high, but she'd been high before. She was a little bit bent, but liquor never made her lose her senses. This was different, and it wasn't just about horny. It was about him. She was brazen now, a borderline ho. Her hand, still fondling the outside of his pants, roved his heated stick and made its way lower to cradle his balls. They were firm, the size of fresh eggs. He groaned as she juggled them. She opened her mouth to speak again, and he covered her lips with his.

Rena's head was awhirl, queuing up all the requisite clichés. "I don't typically do this," "I'm not that kind of girl," "I don't even know your name," "It must be the weed and the liquor," "I don't usually get high."

"Fuck it," he said, pulling back, as if reading her thoughts. "I don't do this either. But I'm doing it now."

Rena had unzipped him and was feeling hot flesh against flesh as her hand searched inside. A vein running along the side of his dick grew fat with excitement, making him pulsate and throb in her hand. She moaned against him and he moaned back. He slid his right hand beneath her silk top, cupping the fullness of her fleshy 36C breast. With his thumb, he fingered the nipple, plucking it rough like the thickest string of an upright bass.

"Twelve dollars," the bartender said with a smirk, placing the drink on the counter behind them.

Mr. Sexy reached into his pocket and pulled out the money. His hand, through the fabric, grazed against hers playing inside his pants. He threw a twenty on the counter and took a sip of the drink.

"Nice," he said. "Nice and mellow, kinda strong."

"Everything with you is nice, isn't it?" she said.

"Nothing wrong with that. Nice is a beautiful thing."

She noted the melody of his voice and asked again.

"Really, where are you from?" She leaned into him and, before he could respond, she cupped his balls with mock threat. "If I were you, I'd give me an answer."

He laughed, deep and thick.

"You'd do that to me, wouldn't you?"

"In a second," she said, quite at ease with his balls in her hand. "I always heard that, if you squeezed them hard enough, you could make a man die."

He pulled her closer, smiling.

"Please. Whatever you do, don't kill me." He hesitated, then had some more of her drink. "I'm from abroad."

She clutched his balls a little closer.

"Abroad is damn big. That pretty much covers everything outside the U.S. Be more specific."

He slid his hands beneath her blouse again and cupped her breasts with the same degree of threat. She laughed.

"Trust me, that won't do me any harm. If anything, I'll just end up coming real hard the more you squeeze them."

"Now that's a visual," he said, and closed his hands around them tighter, this time with both thumbs plucking her nipples.

"Omigod," she groaned, closing her eyes. "Stop it. Don't do that. You're killing me."

He stopped.

She lowered her head, her eyes narrowed.

"If you don't keep squeezing my tits like that, I swear, I'll pop your balls right now."

He kept plucking.

"Where abroad?" she asked, the words enveloped in a moan.

"Africa."

She leaned back a little, dissecting his face. She would have never guessed African. At least, not any African that she'd ever seen. He didn't look like he came from the northern end of the continent, nor did he look Middle Eastern or Egyptian. He wasn't anything tribal and dark, like the images she'd been bombarded with as a child by *National Geographic* and those Save the Nation commercials. He was just a gorgeous black man, period, fuck his place of origin. If she'd had to pick, except for his accent, she would have said American. But what the hell did that mean? Everything in America these days was one big Rorschach blot of confusion.

"Does that satisfy your curiosity?" he asked.

"Yeah, that's better," she said, "but can you narrow it down just a little bit more?"

"Why don't we let that be enough."

He slid his right hand down the inside of her skirt into her panties. She didn't resist. An Asian woman to the left of them watched with unmasked lust. Rena parted her legs a little, giving him clear access to the wetness that was rampant there. He put his finger in it. She felt faint and leaned against the counter.

"You okay?" he whispered, his mouth pressed against her ear, his finger pushing deeper inside her pussy.

"Fuck you," she grunted. "You know damn well I'm not okay."

"Then I'm doing it right?" he asked in that voice. A spasm rocked through her inner thighs and her knees buckled again.

A small group of people near the bar watched them in amusement, but this was L.A., and freaky shit happened all the time. Even though this kind of thing wasn't typical of Rena, that fixture known as the Playboy Mansion, the prevalence of porn at every turn, and an overall cloud tinged with sexuality that seemed to hang in the air had long desensitized folks in this city to the shock of PDF—Public Displays of Fucking. So while the watchers were captivated for a moment, they were soon diverted by a more explicit girl-on-girl scene that was heating up in a private room nearby.

"What's your name?" Rena asked.

"Josef."

"Josef what?"

"Josef from Africa."

She made a sound that was part groan, part chuckle, that bubbled up as he rubbed her clit just the way she liked.

"Africa can't be your answer for everything," she said. "You have to have a last name. Suppose I want to see you again?"

"Then you will."

"He says as he has his hand inside my snatch."

"She says as she has her nails around my balls," he replied with a laugh. "What's your name? I'm in the same position you are."

"Not quite," she said. "My name is Rena."

She had never been this high before. Her head was floating somewhere in the stratosphere and her body was hot as the depths of hell. She wanted to fuck. If she didn't know anything else about herself, she knew that much. She wanted to fuck and she wanted to fuck now. She wanted to fuck a stranger. What would he think? What would her mother think? What would she think of herself in the morning, once the weed and all the Cadillacs wore off?

"Do you have a condom?" she asked.

With bold assertion, she ran her free hand through the rash of curls on his head. The hair was a soft thicket, a mass of blackness that sucked her in.

"Yes."

"Yes what?"

"Yes, I have a condom," Josef said, holding up the silver packet for her to inspect.

Rena grinned and took it from him. She pulled her other hand from the inside of his pants.

"Maybe one of those rooms is free," he said, gesturing toward the myriad private coves that peppered the club.

"Why do we need a room?"

He gave a small laugh.

"Um . . . okay. Well, if we don't need a—"

Rena had torn the packet open and her hands were in his pants before he could finish the words. She slid the thin sheath over his rigid shaft, giving him an extra squeeze when she got to the base.

"Are you sure you want to do this?" he said.

"Just shut up and fuck me."

From the way they were standing, they appeared no different than two lovers at play, fondling, doing the same club tango of hundreds of others around them. It wouldn't have been considered conspicuous behavior. But prying eyes could tell it was not just lovers' play. The Asian woman watched Rena's hands as she slipped Josef's penis beneath her skirt, past her panties that were pulled to the side, into her wetness. She watched him pump, grinding his hips into Rena. They could have been dancing. With the music thumping mad beats, their fucking was in rhythm to the movement of everything else in the club.

The bartender knew what was up, but he'd seen this bit before. The club fuck wasn't original, and it damn sure wasn't new. But it was new to Rena, and as Josef rammed his thick dick into her pliant, slick pussy, she held on to the thatch of curls on his head and stared into his eyes, daring him to fuck her harder, daring him to make her come.

"You're so tight," he whispered.

"Compared to what?" Rena whispered back.

"Tight is tight."

"You talk too much," she said. "I love it. Keep talking."

She grabbed his butt and pulled his firm round ass into her. He thrust harder, the left curve of his dick hitting the right corner pocket of her pink as though it had been there many, many, many times before.

"Look, he's fucking her," the Asian woman said to a buff chocolate could-be celeb who stepped up to the bar.

The guy glanced over at Rena and Josef entangled together. He stared for just a second or so, then turned back to the Asian chick.

"I ain't mad at 'em," he said with a churlish grin. "Fucking makes the world go round." He ran his forefinger along the area just above her breasts. "Perhaps me and you can do like them and take a little spin."

Her face grew perkier with recognition.

"Hey, don't you have that new show on Fox?"

"Yeah, something like that," he said, reaching for the bottle of Cristal the bartender handed over. "C'mon, me and my boys got a private room," he said, pointing to a cove in the back. "Let's go have a drink and maybe get our nice on like these two over here."

He extended his arm. She attached hers and went off with him.

Josef's tongue was making its way down Rena's neck as she held on tight and bucked against him.

"Your pussy is amazing," Josef moaned. "It feels brand new, like it just came out of the showroom."

She laughed. "I love the way you say 'pussy.' Poosy. Poosy. I like you in my poosy."

Rena's body was swirling as she felt the nut building up inside her. The blend of the watchers, the weed, the back-to-back drinks, the pounding music, the hit-and-run love from a stranger, that curved dick rubbing all the right spots, that damn tangle of curls, those hazel eyes, and the threat of impending remorse— all of it was crazier than anything she'd ever experienced. She screamed long and loud as she bust, a wail that made Josef bust right behind her, throbbing, jerking, wiggling deep inside the vibrato of her heated sex. He slumped forward onto her with moans just as raucous.

No one seemed to care about what happened but them. It was an L.A. club, after all. The Asian chick was long gone, in a private room down the way, giving mad heezy to the big black actor with the new Fox show, and some of his boys. The bartender had just plugged a waitress during a quick break five minutes before, so his libido, for the nonce, was a little at ease.

Again, it wasn't a big deal. Sex was no longer as sexy as it used to be for peepers and passersby. It wasn't a surprise to catch fuckers in the act. If folks looked hard enough, it was always happening, somewhere close, right beneath their noses. Random sex in L.A. was ritual. It was ambient sound. A backdrop, like smog or tacos. Like backed-up traffic on the 405.

When Josef came, he didn't pull out right away, which Rena loved. She savored the feel of him inside her. Even though he was limp, she felt plump with the fullness of him as she relished their lingering bond. In the midst of all chaos around them, in that space and that moment there was nothing but the two of them and a little slice of peace.

"You know what's really beautiful about you?" Josef said as he held her, stroking her hair. "This city is full of gorgeous women, but when you look them in the eyes, there's an emptiness, like they're dead inside." He stared into hers. "But you have this light, this twinkle. It makes it hard for me to look at you, but I don't want to look away."

Rena blushed. Josef pulled out of her slow. She could feel every inch of him as he broke their connection.

"I think I'd better find the bathroom," he said.

"Yeah, that might be smart," she said.

"Promise me you won't go anywhere."

His voice, she thought, *ohmigod, his voice is killing me.*

"You promise you'll wait for me?" Josef asked again.

She smiled, knowing that, if it were up to her, she would never leave.

"I'll be right here," she said without a hint of her inner glee. "I need to go to the rest room too, but I'll meet you back here at the bar, in this same spot. Cool?"

"Cool beans," he said, looking just as happy as she felt inside.

They went off in opposite directions. Rena glanced over her shoulder. He was watching her leave as he made his way to the bathroom. He bumped into someone and offered an awkward apology. Rena got chill bumps. This was a stranger in a club. Why in the hell was she feeling this way?

She walked into the bathroom, which wasn't as crowded as she expected, grabbed some paper towels, dampened them, soaped them up, and went into an empty stall. She thought of Josef as she cleaned herself up. What did she expect from this? It was crazy, a literal one-night stand, not even a lay. She was stoned. The whole scenario was about as trite as they came.

But it was nice. Real nice. And he felt like he could be different, like maybe there was some magic there, lurking beneath his surface. She smiled as she flushed the toilet and adjusted her clothes. She walked out of the stall at the exact moment that her girlfriend exited the one beside her.

"Where the fuck have you been?" Anisette screeched, jarring the semisleeping bathroom attendant from her twilight state.

"I was at the bar," Rena said. "Right where you left me."

Anisette's eyes narrowed as she searched Rena's face.

"Well, it's time for you to go home. Your ass is lit like a Roman candle."

"No, I'm not," Rena said, smiling. "I'm fine. I'm chillin'. I'm quite relaxed."

Anisette peered into her face again and frowned.

"You're bent. Whenever you get that stupid vacant grin like the one you've got now, I know you've had enough. Let's go."

Anisette grabbed her by the arm and walked out of the bathroom. She headed toward the exit.

"I'm not ready to leave just yet," Rena said. "I was having a good time."

"Well, I'm not and I gotta get up and go to work in the morning."

Anisette led the way, bumping and elbowing people aside.

"I met a guy tonight," Rena said. "He seemed pretty cool. We had this intense connection and we talked about all kinds of crazy stuff. It's like nothing was off limits for us."

"Yeah, well he's probably played or a liar or gay or some fake wanna-be or has forty babies' mamas just like every other mutha-fuckin' loser in this tainted-ass town."

"Damn, Anisette. Why bother to go out, then? Why bother to get high? I thought this was supposed to be fun and we were supposed to relax?"

Anisette barreled ahead.

"It was. We were. But it never is, and we never do."

"Well, I did."

Rena looked back, searching the club for a sign of him. The sexy hair, the smile. Those incandescent hazel eyes.

"He was funny."

"Who?" Anisette asked. "What the heck are you talking about? I'm not giving you any more weed. Ever."

"The guy. My new friend. Josef. He had me cracking up. He said I looked like I had brand-new pussy. Poosy."

"Oh please," Anisette said. "Whatever. That is so ridiculous. Ain't that a British band or some shit?"

"What?"

"Yeah, The Brand New Pussies. I can't believe you even fell for that shit. His ass ain't even original and you bit."

"You mean The Brand New Heavies. He wasn't talking about a band. And he was original." Rena paused. "He looks like he'd be a fantastic fuck."

"A fuck is a fuck is a fuck is a fuck."

"Not necessarily."

Anisette stopped walking and looked back at her. She studied Rena's bright happy face. There was something different, beyond her usual chipper disposition. There was a glow, a nuclear thing that had Rena's brown skin a little flushed on the surface.

Nah, she thought. Rena wasn't that bold. All the weed in the world wouldn't make her break character and do something crazy like that. Anisette was the one with the wild hairs, and most of those bad boys had long been plucked. She was jaded and angry, disgusted with everything. She got faded to take the edge off a little, because life had gotten way too hard.

"Rena, you need to get rid of that silly, naive look you're always wearing," she said. "People are gonna take you for a sucker with a look like that, and I won't always be around to run interference." She started walking again, tugging Rena along behind her.

Rena glanced back over her shoulder and spotted Josef at last, leaning against the bar where they'd found each other and fucked. He stared as Anisette led her away. He beckoned to her, his hazel eyes large, magnificent, hypnotic.

Anisette was still bitching as they walked toward the door.

". . . and the minute he said 'pussy,' you should have stepped off. He showed you right then that he ain't got no respect for you." She whipped out her valet ticket. "Umma roll another joint when I get in the car. This party was wack. All the same guys, all the same bullshit."

Rena stopped, pretending to rummage through her purse.

"Hey, I think I left my lipstick in the bathroom," she said. "I'm going to run back and get it, okay?"

"Hurry up. I'll be in the car getting blizzled. You're right. I don't know why I even bother to come out anymore."

Anisette burst out of the front door of the club. Rena did an about-face and saw Josef walking her way. She smiled.

The light in her eyes twinkled at the glimmer in his as the two of them made their way toward each other across the crowded dance floor—past the thick smarmy club element and the sideshow freaks—two beacons in the night trying to make sense and order from a bar fuck.

It was possible. This was Hollywood.

Crazier things had happened on an L.A. night.

MICHAEL A. GONZALES

Crazy Love

*L*ester Jones often found solace in the exhilarating arms of full-figured strangers. Moments after Precious, one of the hefty hookers from Hot-N-Tot Escorts, left Lester's space-age bachelor pad the sweetness of her perfume still hovered in the rooms; fruity as fragrant flowers drying between the faded pages of a Henry Miller tome. After weeks of ogling her big booty in the back pages of *The Village Voice,* he'd decided she would be the perfect present for his fortieth birthday.

Precious rang the doorbell of his Harlem apartment at midnight. Her luscious 44DD, 36-44 body was encased in a form-fitting black minidress, a red wig, and tacky platforms. "Hey," Precious purred, walking into the darkened foyer carrying a small backpack containing various costumes.

"Thanks for coming out so late," Lester said.

"It's my job, baby," Precious answered. Sashaying across the cream-colored shag carpet, she surveyed Lester's messy digs. "You got a room I can change in?"

"Sure," he replied, escorting her to the cluttered bedroom in the rear of the massive apartment. Closing the door behind him, he returned to the living room, sat on the crimson velveteen couch and sipped his sixth Grey Goose gimlet.

Emerging minutes later wearing sky-blue crotchless panties, a matching bra, and thigh-high vinyl boots, Precious slinked down the dim hallway toward Lester.

Having always equated sexiness with strength, Lester admired her stalwart legs, sturdy hips, and the few tattoos covering her plump figure. On the small of her slightly fuzzy back was a crudely drawn butterfly, while on her right breast her name was written in script reminiscent of young Catholic girls practicing their penmanship.

"You look beautiful," Lester said, smiling. Pulling two hundred dollars from his leather wallet, he paid her for the hour.

For the next few minutes, Precious and Lester smoked a joint while a Moog synthesizer version of "The Look of Love" played on the stereo. The small Dolby speakers stashed in the ceiling throughout the apartment surrounded them in swelling sound. Stroking her smooth skin, Lester couldn't wait to lavish moist kisses on her bulging belly and bury his face in her Rubenesque rolls.

"What do you like?" Precious asked, her eyes reddening from the potent smoke. "You want a golden shower or Greek or a vibrator in the ass or what?"

"Just regular sex is fine," he said. Unbuttoning his black J. Crew shirt, Lester beckoned her to lie down. His thin body was deeply tanned, having returned from shooting a catalog spread in Miami the week before.

Unlike other men he had spoken to about buying pussy, Lester got no pleasure humiliating women who humped for money. Forcing them to choke while performing blow-jobs just wasn't his thing. Indeed, a few of the whores he had hired over the last year had commented on his tenderness between the sheets. To Lester it didn't matter if he was making love to a hooker or a girl-friend, he tried to treat them with the same respect.

Leaning over he massaged her full hips and rubbed her belly. Tenderly opening her legs, he gently licked the thick stream of black hair that began at her belly button and led directly to her pubic area.

For the next forty-five minutes he was lost in the fleshy wilderness of her massive thighs, floppy breasts, and juicy buttocks that shook like Jell-O. After pulling out of her comforting wetness, they slipped onto sexual highway 69 and Precious worked her tongue over his circumcised cock with perfect skill. Approaching orgasm, cool sweat dripped down Lester's back as every nerve in his body relaxed. Closing his eyes, he tilted back his head and released a blissful moan.

Afterward, as he did with most of the transient women who drifted through his life, Lester asked if he could take a picture of her heavy bottom for his permanent collection.

"Like porn?" she asked wearily.

"It's just for my private collection," he answered. "I like to think of it as more like an art project." Altogether, Lester had approximately five hundred ass pictures in numerous albums stashed in a closet near the kitchen.

He had buttadelious pictures of chicks in thongs as thin as dental floss and snapshots of girls with beautiful behinds spreading their sweet cheeks with bejeweled fingers. There were images of Brazilian hookers with perfect posteriors gripping their asses; jungle-red nail polish setting off their tans, and Jamaican dance-hall girls with bubble butts the size of beach balls. As his lifelong homeboy Oz had once exclaimed, "Nigga, you got your own Booty Museum."

Looking around the apartment, Precious noticed the many framed prints hanging on the bone-colored walls: the gloomy sideshow freaks by Diane Arbus, a Margaret Bourke-White shot of the bombed-out streets of Nuremberg in 1945, Roy DeCarava's Harlem kids splashing in a fire hydrant, and a Gordon Parks shot of a poverty-stricken family.

Gesturing toward the photographs, she said, "Well, I guess. You seem to be really into this photography thing. Did you take all these, too?"

"Naw, those were taken by friends of mine," he lied, amused by her naïveté.

Lester retrieved his wrinkled jeans from the floor and stepped into them. Opening the closet door, he located the old Polaroid he used only for these occasions. Switching on several table lamps, he had great hopes of capturing the perfect picture. Positioning her on the couch, Lester tenderly coached her through several shots.

After posing for the pictures, Precious changed back into her street gear. Standing at the front door, Lester slipped her a forty-dollar tip. "Thanks," she said, stuffing the loot into her bag. "Maybe I'll see you again sometime."

"Maybe," Lester answered, closing the door behind her.

Drunk, melancholy, and still horny, Lester retrieved a photo album from the closet shelf and stumbled barefoot across the floor. Lying back on the sofa, he lit a Newport, then gazed longingly at artifacts of sexual escapades past.

* * *

In all his years as a photographer, Lester's only regret was that he didn't get a chance to take a booty picture of his first real crush. Closing his eyes, he could hear his eighth grade class's childish din, smell the slop steaming in the cafeteria, and see the particles of chalk dust drizzling to the floor. Taking another gulp from his drink, Lester smiled when he remembered the comely moonface of a light-skinned girl from his schoolboy days.

Anna Martinez was much larger than the other girls in his class, but far more beautiful, with her warm olive complexion, budding breasts, molten chocolate eyes, and luscious lips. While Anna got along with the other kids, often overextending herself in hopes of acceptance, this didn't stop the class bully, Tom Lowe, from teasing her during recess. "Fat girl! Fat girl!" he chanted whenever she was within his radar.

Since Lester had a serious crush on Anna, he should have done a few Jim Kelly kicks on the foul-mouthed thug. But he was afraid to speak up in fear that he would become Tom's next victim. He also didn't want anyone to know that he had a thing for a fat girl.

While Anna usually ignored Tom's taunts, one day she snapped. "Leave me alone!" she screamed, her face reddening in anger, her hands forming fists at her side. As Lester stared at her,

Anna's brown eyes revealed a bugged-out wildness that had been absent moments before.

"Or what?" Tom jeered. "Or you gonna sit on—" Before he could finish Anna grabbed Tom around his scrawny neck, and started frantically choking the devil out of him. It took two nuns to finally pull her off of the beat-down bully. As Sister Marquez and Sister Margaret dragged Anna through the steel doors of the school, the young girl's face beamed. Almost thirty years later, Anna's crazed expression remained frozen in Lester's memory.

* * *

Still celebrating his birthday two nights later, Lester and Oz were partying at Brutal, the latest in-crowd watering hole. Slouched in the leather booth, black clouds of chatter, cigarette smoke, and rhythmic symphonies hovered overhead. Twin soul brothers from different mothers, they were dressed like trendy burglars in black T-shirts, black jeans, and black Prada shoes. As DJ Chairman Mao played Slave's post-disco classic "Snapshot," they sipped their chilled martinis surrounded by the nightlife niggarati of players and posers.

"To a new decade and a new job," Oz toasted.

"Forget about the decade, but the new gig is something I'll drink to," replied Lester, lifting his glass.

Having grown up in the same sagging tenement, the duo went back farther than spades and Pro-Keds. Oz worked as the house stylist at *Blur* magazine, a glossy urban-style bible with more attitude than vision.

"Lemme see if I got this straight, Lester," Oz slurred. While he had gained a bit of weight since the days of their youth, Lester was still rail-thin. "Your skinny ass got a gig working for a fat girl mag?"

"It's not a 'fat girl mag,' you insensitive bastard. It's called *Lush* and it's a magazine for plus-sized women. You know, women with a little more flesh than those arty anorexics you work with."

"You sure are sensitive when you're sober. More flesh sounds like fat to me," Oz quipped, draining his cocktail. "Don't hate 'cause I work with fly girls and you're being hired as a chubby chaser. Jesus, just think of how many new installations for the Booty Museum you'll find there."

"Not just any chubby chaser, *chief* chubby chaser," Lester joked. "Anyway, I've been thinking about closing the Booty Museum. I been doing that shit for the last twenty years. I'm forty years old. Maybe it might be time for me to get a new hobby."

"Like stamps or comic books?" Oz asked, laughing so hard he almost spit out his drink. "The Booty Museum is a fucking institution. One of these days those pictures are going to be the topic of intellectual discussions. What Robert Mapplethorpe did for the black man's johnson, you could do for the fat female booty."

"Be serious," Lester laughed. "We both know those pictures are more suited for *Black Tail* than a museum wall."

"What is it about them big chicks you like so much anyway?" It was a question he had asked Lester often, but could never seem to remember the answer.

"I don't know, man. Maybe the nurse that slapped my newborn ass was a chunky mama. Maybe it had something to do with sneaking peaks at the thick R. Crumb girls in your brother's underground comixs. Maybe it comes from watching my buxom god-mother's sway in the sun at summertime picnics. Who knows?"

"Keep the pictures, bro. They're a part of you, a part of your history. What was the name of the first big broad that posed for you? That chick who lived around the corner from us? The one with the pretty face and the Dominican daddy?"

"Devin 'Sweet Ass' Sanchez," Lester answered, with a wicked smile.

"Yeah. Nigga, ya'll looked like the number ten walking into the room." Oz chuckled. "I can still see you now, coming home smelling like snacks."

"You know, for a straight man you sure do act like a faggot sometimes," Lester snapped as a zero body fat, jet-black African model carrying a Lana Marks peacock embroidered pocketbook paused at their table. Making brief eye contact with Oz, she smiled and slipped him her comp card. "I'm not a faggot," Oz said, waving the card at Lester. "I'm in fashion."

* * *

Prior to landing the new gig as "chief photographer" at *Lush* magazine, Lester had done pretty well as a freelancer. Working as an assistant to Gordon Parks the summer after graduating from The School of Visual Arts, Lester had started shooting for various publications. His images of New York City street life were in the sorrowful style of his heroes Weegee and Brassai. From crackhead singers on subway platforms to thugs in Times Square to grizzled grannies eating out of garbage cans, Lester had lovingly documented almost every street in the debauched city.

But, truth be told, constantly staring at despair had started making him feel uneasy. His dreams became spooked by the sadness of the ghost people that haunted the city: of toothless women screaming at invisible children; soiled men staring with vacant eyes; and sickly babies crying from hunger. Other than document these mournful scenarios, Lester felt there was nothing he could do to lessen their plight.

Lester was thankful when Oz had gotten him a few fashion shoots at *Blur* that enabled him to expand his horizons as well as his portfolio. It was his recent neo-blaxploitation spread that had caught the discerning eye of *Lush* founder and editor in chief Nikki B.

A brassy redbone from Baltimore, Nikki had once been down with the Condé Nast Mafia until she'd had the misfortune to gain some weight after a bad breakup. Yet, with the creation of *Lush*, she no longer had to worry about being ostracized by wanna-be Kate Moss waifs. No longer shrouding her ample flesh in all black, Nikki was clad in a skin-tight black-and-gold dress with matching shoes. Half diva and half drag queen with painted bee-stung lips and a husky cigarette-stained voice, Nikki was a former Jack 'n' Jill sister with a "round da way" sensibility who was as comfortable shopping in Paris as she was scoring coke in Washington Heights.

"It's all about shattering the beauty myth," Nikki boasted at their first staff meeting. "We all know that the majority of the women in the country have more curves than they want and less style than they need." The entire staff tittered at her joke. "It's our goal to make *Lush* the sacred manifesto for sizable sisters. When they have no one else to turn to, they *will* turn to us."

Nikki then introduced Lester to the *Lush* team before they retreated to her small office. "Just throw those clothes on the floor," she said, pointing to the modish Cassina couch. Spinning in a black leather chair, she waited patiently for him to get situated, before she continued. "It takes a visionary to recognize other visionaries. I know I am and I know we're going to do great things with *Lush*."

"Thanks, Nikki," he replied. "I can't wait to start working on some ideas I have. Been thinking about maybe doing a film noir theme or maybe even a Swinging London-styled shoot. Something very Emma Peel."

Nikki seemed to be listening intently, but mentally she was trying to locate a lost Chanel bag in her closet. "That's all well and good, Lester, but the key word for this first issue is sultry. We want the big girls of America to know what it feels like to be hot. Just because they wear a size eighteen don't mean they gotta wear floral-patterned trash bags. Victoria isn't the only bitch with a secret."

Nikki reached under her desk and emerged with a yellow-topped Kodak box. "This is our *Lush* lady," she said, tossing the package across her desk. Staring at the pictures, his heartbeat quickened and his mouth dropped open. Inside was a set of sexy lingerie shots of a stunning beauty Nikki introduced simply as Summer Poole.

Wearing leopard-strap stilettos, Summer stared seductively at Lester from the pictures. Her sumptuous body recalled Anna Nicole Smith in her early nineties' Guess girl prime. While Summer had a flawless cocoa-colored complexion and rust-hued tresses swept back in a Bohemian style, it was her tempestuous eyes that caused Lester to swoon. "She's a real looker," Lester said.

"We pledged Delta together at Stanford," Nikki replied. "Summer was like a black valley girl in those days, but now she's just another mad New Yorker."

"That's a party I wish I had been invited to," Lester said, carefully placing the pictures back into the box.

Nikki swung her shapely legs onto the desktop and lit a Marlboro Light. "For our first shoot we're going to feature the new Oscar Dash collection. I want you to think torch singers. You know, give me some Billie Holiday vibe."

Inspired by Summer, Lester thought of the perfect place. "I know a spot uptown called Frankie's Paradise, one of those old-school joints where Max Roach and John Coltrane used to battle, but now it's filled with Japanese tourists yearning with yen for the true black experience." Lester chuckled.

"Everybody wants to be black except black people." Nikki shook her head. "Look, we have Summer booked for next Thursday, so we have till then to make this perfect. And I want a cover shot out of this shoot, Lester." She finished, then shooed him out of her office.

* * *

For the next week, Lester Jones immersed himself in the canon of melancholy songbirds. Roosting on the electric-live wire that separates sentimental visions from romantic redemption, Lester conjured in his mind loving couples sweetly smooching in the summer rain. In his head he envisioned pictures that were a cross between William Claxton's fifties' jazz icons and Henri Cartier-Bresson's atmospheric portraits of Paris. Streaming from the silver Sony stereo speakers in both his office and home was a loop of bygone torch goddesses. Lester found himself lost in the strange fruits of Billie Holiday, staggering down Parisian promenades with Edith Piaf or belting back shots of scotch with Peggy Lee.

* * *

Now that the crack wars were finally over, the once-blighted block where Frankie's Paradise stood was on the upswing. A decade ago, most civilians stayed away when the streets had been filled with dope boys dressed in Dapper Dan suits and gaudy gold medallions.

Sitting on one of the high-backed barstools, Lester watched as the magazine folks straightened mirrors, shined the black baby grand and swathed the tables with crimson cloths. His assistant, a pretty young Goth girl with aspirations of being the next Arbus, arranged his equipment and dressed the one white wall with a textured, plum-hued backdrop. With the exception of Summer Poole, everyone was on the set. On the far side of the room, Nikki B. and the designer were having a heated exchange.

"She's on her way," Nikki screamed. "What do you want me to do?" The expensive silk scarf around her neck fluttered furiously. Without responding, Dash, followed by a one-armed Hispanic stylist, stalked to the clothing racks and began violently sorting through his captivating creations.

Across the room, Lester stood and programmed some songs on the juke. Moment's later Peggy Lee's "Fever" belted from the box just as the bells on the door chimed and Summer swept in like a storm. As she breezed past Lester's chair, he caught the sour fumes of last night's Jack Daniel's mixed with Elizabeth Arden's 5th Avenue perfume seeping from her pores. In Mikli sunglasses, a funky red T-shirt with the Living Colour logo, tight jeans, and sneakers, Summer had obviously dressed quickly.

Sauntering her shapely size fourteen self across the floor, Summer clutched her brown leather Louis Vuitton purse containing her essentials: M.A.C. lipstick, Newport cigarettes, cell phone, two-way pager, Reese's Peanut Butter pieces, a few purple pills of Kaleidoscope ecstasy, a half-gram of blow, boxes of matches, and loose sticks of Juicy Fruit gum.

"The diva has arrived," Nikki said sardonically. Standing with her manicured hands on her wide hips, she impatiently tapped her foot as Summer strolled toward her. Nikki playfully slapped her old acquaintance on the head. "You think you're Naomi Campbell? Tripping the light fantastic again last night, were we?"

Summer paused in front of her and lit a cigarette. "I don't remember tripping, but I do have a bruise on my ass, so who knows what might have happened." She'd broken the ice. They all cracked up. No matter how late she was, her remark endeared her to everyone in the room.

Lester walked over to Nikki. Like an Orchard Street tailor, Summer sized him up from head to toe. "And this lovely gent here is our chief photographer, Lester," Nikki said, introducing him. Smiling, the two shook hands.

"You sure this skinny boy can properly shoot all of me?" Summer joked, seductively licking her full lips.

While he was slightly nervous inside, Lester played it cool. "Don't worry, you don't scare me," he replied. "I've had lots of practice with full-figured women."

"I bet you have," she replied, tipping the chunky frames of her shades down to reveal mesmerizing eyes heavily shadowed by mascara. Lester noticed a strangeness simmering just below the surface of her stare. It was Lester's theory that one could always identify the crazy ones by their disturbing peepers.

Staring at her Living Colour shirt, Lester asked, "So are you a fan or is that just a fashion statement?"

"Of course, it's a fashion statement," she sassed. "But why don't I play you my version of Vernon Reid's solo from 'Cult of Personality' and you can find out for yourself." Lester smiled, impressed by her knowledge of a man he considered a guitar god.

"All right, enough small talk, kids," Nikki said, pulling Summer over to the makeshift makeup/fitting room. For the next hour Frankie's Paradise smelled of beauty products and brewing coffee. After a terse meeting with the designer Oscar Dash, stylist, and makeup artists, Summer was ready.

Watching her emerge from the dressing room, the crew was struck by her metamorphosis from wounded party girl to chic chanteuse. Wearing an earth-toned beaded dress with plunging neckline and matching shawl, her skin shimmered under the golden hue of body powder. Her hair was styled in a Veronica Lake upsweep and the jade pendant around her neck nestled seductively in her cleavage when Summer draped herself across the top of the piano.

"I'm ready for my close-up," she purred.

Unlike those photographers who'd watched *Blow-Up* one too many times, Lester didn't believe in bullying his subjects into submission. To him, women were already visual masterpieces and it was his job to frame and display them properly. As sordid as Summer was when she walked in, none of it mattered now that she was in front of the camera. From the moment she stepped in front of the backdrop, Summer illuminated the room.

For the next five hours Summer styled in strappy stilettos as Lena Horne sang "Stormy Weather" and romped in front of the microphone mimicking Dionne Warwick's maudlin "Message to Michael" clad in a velvet burnout one-shoulder dress and silver mesh mules. Later, wearing a glamorous chiffon tiered gown and wrap, she smiled wickedly at Lester as Dinah Washington crooned "Cry Me a River."

Throughout the shoot, Lester cracked corny jokes and shared silly anecdotes about his Harlem childhood.

"You have more stories than Bill Cosby," Summer laughed. From her constant chuckles, Lester could tell sweetie had a thang for funny men.

With each flash, Lester felt a deeper connection between her troubled eyes and his own sensitive soul. Smoldering in front of thick crimson curtains in a slip dress with white lace highlighting her pretty cleavage, Summer fluttered her feathery lashes and Lester's already excited cock completely hardened.

When the last shot was taken, the entire room burst into applause and Nikki popped the cork of the first of many bottles of champagne. Half an hour later, the first unofficial *Lush* magazine party was in full effect. "My two babies," whooped Nikki, handing Summer and Lester glasses while kissing their respective cheeks. "That wasn't a fashion shoot, that was a religious experience. You guys are gonna be the new David Bailey and Marie Helvin."

Two hours and countless bottles of Moët later, they were more bombed than Hiroshima. Buzzed from the bubbly, they slumped against one another in the velveteen booth and traded war stories from their damaged lives: fucked-up childhoods, fucked-up lovers, fucked-up friends, all compounded by their fucked-up decisions. Including their obvious excessiveness, they had a lot of fucked-up things in common.

"That shoot today took me back," Summer said. "You know, when I was at Stanford I sang in a band. One of those smoky soul groups that did covers of Sade and Prince. We called ourselves Chocolate Suicide, thought that shit was real deep," she laughed.

"I bet 'Smooth Operator' never sounded sexier," Lester said.

After refilling her glass, Summer seductively swigged the golden liquid. With her long piano fingers, Summer gently stroked the bristles on his freshly cut hair. Relaxing beneath the power of her touch, Lester wanted to stretch like a big black cat.

"You couldn't tell a bitch she wasn't the second coming of Tina Turner." Summer continued settling in close to Lester. "When that spotlight came on, I just lost my mind. My real life might have been shit, but at least when I was on that stage I felt loved."

"Sometimes the simplest things can soothe the chaos," Lester said. "That comes directly from the *Intoxicated Philosopher Handbook*," he joked, trying to lighten the mood.

Summer was still wearing the turquoise dress and high-heeled mules that Lester knew would be the cover shot. Lester slid his hands under the table and found Summer's silky legs. Facing her in the booth he lifted her legs onto his and started massaging her shapely calves. Summer could feel his erection against her leg, but neither mentioned it. Lester then slipped off her shoes and gently rubbed her feet, softly stroking her instep.

"I wish my mother could see me right now." Summer eased back into the booth and sniffed, close to tears.

"Is she dead?" Lester asked, draining his glass. They were both a few drinks past drunk.

"Not hardly," she slurred. "She's just somewhere mad that her fat, good-for-nothing daughter became a model. When I told her I was going to model, you know what she said?" Without waiting for an answer, she continued. "'You're too fat to be a model.' That's what she said."

"Why do I get the feeling this isn't the first time you've sung this song," Lester said.

"Fuck you!" Summer screamed, suddenly slapping Lester across the face, her nail leaving a small scratch under his left eye.

And so the seduction dance begins, he thought. With a swift movement he grabbed her wrist, holding her until she calmed down. "Come on, you know I was just joking with you."

"Well, you think you know me, but you don't, so let go of me, you bastard," she yelled, spittle flying in his face.

Releasing her, Lester watched as Summer wobbled to her feet and rudely pushed past him, storming into the bathroom.

"What was that madness all about?" asked Nikki B., rushing over to the table.

Rubbing his face, Lester smirked. "I was just practicing to be a lion tamer," he joked. "It was my fault. Once again, I acted like an asshole. I guess I should be going. Just do me a favor and have my assistant take everything into the office."

Stumbling toward the exit, he turned around and saw Summer emerge from the bathroom and smile coquettishly at him, as though nothing had happened. Rubbing his finger across the scratch, Lester wanted her crazy ass more than any woman he had met in a long time.

*   *   *

The following morning, wearing a tiny Band-Aid on his face, Lester sat at his desk nursing a hangover. The hum of fluorescent lights overhead threatened to drive him bananas. Pushing open the door, Nikki B. sashayed into his office.

"You look terrible," she said. "You shouldn't try to keep up with Summer . . . that bitch drinks like a marine." Nikki, on the other hand, wearing a Gucci T-shirt, vintage jeans, and a gorgeous pair of Jimmy Choo shoes, looked like she'd just left a spa. "How's your face feeling?" she asked.

"I'll live," he answered.

"Between you and me, let me school you on something," she said. "I love that crazy chick like she was my own sister, but be warned that she has more baggage than a bellhop. I know men love them koo-koo for Coco Puffs girls, but Summer can be out there sometimes. You know what I'm saying?"

Under the desk, his cock hardened at the mention of her name. "Did she say anything about me?"

"After she took one of her purple pills, she said you reminded her of a black Fred Astaire. Remember when he played a photographer in *Funny Face?* Well, that's her favorite movie, so I suppose that's a good thing," she sighed.

"I've always thought of myself as a skinny John Shaft. You know, a sex machine." Lester half joked.

"Look, the real reason I came in here was to tell you about this Friday. Oscar Dash is previewing the collection you shot at a fashion show at The Four Seasons. I want you to shoot the show for *Lush*. And have your assistant drop off the contact sheets from yesterday. I'm dying to see them."

After Nikki exited his office, Lester picked up the phone and called Oz. Recounting his misadventures from the night before, Lester rubbed his aching head when Oz howled with laughter.

"And I suppose you're now emotionally charged," Oz stated. "Probably imagined her big-boned ass dancing naked in Manolo Blahniks to 'Baby Got Back' while you jerked off all night long."

"Just until I passed out," Lester groaned.

"You're just a glutton for punishment, aren't you? Am I the only one who remembers that your last crazy love accused you of having sex with her dog? Or when that dusted chick started stalking you a few years ago? And I know you remember that chick Anna from eighth grade. After she flipped out on Tom Lowe you couldn't leave her alone. Then when ya'll finally got together, she damn near blinded you with a pencil because she *thought* you were diggin' somebody else? Why can't you just find yourself a nice bookish girl you can talk about poetry with and leave those drama divas alone?"

"Bookish girls are boring," Lester answered. "You know, a brother needs a sister with an edge. I'll take crazy over boring any day. Especially when they're built just the way I like."

"I heard there's a few sane fine girls floating around the city, too," Oz said, exhaling an exasperated breath. "I'm sure Freud had a name for brothers like you," Oz chuckled. "I just don't know what it is."

* * *

The days crept by with the swiftness of a snail, and not a moment passed when he wasn't reminded of Summer. In her massive Ashley Stewart billboard above Times Square, Summer's voluptuous body hovered like a bronze deity over the mighty metropolis, adding to the *Blade Runner* visage of the cityscape.

By Friday night, the mezzanine bar at The Four Seasons was full of perfectly pudgy women with perfumed skin and sultry smiles holding out glasses to grizzled white men pouring potent cocktails. A creature of the night, Lester relished the art of sipping and small talk as Nikki introduced him into the society of full-figured style warriors at the post–fashion show shindig.

Standing amid the laughter and chatter he was dressed in a sleek black linen Boss suit Oz had messengered from the *Blur* office. Trying not to be obvious, he scanned the crowded room for Summer. Their eyes had locked earlier when he saw her saunter down the catwalk. His body was so tense with anticipation that it took him a minute to realize that the vibrating near his groin was coming from his cell phone.

Without checking the caller ID, Lester put the phone to his

ear. "I've felt you thinking about me, Fred Astaire," Summer cooed.

"Is that a fact," he answered smoothly. "Was I tap-dancing at the time?"

Summer giggled. "You made me look like a princess in those pictures." When she paused dramatically, Lester imagined Summer licking her plump painted lips. "I have a limo parked directly in front of the fountain outside. I'm there now waiting for you."

Coolly flipping the cell phone closed, Lester dashed down the two flights of stairs to the lobby. Standing in front of the glass doors, he saw the grand fountain flowing in all its glory. Through the rainbow mist he caught a glimpse of the shiny black car beneath the glowing streetlight. He was at the car door in a few steps. A moment later, he was inside.

Wordlessly, the two night birds stared at each other. Summer, who was looking at the world through Ecstasy-colored eyes, wore a Marc Jacobs multicolored dress and matching go-go boots. Moving toward her booming body, Lester grabbed her shoulders and kissed her neck, gently nipping her earlobe as she sank into the buttery leather seats. When he had finally worked his way up to her soft lips, she bit his thick tongue sharply.

"What the fuck is wrong with you?" he yelled. Summer giggled. Then hiking up her dress, she pulled her sheer underwear to the side and lay back. Then she spread her freshly shaved legs and caressed her moist clit with the middle finger of her right hand. The same finger she had scratched him with.

Lowering himself from the seat, Lester held Summer's full hips and buried his face in her moist panties before gently pushing them aside to kiss her wet pussy lips. Like a wolf lapping from a fresh spring, he dived in deep as though dying from thirst.

*   *   *

From dawn till twilight, they explored each other's bodies with the precision of poets, speaking in a lost language of lust and love and unbridled desire. With an insatiable hunger he worshiped her ass, dripping melted candle wax and rubbing his swollen penis between her curvaceous crack. Although she wouldn't allow him to put his dick into her behind ("I have to save something for the man I marry," she kidded), it didn't stop Lester from massaging Summer's dimpled cheeks while exploring her curvy derriere with his sensitive fingers and an ecstatic tongue.

For the next three days, the seductive scent of her stickiness lingered through the rooms of his apartment. For once, instead of making love on the couch like some frat boy, Lester took Summer into his bedroom. When they were exhausted from making love, Lester and Summer would indulge in various drugs, order takeout from the Dominican spot around the corner, watch bits of bad Lifetime movies, and share chocolate ice cream from the same spoon. When he told her a joke, the tinkling sound of Summer's laughter was like music to Lester's ears.

"I'm glad we decided to start our friendship from the beginning," he confessed the next morning as they lounged in bed watching Looney Toons.

"Why is that?" she asked, snuggling down deeper into Lester's embrace. Lying close to her, Lester thought that their bodies seemed to fit each other perfectly.

"There aren't many people I feel comfortable waking up next to," he answered, kissing her sweetly on the forehead.

"From this point on, let's not have any secrets from each other," Summer said.

"Don't worry about that, baby girl," he said. "My life is an open book."

Drifting into an exhausted coma Sunday night as he lay close to her warm body, Lester was happy for the first time in a long time.

Monday morning, Lester awoke to the aroma of brewing Bustelo and a strange chemical odor. Getting up from the bed, he pulled on his bathrobe and opened the bedroom door. Sleepily rubbing his eyes, he scanned the spacious flat and heard Summer whistling "You Are the Sunshine of My Life" in the kitchen. It was then he noticed the locked closet door where he kept his prized Booty Museum pictures was open.

Adrenaline surged through his body when he realized the toxic smell was coming from his bathroom. Cringing, he rushed into the vaporous room. The burning chemicals stung his eyes. Through smoke-induced tears he saw countless Polaroids of beautiful backs, enchanting hips, and robust rumps were in various states of deterioration in his bathtub. Luxurious lasses with heavenly asses and divine cheeks that were smooth to the touch and sweet on the lips were crinkling to ash.

Every page from every album representing twenty years of his sexual, wild life sat smoldering in his tub. At some point during the night, he reasoned, a snoopy Summer had discovered the one secret he had kept from her over that long weekend; secrets that she decided to diligently drench with flammable liquid before torching.

Numbly leaning against the porcelain sink, Lester stared silently at the burning ruins, a scream stuck in his throat. Like a lunatic, Summer continued to whistle that damn Stevie Wonder song as though the apartment wasn't slowly filling with toxic smoke and his life hadn't been changed forever.

KAREN E. QUINONES MILLER

Auld Lang Syne

*I*t was ridiculous. It was New Year's Eve, she was getting ready to be all horny because of the Viagra she had popped two minutes before, and she was stuck in the kitchen of her Greenwich Village apartment preparing an ice pack for a homeless woman who was stinking up the place to high heaven. *Yeah, Happy Fucking New Year,* Diane Jennings thought to herself.

"Damn, why did I let her help me upstairs with my groceries?" Diane said under her breath as she grabbed a dish towel and wiped her freshly manicured hands. "If I hadn't let her in, I wouldn't have been so much in a hurry to get her out. And I wouldn't have slammed the door on her damn wrist."

She took a deep breath and glanced at the clock on the microwave oven. Just after eight. Glenn would be picking her up in less than an hour, and she wasn't even dressed.

"Here, Jean, this should keep the swelling down," Diane said patting the woman on the shoulder. As she gave her the ice pack, she tried not to flinch at her smell: a depressing combination of body odor, urine, and stale wine. She was going to have to get the couch fumigated, maybe even the whole apartment, because she probably had lice or bedbugs or worse. The apartment was well-heated in contrast to the twenty-five-degree snowy weather out-side, but Jean still had her raggedy gray wool coat on over what seemed like layers of scarves and sweaters, and a filthy red ski cap pulled low over her matted hair. Diane decided not to suggest she remove her outerwear, afraid of what might be underneath. Jean carefully placed the ice pack on her wrist, wincing as she did so.

"Oh, man, this hurts," she said, her voice so husky it was almost masculine.

She took a deep raspy breath, then looked up at Diane. "I'm sorry for causing all this trouble, Miss Jennings."

"It's no trouble at all," Diane lied as she sat down in the large stuffed chair across from the white plush sofa where Jean sat huddled.

"I just feel so bad, you know, with it being New Year's Eve and all." She gave a weak smile. "I know you must have plans to go out."

"Don't worry about me, Jean. I just want to make sure you're okay," Diane reassured her. *And I want you to get the hell out so I can get ready before Glenn gets here.*

She'd been waiting for this night for two weeks. Glenn Burton was the handsomest man at her law firm, and the most eligible—especially since he'd made partner a few months before. Too bad he was so awful in bed. Three minutes of lousy foreplay, and then two minutes of the actual act. Wham, bam, and not even a thank you ma'am. But he was still marriage material; after all, he was a partner in a law firm. She wasn't going to give up on him too eas-ily; she was thirty-seven now, and never been married. She'd turned down so many men in her life because they didn't measure up to her standards, and she still refused to settle. She wasn't going to wind up like her mother, a beautiful sophisticated woman who fell in love with an auto mechanic, and lived the rest of her life raising a family and barely scraping by. No, she was going to get a professional man, who had the means to treat her the way she deserved to be treated. And Glenn Burton fit the bill. But she had to act fast since forty was quickly approaching and she didn't want to be forty and unmarried.

And there might be some hope for Glenn in bed. Diane was planning on slipping a Viagra pill into his coffee after they returned to her apartment tonight. She figured if it did for him what it did for her they'd be screwing for the next two days.

She'd been seeing Glenn off and on for a few months, but then he'd also been dating at least two other associates besides her at the firm. He was probably screwing the receptionist, too. But it was Diane he'd asked out for New Year's Eve, and that was a real coup.

That's if I can get this old hag the hell out of my apartment.

Diane suddenly felt bad. Jean was actually a nice lady. She'd started sleeping on a subway grate across the street from Diane's apartment building several months ago. Unlike many of the homeless, she never pestered anyone for handouts, seemingly content to rummage through garbage pails for aluminum cans and bottles to cash in. A few days before Christmas, Diane was struggling to her apartment building with an armful of dry cleaning and groceries when someone bumped into her. Before she could turn around, Jean ran past her and tackled a young boy to the ground.

"Miss, he took something out of your pocket," she said as she sat on the squirming teenager.

And indeed he had. Diane had awarded her with a five-dollar bill. Since then, Jean always rushed over to her when she emerged from the building to see if she needed someone to run errands or hail a taxi.

Tonight, when Diane got out of the cab with three bulging bags of groceries, it seemed like a good idea to accept some help. Jean was tall, husky, and amazingly strong. Despite Diane's obligatory protests that they were too heavy, Jean carried all three bags to the apartment door. Diane hadn't intended to ask her in, but wouldn't you know when she looked in her pocketbook, she didn't have any small bills? So she'd allowed Jean into the apartment foyer while she ran into the kitchen to get one of the five-dollar bills she kept in a cookie jar for emergencies. While she was there she popped her Viagra pill so she'd be hot and horny by the time Glenn arrived. She wasn't going to give him any before they left, but she was counting on her horniness turning him on all night.

When Diane returned to the foyer with the money, she'd been in such a hurry to get Jean out of the apartment that she'd slammed her wrist in the door.

"Do you think it's broken?" Diane asked as she sneaked a glance at the wall clock.

Jean wiggled a couple of her fingers, grimacing in pain as she did so. "No, it's not broken. Just bruised, I guess." She sniffed, and Diane noticed her nose was starting to run.

"Let me get you a tissue." Diane stood up, but Jean shook her head, then wiped her nose with her coat sleeve. Diane struggled to hide her disgust.

"No, it's okay, I don't need a tissue," Jean said. "You're doing too much for me already, Miss Jennings. I'm going to go ahead and get out of here, 'cause I know you've probably got plans for tonight." She looked at Diane and gave a small smile. "I see the way you keep looking at the clock."

"Oh well, I mean, I'm not trying to rush you out of here or anything," Diane said guiltily. "But maybe you should go to the emergency room and let them x-ray your wrist. I can give you cab fare."

Jean chuckled. "No thanks. They don't treat people like me too well in the emergency room."

"Well, if you're sure you're going to be okay . . ." Diane let her voice trail off.

"I'll be fine." Jean braced her good arm against the sofa and pushed herself up.

"Well, at least take the ice pack with you," Diane offered.

Jean gave her little husky laugh. "That's okay, Miss Jennings. There's plenty of ice outside."

A pang of guilt shot through Diane. Jean was practically disabled because of her, and she was sending her out to sleep in the snow.

She stole another glance at the clock. Only forty-five minutes before Glenn would arrive.

Diane shrugged her shoulders. "Well, it's your decision."

"No problem, Miss Jennings," Jean said as she walked to the door. "You have a Happy New Year."

"You too, Jean," Diane unlocked the door, but when she tried to open it, it wouldn't budge. She pulled harder, flipping the lock handle back and forth. Then, she realized that she didn't hear the lock disengage. "Shit," she said.

"What's the matter?" Jean asked.

"The damn lock is broken. That's what's wrong," she yelled.

"Oh," Jean stammered. "I'm sorry."

"It's not your fault," Diane snapped. "Just go sit down. I'll call the superintendent." She knew she shouldn't take it out on Jean, but she was pissed.

"Mr. Richardson, this is Diane Jennings in apartment 4G. I'm having a problem with my lock again. Could you come up here and open it with your pass key?" she said when the superintendent finally answered the telephone. "*Fifteen* minutes? Make it five. I'm in a hurry."

"We should be out of here in a bit," she told Jean when she hung up. "I just gave him a big, fat Christmas tip."

"That's good." Jean gave a weak smile. "Could I have that ice pack back?"

"Of course." Diane retrieved the still-frozen ice pack and handed it to Jean. "I would tell you to take off your coat and make yourself comfortable, but the super's going to be here in a few minutes. So why go through all the trouble, right?"

"Right," Jean agreed, not looking at Diane as she took the ice pack.

"Oh, good, there he is now," Diane said as the doorbell rang. She glanced at the clock in the foyer. Only thirty-five minutes before Glenn was due. She was going to have to skip the bubble bath and just take a quick shower before slipping into the slinky red dress she'd blown two weeks' salary on.

"Mr. Richardson," she shouted at the door. "Would you unlock the door?"

"I'm trying, the key's turning but it's not unlocking," he yelled back.

"What?" *This can't be happening,* Diane thought.

"I'm going to see if I can get a locksmith."

"What do you mean *if* you can get a locksmith?"

"Well, it is New Year's Eve, Miss Jennings."

Diane sighed and leaned against the door She couldn't possibly be locked in tonight of all nights. She sighed again and crossed her arms, and in doing so touched her left breast. Her nipple began to swell and harden. *Damn it,* she thought, *the Viagra's starting to work, and here I am locked with some goddamned smelly-ass homeless woman.*

Suddenly angry, she started kicking the door.

"Get me out of here now, Richardson!" she shouted.

"Calm down, Miss Jennings. I'll make some calls," Mr. Richardson soothed.

"Don't tell me to calm down," Diane shouted. "Get me the hell out of here! You hear me?"

"Miss Jennings, are you okay?"

Diane turned to see Jean standing in the living room doorway, concern creasing her dirty forehead.

"We can't get out," Diane huffed.

"I thought the super was going to unlock it from the outside."

"The lock's broken," Diane almost snarled before stomping past her to the living room. The telephone rang.

"What?" she snapped into the receiver.

"Diane?"

"Oh, Glenn. I'm sorry, I didn't realize it was you." Diane purred. "How are you?"

"I'm doing fine. I know it's late to be calling but—"

"Oh, Glenn, you won't believe what's going on," Diane cut him off. "This is turning into the worst night of my life."

"What's wrong?"

"I'm locked in my house."

"What?"

Diane sighed. "You're not going to believe this." She looked at Jean, who was still standing in the doorway. "Hold on a minute." She put her hand over the receiver. "Jean, could you give me a minute?"

"Well," Jean shifted uncomfortably. "Where's the bathroom?"

Diane pointed down the hallway. "Second door on your right." She then uncovered the receiver. "Like I said, you're not going to believe this. My lock is broken and I can't get out of the apartment. My super doesn't think he'll be able to get a locksmith anytime soon."

"Bummer."

"It gets worse," Diane sighed again. "I'm locked in with a homeless woman."

"Come again?"

"You heard right. She helped me upstairs with my groceries, and when she was leaving I slammed her wrist in the door. So I had to tend to her, and now I can't get rid of her."

"You poor baby."

Diane smiled. It was the closest Glenn had ever come to using an endearment. "Yeah, it's just awful. And I feel horrible, because we're going to be late for the party."

"Oh, please, I'm not even thinking about the party. I'm worried about you."

Diane caressed the sofa pillow as she snuggled down into the sofa. Both her nipples were hard now, and her panties were beginning to moisten. "Oh, Glenn, that's so sweet."

"Well, you know you're my favorite girl."

"Am I?" Diane giggled softly.

"Of course you are, Diane. But I'm not going to keep you on the telephone. I know you're busy."

"Busy?" Diane sat up straight. "I'm not busy. You don't have to hang up."

"Well, I mean, I know you have to take care of your homeless woman, and all."

"She's fine."

"Well, you know you're going to have to keep her happy. You don't want her to sue you or anything. In fact, you might want to draft up a quick release form for her to sign to absolve you of all blame for her accident."

"Oh," Diane said. "I hadn't thought about that."

"Well, that's why you have me. So, I'll call tomorrow to check in."

"Tomorrow? But . . . I thought I'd give you a call if the lock-smith gets here before midnight."

There was a pause.

"Glenn, you couldn't have already made other plans. I mean—" Diane stopped, an ugly thought forming in her mind. "Glenn, why did you call me?"

"I was just going to, you know, tell you I was on my way."

"Is that right? What did you mean when you said you knew it was kind of late to be calling?"

"Just that—"

"Glenn, you were calling to cancel on me, weren't you!" Diane almost screamed into the phone.

"Diane—" Glenn started.

"You lousy, no good bastard! You were calling to cancel our New Year's Eve date minutes before you were supposed to pick me up?"

"Diane—"

"Don't Diane me, you fucking creep. You can kiss my ass!" Diane slammed down the phone and threw the pillow she'd been holding across the room. Then she picked up the phone and shouted to the dial tone. "And you fucking suck in bed!"

That bastard. Standing me up on New Year's Eve. How dare he? And what the hell did he mean, I'm his favorite girl? He was letting me know I'm not his only girl. I hope he breaks his leg dancing tonight.

Yeah, Happy Fucking New Year to me.

Diane sniffed back her tears suddenly remembering what Glenn had said. She really should be acting nice to Jean to make sure she didn't get sued.

"Jean?" Diane tapped on the bathroom door. "You okay?"

"I was just coming out," Jean said through the door.

"No rush. Listen. Why don't we make the best of our New Year's Eve? Why don't you take a nice relaxing bath. There are extra towels in the linen closet. Just leave your clothes on the floor. I'm sure I can find you something to put on. I'll make us some nice stiff drinks and a snack or something."

"Oh no, Miss Jennings." Jean opened the door. "I can't let you go through all that trouble."

"Please, it'll be my pleasure. I'm glad for the company."

"Well . . ." Jean hesitated. "Are you sure?"

"I'm sure." Diane gave an expansive smile. "There are bath beads in the cabinet under the sink. You want me to fix your bath for you?"

"No, please. I can do it myself. Um, do you mind if I take a shower instead? I'm not really a bath person."

"Fine with me," Diane shrugged. Judging from Jean's body odor, soap and water hadn't touched her skin in years. "And wash your hair if you'd like. There's shampoo on the shower rack. But be careful not to hurt your wrist, dear."

Diane went to her bedroom, and opened the walk-in closet. She started looking through the racks of designer jeans for a pair she wouldn't mind giving away. It then occurred to her that Jean wouldn't be able to fit into her clothes. Diane was a size nine, and Jean looked like she was probably a sixteen. *Now what?* she thought. *Wait a minute.* She walked over to her bureau and pulled out a pair of brown corduroy pants that her brother had left on his last visit. They should fit. She opened the top drawer and pulled out an extra-large pink button-down man's shirt she used as a nightgown.

She knocked on the bathroom door before entering and spoke to the closed shower curtain. "Jean, I'm going to put clothes for you on the toilet seat."

"Thanks," Jean shouted over the running water.

Diane closed the door and went into the kitchen. "Okay, let's see," she muttered. "I need to get her drunk quick so she'll sign the release." She pulled out a bottle of vermouth and another of gin. "Martinis should do the trick."

She reached into one of the grocery bags and pulled out a tin of Beluga caviar and a box of unsalted crackers that she bought to serve Glenn for breakfast. No use in letting it go to waste, she figured. Better to give it to a bum off the street than Glenn.

She brought the serving tray into the living room, and set it down on the coffee table, then went into her office and quickly typed up an injury release form. She slipped it into a manila folder and placed it on a shelf in the living room. She then took a martini to the sofa and dialed the superintendent's telephone number but the answering machine picked up. The bastard was probably out getting drunk for New Year's Eve. She grabbed the yellow pages and scanned for locksmiths. She didn't bother to look up when Jean walked in, just motioned her over to the loveseat across from the sofa. She tried three different locksmiths before finally giving up. She sighed and plopped back onto the couch. She hoped she'd be able to find one that was open on New Year's Day, otherwise she'd be locked up for two days with a homeless woman. She looked up and smiled at Jean. "Ever had a martini?"

"Yeah, but not in a very long time," she mumbled.

"Well, I've got a couple right here with your name on them." Diane got up and went to the serving tray, picked up the martini shaker and poured two glasses, giving one to Jean. She looked a lot different without all the layers of dirt, Diane noticed. Bushy eyebrows, smooth caramel-colored skin, naturally curly hair that reached the nape of her neck, and a bulging Adam's apple that became all the more evident as Jean took a long swallow of her martini. *What the hell?* Diane's mouth dropped open as she took a closer look at Jean. She was a lot thinner than Diane had originally thought now that the layers of clothes were gone. And very flat-chested. In fact, she had no bosom at all. In fact, Diane gasped and dropped her drink.

"What's the matter?" Jean asked, jumping up from the loveseat to pick up Diane's glass. "Are you okay?" Jean said as she stood up. And there it was, right at eye level, damn near in Diane's face. A bulge in the crotch of the brown corduroy pants.

"You're a man!" Diane jumped from the couch and started backing toward the doorway.

A puzzled look crossed Jean's face.

"Of course I am," Jean said simply.

"But you said you were a woman!" Diane could barely get the words out.

"No, I didn't."

"You said your name was Jean," Diane sputtered.

"It is. Short for Eugene." Realization suddenly crossed his face. "It's spelled G. E. N. E., not J. E. A. N. Miss Jennings, all this time you thought I was a woman?"

Diane nodded; the room was spinning.

The two of them stood there for a moment not saying anything, then Gene sighed and sat down. "Well, this is uncomfortable to say the least. I would offer to leave, but I, you know, can't."

Diane nodded.

"So now what?" Gene asked.

"I don't know," Diane said as she tried to get herself under control. "I'm just, you know, shocked."

Gene nodded. "I understand. But I also hope you know that I didn't try to deceive you. I had no idea that you thought I was a woman."

"Sure, sure," Diane said, inching over to the telephone. She dialed the superintendent's number. "Hello," she said loudly when the answering machine picked up. "This is Diane Jennings again from apartment 4G. I just wanted to say Happy New Year, and to remind you that we're still waiting for a locksmith. I say we because Gene, you know the homeless woman, I mean the homeless man, who's usually across the street, is up here with me. So please don't forget about us, okay?" Diane hung up and gave Gene a weak smile. "Just wanted to make sure he didn't forget us."

Gene nodded. "I understand. I have sisters and they used to do that for each other, too."

"Do what?"

"Whenever one of my sisters brought a man to their apartment who they didn't know very well, she'd call my other sister in front of him and say his full name so that he'd know that if anything happened to her, the police would know who to look for."

"I wasn't—"

Gene held up his good hand. "Don't worry. I'm not offended. And, by the way, my full name is Eugene Arthur Reynolds." Gene smiled.

"Pardon?"

"In case you wanted to call back and give the superintendent my full name."

Diane shook her head. "No, that won't be necessary."

"Yeah, you're right. He probably knows me better as Gene the Homeless Man." Gene gave a little chuckle, then looked at Diane and chuckled louder. "I guess you're really having a messed-up New Year's, huh?"

In spite of herself, Diane began to laugh. "Well, you could definitely say it's not what I planned."

Gene stood up and poured two more martinis from the tray, handing one to Diane. "Here. I'd say you're due a stiff drink." He smiled as Diane took a grateful swallow.

"I really feel I should apologize, Miss Jennings," Gene said with a small shake of the head. "I mean, I'm not sure what I should have done differently. I guess next time I tell someone my name I should spell it for them."

"Yeah, maybe you should. I guess a lot of people mistake you for a woman, huh?" Diane used a finger to swirl her drink.

Gene looked up at Diane. "I hope not."

"Well, I mean, your voice isn't all that deep, and you don't have any facial hair," Diane explained. "And you're so unassuming. And underneath all those clothes you wear, you know . . . well, you can't tell."

"Well, I don't have any control over the timbre of my voice, and I've never been able to grow facial hair. As for unassuming, I've always been the quiet type, I guess. I'd rather observe than participate." Gene gave a little shrug, "And if you're sleeping out in freezing temperatures you need as many layers of clothes as possible. But, Miss Jennings, why would you think I was a woman when I was always offering to carry your bags? And would a woman tackle that guy who picked your pocket?"

"Well . . ." Diane took another sip of her martini. The vermouth and gin were beginning to get to her. "I just thought that you were a very strong woman, who would do anything to make a few dollars."

"I see." Gene took a sip of his martini, then chewed on his bottom lip.

"I didn't mean to offend you . . ." Diane trailed off.

"No offense taken." Gene waved off the apology.

Diane didn't know what else to say so they sat in silence for a few moments. "Do you mind if I ask you a question?" she finally said.

"Please go right ahead."

"How did you end up homeless?"

Gene just looked at Diane for a long while, then he said, "About seven months ago I woke up in my big, comfortable king-sized bed, in my big, swanky Upper East Side apartment, and wondered what I wanted to do that day. I decided that I wanted to see what it would feel like to be homeless."

"You don't have to get smart," Diane snapped. "If you didn't want to answer my question, you should have just said so."

"I wasn't getting smart." Gene took another sip of his drink and looked at the caviar on the small porcelain tray. "Beluga?" he asked.

He knew enough about caviar to recognize it as Beluga? Diane looked hard at him. "Are you serious? You really had an apartment on the Upper East Side?"

Gene nodded and smiled. "Still do, I suppose. I own the apartment, and my co-op dues were paid for a year in advance. I've only been gone seven months. Do you mind if I have some caviar?"

"Get out of here!" Diane's mouth dropped open. "Are you some kind of eccentric millionaire or something?"

Gene chuckled. "No. Just a bored architect. Far from a millionaire, but I was doing okay."

"You're an architect?"

"Mmmhmm."

"And you just decided to give it up and live in the streets?"

"Well, it wasn't my intention to give it up forever, but one day I just decided I was fed up with people being impressed with me simply because I came from a wealthy family, went to the right schools, and had a good job. I wondered how I would be treated if I had none of that. How people would react to just the man."

"So you just walked away from your life."

Gene nodded.

"Get out of here," Diane repeated. "I don't believe you."

"You don't, huh?" Gene smiled. "Look in the white pages for Eugene A. Reynolds on East 67th Street."

Diane flipped through the phone book. There it was. She grabbed the telephone and dialed the number. It rang ten times before the answering machine finally picked up. The voice on the machine sure sounded liked Gene. Diane hung up and looked at him.

"How much longer do you plan to stay in the streets?"

"Well, you may not believe this, but I was going to make this my last night," Gene said shaking his head. "I was planning on ringing in the New Year in my apartment. I was getting ready to start walking uptown when I saw you get out of the cab with all those bags. I figured I'd give you a hand one last time."

Diane shook her head. The homeless woman from across the street was really a rich male architect from the Upper East Side? She felt like she was in the Twilight Zone.

"Miss Jennings, would you mind if I had some caviar? I haven't eaten all day." Gene was hungrily eyeing the serving tray.

"Oh, yes. Please, yes, of course." Diane jumped up and spooned some of the caviar onto one of the crackers and handed it to him. "And please, call me Diane."

"Thank you, Diane," Gene said gratefully.

"I should have known," Diane said. "I mean you're so articulate and everything. I should have known you weren't just some bum."

"There are a lot of homeless people who speak properly," Gene said. "Being able to speak well doesn't mean you've got money. And being homeless doesn't mean you're stupid or a bad person."

Diane shrugged. "I guess that's true." She sneaked a peek at him as he munched his caviar-laden cracker. He was actually really good-looking. And sexy, too. *I bet he would look even sexier in an Armani suit instead of corduroy slacks. And I bet he has a bunch of Armanis in that swanky Upper East Side apartment.* She felt herself becoming aroused. *To hell with Glenn,* she thought. An architect was as good as a lawyer any day. "Why don't I fix you something a little more substantial to eat? It won't take me but a minute." Her New Year's Eve had taken on a whole new spin.

"Oh, no, please. I don't want you to go through any trouble," Gene protested.

"How about a sandwich, at least? It's no trouble at all," Diane said as she headed to the kitchen. "And you know what? I bet I have an Ace bandage somewhere. How about you let me wrap your wrist?"

* * *

"Well, this has really turned out to be a lovely evening," Diane purred after three more martinis and a steak and salad she'd prepared. "Lovely and totally unforgettable."

"It is nice," Gene said with a yawn.

"You're not sleepy, are you?" Diane said in alarm. "I'm having such a good time talking to you."

"No, just a little tired, is all," Gene gave another yawn. "What time is it?"

Diane glanced at the clock. "Oh my God!" She grabbed the remote control and clicked on the television just as Dick Clark started the countdown. "Come over here," she waved to Gene.

Ten, nine, eight, seven, six, five, four, three, two, one. Happy New Year!

Diane threw her arms around Gene's neck and kissed him on the lips. "Happy New Year, Gene," she whispered.

"Happy New Year, Diane," he whispered back.

She could feel the bulge in his pants growing against her stomach. She pressed herself closer to him. "I think this is going to be a really good year. It's certainly starting off well."

Gene's breathing began to quicken, but he tried to step out of Diane's embrace.

"What's wrong?" Diane said, refusing to unlock her arms from around his neck.

"Nothing," Gene said. He tried to give her a quick peck on the lips, but she forced her tongue into his mouth, pressing her hard nipples against his chest. She reached under his shirt and started stroking his chest. Gene groaned in appreciation. Her hand inched down toward his crotch. The bulge had now grown to the point where it threatened to burst through the corduroy material.

She took his hand and guided it to her breast, rubbing his rough callused hand over her nipples. The friction alone almost made her come, but when Gene started biting her gently on her neck, it was too much.

"Oh Gene," she moaned. "You're going to make me come."

"But I've barely touched you," he said. His tongue licked a moist trail from her neck to her shoulder as he unbuttoned her blouse and slipped it off.

"Oh, baby, you're touching me more than you know." She undid the button on his pants. "I want to touch you, too," she said as she started caressing his throbbing penis.

"Oh my God." Gene moved.

"What's the matter, baby?" Diane cooed as she reached for him again.

"Diane, I haven't been with a woman in so long I'm about to explode," he said gently.

"Well, I don't want you to waste all that good stuff on my hand," Diane said standing on her tiptoes and nibbling at his ear. "Why don't we go into the bedroom?"

Gene pushed her away and took half a step back.

"What's wrong?" Diane asked.

"Are you sure you want to do this?" Gene asked, looking deeply into her eyes. "You've had a lot to drink."

She stepped closer to him and slipped her arms around his waist. "I know it's been a long time for you, but don't worry. I'll be gentle," she purred.

"Is that right?" Gene laughed as she slid her hand down and began stroking his penis.

"Yes, that's right." She grinned, slipping her hand into the waistband of his pants.

He moaned deep in the back of his throat. "Let's go into the bedroom, then?"

It only lasted thirty seconds. He came almost as soon as he entered her, and then collapsed on her chest.

Damn, he's as bad as Glenn, she thought. *What a waste of a condom.*

Just as she started to squirm from beneath him, he started licking the hollow of her neck up to her mouth, where he let his tongue lightly flicker over her lips before kissing her long and hard. She moaned as he kissed his way down her body to her waist, then he licked a moist trail down to her clit. He fastened his mouth on the lips he found there and then started licking her roughly. Diane's breathing was coming in short ragged bursts. That orgasm she'd been hoping for was building up inside her. She moaned and pressed her hips into his hand.

"That's it, Diane. Feel good, baby? You didn't think I'd forgotten about you?" Gene whispered. She couldn't answer, could barely breathe. This was just what she'd wanted to do for New Year's Eve. She'd just had a whole different man in mind. But Gene was definitely the better man. There was no more thinking as she felt the first convulsions rack her body. She was coming, her muscles clenching and unclenching against Gene's slick fingers, her own fingers tangled in his hair.

They went through three more condoms before they fell back exhausted. Dawn was peeking beneath the blinds when they finally went to sleep, Diane cradled happily in Gene's arms.

It was almost noon when Diane heard voices in the foyer. She got up and threw her robe on.

"Miss Jennings? I'm sorry, I rang the bell and you didn't answer," Mr. Richardson said when he saw her. "I just told the locksmith to go ahead and fix the lock. He's just finished putting in a new one."

"How much do I owe you?" Diane asked the locksmith, yawning.

"Don't worry about it. He's on retainer with the building," Mr. Richardson said. "And sorry for the inconvenience."

Diane gave him a big smile as she shut the door. "Oh, no inconvenience at all."

"Well, we're no longer prisoners," she said as she climbed into bed and woke Gene with a kiss.

"That's good," Gene murmured, stretching languidly.

Diane curled up into his arms. "Oh, Gene, I know we're going to be so happy together."

"Mmhmm," Gene answered sleepily.

"Yes, the perfect couple," Diane cooed.

Gene sat up in the bed, wide awake now.

"What's wrong?" Diane sat up beside him.

Gene sighed. "Diane, I never meant to lead you on. The truth is I don't see us as a couple."

Diane felt as if she had been punched in the stomach. "You don't?" she croaked.

"No, I'm sorry, but I don't."

"Why?" she stammered.

"Well, honestly, you tend to look down on people who you think are beneath you. And even though I like you, you're not the type of woman I see myself getting serious with. I'm looking for someone with compassion. Someone who would treat a homeless woman just as well as they would an architect." He looked at her and lowered his eyes. "You're not that woman."

Diane jumped out of the bed. "You bastard," she spat.

Gene caught her fist just before it landed on his cheek. He moved toward the door trying to get away from her.

"Diane, I'm sorry," Gene said as he tried to restrain her with one hand while protecting his bandaged wrist.

"Sorry nothing. I'm good enough to fuck, but not good enough to date." She screamed at him. "You think you're better than me or something? At least I didn't throw my life away and start sleeping in the streets just because I'm bored."

"You're right, and I'm sorry," Gene said soothingly.

"Well, I'm sorry, too." Diane stopped trying to swing at Gene and collapsed in his arms. "I'm really not a bad person, and I don't mean to look down on people. Can't you give me another chance?"

"Oh, Diane. I'm sorry, I shouldn't have slept with you." Gene rocked her back and forth. "But I mean, we only just met on any real level. Why are you even thinking about having a serious relationship with someone you barely know?"

Diane looked up at him. "Gene, please, we'd be the perfect couple. A lawyer and an architect. It would be almost like *The Cosby Show*. An architect is almost as good as a doctor."

"Oh, tell me you're kidding. Is that what this is about? Some fairy tale you have in your head?" Gene leaned against the bedroom door and stared at her. He was silent for a moment, then took Diane by the shoulder and gently steered her over to the bed and sat her down.

"Diane, I have a confession to make," he said gently. "I know you're going to be angry, but I want you to try and stay calm."

"What is it?"

He took a deep breath. "I'm not an architect. I made all that up to impress you."

"You what?" Diane looked at him in disbelief.

"I knew you felt uncomfortable being locked up with me, and I figured you'd be more at ease with a successful architect than with a homeless man."

Diane was speechless. She sat there with her mouth open, staring at him.

"I know you hate me, so I'm going to leave now." He started backing toward the door.

"Wait a minute. What about the telephone listing? And what about your voice on that answering machine?" Diane took a few steps toward him.

"That was my cousin. We sound exactly alike."

"Cousins? With the same name?" she moved a few steps closer. "I want some answers."

Gene was just outside the bedroom door now. He looked at Diane with an expression she couldn't read, then he sighed. "Diane, don't you think it best I leave now, without trying to do any further explaining?"

Diane stared at him, finally understanding that there was no way she could win. If he was a homeless man, she didn't want him. If he was really an architect, he didn't want her.

"Get your filthy ass clothes out my bathroom and get the hell out my house. I should never have let you in my apartment in the first place."

"I really do hope you find what you're looking for, Diane," Gene said gently. "Have a Happy New Year."

"Yeah, Happy Fucking New Year to you, too," Diane said, returning to her bedroom and wearily falling back on her bed and closing her eyes. Moments later she heard the front door close.

JOHN KEENE

Sums

This is the year I'll do my own taxes, Augustin kept telling himself right up to the moment he tossed his W-2s and receipts and receipt fragments and fragments of receipt fragments into a plastic shopping bag and headed for Wolfner-Laidlaw Tax Services. He had stacked federal and state tax forms neatly on the table in his messy studio. He'd even purchased a fresh pack of No. 2 pencils, an electric sharpener, and a calculator for the task. As backup, he'd placed the computerized tax software his brother Rafael sent him each September on his computer's desktop. Rafael, who did his own taxes, had reminded him for the thousandth time that this was what most of the tax preparation chains used. Augustin thought, however, that the presence of the paper forms, the pencils, sharpener, and calculator would be a better incentive.

But after two weeks, the orderly, untouched display had begun to remind him of a site-specific installation. So despite his self-motivating mantra, he decided once again on Wolfner-Laidlaw. He would, as he did every year, entrust his earnings statements and written tallies and receipts, as well as selected intimacies of his life and career, to a numbers magician who sifted through them with the care of an archaeologist. So far none of these filings had resulted in serious penalties. In fact, since he'd started using Wolfner-Laidlaw ten years ago, he hadn't been audited once. Nor had he received registered letters filled with litanies of errors made by his tax preparer. That had been the usual outcome when his ex, Stephen, a former financial analyst turned lawyer, had done his taxes. Stephen's ineptitude had led him to swear off lawyers and redheads forever.

One of Augustin's rituals before heading to Wolfner-Laidlaw was to scrub his hands and change into clothes that weren't flecked with paint or blackened by charcoal dust. He also no longer wore the violet ponytail or facial piercings that always provoked inquiries. His artsy getups had led one of his first tax preparers, a stout white matron, to halt her inquiry into his rent rebate to pontificate on the "marvels" of Andrew Wyeth's depictions of rural Pennsylvania and condemn "trash" like Andres Serrano's *Piss Christ. That,* she'd rasped, was a perfect example of why the government shouldn't waste tax dollars on contemporary artists. Augustin, who was hoping to win a state arts council check, simply nodded and tried to redirect her attention to his forms, though he momentarily considered provoking her by mentioning his own infamous photographic reappropriations of Christian imagery.

Another preparer, Mr. Shah, now the tax office manager, had blurted out mockingly when Augustin named his profession, "But what do you *really* do? This is a *job?* If my son, who's at Seton Hall, thought about going into something like this I'd snatch him

out of classes myself! What do *your* parents think?" Surprised by
Shah's outburst, Augustin replied coolly that his parents were not
that happy that he'd chosen to become an artist. But Augustin
loved creating art and since he was able to pay his own bills,
including the one to Wolfner-Laidlaw, he didn't need to answer to
anyone. Mr. Shah had conducted the rest of the session as quickly
and silently as possible.

On his way out, Augustin checked to make sure he had everything. Every year he went through this same ritual, and usually
he had to run back to scour through his files for one thing or
another. This time, for a change, he was getting an early start: Tax
Day was still a month away.

*   *   *

Terry used today's long break between clients to finish his
lunch and polish his Spanish. He cursed himself again for
having chosen French in high school, but growing up in Jersey
City he'd picked up enough of the language to get by when
one of his Spanish-speaking coworkers was busy. Looking up
from his phrase book, he saw bands of late afternoon sunlight
glazing the street. Spring, he realized, was almost here, and
would bring with it the interminable lines of harried clients
lacking the correct documents and offering innumerable
excuses as to why they'd put off till the last minute what
they'd had twelve months to prepare for. In fact, in the two
years that he had worked for Wolfner-Laidlaw, Terry rarely
heard a good excuse, which would have included some mention of incarceration or hospitalization. Since it was still

March, though, he felt magnanimous. Not even a forgotten 1099-R could rile him today.

Terry no longer even thought about his previous job as a junior analyst at a Chelsea dot.com, which he'd hated despite the flexible scheduling and ample food spreads. He'd primarily loathed the persistent management chaos; everything there was free-form and form-free. The result was that everyone had ended up free, as in without a job. Though Terry was planning on moving on, he was satisfied for now. He liked order, particularly in the workplace, and Wolfner-Laidlaw provided that. Like all the other Client Tax Service Specialists at the firm, he'd aced his initial interview, taken a course in tax preparation, and passed the demanding certification exam. The final requirements were two annual tax code update classes, paid for by Wolfner-Laidlaw. It was a far more rigorous approach than many of the other tax consultation outfits. But Terry liked the training, and since he'd studied business as an NYU undergraduate, he found the work fairly easy. If he stayed on, even as a part-timer, he was eligible for promotion based on his performance evaluations in a year to Senior Client Tax Service Manager.

Once this tax cycle was over, Terry figured he'd continue with his other job, working part-time in the accounting department of a video production company. Then he'd go back to school for an M.S. in finance, perhaps even an M.B.A. His goal was to become a financial advisor and set up his own firm. After that, he'd look for a boyfriend. He hadn't dated anyone in a while.

When he heard the front door sing its bright song he looked

up from the phrasebook. A new client was ready to be guided through the tax-filing maze.

*   *   *

Augustin was surprised that there was no line, not even a single other person in the Wolfner-Laidlaw waiting area. Habit, however, led him to snare a number from the dispenser and sign in. Before he could sit down, a young and quite handsome black guy was beckoning him over to his desk. Augustin had seen African-American tax preparers at Wolfner-Laidlaw before, but he had never had one. Russian, Hispanic, Polish, East Indian, and a Filipina—how that *promdi* had pressed him about where in Negros Occidental his family was from, as if he knew—but he'd never had a black preparer. Augustin was both unsure and excited. But was it because the guy was black, or because he was so good-looking, or both?

The young man, flashing a tight smile beneath his trim mustache and offering his hand, introduced himself as Terry Kelly. He guided Augustin to his small cubicle, with its tidy desk and two chairs. Terry was wearing an immaculately pressed blue Oxford shirt with a blue-gray tie, gray flannel slacks, and polished black boots. He looked Augustin up and down as he pointed to a chair. Augustin, in his dingy white down coat, vintage velour sweatsuit, and scuffed work boots, immediately felt underdressed. He also started to feel a bit anxious. Would this attractive, straight-laced guy be another Mr. Shah? He wondered, plopping down facing Terry, the plastic bag of documents and receipts in his lap. Terry smiled again, it appeared to Augustin, even more tightly.

* * *

The new client was a hefty thirty-something Asian man dressed almost like a homeless person, Terry thought. What on earth could his story be? Was he here to get his taxes done or ask for handouts? Terry glanced around the office. Where was Karen Wu? Why was he the only one on the floor right now? What if the client spoke only a little English, and that with a very thick accent? Terry didn't speak Chinese, Korean, or Vietnamese. Or maybe he wasn't Asian. The client had a walnut complexion and his nose and lips were fuller than many black folks'. He even sported a Caesar cut. Looking him over, Terry thought he might actually be Latino. Whatever his background was and in spite of his disheveled appearance, Terry found him sexy.

As the client signed in, Terry could see that what he had originally taken to be fat was muscle. About five foot eight, the guy was built like a Humvee, with shoulders broad as a double axle, a banked chest that molded his hideous sweatsuit top to him, and biceps and calves tight as drums. Terry figured he was probably a garbageman or construction worker; his meaty hands looked liked they'd been rubbed raw by the elements. Except for the velour suit, he was, in fact, exactly the type of guy Terry liked.

"So have you been to Wolfner-Laidlaw before?" Terry asked, as was his routine.

Glancing around Terry's desk, Augustin saw that he was really organized. Not a paper was out of place on his desk, not a hair amiss in his fade. *Wait till he sees the chaos I've got in this bag.* Augustin cringed. He also saw that Terry looked even better up close. His features were perfectly proportioned; his eyes above full cheekbones were almond-shaped and the color of well-steeped tea. *Maybe he's got some Asian in him,* Augustin thought. Terry's straight nose ended in rounded nostrils; his thick and sensuous lips spread atop a solid, dimpled chin. If Augustin had brought his sketchbook, he'd have certainly asked permission to draw Terry. He caught himself staring and focused on the desk. Terry's long, manicured fingers were arranging the forms. Augustin noticed that he wore no wedding or bonding ring, and felt a sudden urge to place his own thick fingers atop Terry's.

"Have we worked with you before?" Terry repeated.

"What?" Augustin looked up. "Oh yeah. Actually, I've been coming here for about ten years."

"So we must have a file on you. Great." Augustin heard some warmth in Terry's voice. Maybe he wasn't as uptight as he appeared.

"I don't think I've seen you here before. You new?" Augustin asked.

"No, it's my second year, but last cycle I worked at the other office, near the waterfront. I didn't get your name."

"Oh. That's right, you gotta have that to find my file. Augustin Pacheco Sum."

What? Terry thought, looking blankly at Augustin. Was his last name Pacheco, or Sum, or Pacheco-Sum? Or had he misheard it altogether? Maybe he hadn't originally been that far off. Perhaps he *was* Chinese-Cuban, or Brazilian, from somewhere in the

Caribbean or South America where combinations of this sort weren't uncommon.

As if he were reading Terry's mind, Augustin answered, "It would be under *S*, I think. Pacheco is my mother's maiden name, Sum is my father's. No hyphen. I'm Filipino."

Terry felt a twinge of embarrassment flush his cheeks.

"Thank you, Mr. Sum—"

"Augustin, please."

"Augustin."

"Well, I just need to get your file, then."

"I'm in no rush," Augustin said, getting comfortable. In fact, he was ready to sit with Terry for as long as he needed.

"Great then, I'll be right back."

"Under *S*," Augustin reminded him.

"Under *S*," Terry repeated, watching Augustin take off his coat. For *scrumptious*.

* * *

As Terry headed away toward the files, Augustin noted how well Terry filled out his shirt and slacks. He had never dated an African-American guy, let alone slept with one. Neither lack of desire nor color had ever been a barrier; most of the black guys Augustin came across were already paired up, only dated black and Latin guys, weren't into Asians, or were straight. Something about Terry suggested he might not fit any of those categories, but Augustin wasn't sure.

He inspected the cubicle. There were no photos of signifi-cant others, no knickknacks or tchotchkes. Just neatly stacked piles of tax forms, nearly empty in–out boxes, and Wolfner-Laidlaw memos all tacked up neatly on the cubicle walls. Then he spotted a small, framed postcard of a Jean-Michel Basquiat painting, sitting behind Terry's phone. He moved closer: It was one depicting Joe Louis. So Terry liked art *and* had good taste.

Augustin untied his bag and began creating his own paper piles on Terry's desk. He was itemizing again this year, because the way the tax code worked, he could deduct his art supplies, as well as the costs of the studio and office he maintained at home. He'd even written up the totals for supplies and equipment.

He then fished out his W-2s for the gallery where he worked part-time. He often cursed the low wages for construction and prep work he did there, but he liked the proximity to artists and art, and the gallery owner had agreed to exhibit some of his work in her midsummer show. Terry probably didn't see a lot of contemporary art despite the Basquiat card. Maybe he'd invite him to the gallery for an opening. If that went smoothly, he'd then invite Terry to his studio to view his male nudes. . . . But he was being presumptuous. He didn't know a thing about this guy. Just the thought of having Terry in his studio, however, was getting him hot. He unzipped his top and wiped his forehead with the back of his hand. He laughed: He was here to get his taxes prepared, but he was instead sweating over some guy. He looked down and saw he was also getting hard. He placed the bag back over his lap and scanned the Wolfner-Laidlaw office. It was still fairly slow, thank the gods!

* * *

Sum, under *S,* exactly where it was supposed to be. Terry pulled Augustin's file and flipped through it. Augustin, Terry read, was an artist. He wouldn't have guessed that; based on Augustin's build, dress, and mannerisms, he'd imagined something more blue-collar. He didn't live too far away from Terry either, though Terry had never run into him on the street or train. He'd definitely be looking for him after today. Augustin was thirty-five. Only a few years older than Terry: perfect. He was single and an artist. Terry wondered if he was gay or bisexual. Had there been a box for it, he would have written in *phyne,* because Augustin definitely was.

Terry caught himself. This was unprofessional, rifling through a client's file, acting like a nosy secretary. He'd been attracted to clients in the past, but he was always professional. He had even dated a few of them, though only after reconnecting in other venues. Plus, there was no shortage of attractive gay men in northern New Jersey or New York, and though he was single, he wasn't desperate. He could get sex whenever he wanted. All he had to do was go online.

But something about this guy was different. Actually, this *guy* was different. Terry had never dated a Filipino and definitely not a practicing artist. There were lots of Filipinos in Jersey City, but he didn't socialize with any, in part because he didn't even know where gay Filipinos hung out. And although Jersey City had a large population of artists and the arts capital of the world, New York City, was just across the river, Terry rarely met any of them either. He'd always imagined artists lived fascinating, even wild lives. As he thought of Augustin waiting for him, Terry knew he'd love to find out for himself.

He wondered what kind of artist Augustin was. Was he a painter? Terry liked paintings, even abstractions. Basquiat and Warhol were his favorite artists. Did he draw? Sculpt? He was certainly built up enough to carve figures out of stone. Or maybe Augustin made the kind of art that was subtle and subversive, or over the top, silly even? Terry had always respected the cleverness—and shamelessness—that it took to come up with that kind of art. When he was at NYU, he'd checked out a performance art piece, in which the artist stood naked between a revolving diaphanous and opaque screen in an East Village storefront for three days. The whole thing was sort of a sham, but he'd been enthralled. He would love to see Augustin standing around in his birthday suit. He could feel he was getting aroused, so he tried to think about taxes. Was there anything less sexy?

*　　*　　*

"So, you planning on running this place someday?" Augustin asked, as Terry checked and rechecked his totals against the receipts.

"Actually, I want to go back to school, then start my own business."

"A go-getter," Augustin said, impressed. "So what would you study?"

"Finance, I think, maybe get my M.B.A."

"Okay. Have you ever thought about working outside of this field?"

Terry paused. "You have a thing against numbers men?" He glanced at Augustin's onscreen tax forms. "You need me, you know."

"Oh yeah, I know I do. No lawyers, though." They both laughed. "So, you love doing this?"

"I don't know about love, but I like it."

"Well, I'm glad somebody does mine, 'cause as my father used to say, I've never been very 'good at sums.'"

Terry looked at Augustin's chest as he spoke. In the unzipped V of his top Terry could see the soft, black down nesting between the massive pecs. If he had the opportunity, he'd gladly teach Augustin about sums. But what he wanted to do first was remove Augustin's sweat top. He'd grab hold of Augustin's huge pecs, just to feel them in his hands. Terry would work the hairy muscled flesh over with bites and kisses till he got to the large, copper-colored areolas. He'd suck on the nipples gently at first. Then he'd massage them with his fingers until they were swollen and tender. With his tongue, he'd draw a line from one nipple to the other, circling each one. Then he'd bite down, gently, then harder, until Augustin cried out. He'd milk each one till Augustin was crying out with pleasure. That's how they'd start the lesson.

"You just need a good teacher," Terry said.

* * *

Augustin smiled. He had no use for accounting or anything else to do with numbers, though he agreed he'd be open to Terry teaching him a few things. He imagined the two of them in the office after hours. Terry would finally take off his tie and shirt, and relax. The main lights would be off as they sat side by side in the soft glow of Terry's desk lamp. Augustin would follow everything Terry said by looking carefully at the relevant equations in the accounting book. As he did so, he would feel Terry massaging his shoulders. Terry's hands would move to the small of his back, then down his sweatpants to Augustin's firm ass. Terry would caress his ass, then lean him forward and spank it. After a few hard spanks, Augustin would climb onto Terry's lap facing him. As Terry grasped his ass tightly and pulled him close, he'd begin kissing Terry's face, his chin, his neck. He'd kiss his shoulders and his smooth dark chest, which he imagined had a clean, spicy flavor. Augustin would slide his hand down past the white band of Terry's boxer briefs, and pull out Terry's erect dick. It would fill both of Augustin's fists. He'd press his own dick, stiff as a pipe, against it. He'd begin working them both, pumping them up and down like an enormous piston. Then Terry would lean him back over the desk, he'd close his eyes and—

"I do need a good teacher," Augustin blurted out. "I do." He was grinning.

"Sounds good to me," Terry said, grinning too.

* * *

After getting most of the way through Augustin's filing, Terry asked, "So what kind of artist are you, if you don't mind me asking?"

"No, that's cool. I do a little of everything."

"You paint?" Terry asked.

"Oh yeah."

"And draw?"

"Yeah, and I sculpt . . . Net art too."

"So you do it all?" Terry was smiling. Augustin nodded.

"Even performance art?"

"So you know a little bit about the art world, huh?" Augustin laughed. "Yeah, I also do performance and conceptual pieces."

Terry stopped typing and looked at Augustin. He tried to imagine what kinds of performance pieces Augustin did. Did he smear chocolate all over himself like the woman who had caused so much controversy? Terry was ready to help him cover every square inch of his thick, gorgeous body.

"What do you draw?"

Augustin hesitated. "Abstract stuff." Terry started typing again. "And nudes." Terry stopped typing, leaned back and put his hands behind his head.

Augustin could see the sweaty pools under Terry's arms, his biceps and triceps pressing against the cotton of his shirt. He wanted to pull Terry across the desk toward him and rip off the tie and shirt, get to those armpits. He'd bury his face in their warm, spicy funk. He'd lick and eat them until Terry begged him to stop.

"Nudes," Terry repeated softly. Augustin nodded. Terry leaned forward in his seat. His dick was creeping down his thigh. "Male nudes?" he asked, his full attention now on Augustin.

"And sometimes live models."

Terry wondered what it would be like to model for Augustin. If he had the opportunity, he'd do so. He'd want Augustin to draw him from behind, as he leaned on a stool. He'd try to keep his pose,

but what he really wanted was for Augustin to stop drawing and just bury his face in his ass. Before he knew it, Augustin would be at his back, his blunt thumbs parting Terry's cheeks. Augustin would carefully guide one of his thick fingers inside Terry. He'd start slowly, pushing until the finger was all the way inside. Then he'd push another finger in, causing Terry to shudder because it felt so good. Next Augustin would bend Terry over the stool, his ass up in the air; then he'd start tonguing Terry's hole. He'd push his tongue in, and Terry, loving it, would moan with pleasure. He'd feel Augustin's face, his lips, his tongue opening him up and he'd begin to pump his own dick, gliding the foreskin back and forth over the swollen head, as Augustin kept licking. . . .

*   *   *

"Maybe you'd pose for me sometime?" Augustin asked. He pictured Terry in his studio, sitting in a director's chair. Terry would stretch out, his shoulders thrown back, his tight abs thrust forward. He'd spread his muscular thighs and calves so that his sleek, heavy brown dick snaked down, and the sweet pink of the head peeked out. Augustin would begin by drawing the dick first, starting from the crotch and tracing a long, continuous serpentine line till he reached the smooth balls beneath it . . . no, he'd have to adjust Terry's pose to get it just right. Before he knew it, he'd be working on the dick himself. Augustin would drop down between Terry's legs and open his mouth as wide as he could. Terry would roll his dick over Augustin's waiting tongue, gliding it back and forth, until he forced it in. Augustin would gag, but he'd take it all. He'd swallow it. He'd feel it sliding down into the back of his

throat where it belonged. Then Terry would thrust his hips forward, ramming his dick down Augustin's throat. Augustin would start jacking his own dick, erect as a pylon, as he swallowed Terry's. He'd feel himself coming, the explosion rising between his thighs as Terry kept pushing deeper. . . .

* * *

Silence filled the cubicle. They sat staring at each other. Each was ready to go for it, right there. Augustin reached his hand across the desk to take hold of Terry's arm as Terry grasped both his hands in his. Augustin stood up now, his fat erection tenting his sweats. Terry stood up with him, his dick poling down the side of his leg. He walked over to Augustin to give him the kiss they both craved. Just then they heard a client walk past. They broke apart and sat back down.

"I think we should finish up here, Augustin," Terry said hoarsely. "Only a little bit more to go."

"Definitely, Terry, definitely," Augustin swallowed, his throat also suddenly dry. "You working late tonight? Maybe we could get together later, and I could show you my studio."

"It's slow, so I'm out of here at five," Terry said. "I'd love to see your studio."

"I could show you some of those nudes."

"I definitely want to see them."

"You'll like them."

"I know I will," Terry said, his smile broadening. "I could even help you with a new one."

"I'm gonna hold you to that, Terry." Augustin grinned.

"And I can take care of any other things you need, too," Terry said.

"As you can see"—Augustin smiled, gesturing to the mess of papers and receipts on Terry's desk—"I could use a little order in my life. I told you what my father used to say."

"Don't worry, Augustin." Terry winked. "I'm very good with sums."

TRACY PRICE-THOMPSON

The African in the American

In the impoverished Kinaksu village where I was born, every male child nearing the age of initiation is taught to view the opposite sex with a healthy measure of fear and veneration. The women of my tribe were glorious. Tall and well shaped, their breasts were pillows of joy; their backsides reigned supreme. Thus, as I had learned, females were often cause for great distraction, and in a community of hunters and warriors we could not afford to relax our guard and become fixated on their delights.

By the age of nineteen I stood just shy of seven feet. Tall, even for a Kinaksu warrior. During a weekly visit to the city of Nairobi where male Kinaksu studied religion, English, arithmetic, and science, my father was approached by a recruiter from an American university who convinced him that I could make a great fortune in the United States playing basketball for his college team.

I balked at the thought of leaving my country. A full-blooded Kinaksu, I was the soul of Africa; its soil I knew intimately, its clear rivers flowed through my veins with the ease and tranquility of my own blood.

But Father insisted I take full advantage of this opportunity, and when he revealed the obscene sum that had been offered in exchange for four years of my life spent at a university, I sat down to ponder it, as my clothes were threadbare and I had already outgrown my father's house. Many of the village's young males had fled the countryside in search of work in Nairobi and other heavily populated cities, and there were very few men available to work the Kinaksu land and maintain the village. This, combined with a recent drought, had caused our food stores to plummet dangerously low. I was the eldest of eleven children, and one of only two sons. My father was aging, my mother ill. My decision was elementary. I accepted the man's offer and agreed to leave my homeland at once.

*   *   *

It was late March when I arrived in California. My benefactor enrolled me at his school and set about searching for a suitable live-in job where I would remain until the fall semester began. I had been in America only six days when I received an offer of employment from the Jackson Manor, a large residential estate in Beverly Hills.

During my initial visit to the manor I stood transfixed, mouth agape. The estate grounds were grand, and all at once I was stricken and intimidated. Commanding myself to rise above my wonderment, I was relieved to discover that my employers, Mr. and Mrs. David Jackson, were good people who had worked hard and were fortunate enough to be blessed with plenty. My father had once told me that there was a bit of African in every black

American, and from the Jacksons' regal bearing and work ethic, I believed he was right.

Mr. Jackson was an executive in the music industry, and his wife of some years, Cynthia, was an actress and a model. I later found out that they hosted frequent parties that were well attended by the most successful black Americans in Beverly Hills. The Jacksons had one child, a daughter named Amira, who was away at college, but whose beauty and aura were illustrated by a proliferation of photos and oil paintings throughout the mansion.

I'd been hired as a handyman, and it was my job to cut the grass, clean the swimming pool, wash the cars, and perform other tasks required to maintain the house and grounds. It was mindless work, but it allowed me the joy of working under a sun that also shone over Africa, so I performed each of my duties meticulously.

As strong as I was tall, I was well suited for physical labor. Quite often I was summoned to lift heavy boxes, or to move cumbersome furniture, or to assist in the landscaping of the grounds by chopping roots away from small trees whose shady leaves were no longer desired. I was all too happy to comply with these demands on my body. In Kenya, men of the Kinaksu were revered for their strength and sexual prowess, and like all men of my tribe, I was physically striking. My skin was flawless and smooth, the color of ripe blackberries. My arms and chest were broad and well muscled. Like most Kinaksu, my features were perfectly symmetrical and topped by angular brows that sloped, piercing and dark.

Our one small flaw was in our testicles. Oddly shaped, the

scrotum of a Kinaksu tended to be underdeveloped and closely retracted to his body. Our penises, however, were legendary. Solid and thickset, they were magnificently elongated, and well proportioned to our great height.

I'd been working at the Jackson Manor for nearly two months when their daughter, Amira, returned home from her university in a city called Atlanta. I'd seen numerous photos of her displayed inside their home, but the first time I actually gazed upon Amira's face I nearly lost my breath.

I had seen beautiful women before. Africa, the birthplace of Creation, overflowed with them. The Ashanti, the Woloff, the Malenta: The women of these tribes were the jewels of Africa, renowned for the purity of their features and the perfection of their flesh. But Amira . . . to label her as beautiful would be quite misguiding. She was exquisite, stunning, striking, and blessed with a backside that had been sculpted by the hands of an African god.

My world had been blessed.

Introductions were made by her father, who, having spawned such a delectable creature, had every right to beam with pride. They came upon me early one morning as I stood raking grass stalks into a large pile.

"Balak Kamboni, meet my daughter, Amira."

The first thing I noticed was her smile. Teeth as white as elephant tusks. Lips the shape of a warrior's bow.

"Nice to meet you, Balak." She extended her hand, and in my disconcertment I released the rake handle and its sharp teeth leaped up to bite my bare ankle.

"Oww!" I yelped, sounding much like an imbecile as I reached down to rub at the small nick in my skin. I recovered swiftly and took her hand, allowing myself only the briefest contact with flesh so supple and smooth it felt like a warm muffin. "I have heard a lot about you, Miss Amira," I replied, "and it is my pleasure to finally meet you as well."

Amira smiled again, her head tilted slightly to the left. She was tall for a girl, nearly six feet, and I delighted in the elegance of her shoulders, her mango-sized breasts, the way her white shorts cut across her firm thighs, emphasizing her broadness of hip. She had the body of a dancer, graceful and muscular. Her eyes were almond-shaped, and her hair was worn natural, in a wild blur of corkscrew twists.

"Your English is very good," Amira said, her eyes boldly roaming mine as she nodded her approval, "and I like your accent. In which of Africa's great countries were you born?"

My heart swelled with delight. Most black Americans I'd met since my arrival were under the impression that Africa was one huge country, its millions of inhabitants nothing more than closely related and often warring tribes. They had little concept of it as a massive continent comprised of fifty-four distinct and diverse countries.

"I am Kinaksu. We are a small tribe outside of Nairobi in the southern portion of Kenya."

Amira, I learned, was two years my senior, and studying biology at her university. She'd taken many tough courses during the semester, and told me she was exhausted and looked forward to relaxing and having fun with her friends during the summer. At the conclusion of our civilities, Amira and her father headed toward the main house for lunch, and I retreated to the carriage house that served as my lodging.

That afternoon I was asked to assist a crew of workmen who'd been hired to pour the concrete foundation for a tennis court. The workmen were fat and lazy, malingering in the shade of their truck whenever Mr. Jackson's attention was diverted. "Hey, now," one called out to me as I lifted burlap sacks filled with powdered concrete from their truck bed and carried one in each arm over to the area designated for the mixing. "Slow down, my friend. You are no longer chasing water buffalo. You are in America now. No need to move so fast."

Ignoring their comments I doubled my load, lifting two, then three of the fifty-pound bags in each of my arms and transporting them from the truck to the mixer. My body was accustomed to tough physical exertion, and my muscles ached in pleasure as I alternately lifted and lowered the heavy sacks. As I turned toward the truck, Amira was standing there. She had changed into a dress made of a light fabric in a flattering shade of yellow. I became conscious of the perspiration that streamed from my head and drenched my face, aware of the damp shirt that molded my frame and revealed the hardness of my abdomen.

"Hey, Balak," she said approaching me. I felt naked as she assessed me from head to toe, her eyes lingering on my chest before snaking downward toward the serpent awakening in my damp trousers.

I turned and walked over to the back of the truck, answering over my shoulder, "Hello, Miss Amira."

With visions of Amira's hips dancing to the pounding of the African drum in my heart, I returned to my task invigorated, slinging sacks of powdered concrete around as though they were as light as the clouds that cushioned my feet and swelled in my head.

*   *   *

I soon learned that Amira's arrival brought with it another dimension to life at the Jackson estate: stunning young women. Girls from her sorority, who, while lovely, did not possess the elegance or the grace of their hostess. Although it was Amira who I immediately desired, it was the others who seemed to immediately desire me. They behaved in much the same manner as silly African maidens when in the company of young warriors, but these American women were far more flagrant in their intentions.

In the presence of Amira and her friends, my manhood was almost constantly on alert, rigid and spouting. They stared and giggled as I pushed the motorized grass-cutter over the lush grass, their tight shorts riding up their shapely thighs. In Africa, a woman's breasts are to be admired as they moved about naked beneath the blaze of the sun. They were like ripe yams baked in an open pit, deep brown and naturally sweet. These American girls had breasts that were different colors, shapes, and sizes. They watched from Amira's window as I pulled weeds and spread mulch, their twin mounds threatening to burst from their skimpy tops, their nipples fat and pointed.

During the heat of the day the girls took to the pool and lay sprawled upon beach towels and lawn chairs as I maintained the

"Do you work out at a gym near here?" she asked, her eyes wide with appreciation. "Or is all of that *au naturel?*"

Facing her, I made a show of pulling the hem of my wet shirt from my waistband and lifting it up to my face, exposing the muscular flatness of my tummy and the dark trail of curly hair that began at my navel and crawled downward toward my groin. Mopping my face and head, I answered, "Where I come from, life itself is a workout. In Africa, we grow our men this way."

"Alrighty, then!" Amira laughed and the sun seemed to glow on the horizon. "Maybe I need to take a trip to the motherland."

"Or," I teased boldly, "perhaps you'll allow me to share my knowledge of Africa and we can explore a few aspects of the motherland right here."

She laughed. "Okay, how about you be the teacher, and I'll let you school me seven days a week." Then she lowered her eyes and gazed up at me through her lashes. I detected a trace of her perfume, tangy-sweet like a ripe papaya. "Seriously, though. I'd like that. I'd like it a whole lot."

"Amira!" Mr. Jackson called loudly from the second-floor balcony. His frown was proof that he disapproved of our flirting. "Come inside, sweetie. Your mother wants you." He disappeared into the house, but not before giving me a warning glance.

"Well," Amira said, turning, "don't work too hard. Save some of that energy for the fun things in life, like taking me to school." She held my gaze pointedly, then raised her right hand and waved. I watched as she walked up the path, the sway in her lower back, the sultriness in her hips, and the roundness of her behind holding me captive.

inviting blue waters. They lay legs spread, stomachs taut, as I fought to avert my gaze from the deltas between their thighs. As if to mock me, they would turn onto their stomachs and grace me with the unabashed sight of their lotion-slick bottoms, thick and golden from the sun. But it was Amira I wanted.

At nineteen, I was far past the age of initiation, and in Africa I had long since been considered a fully grown man. I had not taken a wife there because I had not yet accumulated anything of value to offer one, but certainly, I had lain with girls outside of my village. Yet those furtive encounters in dark bedrooms or thrilling rolls on grassy patches beyond the village borders in no way compared to what I imagined having with Amira. I imagined her naked and moving beneath me, her breasts grazing my chest, her legs spread wide, her sex gyrating against my own.

Each night, immersed in the heat of my cottage, I stood beneath the cascading waters of the shower, and with a soap-softened hand, allowed my rhythmic stroking to bring forth my issue, hot and creamy, my mind plagued with lustful thoughts of Amira. My self-stimulation only heightened my desire. By the time I climbed into the bed, which was several inches too short for my frame, my penis would once again be rock-hard. Groaning, I'd roll over, pressing my organ into the sheets as I shut my eyes and slept, my dreams fitful and restless and filled with images of my village, my family, and of course, my Amira.

*   *   *

It had been barely a week since Amira's arrival and my heart felt like it had been stomped upon by a herd of wild boars. It should have come as no surprise to me that Amira had a male suitor, a boyfriend; yet, it did. I felt wounded. My center was sore and tender. Amira's suitor was called Tre'quan, and his parents were business associates and close friends of the Jacksons. I learned that Amira and Tre'quan had been an item since their early teens, and with the help of Mr. Jackson, Tre'quan had recently landed a recording contract for a rap album.

This young man of Amira's emerged one morning from a sparkling Range Rover with several of his rowdy friends in tow. The men immediately paired up with Amira's girlfriends, who'd spent the morning sunning on the deck, and the entire lot of them began drinking and dancing to a cacophony that attempted to pass as music.

For a long time I studied Tre'quan. *Perhaps Father had been wrong,* I mused. I could not detect the slightest bit of African in this American who was pale of face and weak-willed. He was dressed in the same obnoxious, baggy clothing of his friends, who, to my horror, were leaping into the blue waters of my well-maintained pool wearing nylon underwear and silk head wraps. For the first time, I knew rage. In less than an hour they'd managed to undo many hours of my hard work, leaving lawn chairs overturned and scattered in disarray, and littering the poolside tables and basketball courts with empty beer bottles and gnawed chicken bones.

While it was true that I'd felt an aversion to Tre'quan on sight, it was not due solely to his status in Amira's life. Barely reaching her height, there was something diluted and insubstantial about him. Not enough solidity in his spine to be worthy of the treasure that was Amira.

Although Amira remained friendly toward me and seemed genuinely interested in knowing more about my homeland and my plans for basketball and college, it was obvious that a gemstone like her was well beyond my reach. Amira was privileged, cultured, and sophisticated. She had been exposed to the arts and the humanities and had studied languages and music. Her path had been paved from the moment of her conception. I imagined she'd graduate with high honors, gain admission to one of the country's top medical schools, and then marry a successful surgeon or perhaps a high-powered corporate attorney and live out her American dream.

I, on the other hand, was a simple African man, the hired help who'd been birthed in a village so impoverished it failed to appear on any except the most comprehensive of maps. Although Kinaksu men studied most academic subjects, I'd received the vital facets of my education at the feet of my tribal elders, and while I did not possess any of the material things of Amira's world, I had been carefully instructed in the functions of men. My strength lay in my ability to think for myself, and in my determination to succeed. Still, Amira was destined for far more, and there could be no comparison of our backgrounds or of our futures. The sight of her current boyfriend, swollen with wealth and privilege, was a testament to that.

I did, however, take a small measure of comfort in the fact that Tre'quan's position in Amira's life was precarious at best. She'd been born for a greater man, and I believed this thing she had with Tre'quan was only temporary. He and his friends now visited the Jackson estate almost daily. It was not long before, doglike, we each picked up the other's scent. I was convinced that he sensed my contempt for him and my desire for Amira. Sensed it, and feared it.

"C'mere, girl," Tre'quan commanded Amira one afternoon as he slouched in a lounge chair. Womanish, he wore a jewel in both earlobes and a large medallion hung suspended from his pallid neck by a chain of gold. He was dressed in a pair of brightly colored cotton swim shorts and clutched a frosted bottle of beer. "Come on," he gestured toward her. "Come plop that big fine ass over here by Daddy."

Waving a hose over the flower bed I watered, I glared as Amira sidled up next to him. For all the world I could not understand what it was she saw in such a weak excuse for a man. It pained me to see Tre'quan with his arms draped casually around her shoulders. I cringed at the cavalier manner in which he pawed at her body, rising to his feet and standing on his toes as he thrust his tongue into her mouth, their friends watching and cheering.

I was aghast. Flesh like Amira's deserved to be coddled and pampered, molded and kneaded like wisps of flaked, delicate pastry. Tre'quan caught me scowling and became even more crass. He hurled his beer bottle into the pool, then gripped the pulp of her backside and ground his maleness against her, all the while holding me in his contemptuous gaze.

"What's up, booty-scratcher?" he slid one hand between Amira's legs and gestured aggressively at me with the other. "They don't do this shit in Africa? What? You want some of this, don't you? You think you can pull my girl for yourself?"

Amira broke free of his embrace, pulling him around until his back was to me. I saw the apology in her eyes. "Chill out, Tre'quan, and leave that beer alone."

"Nah, baby." He swung back around until once again he faced me. Releasing Amira, he pounded his chest with both fists. His friends gathered close, bottles in hand. "Every time I touch you this Tarzan motherfucker acts like he wanna do something. Fuckin' jungle-ass Stretch Armstrong! I'll swing on his monkey-ass like a vine if he don't quit glaring all up in my grill!" He slapped the palm of one of his friends. "Crispy motherfucker! Long-ass nigger look like a goddamn exclamation point!"

Amira gasped. "Tre'quan, please! Get with it. Black is beautiful. All of us are part African anyway. Even you." She turned to me and frowned. "Ignore him, Balak. That's his liquor talking. He doesn't mean that crap. This is what happens when the boys get a little too fired up."

"Yeah, ignore me Black, or whatever the fuck your name is."

"No problem," I told Amira, standing my ground and making it a point to stare directly into Tre'quan's bloodshot eyes. African, he was not. "In my country," I assured her, "there is cause for concern only when it is the *men* who are getting fired up."

* * *

After my confrontation with Tre'quan I thought it wise to retreat to the privacy of my cottage. Amira was out of both our leagues, but I, at least, had the wisdom to know it and the grace to accept it. Tomorrow, the Jacksons planned to host a pool party in honor of Amira's exceptional grades, and I decided to wait until her friends left for the evening before going back out to clear their trash and restock the towels in the changing room near the pool.

I forced myself to lie down quietly and allow my internal center to become calm and rejuvenated. I took comfort in the fact that at the end of the summer Amira would return to her university, and my dormitory room would become available. More likely than not, we'd never see each other again. I vowed not to look at her too closely, or to allow her to engage me in conversation. Comforted in a small way, I dozed, and when I awakened the lengthy shadows in the room told me that several hours had passed, that night had fallen.

I rose from the bed and slipped into my sandals. My list of chores was extensive, and I did not want my employers to awaken the next morning to bottles and trash and a poolside in complete disarray. The grounds were quiet as I made my way into the main house, entering the kitchen area through an unlocked door near the breakfast patio.

I opened the large supply closet beside the pantry and took out four large trash bags and a tall stack of white towels that had been ironed and folded the day before. Stepping outside, I headed toward the swimming pool, dreading the task of cleaning up after Amira's guests who were my own age, yet so undisciplined and overindulged.

Setting the towels on a white slatted chair, I went about my work emptying ashtrays and throwing pop cans, straws, and half-eaten plates of food into trash bags. I'd filled up the first bag and knotted its neck, and was halfway through the second when I heard a sound.

I listened with my entire being and then the words reached my ears.

"Give it to Daddy, baby! Oh, yeah. Work that ass, bitch! Now turn over. Whose pussy is this?"

They were in the cabana, a wooden structure equipped with a shower, a toilet, and a decorous dressing room where guests changed into bathing suits and stored personal belongings.

I lowered the trash to the ground and tiptoed over, the male voice assaulting me with his graphic instructions.

"Fuck back, baby! Fuck me back! Swirl it like a roller coaster! Ah, yeah. You know how I like it!"

Standing in the shadows near the door, I reached out and gave a small push. The door swung slightly inward and I was afforded a full side view. Despite the pain growing in my chest I was powerless to tear my eyes from the scene as they coupled atop a mound of crumpled towels: she on her stomach, firm brown bottom high in the air, and him riding her from behind, his yellow skin sallow against hers in the dim light, his muscles meager and unimpressive. Tre'quan moved inside of her with his eyes closed, his expression that of a man who had died and crossed over to bliss. Amira's eyes were closed as well. She lay immobile, and appeared barely affected by his efforts.

I continued to watch as Tre'quan buried himself in what should have been mine. He arched his back and slapped her flanks, her flesh jiggling deliciously beneath his palm. I cringed as he reached beneath her and grabbed at a globelike breast, pinching its nipple sharply between his thin fingers. *Please, not like that. Take your time. Cup them gently. Feel their weight in your hands, the thickness of her nipples scraping the center of your palm.*

Amira's face remained impassive as he pushed her hair aside revealing the back of her neck. Animal-like, he sank his teeth into the soft skin near the juncture of her shoulder. *No, swirl your tongue back and forth like a soft wet cloth. Move forward just a little, right below her earlobe. You could plant a garden there.*

While I marveled at the suppleness of Amira's back, the V of her waistline, the hue of her skin, which shone like the inner bark of a baobab tree, Tre'quan rammed against her, their flesh slapping violently as he strained toward his orgasm. *The lady first! Always, her pleasure must come first. Stroke her flesh, lick the base of her spine, caress her there, then there, then gently, right there!*

A moment later Tre'quan roared and withdrew his minuscule, sluglike organ. His ejaculation spewed in a weak stream as he slumped forward onto her prone form. In that instant Amira's eyes fluttered open and locked on mine as surely as if she'd known I was there. Embarrassed, I turned on my heels and fled, but not before glimpsing the brightness of her smile.

*   *   *

I hardly slept at all that night, so troubled were my dreams, so powerful was my erection. The next day, it was still painful for me to recall what I'd seen the night before without experiencing boiling waves of humiliation. Although Amira's boyfriend was wealthy, a rising star in the music industry, he'd been taught nothing regarding the art of pleasing a woman. I was convinced that Amira was bored with his lovemaking, that at the pinnacle of his orgasm she had looked directly into my eyes and smiled. Surely she thought me a voyeur, a demented pervert who took his pleasure by spying on young lovers. Yet it was obvious by her lack of response to Tre'quan's urgings that she'd derived little to no pleasure from his passionless assault.

I had been commissioned to work Amira's party that evening at a rate one and a half times that of my normal hourly pay. Bartenders had been hired and the meal was to be catered barbecue and cold side salads. My duties were simple: empty trash and discard cups and bottles, and replace the wet towels with clean ones. At three o' clock I double-checked to be sure the shelves of the bathhouse were well stocked with towels, facial tissue, toilet paper, soap, and scented lotion, then I checked the water level and pH balance of the swimming pool before retreating to my cottage to masturbate, sulk, and nap until 6 P.M.

At a few minutes before six I dressed in a pair of designer bathing trunks on loan from Mr. Jackson and left my cottage. Already Amira's guests were partying around the swimming pool, and quite a few older couples, friends of her parents, were present as well. Drinks and marijuana were freely circulated. Everyone was half naked and the aura of sex was in the air. The women wore swimsuits that barely covered their ripe flesh. A swatch of material for the crotch, barely a string to shield the split of their bottoms, and two silver dollar-sized cups that struggled to conceal their round nipples. No doubt, there was a log in the pants of every heterosexual male on the grounds, and quite a few swimming trunks appeared tented and extended.

As a young deejay played rap music at an obscene volume, I

found an empty lawn chair and dragged it toward the shrubbery. I sat alone along the perimeter where I could observe the happenings unobtrusively. Sullen and dejected, I stewed in self-pity, lamenting my lot in life. I glared at Tre'quan as he grabbed a microphone and rapped along with the music, performing his routine like a hooligan in a music video. His hips gyrated wildly as he waved a beer bottle and clutched at his crotch. Young men and women gathered around him, clapping as though he was the Second Coming. And why not? He had a recording contract and stood to make a fortune. He and Amira were of the haves, and I was of the have-nots. Tre'quan was a longtime friend and an honored guest, while I was simply the hired help.

About an hour later the alcohol began to do its job. The crowd swelled and the couples began to mingle. From my vantage point I saw rolling buttocks patted and caressed, high, firm breasts pressed against muscular backs, and swollen crotches, throbbing and on the ready. I also saw Amira, who seemed to tease me with her eyes and take great pleasure in turning her back and allowing me a good look at her sultry hips, then bending over to pick up a towel as her breasts strained to be free. Once, when no one but me was watching, she lifted a clear bottle of water to her lips and looked into my eyes as she teased the throat of it with her tongue, then opened her mouth wide enough to fit half of it inside.

From time to time, Mr. and Mrs. Jackson ushered in a new guest and gave them a tour of the gardens, introduced them to friends already poolside, and then showed them to the cabana where they could change into their swimsuits. With one eye on

Amira, I counted close to fifty guests, quite a few splashing in the pool, and certainly more inside the manor.

At 7:45 I made an obligatory trip poolside, and armed with a trash bag, conducted a full sweep of the area. I emptied several ashtrays and retrieved about a dozen damp towels. As I headed toward the bathhouse for fresh towels, I felt a soft hand light upon my arm.

"Hello, Balak." Amira stood so close to me I could have kissed her. She smiled up at me, her teasing touch sending warmth radiating through my skin. "You haven't been around all day."

Her thick hair stood out in velvety spirals and she wore a white bikini that illuminated the caramel of her skin. Her breasts were full and plump, her buttocks curved and thrusting. "Amira," I breathed. "Are you enjoying your party?"

She gazed at me with heat smoldering in her eyes. A slice of pink emerged from her mouth as she moistened her lips. She leaned in closer, her breasts grazing my arm. "You were watching last night," she said. "I saw you."

Embarrassment flooded me, and as dark as I was, I blushed. "Please, forgive me. I heard noises . . . didn't know who was there . . . thought maybe you needed help . . ."

Amira grinned at me, and at that moment she was undoubtedly the sexiest woman I had ever seen. "Come, Balak. There *is* something you can help me with." With her hand still blazing a trail on my arm, she pulled me into the bathhouse. Wordlessly, I followed her, the hair on the back of my neck on end, my penis leaping and jerking against my thigh.

She led me inside where there were two all-weather benches, a low table covered with magazines, and several hooks draped with an assortment of bathing suits and swimming trunks. Amira reached behind me and pulled the door shut, locking it. Stunned, I let the damp towels fall to the floor.

"Balak," she murmured, pressing, teasing, molding her softness against me. "I've been dreaming about you, baby. I want to feel every inch of your fine, hard body." Her hands were clutching the small of my back, traversing over my muscular flanks, and pulling my hardness closer to her. She reached into her swimsuit and held out a silver square. "Do you want me? Do you want some of this?"

"Y-yes," I murmured, accepting the condom and gathering her close and gripping her hips. "I want you more than anything, Amira." I remembered the disapproving look in her father's eyes and nearly froze. "But are you sure?" I asked as my hands found her hair. My fingers slid down her neck and back, then up to cup the fullness of her breasts, teasing her nipples until they were stiff. "What about your father? And Tre'quan?"

Her hands climbed the mountains of my shoulders. "What Daddy doesn't know won't hurt him," she whispered. "And forget Tre'quan. He's nothing compared to you. I want *you*." She planted feathery kisses along my chest and when her lips found my nipples I moaned out loud. "You, Balak. Your delicious black skin, your rock-hard body and sexy smile. I've dreamed of touching you since the moment I met you."

I let out another low moan and then claimed her mouth, my tongue snaking in and out to a sensuous rhythm, exploring her lips and reveling in her flavor. Fire pulsated in my scrotum as my manhood strained, pressing deeply into her stomach. She parted her legs and rubbed her vulva against the muscle of my thigh, dampness seeping from the thin cotton of her suit bottom and leaving streaks of her essence on my skin. Using both hands, I grasped that firm, heavenly bottom of hers that, for days, had driven me to distraction. I kneaded and squeezed the soft roundness of it, my hands marveling at its fullness, its perfect outline, its soft, yet muscular tone.

She pulled away from me and lowered herself to a bench. Leaning back, Amira exposed her breasts and I gasped at their sheer perfection. Moaning, I freed my erection and she sucked in her breath, overwhelmed by my measurements.

"My God," she moaned, her eyes locked greedily on my organ. "So big."

"And all yours."

I guided my penis to her right nipple and massaged it, flicking its stiffness back and forth, swirling my slipperiness around her areola before burrowing my crown deeply in the valley between her fleshy breasts.

She took my organ in both hands, measuring its girth, marveling at its circumference, anticipating its power. "Right there," she moaned, squeezing her mounds together, trapping my thickness between them. Her breasts felt like wondrous satin pillows, and I slid the full length of my penis back and forth between them until I thought I would explode.

When I withdrew Amira stood and stepped out of her bathing suit. The last time I'd seen her naked Tre'quan had stood bucking behind her. I banished that image from my mind and replaced it with this sight of her bare body, brown and oiled, waiting to be worshiped in a manner befitting a queen.

"Amira," I breathed, my eyes feasting upon her flawless flesh. "I want to make you feel good. I want to give you more pleasure than you know is possible."

She reached for me. "Show me how a real man does it, Balak. Make me come all night."

In my fantasies I'd imagined her mouth upon my organ, her tongue lapping, her lips sucking. I'd dreamed of kissing her womanhood, of parting its folds and exploring her crevices, bathing her with my tongue.

She pulled me downward, indicating that I should lie back on the bench. I complied, my back against the hard wood, my legs bent, feet on the floor. Amira straddled me, inching her glorious womanhood up the length of my body until it hovered just above my lips. I inhaled its scent, flavorful and sweet, then grasped her buttocks and prepared to drink from her fountain.

As my lips delved into her, Amira rocked her pelvis, smearing my face with her juices. "Oh," she moaned, head back. "Lick it right there . . . yes, right there . . ." We were performing in concert, when we heard voices. We froze. On the other side of the door her parents were giving their guests a tour. Fear burrowed like a cannon in my stomach. The doorknob turned, but did not give.

"Shhh." Above me, Amira touched one finger to her lips, and then smiled reassuringly as my eyes darted toward the door. "It's locked. They can't get in."

She slid her wetness back and forth against my lips as I lay immobile, listening to the voices on the other side of the door.

"David, this door is locked."

Fists pounded.

"Keep going," she commanded, her whisper thick with need.

Amira gyrated her hips and despite my fear, my tongue snaked out to explore her folds.

"Damn. I'll have to ask Martha to look for the key."

Key? I froze again and Amira growled. Chastened, I gripped her small waist and allowed her to move her hips to her own satisfaction. As my tongue darted in and out of her warmth, massaging her clitoris and teasing her anus, Amira moaned toward her orgasm.

With her parents on the other side of the door, Amira bucked wildly, grinding herself into my mouth. I reached up and cupped her full breasts, teasing her nipples as she snagged her bottom lip between her teeth, suppressing a joyous scream.

At the sound of retreating footsteps, I opened my mouth wide and licked the full length of her wetness from her anus to the height of her mound. Amira rocked back and forth, impaling herself on my stiffened tongue, her breath coming in short, harsh heaves. I felt her insides clenching, a storm gathering at the base of her spine, and I pushed her away, freeing myself. The time was now.

I sat up, her scent on my lips, and she faced me, sitting upon my lap, our bodies colliding in heat. The music outside became amplified, the base running along the floor sending tremors pulsing through my feet. "I want to feel that big dick," she whispered, her fingers playing in the smooth hair on my stomach. "Right now, Balak. Inside me, I want to feel all of you."

As I remembered, Tre'quan, with his diminutive organ, had taken her like an animal. Unceremoniously on the floor, atop a pile of soiled towels. As humble and indigent as I was, I, at least, knew she deserved much better. I would give it to her so much better.

I tore the condom wrapper with my teeth and rolled the slippery latex over the head of my penis and down its length. Then I gathered her close and placed my hands below her armpits, near the top of her breasts. Using the muscles in my thighs, I stood in one sure motion, lifting her with me and into the haven of my arms, one hand at her back, the other beneath her bottom, holding her like a child. Tre'quan's voice blared from the microphone, a jumbled melody of unintelligible rhymes rolling from his liquored tongue.

I pressed my back against the coolness of the wall as Amira wrapped her lithe legs around my waist. My hands cupped the meat of her bottom, guiding her wetness toward my rod. With my arms extended, I lowered her onto my penis, entering her bit by bit. I was a large man, and she struggled to accommodate me as I kissed away her murmurs of pain and protest until there were only whispers of passion left on her lips.

She moaned into my neck, nibbling at my earlobes as I alternately lifted and lowered her to the beat of her boyfriend's rap, my muscles coiling and undulating, her vagina making heavenly wet sounds between us. Amira clenched my waist with her legs, her feet locked behind my back, spurring me faster, her body blossoming to accept the gift of my magnificence. Heat swirled in my testicles and bubbled up through my penis.

Her pleasure must always come first.

I pounded into her as she arched her back and cried out for more. My penis plunged into her with long, bucking strokes, and she clung to my shoulders and held on for the ride. My time was near. Cradling Amira in one arm and deepening my strokes until I felt her slickness dripping onto my scrotum, I reached between us and massaged her clitoris until she exploded, a scream tearing from her throat, her body shuddering with orgasm after orgasm until she lay limp, legs dangling, head lolled against my shoulder.

Minutes later, with Tre'quan still gibbering nonsensically over the microphone and my penis still semierect and buried deeply inside his woman, I lowered myself back to the bench, enjoying the feel of Amira's body straddling mine. I stroked her back and teased her buttocks as she slept, a tiny smile playing across her lips.

And then I closed my eyes and savored the moment, doubtful it would ever come again. Though our lives were polarized and distant, we'd managed to connect at a crossroad of passion. The African and the American. The African in the American.

E. ETHELBERT MILLER

Korea

*Maybe you thought I would exaggerate
the fire of the stars*

—June Jordan
After All Is Said and Done

*D*on and Kim sat on a green park bench looking at the river. It was morning and the city was just kicking off its covers. One could see three boats slowly moving in the distance as if they had lost their destination. Don was lost. This is what Kim had told him just a few hours ago. Her lips had surrounded his penis as if it were the Alamo. Her tongue made him feel as if he were blind-folded and being led out of a building in Iran. Don was a hostage with the wrong passport. Kim was angry and so she sucked him like a terrorist. Don had felt her teeth.

Years ago many men had disappeared after loving Korean women in Korea. They were soldiers who sought comfort to

336

escape the war. They needed women to remind them that the blood on their hands could be kissed away. In small rooms near military facilities women who were already ghosts in their own land undressed.

Kim watched the boats on the river. If she were back home she would have leaped into the water long ago. Some of the women gave birth to babies as dark as the earth. Kim had listened to Don repeat the stories he had heard from his grandfather in North Carolina. He told Don that right before he was sent overseas an officer told him "every woman's pussy is a mine ready to explode."

What made Don almost weep on this last day with Kim was how good she felt pressed against his side. In a world divided into colors Don was a black Columbus discovering Asian women. He had met Kim a year ago in a Portland bookstore. He hated the city as well as the entire state of Oregon until he saw Kim sitting in the front of the poetry section. She was holding a copy of *Otherwise* by Jane Kenyon. Kim liked to sit with her legs open when wearing short skirts. It was her way of making a political statement. Don stood in the aisle looking between her legs. Her eyes caught his and she smiled. She went back to reading her book and opened her legs a little more. Don could see she was wearing nothing underneath.

The poetry aisle was narrow and in the back of the store. When Kim looked up again from her book it was impossible to ignore Don's erection. He was wearing tight jeans. "Is that a metaphor for something?" she asked with a sly grin. Don was struck by how casual and soft her voice was. He prayed she was single and not a Buddhist. He didn't want to believe the stereotype of all Asian women being quiet and exotic. He had never gone out with one. Now he was in a bookstore, in Oregon of all places, staring at a woman who was staring at his zipper. Don looked over Kim's head and scanned the paperback volumes of poetry. He knew he had to read some love poems by Neruda tonight.

*   *   *

Three months passed until Don saw Kim at the bookstore again. During the intervening months he had dreams about her legs and what he had caught a glimpse of between them. He had wanted to fuck her in front of the shelves filled with Whitman, Pound, Frost, and Rich, or maybe just lick her silly. Instead he woke several mornings with a headache and the voice of an old woman warning him to be careful. Sometimes he would look into the bathroom mirror and notice red scars on his chest and shoulders. How did they get there? Didn't his mother or some aunt warn him about the demons from the spirit world? The female ones could climb on a man's back when he was sleeping and ride his soul.

Don stood and looked at Kim. He wanted to remain on the bench with her and never move, but it was best to let everything become a memory. He was leaving for the airport in the evening. He felt like one of those American soldiers going home to his wife and kids. There was Kim sitting on the bench staring at boats. Was he escaping the war? There was too much silence between them. What started with poetry, jazz, and great sex on tables and floors was ending with something that needed to be translated.

*   *   *

Don was addicted to Kim's body. It was on the nights when he slept alone that he felt her hair falling down on his face. She loved being on top when they made love. Don would lie on his back watching her. Her eyes would open now and then as her face changed to an autumn red from its summer yellow. She would scream "fuck" over and over. One afternoon she screamed out "Fuck me, you black bastard!" It was the day Don knew he would never stay with her. If he did he would be walking into a mine-field.

Kim had lived close to the American military bases south of Seoul. She had two older sisters who believed black soldiers were the best to bargain with. "How wide can you open your mouth?" They laughed and stuck their tongues out at her. "If you suck them well, they might even say they love you." For many years Kim tried to ignore them. The good life for her consisted of reading and writing poetry. She daydreamed about one day becoming a muse and waking up inside a poem or maybe in America.

"What do you think about when you look at the river?" Kim asked Don as she rose from the bench. She knew they needed to head back to her apartment so Don could pack for his flight. Kim decided small talk would keep her hands out of his pockets. She wanted an endless fuck. She knew he was never returning to Portland. Don looked at boats the way black men looked at railroad trains. Kim wished she were his blues guitar so she could go with him.

She has a mine for a pussy, Don thought as he recalled old war movies where a soldier was too afraid to move, knowing he could be blown to pieces. Don laughed to himself as he thought about folks finding every part of him except his dick. *I bet Kim would find it.* He chuckled. He tried to remember the name of the movie in which a woman loved a man so much that she cut off his dick so that it would always be hers. Don thought of Kim shopping for silk and a nice box to keep it in. Maybe she would burn incense and candles like the woman he married years ago.

Kim unlocked her apartment door. Don stood behind her wanting to touch her neck. How could he leave her? He was struggling to find a word in Korean that would capture his emotions at this moment. Kim had taught him a new word every time they made love. Many words and thoughts were in his head right now. It was difficult to think and impossible to speak. So he placed his arms on her shoulders and followed her into the room like a blind man. They had only taken a few steps when Don felt Kim's hand's searching for his zipper. "You should leave this here with me," she said.

The lovemaking came in waves. For a moment Kim felt she was swimming. Don was a boat. Kim moaned and scratched and bit. When she felt Don become soft inside her she prayed she was pregnant. She wanted to give birth to blackness and maybe a poem that would one day love her back.

*   *   *

Sometimes after making love Don had the feeling he was flying. This time he was. He looked out the airplane window. He could see nothing. He was tired of the emptiness he felt. Pressing his head against the back of his seat he closed his eyes and thought of Kim. He could sketch every detail of her body if he had paper right now. His thoughts were about to touch her nipples until Aretha interrupted everything. Despite all the hip-hop he was surrounded with, Aretha's voice was still tops. Don's love for Kim pushed him beyond the blues. His head was filled with the Queen of Soul singing "Ain't No Way." Aretha's voice made him feel guilty for all that he had said or had never said to Kim. He had been oppressed by sex. He had failed to love the only woman who had really wanted to touch him. Don listened to the song that was in his head and realized he was flying back into nothingness.

Kim decided to stay in the airport until Don's plane left the runway. She kept looking out the window until she saw his plane enter the night's sky and become a star. The sky was divided into light and darkness. Everything was divided into two. Why? People were divided like nations. Kim felt like Korea, a place divided because of history. The American soldiers she remembered from her childhood had changed everyone in her family. Had she fallen in love with the enemy? Don's face had been a mirror reminding her to love herself first. Now she was alone in her own blackness. Kim turned from the window and headed home.

CONTRIBUTORS

Preston L. Allen is a black Caribbean born in Spanish Honduras on Roatan, an English-speaking island. He is the 1998 recipient of a State of Florida Individual Artist Fellowship in Literature, and a winner of the Books and Books Poetry Prize. His short works have been published in numerous literary journals, including the *Seattle Review, Crab Orchard Review, Gulfstream, Drum Voices Review,* and have been anthologized in *Having a Wonderful Time: An Anthology of South Florida Writers* (Simon & Schuster, 1997). His first short-story collection, *Churchboys and Other Sinners,* is the winner of the 2000, Sonja H. Stone Prize in Literature and is forthcoming in 2003 by Carolina Wren Press. A versatile writer of short prose, Preston L. Allen's first novel, *Hoochie Mama,* is a mystery/thriller set in Opa-Locka, Florida, the Baghdad of the South, where he grew up. His erotic fiction has been published in *Brown Sugar* (Plume, 2001) and *Brown Sugar 2* (Simon & Schuster, 2003). He is currently completing a novel, *Nadine's Husband,* in which the selection *Who I Choose to Love* appears. He can be reached at pallenagogy@aol.com. His web-page is: Community.webtv.net/pallensky.

Lori Bryant-Woolridge is the author of the popular novel, *Read Between the Lies* (Doubleday, 1999), which was nominated for the Golden Pen Award for Best Contemporary Fiction of 2000. She has contributed to several anthologies including: *Best Black Women's Erotica* (Cleis Press, 2001), and *Gumbo,* edited by E. Lynn Harris and Marita Golden (Harlem Moon, 2002). Her next novel, *Hitts and Mrs.,* will be published by Avon in 2004.

She is a fifteen-year veteran of the television broadcast industry, having worked in various production and management positions at the ABC Television Network, Public Broadcasting System (PBS), and Black Entertainment Television (BET), and is the recipient of an Emmy Award for Individual Achievement in Writing. Lori is also the cofounder and president of the non-profit organization, Mothers Off Duty, Inc., a group committed to helping teen mothers continue their education. She lives with her family in New Jersey, where she is at work on her third novel.

Raquel Cepeda, an award-winning journalist for political reporting, is the editor in chief of *Russell Simmons' OneWorld* magazine. She has contributed to *MTV News* and *The Village Voice, The Source, Vibe, Essence, Jalouse*, and many other publications. *And It Don't Stop: The Best Hip Hop Journalism of the Last 25 Years,* edited by Ms. Cepeda with a foreword by Nelson George, will be released in the fall of 2004 by Farrar, Straus and Giroux. She lives in New York City with her daughter, Djali.

Wanda Coleman is known as "the Los Angeles Blueswoman," and is featured in *Writing Los Angeles* (the Library of America, 2002) and in *Poet's Market* (2003). She has been a Guggenheim fellow, Emmy-winning scriptwriter, and a former columnist for

Los Angeles Times magazine. Coleman's fiction currently appears in *High Plains Literary Review, Obsidian III, Other Voices,* and *Zyzzyva.* Her recent books from Black Sparrow Press (David Godine, Publisher, Inc.) are *Bathwater Wine* (1998), winner of the 1999 Lenore Marshall Poetry Prize, *Mambo Hips & Make Believe* (a novel, 1999), and *Mercurochrome: New Poems,* bronze-medal finalist for the National Book Award, 2001. *Love-Ins with Nietzsche: A Memoir* (Wake Up Heavy Press, 2000) was nominated for the Pushcart Prize. She is featured in *African American Writers: Portraits and Visions* by Lynda Koolish (University Press of Mississippi, 2001).

Michael Datcher is the author of the critically acclaimed *New York Times* best-seller, *Raising Fences: A Black Man's Love Story* (Riverhead, February 2001), which was also chosen by Terry McMillan for the *Today Show* Book Club. His latest play, *Silence,* was commissioned by and opened at the Getty Museum in February 2001. Datcher is the Director of Literary Programs at the World Stage Writer's Workshop in Leimert Park.

Patricia Elam received her M.F.A. in Creative Writing from the University of Maryland. Her short stories and articles have appeared in *The Washington Post, Essence, Emerge, Newsday, Mid-American Review, Epoch, Father Songs: Testimonies by African American Sons and Daughters* (Beacon Press, 1997), *New Stories from the South, the Year's Best, 1997* (Algonquin Books of Chapel Hill, 1997) and *Gumbo: An Anthology of African American Writing* (Harlem Moon/Broadway Books, 2002). She has also been a commentator for National Public Radio, CNN, NBC News, and the BBC. Patricia has taught creative writing at The Writer's Center, the University of Maryland, Goucher College, the Black Student Fund, the Hurston/Wright Summer Workshop, Manhattanville College Writers' Week, and Duke Ellington School of the Arts. She has served on the board of the Hurston/Wright Foundation and is a current board member of the PEN Faulkner Foundation. Patricia has won numerous awards, including a 1997 O. Henry Prize. Her first novel, *Breathing Room,* was published by Pocket Books in January 2001, and was nominated for a Hurston/Wright Legacy Award in the category of debut fiction. She lives in Washington, D.C., with her three children.

Lolita Files is the best-selling author of four novels, *Scenes from a Sistah* (Warner Books, 1997), *Getting to the Good Part* (Warner Books,1999), *Blind Ambitions* (Simon & Schuster, September 2000), and *Child of God* (Simon & Schuster, September 2001). She lives in Los Angeles, California, where she is writing and developing projects for television and film. Her next novel, *Tastes Like Chicken,* a follow-up to her popular Misty and Reesy series, will be published in 2003 by Simon & Schuster.

Michael A. Gonzales, a writer and journalist whose fiction has appeared in *Ego Trip, Russell Simmons' OneWorld* magazine, *Brown Sugar* (Plume, 2001), *Brown Sugar 2: Great One Night Stands* (Simon & Schuster, 2003), *Parables for the People* (Dafina Books, 2003), *Trace,* and *Untold* (U.K.). A former writer-at-large for *Vibe* and former senior writer at *The Source* and *Code,* he currently contributes to *XXL*. His work has appeared in *Essence, Mode, New York Press, The Village Voice,* and various other publications. He is the coauthor of the classic book on rap music and hip-hop culture, *Bring the Noise* (Harmony Books, 1991). Gonzales lives in Brooklyn.

John Keene is the author of *Annotations* (New Directions, 1995) and, with the drawings of Christopher Stackhouse, of the forthcoming *Seismosis* (Lush, 2003). His poetry, fiction, essays, reviews, and translations have appeared in an array of periodicals and anthologies. Among his awards is a selection for Best Gay American Fiction, Vol. II, and the 2001 Solo Press Poetry Prize. He teaches at Northwestern University, and lives in Jersey City, New Jersey, and Chicago.

Miles Marshall Lewis is the grandson of the late Harlem numbers runner Amsterdam Earl Benton. During the late nineties, he was the Music Editor of *Vibe,* and the Deputy Editor of *XXL* magazine. His essays and criticism have appeared in *The Nation, The Village Voice, Index on Censorship, L.A. Weekly,* and *Rolling Stone,* among other periodicals. A Bronx native, Lewis now resides on Sugar Hill in Harlem. Lewis is an internationally recognized expert on hip-hop music and culture whose commentary has been featured in print, television, and radio, including the *Daily News, USA Today,* and *The Los Angeles Times.* Lewis was recognized for writing a Notable Essay of 1999 by *Da Capo Best Music Writing 2000.* A graduate of Morehouse College with a degree in Sociology, Lewis also studied at Fordham University School of Law. He is finishing his first novel, *The Magic Kingdom of Christmas Muse*. It is the follow-up to his essay collection entitled *Scars of the Soul Are Why Kids Wear Bandages When They Don't Have Bruises* (Akashic, 2004). For more information visit www.MilesMarshallLewis.com.

E. Ethelbert Miller is the former chair of the Humanities Council of Washington, D.C., and a core faculty member of the Bennington Writing Seminars at Bennington College in Vermont. He has been the director of the African American Resource Center at Howard University since 1974. Author and editor of several books of poetry including *Where Are the Love Poems for Dictators?*, *In Search of Color Everywhere,* and *Beyond the Frontier.* His memoir, *Fathering Words: The Making of an African American Writer,* was published in 2000. Miller was one of sixty authors selected and honored by Laura Bush and the White House at the First National Book Festival.

Karen E. Quinones Miller is a former reporter with *The Philadelphia Inquirer,* and is the author of *Essence* best-sellers *Satin Doll* (Simon & Schuster, 2001) and *I'm Telling* (Simon & Schuster, 2002). Her third novel, *Using What You Got,* was published by Simon & Schuster in July 2003. She is currently working on *I've Known Rivers*, a coffee-table book that will profile African-American centenarians.

Nick Chiles and Denene Millner, a husband-and-wife writing team, are the coauthors of five books: the three-book series *What*

Brothers Think, What Sistahs Know (William Morrow, 1999), *What Brothers 'Think, What Sistahs Know About Sex* (HarperCollins, 2000), and *Money, Power, Respect* (HarperCollins, 2001), and the novels *Love Don't Live Here Anymore* (Dutton, 2002) and *In Love and War* (Dutton, 2003). Millner is also the author of *The Sistahs' Rules* (William Morrow). As a journalist, Millner has written for the Associated Press, the *New York Daily News,* and is currently senior editor at *Honey* magazine. Chiles has written for *Essence,* the *Dallas Morning News, The New York Times, Savoy,* and *New York Newsday,* with whom he won a Pulitzer Prize. Millner is a graduate of Hofstra University; Chiles is a graduate of Yale. They live in South Orange, New Jersey, with their two daughters.

Leone Ross, 33, is an award-winning novelist, short-story writer, editor, and teacher of fiction writing. She has written two critically acclaimed novels, *All the Blood Is Red* (ARP, 1996) and *Orange Laughter* (Picador USA, 2001). Her work has been widely anthologized in Europe and the U.S.A., collections include *Dark Matter, Brown Sugar, Brown Sugar 2: Great One Night Stands, Catch a Fire, The London Book of Short Stories Vol. II,* and *The Best of Horror and Sci-Fi: 14th Annual Collection.* She works as an associate lecturer at Cardiff University in Wales. Leone is Jamaican/British and lives in London.

Tracy Price-Thompson is the author of the *Essence* best-seller, *Black Coffee* (Random House, 2002) and *Chocolate Sangria* (Random House, 2003) and the coeditor of *Proverbs for the People: An Anthology of Contemporary African-American Fiction*

(Kensington, 2003). A Brooklyn, New York, native and retired army engineer officer, Tracy is a Ralph Bunche Graduate Fellow who holds degrees in business administration and social work. Tracy was recently awarded a Zora Neale Hurston/Richard Wright Finalist Award for literary excellence. She lives in Hawaii with her husband and their children.

Sharrif Simmons has been called today's answer to Gil Scott Heron, The Last Poets, and Amiri Baraka. His first collection of poetry, *Fast Cities and Objects That Burn* (Moore Black Press, 1999), was hailed by Abiodun Ayewole of the Last Poets as "an invaluable contribution to his generation." His album, *Echoeffect,* was released in March of 2003. For more information visit (www.SharrifSimmons.com). Sharrif has toured throughout Europe and the United States with his *Echoeffect* band. A staple in New York's underground arts scene throughout the nineties, he has performed at the Nuyorican Poet's Cafe, S.O.B.'s, CB's Gallery, Sweet Basil, and the Bowery Bar, to name a few. His poetry has appeared in the anthologies *In Defense of Mumia* (Writers and Readers Press, 1996) and *Role Call* (Third World Press, 2002). Sharrif's music is like listening to an echo. His poetry is steeped in the tradition of conscious struggle, his sound, according to the legendary David Bowie, "is a mix between Sun-Ra and Gil Scott Heron." Sharrif lives with his eight-year-old son, Omari Simmons, in Jersey City.

Lisa Teasley's work appeared in the first *Brown Sugar.* She is the author of *Glow in the Dark* (Cune Press), winner of the 2002 Gold

Pen Award for Best Short Story Collection, and the Pacificus Foundation Award for Outstanding Achievement in Short Fiction. Ms. Teasley's past awards include: the May Merrill Miller Award for Fiction; the National Society of Arts & Letters Short Story Award, Los Angeles; and the Amaranth Review Award for Fiction. Forthcoming is the paperback release of *Glow in the Dark,* as well as her novel, *Dive,* both from Bloomsbury in 2004.

Trisha R. Thomas is the author of the best-selling novel, *Nappily Ever After* (Crown, 2000), a finalist for the NAACP Image Award for Outstanding Literary Work and a finalist for the Gold Pen Award for Best Mainstream Fiction in 2001. Her novels have been featured in the *Washington Post, Essence,* and *O* magazine. Her new novel, *Finding Love Finding Venus* is the much-awaited sequel to *Nappily Ever After* and will be published in 2004 by Crown.

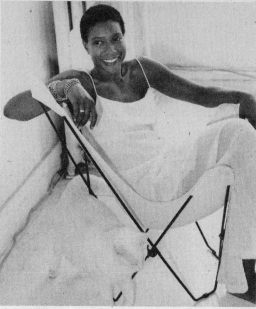

Bob Myers

About the Editor

Carol Taylor, a former Random House book editor, has been in book publishing for over ten years and has worked with many of today's top black writers. She is a contributing writer to *Sacred Fire: The QBR 100 Essential Black Books*. She is also the editor of the first best-selling *Brown Sugar* erotic collection, and *Brown Sugar 2: Great One Night Stands*. She has been featured in *Essence, Ebony, Black Enterprise, Honey, BET, Heart and Soul, The Boston Globe, Upscale, The Daily News, The Chicago Sun-Times,* and *Publishers Weekly,* among many other publications. She has also appeared on *BET Tonight with Ed Gordon* and *ABC Eyewitness News.* Her fiction and nonfiction have appeared in many publications. Her online relationship column, *Off the Hook: Advice on*

Love and Lust, is featured on Flirt.com. She lives in New York City and is at work on *Brown Sugar 4,* and on a collection of her own stories. She is the CEO of Brown Sugar Productions, LLC, and can be reached at Carol@BrownSugarBooks.com. For information on all the *Brown Sugar* books visit www.BrownSugarBooks.com.